THE SANCTUARY MAN

Also by A. R. Beven

The Seldom Girls

THE SANCTUARY MAN

A. R. Beven

Hodder & Stoughton

First published in Great Britain in 1995
by Hodder and Stoughton
A division of Hodder Headline PLC

10 9 8 7 6 5 4 3 2 1

British Library Cataloguing in Publication Data

Thorne, Alexandra
Sanctuary Man
I. Title
813.54 [F]

ISBN 0-340-63803-6

Typeset by Hewer Text Composition Services, Edinburgh
Printed and bound in Great Britain by
Mackays of Chatham PLC, Chatham, Kent

Hodder and Stoughton
A division of Hodder Headline PLC
338 Euston Road
London NW1 3BH

For Colin and John

Acknowledgements

Thanks to Lisa Eveleigh, Carolyn Mays, Norah Child Villiers, Andi Blackwell, and Patrick Donovan.

It's so rare to see
the whole of the moon
it's a waste to bay at it –
better just bathe in its glow

Chapter One

If I said that on the day in question I was watching the cricket at Lords, that could give a misleading impression. In fact I know very little about cricket but my brother was a member of the MCC and often entertained clients there. It was his unexpected decision to take a couple of days off that found me deputising for him, watching Middlesex struggle against Surrey in the Cup.

As an introduction to the game it could probably not have been bettered. Both sides concentrated on scoring runs, the sun was warm, and after a couple of pints at lunchtime I was happy enough to let the Baring brothers explain to me, a confessed novice, why so many matches end in draws. The desultory drone of their voices above the distant exclamations of players and the genteel approbation of midweek middleclass spectators was only marred by the insistent trill of my mobile phone.

I have always detested the type of poser who bolsters his self-importance by making calls in the middle of a restaurant or wine bar, at least in part because in my experience they are more likely to be telling their spouse when they will be home to supper than clinching a deal in another time zone. I had reluctantly accepted that in our business, where we are either travelling or on half-built exhibition sites for much of the week, a mobile is essential but I still found them somewhat embarrassing and hated being rung without good reason.

So when Dorothy called that afternoon I would have been brusque had the Barings not been within earshot.

'What's the problem?'

'I can't get hold of Stuart.'

'Leave a message on his answerphone.'

'It's not on. Neither is his carphone or the mobile.'

'He must have popped out, then. Into the garden or the village. I'm sure he won't be long. Can't you try him later?'

'I've been trying for two hours, Alex. I wouldn't have bothered you otherwise.'

It was true; Stuart's PA was intelligent and reliable. I stood reproached. 'Of course not.'

'I just thought he might have changed his plans at the last minute.'

'You'd have been the first to know. As far as I'm concerned . . .' I paused momentarily. I hardly wanted Stuart's clients to know that he considered a couple of days in his study thinking through some ideas in peace more important than seeing them, and I'd already implied a man at leisure, '. . . David's plans were unchanged.'

'The Barings are with you,' she said, quick on the uptake.

'Uh huh. There must be a fault on the line.' This was far more likely, as we both knew, than Stuart forgetting to be contactable. Even when he went on holiday he furnished Dorothy with hotel phone and fax numbers. 'Get Telecom to check it. In the meantime, is there anything I can do?'

Having sorted out the matter on which the printers were clamouring for a decision, I turned back to the game. 'Sorry about that.'

'Shame you missed that last wicket,' Roy Baring said. 'Your lot will be lucky to win now.'

He was right. 'My lot', so-called only because I lived within a mile of their home ground the Oval which for some reason was not in Surrey at all but in south London, duly lost. I saw the Barings into a taxi and rang the office. It was after seven and Lynn, my own secretary, had gone 'but Dorothy would like a word,' said Polly who had answered the nightservice phone, and transferred me.

'You ought to be on your way home,' I said. 'What's keeping you?'

'Oh, just catching up on some typing,' Dorothy said.

'Did you get through to Stuart in the end?'

'No. But the engineers insist that there's no fault. Just no answer.'

'Well . . . don't worry about it. I'll call him later. He must have taken advantage of the fine weather and gone on a jaunt. Is there anything that can't wait till the morning?'

There wasn't but she was reluctant to go, a mother hen whose chick has done something unpredictable. Dorothy had been with Buccaneer since the start and seen Stuart through the death of his first wife and the difficult time afterwards; they had grown middle-aged together. I had suspected that she would disapprove of his remarriage but she was all in favour of him having a 'proper home' again. The chief cause of her concern now was probably that he was fending for himself as Nicole, his second wife, and Katie, his daughter, were both on holiday.

I caught the tube home, opened some windows to let out the heavy heat of the day, and made a pot of tea. I felt vaguely dissatisfied – too lazy to start on any real work but debarred from slumping in front of the TV by the fact that I had done nothing but watch cricket since breakfast. I knew that the point of taking the Barings to Lords was precisely not to discuss business with them; I just wished Stuart had done it rather than me.

I rang Stirton Hall again but there was still no reply. Below the drawing room windows the traffic on the Camberwell Road had slowed to a drizzle; the rush hour – a euphemism for a tidal wave three times that length – was spent. I decided to drive down to Kent and see what had happened to Stuart.

I wasn't particularly worried but I had nothing better that I wanted to do, it was only a forty minute drive, and assuming that he was at home I thought we might repair to his local and watch the sun set along the valley from its garden.

I nearly changed my mind when I opened the Saab and the foetid warmth that had been cooped up within it all day rolled over me like a damp duvet, but instead I wound down the windows and let the carbon monoxide breeze clean it through as I drove. The route from my place to Stuart's is not picturesque but it does reflect the gradual outward sprawl of London and a soft summer dusk is the best light in which to see it.

From the heavyweight Regency and tawdry Victoriana of Camberwell you pass through the Edwardian yellowbrick villas of Dulwich and eventually come to the cheapskate neo-Tudor of the Sidcup bypass, the tenuous charm that these semis once had lobotomized by double glazed picture windows and front gardens concreted over to create parking for the family cars.

Quite suddenly then London is over, with enough fields to qualify as country and a green belt of sorts before a newer sort of sprawl, the pygmy estates surrounding the north Kent villages. This was where Stuart and Nicole had realised his midlife ambition to become a latterday squire and reconciled that with daily commuting to our office in the city.

Of course some compromises had been necessary; while Stirton Ash had a fourteenth-century church and a quaint corrugated-iron village hall where the Dramatic Society and the Women's Institute enacted ancient rituals, one of its two pubs now boasted a carvery and three quarters of its inhabitants were also commuters who had no need of or desire for a paternalistic figure in 'the big house'.

This suited Stuart who had enough responsibilities and was more in love with the historical resonance of his house than its standing in the community. Stirton Hall was no stately home but it was substantial and pretty, a sixteenth-century L-shape turned into a C by Victorian addition. It stood in four or five acres of grounds, screened from the road by high flint and brick walls and from the village below by trees at the bottom of the garden. There was only one gateway with, inevitably, white balls on its posts and heavy wooden gates. These were open. I turned around on the looping gravel drive before stopping close to the porch.

The door of the wooden coachhouse where they garaged their cars was ajar and I could see both Stuart's Jaguar and a small red hatchback parked inside. I rang the mechanical doorbell and waited, smelling the wistaria and batting at the insects that danced beneath the portico. It could take several minutes for someone upstairs in the Victorian wing to get down here but there was no twitch of a curtain, no light came on, no one answered.

Through the sitting room windows I could just make out the jumble of magazines and an empty coffee cup or two on the occasional table, not the kind of thing to have escaped the ministrations of their daily, Mrs Cuttifer. I thought I would take a look around the back – it was possible that he was listening to music and had not heard the doorbell.

I went under the arch that led into the walled side garden where they set up the croquet hoops for summer parties, past the diamond-panes of his study windows and onto the terrace at the rear of the house. There were two sunloungers by the wrought iron table, their striped cushions already wet with dew. The twilight had closed in to the point where, unless they were sleeping, anyone in the house would have switched on at least a lamp, but its façade was dead.

I did feel perturbed then, but not certain that there was really anything to worry about. He might have taken a car other than the Jaguar – I wasn't sure how many others the family possessed. It was unusual, very unusual, for him not to have left messages or switched on his answerphone, but everyone makes mistakes or gets forgetful once in a while. He might have popped down to The Greyhound for a beer. . . .

When I noticed the open windows I knew that wasn't the case. There were two upstairs, one sash in the Victorian wing and one at the older end behind which a closed curtain rippled. More importantly there was another gaping casement on the ground floor, just to the right of the door in the building's backbone. Nobody with an expensive and isolated rural house goes out and leaves the windows open.

I tried the door, which was on the latch, and admitted me to a small boot room, heavy with the scent of Barbours and wellingtons. I would have called out an experimental greeting but somehow the overwhelming silence did not allow it.

I passed into the kitchen and back into a real world of sound, the hum of refrigerator and throatclearing of a distant boiler. I felt for the light switch and the noises receded as they were superseded by visual information. It was a long low farmhouse kitchen, neither in the correct style nor position for this sort of house, but painstakingly recreated by Nicole and the builders right down to the flagged floor. It was so tidy that the litter – a couple of plates with a residue of salad, a wine bottle, a cafetière with its dark silt of grounds and attendant cups – jarred against the slate and elm worksurfaces like an oil disaster. The open window was above the double sink.

I went out into the narrow passage which looked out onto the drive. The kitchen and this parallel corridor formed the bridge between the grand nineteenth-century reception rooms to my right and the more cosily proportioned sixteenth-century quarters. I turned left, past the sporting prints and the long-case clock ponderously ticking at the foot of the stairs. I called out, 'Stuart. Stuart.'

I switched on the lights in the sitting room, the study and the garden room, transforming the last glow of evening through its French windows into a fragmented reflection of myself which made me jump.

I climbed the stairs, dark once I had turned the bend, boards creaking beneath my feet. I stopped on the landing to get my bearings. The light switch did not seem to be in any of the obvious places but I remembered that their bedroom looked over the lawn at the back, so I made for that and was relieved when the switch there was exactly where it should have been. The bedspread on their fourposter was unruffled, its drapes invitingly hooked back. The matching curtains at the windows were drawn for sleep. Out of the corner of my eye I saw one of them move.

I froze, staring at it, unable to believe in a malign presence but equally unwilling to test my theory. The next time I was sure no human could have induced its delicate billow. I strode over and swept it aside to reveal the open casement. 'Silly bugger,' I said. My voice sounded as absurdly loud as a cough in a reading room.

Reactivated, I quickly checked the dressing room and ensuite bathroom and went back onto the landing where the light switch was now immediately apparent. The bowls of pot pourri and watercolour landscapes that it illuminated were comfortingly homely. I turned to the corridor above the kitchen, a black tunnel hardly penetrated by the landing's weak bulb. Just on the edge of darkness was a bare foot, sole towards me, its owner therefore lying on his back.

As I stumbled forward I knew it would be Stuart's, and that he had to be unconscious if not dead. I knew with the benefit of hindsight that I had half expected it. What I was not prepared for was the nature of his injuries.

He was wearing a towelling robe, jauntily striped, but the top half was soaked with blood. It looked as if some creature had tried to burrow into his chest cavity. The amount of blood beneath the body, dried now on the carpet, suggested that it had got out the other side. I didn't lift him up to look.

After the initial nausea I felt quite calm. He was obviously dead, had been since – judging by the dressing gown – last night, and he wasn't really my brother any more.

It wasn't just the runnels of blood that had oozed from the corners of his lips and coagulated in Draculian parody on his chin; his whole face was a pale imitation as if he had been famous enough to have been cast in wax at Madame Tussaud's. You could see who it was meant to be but, for all the accuracy, it wasn't.

I understood now why people believed in the soul leaving the body. There was nothing left behind those dull eyes. I took some deep breaths.

I should do something. Ring the police. There was a phone in the bedroom. What to tell them?

There was no weapon but I thought I knew what had killed him.

The centre of the wound might have looked like the work of some supernatural assassin, but its extremities were speckled with tiny dark holes like those caused by shotgun pellets. I'd never seen them on a human before but the effect was remarkably similar to that on the skin of a plucked pheasant. For the spread not to have reached his face, and for it to have caused such devastation, the gun must have been fired at point blank range.

I dialled 999 and discovered that my hands were shaking. Conditioned by the usual folklore I went downstairs and poured myself a cognac from the tray in the study. I was having a first sip, well, more a gulp if I'm honest, when I heard this dull thud from upstairs.

Absurdly my first thought was that it was Stuart, that miraculously he was alive. More absurdly when I was standing by the motionless corpse I realised that I had galloped up the stairs still clutching the balloon glass. Reflexively I took another swig, making my eyes water. What had thudded? Momentarily I wondered whether the gunman was still lurking in the shadows, both barrels loaded, prepared to blow me too away, but that would have been crazy. No murderer in his right mind would have hung about waiting for the body to be discovered.

I didn't stop to question the rationality of murderers but waited for my heart to slow and went in search of the other open window. A fluttering curtain had obviously twitched some ornament off a ledge, but I couldn't relate its position outside to the closed doors in here. The first two were inert guest rooms, but when I pushed at the door of the third I met resistance. I gave it a shove with my shoulder and consequently lurched into another bathroom. This time the glass fell from my fingers. On the floor, tied to an overturned chair, was a woman in a nightdress.

I lifted her upright, as decorously as was possible under the circumstances, and the long black hair fell away from her face revealing wide, dark eyes and a gag over her mouth. It was Deborah, Stuart's stepdaughter. She looked terrified.

'Hang on,' I said, squeezing her arm as I felt for the knot behind her neck, 'and I'll get you out of these.' I pulled away the scarf and started on the line that secured her wrists. 'Are you all right?'

Her reply was a muffled grunting; her mouth was stuffed with a handkerchief. Removing it was a strangely intimate act. 'Thank you,' she said thickly, and burst into tears. I released her arms and legs and she lifted a hand awkwardly to brush away her tears. 'Gone dead,' she added, rubbing her hands together. 'Can I have some water?'

'What happened?' I asked, handing her a glass.

She swallowed. 'Where's Stuart? Is he OK?'

I squatted down so that our heads were level. 'He's dead, I'm afraid,' and it hit me then properly that he was and I was as glad to hold onto her as she me. Through her sobs she started to gabble.

'I just got up in the middle of the night for . . . a drink of water or a pee or something and I came in here and somebody grabbed me and put this pad over my face and it smelt sickly sweet and then . . . everything just went black like having gas at the dentist's . . . and when I woke up I was here. At first I was frightened they would come back and then it got light and I decided they must have gone and I waited and waited for someone to come and let me out but nobody did so I tried to move the chair to the door by rocking backwards and forwards but it fell over and I've been on the floor ever since. Why did it take you so long?' she ended, with a kind of groan.

'I'm sorry,' I said. 'The police are on their way.'

'Where . . . where is Stuart?'

I wasn't certain that she had understood. I decided to make it clear. 'His body's in the hall. Better not to look.'

She seemed relieved. 'How did he die?'

'He was shot.'

She struggled to her feet. 'I want to clean myself up.'

I wasn't surprised. Close to her I had smelt the sharp ammoniac scent of dried urine. Sometime earlier, either from fear or simply because she had been restrained for so long, she had wet herself.

'You'd better not do it in here,' I said. 'It might destroy – well, clues or something.' I was amazed that I was thinking so logically.

'It's all right, there's a basin in my bedroom.' She stopped. 'When did you ring them?'

I looked at my watch. 'I don't know. Five minutes or so.' I went with her onto the landing, creating a screen between her and the corpse but she didn't look, just crossed into her room, affording me a glimpse of red bedclothes before she closed the door. I fancied another drink but I didn't want to leave Deborah in case she stumbled over Stuart when she came out, so I waited at the head of this more grandiose staircase; beneath the sound of running water I could hear her moving about.

'Have you rung Mummy as well?' she asked when she emerged, shortly afterwards. She was very pale but her hair was brushed and she was wearing a cotton summer dress and carrying a large Mulberry bag, as if she was on a day out.

'I hadn't thought. When the police come—'

'Let's wait for them downstairs,' she said and, aware of the uncovered corpse behind me, I was glad to agree. She made for the kitchen and sat at the table. She was trembling. 'Could you get me a drink? Brandy's good, isn't it?'

'It's what I had,' I said. 'I'll join you.' While I was in the study I heard the cars pulling into the drive.

After that it was a bit of a blur. Blue lights flashed outside. I explained to a uniformed sergeant what I knew and then a policewoman ushered Deborah away somewhere. Feet pounded up and down stairs and in the corridor above my head. I sat on in the kitchen until a constable moved me to the small sitting room and brought me some tea.

Eventually the man in charge, Superintendent Cromarty, introduced himself.

'How's Deborah? Miss Makepeace,' I added, falling into the cod formality of Agatha Christie. I had watched an ambulance arrive and depart, presumably with her on board.

'Almost certainly perfectly OK. But it's as well to be sure. And to get her away from here. What about you? You've had a bit of a shock yourself.'

He was an ugly man, thick-necked and pockmarked with small eyes that flicked back and forth, in animal terms a cross between a boar and a lizard, but in spite of his appearance his voice was soft, not brutish.

'OK. Odd. I'm not sure. The whole thing's a bit surreal. I'm not sure it's sunk in.'

'Would you mind me asking you a few questions?'

I said of course not and he got me to retrace the night's events, occasionally prompting or interjecting.

'Was it unusual for your brother to work from home?'

'Fairly, during the week, but not unprecedented.'

'Was he celebrating anything in particular?'

'Not as far as I know. Why?'

'Just that there was an empty champagne bottle in the kitchen.' I didn't remember that.

'But perhaps that was a favourite tipple?'

'Not really.'

'Of Miss Makepeace maybe?'

'I don't know. Because Stuart and I see – saw – each other every day at work I didn't come down here often. We didn't live in each other's pockets. And besides, Deborah has a flat in London, Clapham – I don't think she's here much. I don't see her more than two or three times a year, I shouldn't think.'

'Doesn't your brother have any staff? It's a big place and, forgive me, I'm assuming he was a wealthy – reasonably well off anyway – man.'

'Mrs Cuttifer came in every day.'

'But apparently not today. Do you know of anyone who might want to kill your brother?'

I stared at him. 'But . . . wasn't it burglars?'

'Probably. Miss Makepeace says he kept cash in his desk and there's none there now, but the place hasn't exactly been ransacked. We have to consider any possibility.'

'Not that I can think of.'

'Something to do with the business? You might know about that, being a partner.'

I couldn't help smiling. 'I'm sorry. The design business might be tough at the moment but not in that way.'

'He was a shooting man, your brother. Were you?'

'Yes.' Something bizarre occurred to me. 'He wasn't, I mean, was he killed by one of his own guns?'

'We don't know. Same type of cartridges as those in his cabinet which was unlocked. A gun, fired, found in the garden, which may be the murder weapon. Tests should confirm. Would you recognise his guns?' All the while he was speaking I was aware of him watching me intently.

'Yes, I should think so.'

'How many did he have?'

'Two . . . . as far as I know,' I added when he raised an eyebrow. I'd obviously got it wrong but he showed me the suspected firearm anyway. I hadn't seen it before.

'So Mrs Buchan is his second wife?'

'Oh god, I'd forgotten about Nicole. Has Deborah told her?'

'No sir. She left the number. She thought you would ring her.'

'Er .. of course.'

'She is in a bit of a state herself.'

'Of course. Shall I do it now?'

'We're setting up a line. Perhaps I could just get a bit more background, while we're waiting. Is the first Mrs Buchan still alive?'

'No, Angela died in . . .' I counted back. '1981. A skiing accident. Stuart married Nicole three years later.'

'Did he have any children of his own?'

'Of course . . . sorry, how were you to know. Katie.'

'And where is she?'

'On holiday too.'

'In Corsica with Mrs Buchan? I thought Miss Makepeace said her mother was alone.'

'Oh no. Katie's with the family of some schoolfriends. Greece, I think.' I wondered what opinions Cromarty was forming of this family, my family I supposed, of wives who holidayed alone and husbands who opened champagne without just cause.

'And how old is Katie?'

'Eighteen.'

'Younger than Deborah, then.'

'Yes, she must be . . . twenty-one, twenty-two.'

'I think we're ready to make that call now.'

There was nothing difficult about phoning Corsica; like almost everywhere else in the world it was direct dial. The delay had been for installing a special handset with an extra earpiece. Cromarty picked it up. 'I hope you don't mind me listening in. But it will help me to judge whether we should send the local police round to get her to the airport or whatever.' This sounded lame; I assumed that Cromarty was merely exercising his nosiness but I didn't begrudge him. It must be an occupational necessity for a detective.

I had never been to the villa so I had no mental picture of the room in which that bell, more reminiscent of Hollywood movies than France, jangled. Time passed. My watch said one which meant two there; Nicole must be in bed.

'Hello?' Her voice was tense, almost as if she expected bad news, but then what other news did you get unexpectedly in the middle of the night?

'Nicole, it's Alex.'

A pause, as if she was trying to compute this fact. She was probably still waking up. I couldn't imagine her rumpled by sleep. 'Yes?'

'I'm afraid there's been an accident,' I said as levelly as I could, following the line agreed with Cromarty. 'A very serious accident.' I wanted her to have time to adjust a little rather than hitting her with an immediate hammer blow.

Another pause. 'What's happened?'

'I'm afraid Stuart's dead.'

An intake of breath. Silence.

'I'm very sorry,' I added inadequately.

'How?' she said eventually.

'A shooting . . . incident. They think he died instantaneously.'

I doubted this but didn't want to dwell on it. Better to accept the comforting fiction.

'What shall I do?'

I chose to take this as a specific and practical rather than a general or philosophical question. 'There's a flight from Ajaccio at seven. Can you catch that?'

'Yes.'

'OK. I'll meet you at Heathrow. Will you be all right on your own?'

'Yes. Is . . . is Debbie all right?'

'Yes . . . yes, fine.'

Silence again. 'OK, I'll see you later,' she said and put the phone down.

'I knew she'd wonder,' I said to Cromarty, 'why I was ringing and not her own daughter.' It was he who had counselled against any mention of murder and therefore of Deborah's involvement. I felt very tired. 'Can I go home now?'

Chapter Two

For some reason it only seems possible to arrive at or depart from Athens airport at odd times of the night. When I stepped onto the tarmac and forced my way through the inevitable soggy heat to the terminal building it was two a.m. Inside, the air conditioning condensed the sweat beneath my shirt and my nostrils were assailed by the familiar odour of inadequate drains poorly disguised by cheap disinfectant. To blot it out I smoked a cigarette, in the discontented way that you do when you're tired but not sleepy and you've already smoked too many. I drank a cup of thick sweet coffee and took a typically suicidal taxi to the seafront at Piraeus where the driver recommended a 'hotel' – I use the inverted commas advisedly – and I lay down on a thin mattress in a tiny room which would have made a perfect cell for some particularly masochistic order of monks.

It had been a long day. When I got back from Stirton Hall I was frightened to go to bed, suspecting what my dreams might hold, so I sat on the sofa to read with a tumblerful of Scotch. I must have dozed almost immediately and woke, head resting uncomfortably on the book, with nothing more than a stiff neck. I drove into the office and made temporary management arrangements, having in the process to tell at least some of the staff what had happened. Then I drove to Heathrow, rendezvoused with the police and met Nicole off the plane. There, in a room whose seedy officialdom was emphasised rather than ameliorated by a vase of flowers, I told her. Accompanied by a policewoman who sat watchfully in the back, and escorted by a police car unafraid to use its siren and lights, we circumnavigated the M25 in record time and I left her at Stirton before driving on to Eastbourne to tell my father.

It was a tight schedule. The matron of the nursing home in which he now lived had agreed to divert him from the lunchtime news but couldn't guarantee that some other resident wouldn't pass on the bad tidings, and I was afraid that they might prove a fatal surprise. In the event he sat in a wingbacked chair and stared into the middle distance, his rheumy old eyes watering no more than they did on a normal visit. He was eighty and his grasp of events wavered from the apparently complete to the obviously tenuous. We drank a lot of tea and I explained that I couldn't stay as I had promised to fly out to Spetse and tell Katie.

Neither Nicole nor I felt she should find out from the Cliffords with whom she was holidaying.

Which was why I stood at this window watching the neon signs fade into the dawn and the first clanking trams herald another ordinary day for port workers and wheeling gulls alike. The sense of being in a time warp that the trams and the archaic lines of ageing trucks conveyed was perpetuated by the travellers on the island-hopping ferry. On its decks backpackers were outnumbered by old women in black coats and headscarves, chattering to their gnarled and goldtoothed consorts or munching the feta cheese pasties sold in the humid bar.

In every harbour that we docked, bundles of newspapers, along with anonymous crates and the occasional vociferous goat, were disgorged onto the quay. I wondered whether amongst the Athens dailies there lurked an occasional *Daily Telegraph* carrying Stuart's story 'by our Crime Correspondent' for the mild tittilation of British tourists; something to be left on a café table or smeared by beachy fingers coated with Hawaiian Tropic. I was aware of how often I had skimmed through similar accounts, drawn only by a familiar name or place or a hint of sexual irregularity. I doubted that a straightforward shooting by burglars would have detained me long, even with the added lucky escape of the stepdaughter.

It was commonplace. Another unfortunate crime added to the statistics, the subsequent conviction of its careless perpetrators eventually rating a scant line or two. It even seemed unreal to me, the deceased's brother. What I had witnessed bore little relation to my other memories of the victim. The post-death practicalities had kept these at bay, just as they had when my mother had died. It was only now, with nothing to occupy me on this sunny Aegean boat trip, that they crowded in.

We had not been close as children because the age difference, Stuart being ten years older, was too great. My first memory of him was in grey flannels, maroon blazer and cap, swinging his shiny black briefcase into the kitchen, home from Grammar School. Most younger siblings are an irritant to their elder brothers and sisters and I'm sure I was no exception. Not because I wanted to join in his games – I never even aspired to that – but because I hero-worshipped him. That gangly adolescent with the coxcomb above his double crown was a figure of mythological significance and courage to me. When he dived beneath the waves at Hastings or Bexhill and our mother, anxiously scanning their surface, began to panic I, scarcely more than a toddler, remained calm. My brother Stuart was not confined by the normal lung capacity of *homo sapiens*; he could swim underwater for ever. When he was ready to return to us he would, and of course he always did, popping up and waving cheerfully, halfway across the Channel.

Much later, when he wanted to emphasise my failure to grasp some physical principle or other, he would remind me of how, on one of those holidays, I had spent hours in the futile, frustrating and eventually tearful enterprise of attempting to turn out sandcastles from a plastic bucket filled with uncooperative pebbles. I wasn't quite as stupid as that anecdote made me sound. Selling buckets on that part of the coast was pretty fraudulent, as the only sand there was appeared at low tide when it was far too wet to stand up. I was simply trying to do what the kids in the comics did with the only raw materials available.

As we grew older my adulation, if anything, increased. When I in my turn was a gawky teenager he was the personification of the swinging sixties, an unbelievably glamorous character who sometimes blessed us in Watford with a Sunday afternoon visit. A halo of sophistication adorned his suede-jacketed shoulders, and his open-topped Triumph sports car radiated the excitement of his usual hunting ground – the King's Road. When he came alone my pleasure was unalloyed, but when one of his exotic and beautiful girlfriends (in those days I think the expression might actually have been dolly birds) was in tow I inwardly, and quite possibly outwardly too, squirmed with embarrassment. I was ashamed of the meatpaste sandwiches, the cling peaches and Carnation, the surreal yellow and pink squares of Battenburg cake. In my imagination these gilded couples were desperate to escape from my suburban parents and return to the hissing cappuccino machines and straw-jacketed wine bottles of Chelsea. In reality what they were probably keenest to get away from was my scowling and spotty face.

We only really became friends, or something akin to equals, when we began working together. Ever since I had picked up my psychology degree and enrolled on a postgraduate arts course in London he had been asking me what I was going to do with my life. He was already a successful advertising executive who believed that fun and what he called creativity (my own definition of this word was still academically high-falutin') could be mixed with business. A year later he set up his own marketing services and design company and started pushing me with apostolic zeal to join him. Still smarting at having just missed the golden age of student radicalism I held out until the oil crisis, the three day week, and the rise of the ultra right National Front persuaded me that the world was a more serious and unforgiving place than I had supposed. In 1976 I became the junior partner at Buccaneer.

This play on the Buchan surname looked somewhat less appropriate after the late eighties tarnishing of the image of bright young capitalist adventurers, but we'd been around long enough for the name to have lost its symbolism for clients, and although we have expanded we were never tempted by the Stock Exchange. Consequently no one outside the trade press has ever heard of us or, as far as I know, criticised us.

The reverberations of my youthful admiration and the unobservant familiarity that comes from seeing somebody virtually every day meant that only recently had I realised Stuart was a stocky middle-aged man with a rapidly receding hairline. He wasn't quite short enough to be realistically accused of having a Napoleon complex but I was four or five inches taller, and thinner. In this physical way he had become my little brother and his recognition of the combined disadvantages of size and age made him . . . sensitive. He looked hopefully for signs of incipient baldness in my flourishing thatch and for opportunities to emphasise his greater commercial experience. And I let him without rancour. It was too late for sibling rivalry. Our blood tie was far more remote than our business connection. We were less brothers, more old friends and allies.

I could hardly believe he was gone, despite having had to tell so many people. That repetitive formality should have normalised the event, allowed me to absorb and accept it, but it didn't seem to have done. And now I had to tell Katie who had become an orphan.

The last island at which the ferry had called had been high and rocky, the pale stone houses above the narrow harbour blending into the barren landscape; but Spetse was pine-clad, its interior peaks hazy in the noonday sun. From beneath canvas awnings Greek café society watched us dock. Donkeys and traps were lined up on the cobbled quay to take disembarking tourists to their hotels; there were no taxis. Following the instructions I had been given in London I looked for the tour company's local office. On the flaking blue door of a building at the corner of the square was the incongruous parrot and palmtree symbol of Aegean Hideaways.

I knocked, and it swung open. Inside, behind a ramshackle desk and making the most of the breeze created by an ancient fan, was a Greek woman with the statutory smouldering eyes and deep tan, offset by a startling puce bikini. She raised an inquisitive eyebrow.

'I'm looking for Dimitri Papandreou.'

'Are you one of ours?' she said eyeing my small shoulderbag. 'He should have met you from the boat.' She picked up a grubby list of their arrivals. 'Your name, please?'

'I'm not on holiday. I'm looking for someone who is staying in one of your villas. Your head office said Dimitri would direct me to it.'

'Oh.' This unorthodoxy seemed to have defeated her. She lit a cigarette. 'He is busy with the transport at the moment. You had better wait for his return. You would like to wait here or in the bar across the street?' She gestured vaguely. 'I will bring him.' That seemed to indicate which of the alternatives she preferred.

I looked around. There was nothing to sit on apart from a half-deflated rubber dinghy. 'OK. Thanks.' I found an empty umbrellaed table by the sea wall and ordered a beer. I had forgotten that the waiters were not as promptly attentive as their French counterparts and by the time the cold Amstel came the sight of Greek salads at the next table had made me hungry. I ordered one and another beer, knowing that I would have finished this one long before it arrived.

While I was eating, the girl and Dimitri locked their office and ambled over. She called for a couple of Sprites and was served immediately.

Dimitri looked just as Hellenic but when he opened his mouth the accent was pure North London.

'My dad's got a baker's on Green Lanes, just up from the old Haringey dog track. But my uncle has a restaurant up the road here so I could claim local knowledge. It's a good job; nice sun, nice hours, nice girls.' His companion sucked haughtily on her straw.

I explained who I was looking for.

'Perhaps I should telex head office,' he said. 'Sorry, but I ought to make sure it's OK.'

So I told them too. Bereavement must be a great weapon for con men; the mixture of sympathy and embarrassment it induces stunts any further questioning. He explained how to find the villa.

'There don't seem to be any taxis.'

'That's because nobody really needs one. The road runs out after a mile or so, and so do the hotels and stuff. There's a track that goes round the island and a bus; otherwise you can hire a motorbike or Vani has got a jeep . . .' He tailed off, realising that this comprehensive rundown of Spetse's transport arrangements was not required.

'It is only a kilometre,' said the puce bikini.

'I'll walk then.'

'Ciao.' She went back to her Sprite.

'Well . . . good, you know, luck . . . if there's anything we can, you know, do . . .'

'I don't think so, thanks,' I said and set off up the street.

The supermarkets and cocktail tavernas that ran down to the town's crowded beach gave way to a mixture of traditional hotels and holiday villas, their small gardens bursting with sweet-smelling shrubs. The high rise had yet to reach this island, although the unfinished building work that characterises the Greeks' own dwellings was much in evidence. Every modest house, whatever its age, featured a stumpy and incomplete breezeblock extension.

The sun was so strong that it had bleached the colour from everything apart from the sky. I stopped under the dusty awning of a shop and contemplated a selection of weary fruit and vegetables just to get away from it for a moment or two. A fat cat and equally rotund old woman gazed implacably at me from the murky interior. A radio jabbered, apparently using up the entire household's energy quota. I toiled on my deserted way, feeling like the stranger in a western until, turning a corner, I reached the short avenue of trees that marked the town's boundary and the relief of dappled shade. The metalled road gradually disintegrated into a mixture of sharp stones and parched earth. Poking out of it, as Dimitri had said, was a wooden sign for the Villas Hetaxion.

There were two, white painted, and the one on the right had been rented by the Cliffords. As it was three in the afternoon I thought there was a possibility that some at least of its tenants might be taking a siesta, but the louvred door was locked. I followed the terrace around until I was overlooking a small sandy beach. The distance from the centre of town was clearly a deterrent but there were still twenty or thirty territories staked out with towels and beach mats, and another four or five parties occupying tables outside the bar café situated in the scrub that bordered the sand.

My ideal scenario would have been to explain quietly to the Cliffords before taking Katie aside but, as I hadn't the faintest idea what they looked like, that was out. Either I waited here for them to return or searched for her on the beach. Whichever, I would have to tell her the truth straightaway. In an obscure cove on an out of the way island I could hardly claim to be just passing.

I left my bag and jacket by their barbecue but felt selfconscious even so in shirt, trousers and deckshoes amongst these predominantly topless sunbathers, particularly as my task entailed a voyeuristic study of any likely female form. I hoped that my sunglasses helped to conceal this. At least the partial anonymity they provided should give me some moments' recognition advantage over my niece.

What drew my attention to Katie and Jane Clifford, walking by the water's edge, deep in conversation, was that they were not topless. As Germanic matrons were beefily baring all I was surprised at this pair's modesty until I realised who they were; exposure in the presence of parents or the parents of your best friend was presumably unthinkably embarrassing.

Katie was tall and loose-limbed which, together with the sprinkling of freckles on her strong shoulders and across the evenly spaced and well constructed features of her face, gave her the open attractive look and healthy femininity peculiar to some Australian sportswomen. A tennis player or, in her black one piece costume, an Olympic swimmer. The grace of her movement was only marred by the slight stoop that is unconsciously adopted by women who feel too high or too busty. Her stance made the shaggy brown hair, a little streaked by the sun, its lower tendrils curlingly wet from the sea, fall across her cheeks.

Neither girl noticed me until I called her name. They both looked around, but until I removed the glasses Katie's expression was as questioning as Jane's. Then her blue grey eyes blinked rapidly. 'Hello. It's all right,' she said to Jane who was standing, arms protectively akimbo, in unconvincing imitation of a fishwife. 'He's a relation. What . . . what are you doing here?'

'Sorry,' I apologised to Jane. 'I just need to have a private word.' She backed off uncertainly. Katie stared at me. 'I've got some bad news, I'm afraid.' I felt as if I'd been saying this all my life, working up to the punchline of my routine like some stand-up tragedian. Her eyes flickered around, as if by avoiding mine they could stave off the information. 'I'm afraid your dad has been . . . has . . . died.'

She put her hand to her mouth, as if she was about to be sick. I held out an arm to her, pressed her shoulder gently, offering her the opportunity of a hug if she wanted one, waiting for the supplementary questions.

She turned and ran into the sea.

This was so unexpected that I just watched her until she was in deep enough to start swimming, breaststroke, away from the shore. What was she doing? I called out 'Katie' but she didn't look round. She had the dogged determination of someone trying to escape . . . the fact? . . . life? Suddenly I was convinced that she would drown, that she was suicidal and even if she changed her mind it would be too late. I tore off my shirt and trousers and charged in pursuit.

The temperature of seawater is always sufficiently lower than the air above to shock, but after the initial gasp and tightening of the skin its cold was soothing and I calmed down somewhat, settling into the rhythm of stroke and breath. Katie was a strong swimmer but, adopting the crawl, I gained on her inexorably and, as she was passing between the brightly-painted boats moored in the cove's mouth, I drew level.

'Katie,' I puffed, taking in some stingingly salty water. She looked but did not slow. I renewed my efforts and nosed far enough ahead to swing round and block her path. 'Stop for a minute. Please.' She trod water. 'I know how you feel. He's my brother, remember, as well as your dad. If you want to be on your own you can be, but not out here. There isn't an easy way to tell someone or for them to find out, I'm afraid. Do you want me to tell the Cliffords for you?' She sniffed, nodded. 'You'll have to point them out to me then. I don't know what they look like. Otherwise I'd have warned them first.'

'OK. Can we just stay here a bit longer?'

I said yes, although I could now feel the cold seeping into my bones. We both hung onto the anchor line of one of the boats and she asked me how and when but thankfully not why – as in why him? why us? why me? As we turned for the shore I identified the Cliffords for myself, unmistakeable even at this distance, the trio hovering uncertainly in the shallows, staring seawards, debating what to do, English rectitude overcoming concern and curiosity. 'Why don't you cut across to the villa, and when I've explained to them I'll meet you and you can decide what next?'

The Cliffords – 'Call me Tim' 'And Joan' they said heartily when I apologised for the unorthodox manner of our introduction – were sympathetic and accommodating, offering me the sofa in the villa that night and dissuading their daughter from running after Katie. I asked them for a key so that we could get in and dry off. Joan handed me one and, as I picked up my discarded clothes, nudged her husband. The pink of her sunburn perceptibly deepened.

'Perhaps you'd better have this, old man,' he said, discomfited, brandishing a towel and nodding downwards. I followed his gaze. Immersion had rendered my shorts transparent.

The sun was strong enough to dry my back before I reached the villa but, sitting in its shadow, Katie remained dripping wet, and when she spoke her teeth chattered. I hustled her inside and encouraged her to take a shower while I dressed and made some Nescafé.

There was no ferry until the next day so somehow we had to fill the time until then. I had no intention of leaving her alone, but would have accepted her opting to be with Jane, who she knew far better. As it was she said she would like to go for a walk, and didn't question my accompanying her. I scribbled a note to the Cliffords, and in silence we followed a footpath over the headland and onto an esplanade which took us to the old harbour. Too narrow and shallow for ferries, it was used by smaller sailing boats, and the tavernas catered for a more select class of holidaymaker.

'Let's have a drink,' Katie said. She ordered a cocktail of disturbing complexity which arrived with the obligatory umbrella and maraschino cherry. 'It's lovely, taste it,' she offered when I queried her choice. The mixture of rum, grenadine and I think Grand Marnier with fruit juice had created a potion which, while sickeningly sweet, managed to sting the back of the throat. I swilled my mouth out with my own ouzo.

'Not my cup of tea. Have you had it before?' It wasn't the time to be authoritarian but I didn't want her drinking spirits if she wasn't used to them.

'Of course. Last night, and the night before. We come down here for a drink before dinner.'

'Somehow I can't imagine Tim and Joan getting stuck into Grasshoppers or Brandy Alexanders.'

'They don't.' She smiled. 'Joan's strictly G and T and Tim would like a Scotch but for some reason it's very expensive here so he grits his teeth and has a beer.' She looked out over the water. Her eyes were red-rimmed and bloodshot but that could have been the sea salt.

A man in denim shorts was windsurfing in from one of the yachts, a black dog standing excitedly on his board, threatening the balance. As they approached the steps it could contain itself no longer and jumped ship. We watched it bark its master ashore and them both disappear amongst the half-finished wooden hulks in the boatyard opposite.

'I'd forgotten,' I said, 'how the sky and the sea both fade to the same shade of silver at the end of the day.'

'Yes, makes me think of King Arthur. I know that's the wrong type of legend but . . .' She shivered. 'Mysterious. Ghostly.' There was a hiccup of silence. 'When did you last come to Greece then?'

I told her and we ordered more drinks and all of a sudden the sun was gone and it was night.

'Shall we eat?' I asked. I mentally totted up her alcohol consumption. 'We'd better eat.' She was only wearing shorts and a vest. 'Do you want to get a jacket or something first?'

'No,' she said quickly. 'We can go inside if it gets too cold.' Which we didn't in the end. We stayed out where the chirpy bouzouki music from the taverna was a background to the melancholy clanging of metal masts, and the courses of our meze came and went almost as often as the glasses of retsina.

At one point I said, 'We're going to feel like shit tomorrow,' and she nodded. I thought about it. 'What the hell, we would feel like shit anyway.'

At another she said, 'Don't call me Katie. Please. That's a child's name.'

'It's what you've always been called.'

'Not by anyone but you and . . . Daddy . . . for years. Now it will just be you. So it's a good time to stop.' She put her knife and fork down shakily.

I squeezed her hand. 'OK.'

'You never spelt it right anyway. Catriona begins with a C.'

'You'd better remind me nearer your next birthday. Old habits die hard.'

'And would it be all right for me to call you Alex?'

'I thought you did.'

'No, I don't call you anything. It avoided arguments. When I was little I was made to call you Uncle Alex and I think Daddy thought dropping the "uncle" was a bit trendy or disrespectful or something.' Into my mind came a picture of the erstwhile demon of the King's Road, translated into the upholder of Victorian values. Presumably this hardening of the social arteries would happen to me in time. 'But I've never thought of you as an uncle. I mean I know you are my father's brother but you're not an uncle uncle.'

'Is that good or bad?'

'Oh good. Uncle uncles have pot bellies and red noses and chuck you under the chin while making stupid jokes.'

She negotiated the esplanade under her own steam but stumbled twice on the footpath, weaving off into the scrub and frightening the cicadas before I put her arm over my shoulder and mine round her waist to guide her home. By the time we had careered off the patio table she was on automatic pilot, virtually asleep. I lowered her onto her bed and put her on her side in case she was sick. I knelt down so that our faces were close enough for whispering, although I didn't see how Tim and Joan could have slept through our return. 'I'll only be next door if you need me.'

'OK.' She nodded and leant forward. Preoccupied by the possibility of her vomiting I reached for the bucket, but she was only trying to kiss me on the cheek.

'Goodnight.'

She smiled seraphically. 'Sleep tight, don't let the begbuds . . .' She giggled and stopped herself. 'Shhhhhh.' She tried again. 'Bed bugs bite.' Her eyes closed and by the time I had stretched out on the sofa she was letting out the occasional snore.

Our hangovers lasted all the way to Heathrow, aggravated by the airconditioning on the plane, and then it was back round the M25 – no police escort this time. It scarcely seemed possible that it was less than forty-eight hours since I had discovered Stuart; I felt like a man condemned to repeat the same journeys with the same information over and over again. When we arrived at Stirton Hall to find it locked and lifeless this sense of *déjà vu* intensified.

Chapter Three

By this time we were already in the hall, Cate having used her front door key. 'Don't wander round,' I said, feeling desperate, part paranoia, part fear of her finding the bloodstains upstairs. 'I'll ring the office. But let's stick together.'

She looked at me curiously. 'If we use the phone in the kitchen I can make some tea.'

It turned out that Nicole had left with the police on Thursday afternoon, not long after I'd gone to Eastbourne, and was staying with friends in Primrose Hill. 'I couldn't face sleeping in the house. I'm sorry you had a wasted journey. I thought you'd call the office before you drove down. I couldn't think who else to leave a message with.'

'It's all right.' I looked at Cate. She was looking out of the window, mug clasped in hand. 'Have there been any developments on the police front?'

'If there are they haven't told me.'

'What shall I—' I realised I was about to discuss Cate as if she were a piece of luggage. 'Would you like to speak to Cate?'

Nicole hesitated. 'Yes, you'd better put her on, Alex.'

I retreated ostentatiously to the sink. From this end, the conversation was a series of expressionless monosyllables. Eventually Cate put the phone down. 'I've got to go to the Brewsters with Nicole,' she said.

'Well, yes,' I said, a little surprised. 'I know this was . . . is . . . your home but—'

'Oh no, I don't want to stay here. I can get a train, but could you run me to the station?'

'Don't be silly. I'll take you all the way.'

'Thanks. I'll just get some stuff from my room. Don't worry. I won't go astray.'

Nevertheless I went up with her and mooched about while she packed a fresh suitcase. Her room was bedecked with posters and stacks of Penguin paperbacks. Deborah's, next door, was spartan by comparison – the few books left behind were those that she did not care to display in her flat. It might have been a roomset in a smart furniture store with its jazzy black-and-white duvet and rich red walls.

When I got home all I really wanted to do was get under my own duvet, but the light on the answerphone flashed insistently. Some more or less fluent expressions of condolence, and a raucous drunken harangue from my old friend Danny who clearly hadn't heard of the murder; his message contained a couple of casual insults directed at Stuart which, if he remembered them, would make him squirm with embarrassment. Too late now for retractions. Three requests to call the office and finally Saro.

'Alex, Lynn said you'd be home this afternoon. I'll try and slip out to call you again later but I can't promise. We have a dinner party. I'm so sorry about Stuart. I've been thinking of you. Bye.'

Stuart had introduced me to Saro four years previously, at a private view of an exhibition sponsored by Pasco, the edible fats to hairspray conglomerate. She was the wife of Henry Beaumont, a merchant banker of his acquaintance, and unusually she was looking properly at the paintings rather than giving them the customary cursory glance in between canapés. We struck up a conversation and, finding that she knew something about photography also, I invited her to another exhibition preview.

'I'd love to come.'

'What about Henry? I mean, I only have two tickets but I'm sure I can get . . .'

'Oh no,' she had said. 'These things are strictly in the line of duty for him. Besides, he'll be in New York by then.'

I hadn't given her any clue but she must have known that the Photographers' Gallery, a whitewashed space in a Clerkenwell backstreet, did not have the same dress code as a Royal Academy corporate bash. Instead of the tailored navy suit in which I had first seen her she wore an equally expensive-looking gauchoish outfit – the kind of Peruvian chic that was doing the rounds then. I subsequently realised that, while far from a clothes obsessive, Saro was always appropriately dressed; couture as camouflage rather than attention grabber. But despite her best efforts that night she failed to merge into a crowd which chose to disguise its affluence behind egalitarian 501s and black minis, and therefore attracted several intrigued appraisals from the organisers who could smell money but weren't sure what kind it was.

Saro wasn't a beauty but she was good-looking in an upperclass way. She was tall and thin and pale. Her skin was pale – not white but very faintly and permanently tanned; her eyes were pale blue; even her shoulderlength hair was a shade of pale mouse which I might have called beige if it hadn't sounded rude. She had a Roman nose, thin lips (also pale) and a pointed chin. She was all of a piece apart from the voice, her most startling feature. Not the accent which was, as one might have expected, cut glass toned down for everyday use, but the timbre – deep and slightly cracked as if she might be about to cry, or shake with some sort of emotion.

I had taken her out for supper after the viewing and tried to think of a pretext for seeing her again. She had suggested a weekday lunch to take in something at the Hayward, and while we were sitting on a couch there looking, as I recall, at an installation composed chiefly of ladders and buckets, I had asked whether she and Henry would like to come round to dinner. 'No,' she had said. 'Or at least not if we are going to have an affair.' She stared straight ahead. 'I haven't told him I'm seeing you today. He's not a suspicious man as far as I'm concerned but two people of opposite sexes meeting to look at pictures he would find far-fetched. Whether he believes it or not doesn't matter if our . . . relationship . . . is going to be platonic, but if not they must be secret assignations from the start.' She took a deep breath. 'So . . . do you want to?'

When she turned to look at me she must have mistaken my expression, surprised into imbecility, for a tacit refusal because she stumbled slightly as she said, 'I've been very forward. If the answer's no I do hope you can forget this conversation and that we can still meet . . . although I can see that would be impossible so—' She made to stand up.

I took her leather-gloved hand. 'It's irrelevant. I do want to. I mean I don't want it to be platonic,' I waffled. 'I've lost track of the syntax but not the meaning. Shall we go?'

And that was how it started. It was a long time before I asked her whether she'd ever propositioned anyone else.

'Never. But when we had supper together I realised I wanted to and I thought you did too, there was a certain . . . electricity. And then I thought you might, being' – she kissed me – 'the sensitive soul you are, take ages to broach the subject, what with me being a housewife and mother. And then it would have been too late. For secrecy. So I steeled myself to take the bull by the horns and hoped that if I was wrong you would be decent enough not to tell anyone what I had suggested.'

When she had married Henry she was twenty one and he was twenty eight. They had three sons – Hugo, Henry junior, known as Harry, and James – who, when we met, were nine, seven and four respectively. James was their attempt to have a girl, an enterprise that they had abandoned on statistical grounds after his birth.

The boys, as befitted their tradition, were despatched to boarding school at the appropriate age and Henry travelled on business frequently, but at the time of Stuart's death James had yet to begin his first term at prep school and so our meetings were confined to the occasional weekday lunch and afternoons at my house.

Discretion was absolute. I never rang Saro at home in Campden Hill Square, and although Stuart had to know the reason for my absences, and my secretary Lynn might have speculated on the precise nature of my relationship with Mrs Beaumont, I had told none of my friends. They, after abortive attempts to pair me off with single women of their acquaintance, presumably believed that I had sunk into celibacy or possibly that I was a closet gay, plying for rough trade on Hampstead Heath or in the public conveniences of Southwark.

Stuart, after ritual disapproval, simply said that if the imbroglio ever came to light he would deny everything. When visiting, Saro always parked her car round the corner although, as she remarked, 'I don't suppose any of my friends come south of the river except during Wimbledon fortnight, and if they're so lost that they're driving past here the last thing they would notice is the Golf.'

She had an au pair, a daily, and sat on various charitable committees. Otherwise, as far as I knew, she shopped, lunched, rode, cinemaed, and entertained Henry's business contacts. I lived on the fringe of her life and she on mine. I had never had an attachment like it but it seemed to work. We never spoke of love but we shared this satisfying secret. When she rang, as she eventually did that Saturday night I returned from Spetse, my heart jumped with anticipation.

There was no preamble so I guessed that it was a snatched moment of solitude. 'I'm so glad you're home safely. Listen, tomorrow we're taking the boys down to Tewkesbury' – Henry's parents – 'and I have to drop him at the airport, he's off to Bulgaria again' – like so many of his calling, Henry was heavily into the investment potential of the newly democratised Eastern Europe – 'so I could see you in the evening. Is that convenient?'

'Yes.'

'OK.' She was gone.

I spent the day catching up at the deserted office, and prepared a salad for our supper. I was at the window with my first glass of chilled Chablis when their Mercedes estate, dusty from its country outing, passed the house and vanished along the side street that led to the square. Seconds later she was on the doorstep in a sleeveless cotton frock, handbag tucked beneath her arm, cool and composed.

'How do you manage it?' I asked. 'If I'd just done that drive I'd be grimy, pink, and perspiring.'

'I don't suppose you would powder your nose before leaving your car. And I wouldn't advise you to test the perspiration hypothesis.' She put her arms around me, and I smelt the familiar cucumber of her perfume. 'How are you?'

'OK.'

'Don't you want to talk about it?'

'I'm not sure. Maybe it will just spill out as we eat. Tell me what's been happening to you.'

Dutifully she did, and in far more detail than I might normally have expected, picking at her salad and taking the merest sips of wine, watching me warily. 'Are you looking for symptoms of shock?'

'I'm sorry,' she said. 'I don't know what to do or say for the best. You're not a child, to be comforted easily. We haven't had to contend with this much unpleasant reality before.'

'Have you finished?' I indicated her plate.

'Yes – Henry's mother is convinced I'm anorexic now that she's discovered the word, although why they're writing about it in *The Field* I can't imagine. And she makes no concessions to temperature so I've had enough of the roast beef of old England to blow out Falstaff.'

'Can you manage the stairs?'

'Yes, if you—'

'Feel up to it?' I grinned. 'I'm bereaved, not paralysed. Don't worry; it's not disrespectful.'

She smiled back. 'For once I can stay all night so there's no rush.'

'Oh, I think there is.'

I don't know whether Henry was a confirmed missionary position man, but with me Saro almost invariably ended on top. Sometimes, just sometimes, eyes closed and her muscular thighs gripping my flanks, I understood the horse and rider analogy, although the occasional snorted breaths, which were the only noise she made as she galloped towards conclusion, confused our roles slightly. Conclusion rather than orgasm; when I was twenty I would have claimed to know an orgasm when I heard one, but now I wasn't so sure. Then I thought I knew all about women; now I suspected I knew nothing at all.

I slept fitfully, and when I dreamed I was standing in my drawing room, in the dark. The curtains billowed. There was something behind them, rustling and whispering. I knew that whatever it was meant me harm, and that I should defend myself, but I could find nothing to defend myself with. No poker in the hearth because the flames were gas-generated, no knives, not even a vase. Ostrich-like, I put my hands over my eyes.

When I parted my fingers a figure was gliding from behind the drapes. It was Stuart in his bloodstained robe, but the head on the shoulders was his as a young man. Behind him came his first wife, Angela, with the snow on her hair of that final fatal run down the piste. She was laughing, but not the girlish peal I remembered; this was the cackling of an old crone. Then my mother, sunken-cheeked as she had lain in her coffin, mouthing and dentureless. I backed across the room, tripped over the captain's chest that served as an occasional table, and fell on the sofa. They crowded in on me, muttering, threatening. The light was bright above them but I could just make out another head, balaclavaed, in the background. They bent towards me. I woke up.

'God, Alex, are you all right?'

'Yes, I'm fine.' I was soaked in sweat.

'What was it? A bad dream?'

I told her.

'Do you think they were trying to tell you something?'

'No, they were threatening me. That's the worst thing. All the people who've been closest to me that have died, and when I see them they're out to get me. I mean, I know they weren't in life so what does that say about my psyche?'

'Nothing. You've had a disturbing time. It's bound to jumble things up a bit.'

'I'm sorry. The first time you stay here overnight and you're subjected to the ravings of a nutter. I'm not normally like this.'

'Of course you're not.'

'Perhaps it's just that I'm so unused to sleeping, I mean literally sleeping, with anyone.'

'How long, since you did?'

'Four years.'

'You don't have to be faithful to me, you know.'

'I know. I just happen to have been.'

'Happen to have been, or chosen?'

'Chosen I guess.' I pushed the duvet away from my chest. 'Christ, it's hot in here.'

'As they say in the movies,' she added, smiling.

'I'm really sticky.'

She licked my ribs. 'Nice and salty.' She ran her finger along my cheekbone. 'Are you feeling better now?'

I nodded.

'Do you want a glass of water or something?'

'No.'

'Then as we're both so wide awake, perhaps you can do something to put me back to sleep.'

'What?'

She kissed her way down my stomach. 'Let's see,' she said, her voice muffled beneath the bedclothes, and I felt her wet lips on my flaccid penis. She peeled back the skin and sucked until I was stiff. Then she wriggled back up my body and, kneeling above me, deftly slipped me inside to begin another canter towards oblivion.

I woke, as always on a Monday, to the sound of the bin-men in the basement area. Saro stirred when the lid was clattered back into place, drawing her knees more firmly up against her body. This position is normally described as foetal but in her case the lean limbs were more reminiscent of the racing posture of a National Hunt jockey.

A delivery truck reversed into the yard of the Iceland freezer centre opposite, bleating electronically. That reminded me to switch off the radio alarm. I had to get up but there was no reason why she should be woken again.

While I was in the shower the phone rang, and a frisson of excitement traversed my gut. Whenever Saro was there I always half-imagined it would be Henry; that he had somehow discovered what was going on. But it never was. By the time I had answered it, she was sitting up.

'Why didn't you wake me?'

'You were sleeping the sleep of the innocent.'

'Innocent? I'm an adulteress.'

'The sleep of the amoral then.'

'Have you finished in the bathroom?'

I shaved while she showered, watching her in the mirror to the detriment of my chin which I snagged twice with the razor. Female friends had complained that having babies ruined their figures, but to my admittedly inexperienced eye no havoc had been wreaked on Saro. Her breasts were self-supporting and her belly flat. I wasn't quite certain what stretchmarks looked like but hers bore no markings of any sort, apart from a mole just below the navel.

'Perhaps I could keep a few clothes here. I don't like going home in yesterday's dress but I couldn't really conceal another in my handbag. It was hard enough hiding the knickers.'

'You sat through lunch at your in-laws with spare knickers for illicit purposes in your handbag?'

'Well, I draw the line at wearing the same ones twice, even for you.'

'Keep as many as you like. There's plenty of wardrobe space. Bring some when you next come round. When will that be?'

'I'm not sure. I'd better call you.'

When I got to the office I rang a locksmith. I knew that in my dream the apparitions had come through a first-floor window, but bars over those in the basement seemed a sensible idea, something I told myself I'd anyway been contemplating for ages.

Chapter Four

Stuart had specifically requested that he be buried in the churchyard at Stirton, which was just as well since, left to her own devices, I thought Nicole would probably have opted for a North London cremation. Under the circumstances I couldn't say that I blamed her.

Apparently neither she nor the girls had been back to the house before the day of the funeral, and we assembled there barely half an hour before the undertaker's cars arrived. It was hot and the floral tributes on the front lawn already looked tired.

The place had been opened up by Mrs Cuttifer who, assisted by a couple of other middle-aged ladies, was preparing a buffet lunch. From somewhere they had found a couple of ornamental ropes which barred access to the upper storey and these, together with the smell of uninhabitation, gave the building the air of a National Trust property.

St Michael's was only four hundred yards from the house and so there was some confusion as to whether we should walk or ride in the limousines. The chief pall-bearer approached Nicole and asked in hushed tones which she would prefer.

'Walk,' she said.

Deborah stared at her. 'No,' she said. 'Definitely no. I don't want people staring.'

'They'll only be paying their last respects. It's ridiculous to drive that tiny distance.'

Both of them were tight-lipped and desperately pale beneath their make-up; I thought this might be the blue touchpaper of an emotional outburst. I moved in to defuse the situation, glad that Cate was out of earshot, sitting with my father. The funeral director hovered uncertainly.

'But what about reporters?' Deborah was saying.

'The thing is,' I said quietly, 'Dad isn't really up to the walk, so he at least will have to go in the car, and someone ought to sit with him . . .'

Nicole gave me a very cold look. 'In that case we must all do the same.'

'Well,' I said, 'if you feel strongly I'll walk with you.'

'No thank you. It will look absurd if we are straggling all over the place.'

To my amazement there were a couple of photographers at the lych gate, but as the Daimlers had to halt in an orderly queue on the village street we were forced to run the gauntlet of the gaggle of onlookers in any case.

I had collected Dad from the nursing home very early that morning and, coming up through the iridescent Sussex countryside, he had been extremely lucid, recalling with great clarity the day that Stuart had been given his racing bike, and how Mum, which is what the old boy still called her, had stood at the window with her knuckles pressed to her lips as her eldest son had ridden away. She was sure that he was going to take the skin off his knees and elbows at the very least, and she blamed this anxiety for the fact that his birthday cake had turned out somewhat soggy and heavy.

Rather touchingly Dad, or the matron, had pinned his service medals to the pocket of his blue suit, and they clanked as he clumped across the uneven grass to the graveside. He had sung the hymns as lustily as his aged larynx would allow, and nodded sagely at the vicar's brief eulogy. I was therefore completely unprepared when he turned to me and asked in a penetrating voice, 'Young chap, was he?'

'Who?'

'This fellow we're sending off.' He gestured to the empty grave, with its adjacent blanket of emerald plastic grass covering the earth that would smother the coffin.

'He was forty-eight.' I didn't know whether to laugh or cry.

'Unlucky to be taken so early. Or careless.' He tutted, shaking his head a little, but thankfully the rambling stopped.

Nicole, Deborah and Cate stood on the opposite side of the grave in a row; strangely it was Deborah who seemed the odd one out, being several inches shorter than her mother or step-sister. The flared black skirt beneath the bolero jacket, and black lace holding back the long black hair, made her more of a Mediterranean femme fatale than ever, the dark eyes challengingly sulky despite being red-rimmed from crying. Her build and looks – sallow skin, wide and pouting mouth – she must have inherited from her father. Only her dress sense marked her as her mother's daughter.

Nicole's eyes were partly hidden by the net veil of her hat, under which her blonde hair had been gathered to leave the shape of her face exposed. She was strong-featured and muscular without being masculine. Her elegant dress accentuated the benefits of a strict regime of swimming and squash. Unlike many tall women she was not embarrassed by her height, neither stooping nor eschewing heels. The shoes that she was wearing now must have added an extra couple of inches.

Cate was shod in a pair of heavy black loafers, of the type which only a man would have worn until recently. In defiance of the heat her black tights were thick, and the unstructured jacket that topped her short black stretchy skirt was reminiscent of a school blazer waiting to be grown into. Everything about her appearance distanced her from the others; sullen adolescent acquiesence in the face of unwelcome but unavoidable events.

When they lowered him into the ground Deborah sobbed audibly and Nicole, sternly in control until that moment, dabbed ineffectually at the delicate tear tracks on her own cheeks. Cate looked above our heads, perhaps at the church, her gaze more a disinterested glare than anything else.

When, at my mother's funeral, the coffin had trundled behind the crematorium curtains, I had experienced some kind of cathartic release, and I had expected the same to happen here; even perhaps for it to be more intense given that a hole in the ground was less banal than the mechanics of the municipal chapel of rest. But nothing came to shift the dull weight of anger, frustration and regret.

As we were leaving the church and the photographers were snapping away – one even having the gall to call, 'Deborah, this way' – I saw Superintendent Cromarty. He was sitting in a car along the lane, window down, a summer-shirt-sleeved elbow poking out. He must have seen me looking in his direction but made no acknowledgement, perhaps uncertain of the etiquette of greeting the bereaved while on duty and inappropriately dressed. What was he doing there? He could hardly expect the burglars to turn up at the funeral for old time's sake.

But there were plenty who had. Back at the house the awkward whispering of the guests rose with the food and drink to normal party level. I accepted condolences from a string of Stuart's friends, including Henry and Saro. She, of course, did not betray by so much as a flicker that we had met since Stuart's birthday party. In a corner of the room my father was regaling some distant cousins with an eye-witness account of a Zeppelin raid. I wondered whether any of them knew enough family or world history to calculate that he had been a small child living in Saltcoats on the Ayrshire coast during the First World War, and therefore not a potential victim of the German airforce, with whom he had only made acquaintance twenty years and a global conflict later.

I left him to it and went into the garden. One or two groups were dotted about the terrace and on the sloping lawns. Deborah, make-up impeccably repaired, jacket discarded to reveal a white silk shirt, sat at a wrought iron table, nursing a glass of white wine and nodding at the monologue of a middle-aged man with a bald pate and a goatee beard. I pulled up a chair, and the monologue tailed off.

'Thanks,' she said, when he had made his excuses and left. 'He has always been able to bore for England.'

'Who is he?'

'Bill Starling. He's an old friend of Mummy and Daddy's.' By which she meant her natural father, Charlie Makepeace.

'An actor then?' Charlie had been a promising Hamlet who had degenerated – or risen, depending upon your cultural point of view – to the mini-series and portraying the occasional well-spoken villain in a Hollywood blockbuster.

'No, a journalist. A critic. Actually,' she smiled, 'more Mummy's friend. I'm not sure that Daddy ever much cared for him. We used to call him Merlin. After the wizard.'

Charlie had left home ten years ago, abandoning Nicole, then thirty, for an eighteen-year-old aspirant actress very similar to the girl she had been when he got her pregnant with Deborah. And Starling had remained friendly enough to be invited to the funeral of Nicole's next husband. He had the look of a courtier.

'Have you seen your father recently?' I asked.

'Yes, he was over for the premiere of *Extreme Prejudice 3*. Did all the chat shows.'

I had heard him – on *Start The Week*, *Midweek*, and possibly even *Stop The Week*. I had also seen him on *Churchill's People*; tanned, white-haired, the nascent jowls not quite hidden by a beard, the incipient paunch just disguised by the Versace suit, the roisterer with a twinkle in his eye poking through the surface of Californian chic.

'I went out with him and Staten,' she said bitterly.

'Is that his wife?'

'No, not even his third wife. Dory was at home in Bel Air. Staten had a small part in the movie. She must be about seventeen.'

'Oh.' There wasn't much to say. I thought, and perhaps she did, about history repeating itself. On the other side of the lawn, by a gate that led in to the kitchen garden, Cate was standing, watching us. When she realised that I had noticed her she turned, went through the gate, and disappeared.

'In a way,' Deborah was saying, almost plaintively, 'I suppose Mummy was the luckiest. I mean she had twelve years, whereas Rachel had seven, and Dory looks like she may not make the four.'

Did they look at his pedigree? It wasn't really a question I could ask his daughter, who also seemed to regard him as a loveable rogue.

'Would you like another drink?' Deborah asked.

'No thanks.'

'OK. I'll just nip inside and get myself one.'

I knew, and her tone implied, that I should have gone for her, but I thought I should find Cate. I hadn't seen her talking to anybody since we had returned to the house.

The kitchen garden was big, originally designed to feed a very large household. Stuart had laid a tennis court here, where it could not be seen from the house, and much of the rest was given over to shrubs and flowers. But there were fruit cages and runner bean poles, and an enormous greenhouse with some of its panes whited out. I opened the door and was overwhelmed by the smell of ripening tomatoes.

Cate was sitting on a wooden box at the far end. She didn't look up.

'Hello.'

'Hello.'

I walked down the aisle. 'How are you feeling?'

'OK.'

'But not like company?'

'Not really.'

'Can I get you anything?'

She flashed me a tiny, conspiratorial grin. 'I've had some tomatoes. Mr Cuttifer will be cross. It's always been a condition of his working here that no one but he picks the produce.' She paused. 'I'm all right. I just don't want to talk about it. I couldn't face all those people sympathising.'

'I know what you mean. Listen, I'm going to have to take Grandad back to Eastbourne soon, before he starts telling people he was with Nelson at Trafalgar and they realise he's been fantasising all along. But I'll see you tomorrow. Don't stay out here so long they raise the alarm.'

She raised a worldweary eyebrow.

'Bye then.' I gave her shoulder a squeeze. I had already reached the door when she said, 'Alex . . .' I waited. 'Drive safely.' I felt a bit of a traitor when I told Nicole where she was.

Chapter Five

Boy Chippenham, a university friend of Stuart's, had been Buccaneer's solicitor from the start, and had apparently handled all of his personal affairs since, including the drawing up of the will. Although Stuart had asked me to act as an executor I had not seen it, and at the time had given the matter no thought assuming, as one does, that it would only be needed in some dim and distant future.

Boy had requested that executors and beneficiaries assemble in his office on the morning after the funeral. Unlike the previous day it was grey and, at least on the Embankment, blowy – appropriately gloomy weather for such an occasion. The neo-classical facades of the Temple, set around lawns and with the names of barristers in chambers painted at their doors, were reminiscent of the Oxford and Cambridge colleges from which so many of the lawyers came. Boy's office was on the edge of this insular community, convenient for the Law Courts in the Strand, and the Old Bailey.

I was the first to arrive and, having been given a coffee and a custard cream, which seemed too irreverent a biscuit for its setting, sat before his battered partner's desk. 'I didn't realise the reading of the will happened in real life,' I said. 'I assumed it was a convenience for the plots of detective stories.'

Boy reclined in his chair. Against the backdrop of legal reference books, gilt dusty on their fading crimson spines, he looked more youthful than ever, a schoolboy pretending to be middle-aged. As the disparity between standing and appearance which had given rise to his soubriquet grew wider, he had affected ever more accoutrements of stolidity, but to no avail. The pinstripe suits had acquired double-breasted waistcoats, and the waistcoats had acquired a watch-chain. His haircut positively emphasised his receding hairline, and as a last desperate attempt at *gravitas* he had grown a moustache – but it resolutely refused to look realistic. The temptation to test the strength of spirit gum and pull it off was sometimes overwhelming. 'It's not common,' he said. 'But where those involved are all family, it's quicker than contacting each one separately.'

That may have been so, but a predilection for drama, which can often be seen in solicitors coveting the barrister's ability to strut upon the stage, was also a factor. For when the beneficiaries were all assembled – apparently only Nicole, Deborah, Cate, and I – Boy ignored the copies at his right hand and simply declaimed from the original.

It was a simple will. Stuart had left the whole of his estate to Nicole with two exceptions – but the exceptions turned out to be substantial. He had owned 700 Buccaneer shares, the remaining 300 being mine. 500 of Stuart's shares went to Cate and 200 to me, which meant that now we each controlled 50% of the company's stock.

It would be a lie to say that I hadn't given any thought, since Stuart's death, to the disposal of his shares and therefore the effective future ownership of Buccaneer, but this was one outcome I hadn't envisaged. I had always assumed that there would be a wider division involving Nicole, and apparently so had she, judging by the faint look of surprise on her face.

'As the sole sur—director at present, Alex is probably best placed to explain the implications of this inheritance,' Boy was saying. 'There are certain limitations on your voting rights, although not, of course, on your entitlement to income. We can perhaps discuss these in greater detail at another time.' Cate remained taciturn, nodding minutely.

The only other provision was that Deborah received a portfolio of investments. 'The income from that is rather easier to evaluate,' Boy said. 'Last year it amounted to about £20,000.' Deborah looked shocked. Nicole, who had darted her a glance, now appeared slightly perplexed. 'Were those Stuart's only investments?'

'No,' Boy said. 'There are two portfolios, both composed of similar blue-chip stock, and both generating a similar income. The second is yours.' As if she had asked what else he continued. 'The other main components of the residue of the estate, which of course are also yours, are: Stirton Hall and all its contents, a life insurance policy with a surrender value of approximately £200,000, and various bank and building society accounts amounting to a further £33,000.' Nicole thanked him, gravely, as if he were the provider rather than the messenger.

'Well,' Boy said, once the papers had been handed round. 'If there are any questions you can contact either Alex or myself at any time, and I will, in any case, be in touch. Thank you for coming.'

As they filed out I said to both Nicole and Cate, 'I'll call you,' and then felt guilty at having left out Deborah, although I had never had any reason to call her before. As soon as we were alone Boy said, 'I think we can finish our business for today over a bottle at El Vino's, if you feel so inclined. More convivial place for a chat than this hole, anyway.' Cautiously he collected his umbrella and a light raincoat for a walk of two hundred yards.

At one time, when Fleet Street was the real home of newspapers, the darkly panelled bar at El Vino's had been a hive of loud, scabrous gossip and backbiting journalistic bonhomie. Now that the clientele was almost entirely legal the same sentiments were expounded in more muted tones and by more muted suits. We ordered sandwiches, and Boy extolled the virtues of the wine that we sipped before changing the subject with scarcely a pause for breath.

'How much, more or less, is Catriona's stake in the company worth?'

'It's hard to say exactly but, assuming that we do as well this year as last, then the profit was £200,000. We normally retain half and split the rest in proportion to shareholding. On that basis she would collect £50,000 a year.'

'That's about what I thought,' Boy said, 'from the accounts. I'm not terribly good at reading balance sheets, but even I can just about spot the bottom line.'

'I suppose it would be more,' I said, 'because whoever I recruit to take over the parts of Stuart's job I can't manage, they won't be paid more than about half his salary.'

'Which was £120,000?' He had read the balance sheet. 'But surely, if you're becoming chairman or chief executive or whatever you'll want to pay yourself more. I mean at present you're paid . . . what . . . eighty grand?'

Being English I wasn't particularly comfortable discussing my personal finances with a friend. 'Yes. Plus my profit share. It's enough. I might leave things as they are at present; there are plenty of more important adjustments to make.'

Boy nodded approvingly. I presumed he was tactfully keeping an eye on Cate's interests.

There were a lot of things to be sorted out. Aside from keeping happy the clients that Stuart had handled, I knew that a limited company such as ours needed at least two directors but, as they had always been Stuart and me, I didn't know whether any new appointees had also to be shareholders or, if not, what voting rights they would have.

The sandwiches arrived and Boy set about them with relish. He ate in a way that reminded me of a frog or toad, popping each delicate triangle entire into the pink hole of his mouth which then snapped shut. Whilst chewing he crossed his equally pink hands over the buttons of his waistcoat, eyes occasionally blinking, jaw working, otherwise immobile.

'I hadn't expected to get extra shares myself,' I said. 'But nor had I expected all of the others to go to Cate.'

'What had you expected?'

'I don't know. Cate to get some, Nicole to get some, Dad to get some, I don't know who else.'

'Divide and rule.'

'That sounds very cynical.'

'I thought business was cynical. And before you say so, let me make it clear that I realise that is very much a case of the legal kettle calling the commercial pot black.'

'I just want the company to go on as before,' I said, without forethought.

'Then I think you have the best outcome. Share splits are usually messy and so often those who try to divide and rule can end up ruling nothing as the company gets sucked down in the politics. In terms of control, I don't think you need have any worries, at least in the short term. It was clearly Stuart's intention that Buccaneer should stay not only within the family but within the bloodline. Even his own daughter is not allowed to rock the boat until she's crewed it for at least three years. Stuart obviously trusted you implicitly.'

The will had stated that Cate's shares entitled her only to income until she had worked for the company for three years, which seemed to leave me in sole charge. It was ironic that Stuart's wholehearted confidence in me was only revealed by his death.

Thinking about this girl that I hardly knew, and trying to imagine what I might have wanted if I'd inherited half a capitalist enterprise at idealistic eighteen, I was glad of the three-year safety net before she was entitled a vote. Maybe six years if she went to university first which, as far as I knew, she would if she hadn't messed up her A-levels.

'The only potential problem that I can see, speaking as your friend,' Boy said, 'is if she should want to sell. To finance something else or to help out a husband who might exert undue influence.' Boy held rather old-fashioned views on the susceptibility of wealthy women to fortune hunters, and indeed on the mixing of women with money at all, although if these were something more than pure prejudice he had never produced any evidence of it. 'I suggested to Stuart that he put in a clause giving you first option to buy at a fair price, but he was so convinced that she would not want to sell once the company was part of her life that he said it would be an unnecessary complication.'

'It's very hard to fix a fair price on the shares of a private company.'

'That's what he said,' Boy smiled. 'But as I pointed out, if in the end you can't agree, then—'

I laughed. 'Don't tell me. You can always go to law.'

'There's nothing wrong with that. I've got a wife, three children and mortgages in Barnes and Devon to support.' He lifted the empty bottle mournfully from the table. 'Do you think we should have another?'

'Can you afford it?'

Boy sighed over the wine list. 'If only I'd become a libel lawyer, we could be drinking the Chateau Lafitte '85.'

'When did Stuart make this will?'

'First draft, just after they got married.'

'But substantially the same?'

'Pretty much. Everything to Nicole apart from the shares which were split, as they still are, between you and Cate. Of course, had he died before she was eighteen they were to be held in trust for her by me.

So I would have been demanding a seat on the board. Sorry, that's in very poor taste.'

'Don't worry,' I said. 'Graveyard humour helps. I know you were fond of him. You didn't mention Deborah. Was she included in the first draft?'

'No, as a matter of fact. He only split his share portfolio in two this April.'

'So until then Nicole stood to get the lot.'

'Yes.'

'Do you think she knew, or thought she knew, what was in the will?'

'Who knows what other husbands tell their wives. Why do you ask?'

'She looked a bit taken aback, that's all. Deborah even more so.'

'Nicole's been left a very tidy sum anyway,' Boy mused. 'Particularly if you count the house, and the contents.'

'That doesn't have any monetary value if you need to live in it.'

'She might choose to sell it. I know the property market's rather uncertain at the moment, but it can't be worth less than what – four hundred? Five?'

I supposed this type of speculation was what being an executor was all about. I decided to change the subject. 'That policeman – Cromarty – was at the funeral.'

'Was he? Paying his respects; that's civilised for the boys in blue.'

'No. Just sitting in his car. Outside the church.'

'Oh.' Boy looked thoughtful. 'It's a shame there was no provision made for your father. Obviously Stuart never contemplated the possibility that the old fellow would survive him.' He was referring to the fees for Dad's nursing home, which had been split between us. 'I presume there's no difficulty there, because I'm sure he would have wanted—'

'It's not a problem,' I said hastily. What did he think – that I would see Dad thrown out for want of an extra two hundred a week? My extra shares would produce twice that much anyway, God or whoever – me – willing.

Discovering that Boy perceived me as a potential skinflint irked somewhat. But he had probably seen so many rapacious relatives of his clients transformed from apparent decency to slavering avaricious bastardy by the sight of an estate they considered to have been unfairly distributed that he was entitled to be jaundiced.

In a taxi on the way back to the office I wondered how Cromarty was getting on. I imagined that if he had made any real progress I, or at least Nicole, would have heard. And if he hadn't . . . somewhere I had read that the chances of the police solving a murder committed by persons unknown diminished dramatically after the first forty-eight hours, as forensic evidence disappeared. So it was quite possible that we would never know who had topped my brother for the pathetically few pounds that he kept in his desk.

'Alex.' Lynn, my secretary, was hovering in reception. 'I thought I should warn you that your niece is in your office. We didn't think you'd want her left waiting down here.'

'No. Very considerate of you. Thanks.'

Cate was sitting on my sofa, reading a paperback.

'Come for a look round?' I said. 'Might as well get a feel for the place. There's one or two things I have to do but they won't take ten minutes, and then we can have a chat about the business if you like.'

She flushed. 'It's not that. I mean, I am interested, of course, but that's not why I came today.'

I sat on the edge of the desk. Somehow sitting beside her on the sofa seemed aggressive. 'Would you like to talk about something else?'

'I wanted to ask you something.'

'OK.'

'Can I . . . come and stay with you?'

I was taken aback, but attempted to be light hearted. 'Will it be a flying visit?'

'Well, I hoped . . . until I go to university in September.'

'If you want to, of course you can.' Whatever the reasoning or implications I thought it was important not to reject her.

'Thank you.' She stood up. 'I'll go back to Primrose Hill and get my things.' She gave me the tiny, complicitous smile again. 'I knew you'd say yes.'

'Hang on a mo.' Her expression immediately regained its normal, bland watchfulness. 'Does Nicole know?'

'I couldn't see any point in telling her until I'd asked you. She'd only have told me not to.' She sniffed, and then gave a gulping sob. Tears filled her eyes and she grubbed for a tissue in her pocket. 'Fuck. I knew this would happen,' she said angrily.

'It doesn't hurt to cry. I mean, it does, of course, sometimes, but it's better to let go in any case.'

'It's just such a little-girlish thing to do.'

'Bloody hell. Your father's just died. It would be unnatural if odd things didn't make you weepy. They do me.'

'Do they?'

'Of course. And I expect Nicole feels the same. If you come to me I'd just be a little bit worried that she might feel even more lonely.'

'She won't. She's reverted to her old life.'

This seemed like an expression from some nineteenth-century moralist tract. 'What do you mean?'

'Her old friends. It's as if the last six years didn't exist. Not that I mind,' she added almost grandly. 'But she doesn't want me with her. I'm not even her own daughter.'

Nicole rang me about an hour later – more or less the time I'd estimated it would take Cate to get back to Primrose Hill. She apologised for her stepdaughter having bothered me.

'It wasn't a bother,' I said. 'And I'm happy to have her. It seems a radical decision but she must be very shaken up and confused. I'm sure it's not meant as any kind of slight to you.' I couldn't quite think what else to say.

'Won't it be hard for you, having somebody else around the house, particularly an adolescent girl? You've lived alone for a long time.'

'Don't worry, I'll take care of her.'

'I'm sure you will. But you shouldn't have to unless you want to.'

'Is she there with you now?' Once again Cate was being discussed like a possession.

'No; give me some credit for sensitivity, Alex. I'm not the wicked stepmother, you know, despite what Cate might say.'

'Of course you're not . . . and she doesn't,' I added somewhat hopelessly.

'Well, if you're sure you can cope with her, perhaps it's best that we have a break from each other.'

'Yes. I'm sorry.' I didn't know for what precisely, just that it needed to be said. I'd begun to feel that I didn't know these people at all. Contrary to my expectations Nicole didn't seem distressed at losing her child – all right, not her natural child, but one that she had seen through adolescence, amicably as far as I had been aware, and her strongest living link with a dead husband. Maybe that was it; Stuart's death had turned the world topsy-turvy for both of them. Perhaps Cate was domestically the spoilt brat that Nicole now implied rather than the slightly gauche young adult that I had seen. Still, I must have been insufferable to my parents at eighteen but they had given every appearance of missing me when I left home. Maybe that had been an elaborate bluff.

When she arrived she had two suitcases – one new and clearly her own in a tapestry pattern that matched her shoulder bag, the other a battered cardboard affair held together with a trouser belt.

'I'm amazed that's still in use. It's been in that state ever since your dad went on his first package holiday.'

'I found it in the loft when we were clearing out the house in Fulham, and I've used it ever since. Much to Nicole's distress.'

That sounded unfair; Stuart would have been just as keen to replace it with Louis Vuitton. 'And his as well I should think,' I said.

She shrugged in rueful acknowledgement. 'You're right.'

'Do you want a drink or something?'

'Can I have a look round first?'

'Yes, go ahead. Do you want a hand with the luggage?'

'Please. And I'd like you to show me where everything is.' She smiled. 'I think you've forgotten. I've only been here once.'

It must have been true. Stuart had sometimes popped in on his way home, and he and Nicole had occasionally been to a party here but I could not remember Cate in this setting at all. 'When was that?'

'I think I must have been about ten. It wasn't long after Mummy died.

I don't remember much about it except it was dark and there was no proper furniture. I was terribly impressed by that, and by the electric guitars and stuff lying about. I think you'd just bought it, and I think Dad thought you'd made a mistake.'

She was right. In 1982 Stuart had advised strongly against taking out a mortgage on this decaying early-Victorian terraced house on a main bus route in unfashionable south-east London. Even Battersea was hardly acceptable then, let alone the fastnesses beyond the Elephant and Castle. The most that he could say for it was that it was convenient for work, being less than half the distance and journey time from Buccaneer than his own north-of-the-river piece of Fulham Edwardiana.

I'd lived in the house ever since I'd moved to London to do my post-graduate course in 1973. It was being rented out then by a displaced Lebanese named Girsoy Hassan. There were two double rooms – one in the basement which had the advantage of being next to the only bathroom, dank and mildewed though that was, and the other where I had my bedroom now, which had the advantage of daylight through large windows and a view, although only of a used car lot and a pub called the The Knobkerry, since demolished to make way for the freezer centre.

The other four rooms were singles and, being the new boy, I had had the smallest – now the guest room on the first floor. They all commanded the same rent and so, the next summer when the inhabitants turned over in accordance with graduations and exam failures, I had moved to half of my present drawing room. In 1976 when I joined Buccaneer I took advantage of the ensuing personal economic boom to annexe the upper double room for myself. I could of course have moved out altogether but I wasn't entirely sure that I was ready for the world of work, and the top floor front gave me more space and privacy within the security blanket of a familiar community.

You could measure my progress to a kind of adulthood by the proportion of that house that I paid for and occupied. By the time that I was thirty, in 1982, I had the whole of the top floor and therefore the attic, which had previously been communal. I also had access rights to one of the bedsits below, ever since Julia had moved in and we had become lovers. The whole idea of group living, and my place within it, had finally become anachronistic. Coincidentally, apart from Julia who still had a year of her degree course remaining, the others were destined to leave that summer. So I went to Hassan and made him an offer for the place.

Although we'd discussed it, neither Julia nor I had understood how profoundly my owning the house, and us being the only two in it, would change our relationship. Instead of being co-tenants we became landlord and lodger, except that if you are also lovers then it seems an absurdity for one of you to retain a separate room and pay for it. We lasted another two years, but the writing had been on the wall ever since we'd pulled down the plywood partition that had created Julia's bedsit out of half the drawing room, amused by the symbolism of the fact that the other half had at one stage been mine.

'It must have changed a lot,' said Cate. It had. The room in which we now stood was still the kitchen/dining room, but the white-painted oak units and marble worksurfaces were a far cry from the grimy Belling and chipped formica of the seventies. The walls were now an oxblood red and on the silk Kashmiri rug at the dining end of the room stood a highly polished Georgian table and eight chairs. It was in front of those windows, on a large bean bag and overlooked by Che Guevara, that Nicky and Lindy, the dopehead anthropologists, had sat in their tatty kimonos and rolled their first joints of the day.

We went out into the hall where I saw, leaning against the striped Colefax and Fowler wallpaper below the dado rail, the faint wraiths of bicycles past. Up the stairs to the first floor where, on the present site of an enormous sofa in the pale yellow drawing room, the ghost of Julia sat hunched on her mattress in an old sweater, blonde rats' tails hanging across her face, bitten nails tapping in time to some jazz rock track. Off the same landing was the guest room. 'It's good,' I said. 'Apart from the bathroom it's the only other that faces the rear and looks over the park.' The kitchen window was just too low to let you see over the high brick wall that boundaried the bottom of the garden.

'You've got your own private gate,' she said. 'Do you use it much?'

'I don't suppose I've opened it for years. So unless Mr McGinty keeps it oiled, the hinges have probably rusted up.'

'I'll try it tomorrow. Who's Mr McGinty?'

'The man who does the garden.'

She wasn't fazed by the idea of having a gardener – after all, Mr Cuttifer had spent his retirement from the County Council's playing fields department in the grounds of Stirton Hall, trimming hedges and raising produce – but by the fact that I needed one for my meagre plot. I looked down on the mossy brick patio and path, the thin strip of lawn surrounded by sweet-smelling shrubs and bushes, the inevitable lime tree in one corner. 'I can't tell a wallflower from a rhododendron, but I like somewhere nice to sit,' I offered by way of explanation.

'It is nice. Sort of cosy and enclosed.'

We went up to the second floor, which was entirely taken up with my bedroom, an attached dressing room and a bathroom in which I had further indulged an affection for marble.

'Gosh,' she said, which was an appropriately outdated exclamation. 'It's like a very posh hotel.'

'There's another bathroom in the basement, but that's rather a long way, so feel free to use this one.'

'I certainly will if you're out. Mind you, I haven't seen the other yet. That might be full of potted palms and a . . . a Mediterranean wall painting for all I know. In which case I shall alternate.' She got up off the Lloyd Loom chair and wandered back into the bedroom. 'Brilliant colour.' The walls were somewhere between jade and emerald.

'You need to be a bit careful. Show them a sporting print and they'll start thinking they're a billiard table.'

She looked through the open door of the dressing room and gestured at the engravings of hare and hounds on the wall. 'Is that why you keep them all in here?'

'Oh yes. They go with putting on my soup and fish.'

She stared at me blankly.

'Dinner jacket,' I explained. 'Allows me the illusion that I'm not only doing it for some lousy bunfight at the Grosvenor House Hotel.'

'Why are correct explanations always less interesting than imagined ones? Soup and fish sounds really surreal.'

'So is an evening at the Grosvenor House.' We went out onto the landing again. 'I'll leave you to unpack while I get some supper. Is pasta OK?'

'Lovely.' She pointed to the small flight of stairs that continued upwards. 'What's at the top?'

'Attic. It's the only part of the house I haven't done.'

'Can we have a look?'

The room, with unvarnished board flooring and walls of pitted plaster, was lit from skylights in the flat roof – enough to pick up the dust haze created by our intrusion but not enough to penetrate the shadowy spaces between the racks of old clothes and piles of discarded artefacts.

Cate picked up the trumpeter from an ensemble of Robertson's golly musician figurines.

'Not the full set. I never managed to get the banjo-player,' I said.

Behind the gollies was one of those ugly oil-filled table lamps, the heat of which makes globules rise and fall within the illuminated glass cylinder. 'It's like an Aladdin's cave,' she said.

'Of crap, perhaps.'

She brandished the lamp. 'This psychedelic stuff's back in fashion, you know.'

'I know. You can't imagine how depressing it is to see it come round for the second time. I'm going to get the dinner.'

'OK. Can I have a poke around in here? I don't mean now; I'll unpack now. But sometime?'

'Yes. If it's your idea of a treasure trove, go ahead.' I paused on the head of the next flight of stairs. 'Talking of things coming back into fashion, you might even find some loons and embroidered cheesecloth kurtas on those racks.'

Cate looked dubious.

I laughed. 'My faith's restored. Some things can never come back, thank God.'

After we had eaten, she said she would go and have a look at the other bathroom. 'Don't hold your breath. It's a basic black-and-white tile job.' I started to make some coffee, but heard her call out over the noise of the electric grinder. 'What's the matter?'

'Nothing. I want you to come and demonstrate this lot.'

For a moment, knowing that she had been brought up in relative affluence, I wondered whether she meant the intricacies of the washing machine and tumble dryer which were plumbed in down there, but when I reached the basement she was standing in the other room – my office and studio.

When, sometime in the mid-seventies, I'd realised I was not blessed with the fingers of a guitar hero, I'd reverted to playing keyboards. I was no more proficient at the piano than the guitar but, as successive synthesisers became capable of an increasingly diverse range of sounds, writing and recording music at home became easier. With the advent of first the drum machine, then the sampler and finally the dedicated composition computer, the illusion of technical competence and orchestral omnipotence was complete. I'd established a studio down here in which, alongside my own stuff, I produced soundtracks for videos and commercials with which Buccaneer was involved.

'It's like a musical equivalent of the Starship Enterprise.' Cate touched the ranks of faders on the mixing desk. 'Can I see how it works?'

I switched on the power and the black boxes lit up, VDUs glittering green and red. The computer screens followed, their bluer-than-white bright enough to make a hardened TV washing powder housewife blink. 'Maybe we'd better do something then. You play, don't you?' I gestured at one of the banked keyboards.

'Well, you know, Grade 5, Chopsticks, that sort of thing.' She rubbed one shoe against the other leg of her jeans.

'OK. Chopsticks then.' I found a piano sound.

She hit out the tune in an embarrassed way. 'I'd better do it again.'

'No need. Let's clean it up on the computer.'

I brought up the score of what she'd played on the screen and corrected her mistakes. Then we ran it over on a variety of other sounds. 'I like that one,' she said. It was an echoey mixture of tribal bottle-blowing and Colombian woodflute.

'Too melancholy for the speed.' We slowed the tune to something like a tenth of its original pace and added some drum sounds and an arpeggiated backing track. The result was soulful and remarkably spooky. 'Your first composition,' I said.

'Yours.'

'A collaboration, then. Our first collaboration. Shall we put your voice on it?'

'I'm not singing.'

'You don't have to.' I put her in the glass sound booth in the corner. 'Just speak into the mike.'

She giggled. 'What shall I say? Let me think. Now I'm here I can't . . . are you running the tape machine and things on this load of twaddle?'

'Yes. You can come out now.'

She stood behind me, laughing at the sound of her own voice on the sampler. 'What are you doing to me?'

'Cutting you up. Editing you for public consumption.' I twiddled the knobs, pulling selected words together. Then I detuned her to harmonise with the music. 'Listen.'

Across the pattern of noise, as fresh and bright as distant sheets of glass, came her giggle, tinkling against the snare drum, repeated sepulchrally on every twelfth beat. Then, in a rhythmic lull, a new single halting sentence. 'Let me – now I'm – running – running – running – things.'

'But I never said that,' she said finally. 'Isn't it weird?'

'Yes,' I said. I reactivated it. 'What shall we call it? *Sub Text*?'

'That's not very poetic. Also it reminds me of my A-levels. *The Sorcerer's Apprentice*?'

'It's been done, I believe.'

She thought. 'What about *Hidden Meanings*?'

Chapter Six

It was strange having someone else in the house, but not difficult, which I had suspected it might be. For the first few days I kept expecting to find tights and knickers strung above the bath in the basement, but that was just another memory hangover from the time before there was a washing machine, when Julia felt unable or disinclined to wait for our weekly trip, laden down with black bags, to the laundrette.

I asked Cate to treat the place like home, and then wondered whether that had been wrong – not because it immediately filled up with crowds of her friends helping themselves from the fridge, but because there seemed to be a dearth of them. Perhaps Stuart and Nicole had run a prohibitive regime. Once or twice a couple of girls were there when I got in, and occasionally a mixed foursome, but as far as I could make out neither of the boys fulfilled a traditional boyfriend role, or if so it was discreet to the point of invisibility. I never interrupted a sofa-bound grope or goodnight snog in the hall, nor did I bump into a visiting youth in the kitchen at breakfast time.

'Not having been a parent,' I said, 'and not wanting to act like one, I don't want to impose a curfew but—'

'There's always a but,' Cate said with apparent good humour.

'It's just that if you give me some idea of where you're going and when you're likely to be back it will save me from worrying and you from the embarrassment of being accosted by the Metropolitan Police as a reported victim of suspected kidnap or rape.' She nodded assent and, if she didn't tell me in advance, there was always a note on the table or the answering machine informing me of her whereabouts.

After a couple of days she had asked about cooking and cleaning. 'The thing is I can't really cook anything very useful or interesting. At school they specialised in Victoria sponges and lemon meringue pies, and they don't seem to form a staple part of your diet.'

'We could always invite some people for Sunday lunch and tea if you're looking for a showcase.'

I told her about Betty, who came in three mornings a week, and on the first of those waited in to tell Betty about her, not wanting there to be any misunderstanding about Cate's status or our relationship. Betty sang in the gospel choir of the Tabernacle church and carried

Bible scholarship notes in her voluminous handbag. I didn't want her seething with silent disapproval or praying for my forgiveness.

Similarly I didn't want Saro to be landed with the *fait accompli* of arriving for an afternoon tryst and discovering that I had already told Cate about us, or that Saro's presence had to be uncomfortably explained on the spot. Consequently when she next rang I suggested meeting at a wine bar. There was a silence. 'There's nothing wrong,' I said hastily. 'Just that I've unexpectedly got someone staying.'

Over a bottle of wine I elaborated. 'If you come round she'll have to know, which will make her the first person. It shouldn't matter because she doesn't see any of your friends or family, I shouldn't think, but I felt you should be able to decide about that, not me. I mean, it doesn't matter to me, obviously . . .' Was that true? There was something disconcerting about the idea of making love in the middle of the day with Cate beyond the bedroom door engaged in some mundane activity like reading, or watching TV, or making a sandwich.

'She might tell Nicole. Then it would be out.'

'I don't think so. I mean they've spoken on the phone but I don't get the impression that they're confidantes at the moment.'

'But you can hardly ask her not to mention to her stepmother that you're having an affair with a business chum of her father's. And she does know me. We've been to dinner at Stirton . . . we were at the funeral for heaven's sake. We're closer than you think.'

'I'm sorry,' I said. 'It's a complication.'

'Don't be. You did the right thing, the only thing. How long is she staying?'

'Until university.'

Saro calculated. 'Five weeks or so. It's not an eternity. Of course she might not get in. When are her exam results due?'

'Couple of days, I think.'

Saro raised her glass. 'Well here's hoping, for all our sakes. How are you coping?'

'Fine. She's not a child.'

Saro raised an eyebrow.

'And she's not always in. With any luck one of your free periods might coincide with one of mine.'

'That would be nice. If she's taking up semi-permanent residence obviously we'll have to tell her . . . or work out some solution. I mean I'd rather do it in the back of the Mercedes than scuttle into some hotel . . . which isn't an offer.'

'It would have a certain novelty value.'

'Not if you can still remember your teenage years. No, until circumstances change it will have to be civilised lunches.' She grinned. 'I'm sure you can think of a pun to cover the situation.'

I tried. 'Abstinence makes the heart grow fonder?'

'You're a boy at heart, Alex.'

Cate was on tenterhooks the next morning. She had rung her school and asked them to forward the results to my place, but they weren't in the first post.

'Can't you get them over the phone?'

'I couldn't bear that.'

'I suppose there is another delivery, but I've never been here to witness it.'

'It's at about half eleven,' she said promptly.

When the time came I wondered whether to ring her from the office, but decided against it. Either way she would probably want someone there, which I could not be, and a disembodied voice of sympathy or congratulation seemed worse than nothing. I left as soon as I could after six, telling myself as I drove home that she would be out anyway, celebrating or drowning her sorrows. I hoped it was the first. To fuck up her A-levels and the possibility of a degree on top of everything else would be too awful. I realised I didn't know what chance she stood of getting the passes she needed. Stuart had referred to her sometimes as a dunderhead but she clearly wasn't, and presumably he had not thought so either, given that he had entrusted her with the future of his company.

At first, in the dim light of the hallway, I thought that the woman must be a friend of Cate's, and she stood so gravely still that I feared something awful. Then I realised it was Cate herself.

She was wearing a longish skirt and baggy, formal shirt – not clothes in which I was used to seeing her – but it was the hair that had changed her beyond instantaneous recognition. What had been shoulder-length and chestnut brown was now boyishly short and strawberry blonde.

'Well? What do you think?'

'It looks great. Let's get into the light where I can see it better.'

We went into the kitchen. Half-unwilling to be scrutinised she walked away, into the evening sun from the front windows, and turned by the table. The signals of her new style were a mass of contradictions. The urchin cut, which ought to have done the opposite, emphasised her sex and gave her a sophistication to which the clothes added.

I chose my words carefully. 'It's a success. Unqualified.' She smiled broadly, and then looked down at her feet in a gesture that broke the spell of adulthood. I felt on sure enough ground to continue. 'And talking of success and qualification, has there been any other news?'

'Yes. I've got them. Two As and a C in bloody old French.'

I whirled her round in a hug. 'Is it enough?'

'It's enough,' she said rather huskily into my left ear.

It occurred to me that the huskiness might be the gasp of someone being squeezed too tightly. I let go. 'Great. Just in case – no, not just in case, because I knew you would, I put some champagne in the fridge.'

'I know. I looked. I've been chilling the glasses.'

We toasted and drank. 'Have you told Nicole?'

'Not yet.'

'Why don't you give her a ring now?'

Cate frowned. 'I'll do it tomorrow.'

'Be a sport. Do it now. She's bound to be on tenterhooks too.'

'Can't I just keep it to myself for one evening?'

'Yes. If you want to,' I said, although of course she wasn't. 'What shall we eat? I'm afraid my forethought didn't run to fatted calves.'

'I don't mind.'

She had thought about champagne, but not about food. It suddenly occurred to me that Cate probably rarely ate in restaurants – that for her they were associated with celebrations rather than business. 'Shall we go out?'

'Oh . . . yes.'

'What sort of food? What sort of place?'

'I don't mind. You choose.'

I tried to second guess. Perhaps a quiet eaterie in Herne Hill wouldn't be triumphal enough for this occasion. 'OK. I'll book.'

'Will I be all right like this?' She indicated her clothes.

'Of course.' I didn't want to advise her on a change so now I had to pick somewhere she would look at home. There was a post-modernist place in Covent Garden where, although the service was erratic, the interior was bizarre and the atmosphere suited high adrenalin levels, but the sombre maturity of Cate's costume suggested that wasn't the ambience she expected. What we needed was smart unfussy service, a certain chic, a little buzz, and fellow diners who were neither tired businessmen nor couples celebrating their twentieth wedding anniversary.

The Braganza had an enormous bronze mask over the street, a lifesize replica of a waiter dropping a tray of glasses on the stairs, and the first floor was all glass, steel, and over-bright abstracts – but the galleried second floor had a baroque ceiling and boardroom-heavy tables and chairs. The contrast of these with the pony-tailed waiters in their designer uniforms and the Cole Porter tinkling up from the grand piano below was appealing. It seemed only fitting to have another bottle of champagne to sustain the mood.

Cate studied the transparent plastic menu with the attention necessary to decipher the cramped black heiroglyphics upon it.

'Is it OK?' I asked.

'Oh yes. I can't decide what to have. What are you having?'

'I'm going to have the gravadlax and the duck breast.'

She wavered for some time over salmon and the lamb until the waiter arrived when she promptly said, 'Goat's cheese salad and I'll have the *canard* as well. What are you smiling at?'

'Last minute decisions.'

'It's a woman's prerogative to change her mind, or so I keep reading.'

'What made you decide to go to Durham?'

'The school suggested it. And I remember you once telling a story about when you went for your interview, going into the cathedral and it was snowing and the organ was playing Bach and that deciding you.'

She'd remembered the story very well. 'You didn't think about Oxford or Cambridge then.'

'No, well I did, but I didn't want to go. Cambridge is flat and windy, and I liked Oxford but . . . I thought if I went to Oxford then Daddy would constantly be comparing it with when he was there and how it had gone downhill or how I wasn't living up to his own achievements, you know.'

It occurred to us both at the same moment that that reason no longer existed.

'He'd have been very proud of you,' I said as she slurped from her glass.

'Yes. But all he'd have said was, how did you manage to cock up the French.'

Sometime later, locked in combat with a Death by Chocolate, Cate said, 'Do you know what happens about my grant? I mean, I know I only qualified for the minimum but do I have to pay the rest myself now, well, now I'm sort of parentless?'

'I don't know.' A sudden thought struck. 'What are you living on at the moment?'

'Well, I haven't needed much because your house has always got everything. I've been using my building society money, but there's not much unless I break into my car fund. I'm sorry, I should have been paying you housekeeping I suppose.'

'No. But we do need to sort out your financial position.' As far as I could remember she had nothing except what Buccaneer would pay her. 'Don't worry about it. We'll talk to Boy and the accountants on Monday. I'm sure we can organise an advance against profits or a salary of some sort. What's the car fund?'

'It was a bit of a joke really. When I passed my test Daddy said I could have a car when I left school, but he would only put half of the money towards it. I had to save the rest. I've only got four hundred. I don't suppose he would have held me to it.'

Neither did I. I couldn't imagine Stuart allowing her to drive an £800 jalopy, unless he had been further down the road to a Victorian belief in offspring self-sufficiency than I had imagined. 'I don't see why you shouldn't have a company car.'

Cate snorted.

'Well,' I added. 'It's half your company.'

'Are you busy tomorrow?'

'I'm out for dinner. Not during the day. Why?'

'Can we go and have a look at some cars?'

It was dark when we left, or as dark as Soho ever gets with its street lights, car headlights, and glowing pub and restaurant windows. The air was soft and warm. I scanned the road for a taxi.

'This is nice,' said Cate. She was peering through the windows of a small Mazda sports coupé with the pointed bonnet and tail fin of a high-tech insect. 'Is it out of my price range?'

I hadn't really thought what that might be. I supposed in fairness it should be the same as mine. What had my Saab cost? The Mazda wasn't cheap but on the other hand it wasn't a Porsche or a Ferrari. 'Don't suppose so.'

Suddenly she grabbed me by the hand and hauled me into the nearest doorway, looking out over my shoulder.

'What's the matter?'

'Don't turn round. It's Nicole.'

I compromised by leaving my body facing inwards and twisting my neck at an extremely uncomfortable angle. Nicole was standing on the doorstep of a Thai restaurant across the street, one of a small group including Bill Starling who was nodding and stroking his beard, his bald pate shiny from the heat and reflecting the red-and-white neon of the restaurant's sign.

'Don't move. She mustn't see us.'

'Don't be silly. She's your stepmother, my sister-in-law. We can't hide from her. I've got no reason to – don't want to. Come on.' I began to pull away.

'We can't. She'll ask about the results and then it will have to come out that I haven't rung her and we've been out celebrating. Or we'll have to lie.'

I was irritated, and then nearly laughed with the absurdity until I realised that she was on the verge of tears. 'All right,' I said, 'tell me when they've gone.'

'Sorry.'

'What a tangled web.'

'What?'

'What a tangled web we weave, when we practise to deceive.'

'I've never heard that before.'

'There's not much hope for your character then.'

The next morning I went down to make some tea and found Cate already up and dressed at the dining table.

'There's a pot under the cosy,' she said, and went back to her reading. The *Guardian* that she had brought back from the newsagents was untouched; she was absorbed in a pile of car magazines.

'Got enough information?' She failed to notice my sarcasm.

'Yes, I'm making a shortlist.' She was her father's daughter. She showed me the five possibles.

'Have I got time for a bath before we hit the road?'

'Of course.' She surreptitiously glanced at the clock.

'I won't be too long. Why don't you look up the nearest dealers in the Yellow Pages and make sure they've got one in stock to test drive?'

By the time we returned from our run in the Mazda, the salesman forced to squeeze into the back and thereby demonstrating that the car's claim to have a rear seat was false, it was five o'clock.

'Well,' Clive said, 'I'll leave you to have a little chat, shall I?' and walked away stretching his cramped legs and rubbing the numb bottom of his Wall Street money dealer's suit. I felt marginally sorry for Clive. He had started off adopting a matey tone with me and a patronising one with Cate before twigging that the balance of purchasing power was not necessarily as he had assumed. He had worked out that she was neither my daughter nor my mistress but was clearly at a loss for a replacement relationship.

'What do you think? Do you like it?' It was patently obvious that Cate did.

So did I. The low cockpit, with its leather seats, felt like a go-kart after the high dashboard of the Saab. It was the kind of car I would have loved to have owned as a toy. 'It's fun,' I said, 'but . . .'

'There's always a but.'

'There is. But it's your choice. I'm just playing devil's advocate. If you get this one you'll only ever be able to travel with one suitcase . . . and one friend. What about the Golf? That was bigger, but quite sparky.'

'I expect I'll want one when I'm twenty-something.' A stiletto of a dismissal. 'Wouldn't you have wanted a car like this when you were my age?'

'Truthfully . . . probably not. I mean I liked riding in Stuart's sports cars when I was a kid, but in my day most students didn't have cars, and if they did they were battered Morrises, or Beetles. If I'd had anything I would have chosen a Mini.'

'With a Union Jack painted on it?' she teased.

'Have a heart. I was seventies – just – not sixties.'

My real worry was that the Mazda would seem too flash. I didn't want her starting college with the disadvantage of being thought a poor little rich girl – although I supposed she was now.

'What are you worried about? I won't drive it any faster than I would drive anything else.'

'It's not that. Just that in my Calvinistic soul I wonder whether the image is a mite decadent for a first year English undergraduate. Perhaps it would be more politically correct to have a small Citroën.' I smiled. 'And a lot of stickers.'

'You forget – we're Thatcher's children. Fast and expensive is politically correct.'

We looked at colours. 'White,' she said, and glanced at me, waiting for any sign of disapproval. Scenting parenthood, I forebore to mention that white looked awful unless it was kept clean. The gunmetal grey of my own car had been chosen as much with neglect as aesthetics in mind.

'So can we just – like – get it now?'

'No. The sad bit for Clive is that we won't get it from him at all but from Buccaneer's leasing company.'

'So will that take long?'

'No, a couple of weeks.'

'It's like going into Hamley's a fortnight before Christmas.'

'Never mind. You can keep its photo under your pillow until it comes.'

It transpired that it was going to take six weeks to acquire unless Cate was prepared to take navy blue, but when I came home with this news she seemed preoccupied by something else. I didn't find out what until after supper.

'That policeman Cromarty rang up.'

I waited.

'Asked if he could pop over and check a few things.'

'Oh. When's he coming?'

'He came – this afternoon.'

I thought of Cromarty standing in my drawing room before this fireplace, four-square in his shirtsleeves, evaluating me by my goods and chattels as he had evaluated Stuart. It made me uncomfortable. I wondered what his own taste in interior furnishing was. Or perhaps they had stayed downstairs. I saw him ponderous by the kitchen window, wondering why I didn't grow rose bushes. I wanted to ask where the interview had taken place but it seemed such a stupid question. Cate was silent. 'Have they arrested anyone?'

'No. I don't think they're any closer to finding who did it. He just asked me to go through what happened on the evening before in case I'd remembered anything else.'

I poured us some more coffee, and lit a cigarette. 'What did happen?'

'Nothing unusual. Dad was home from work. He was in the study most of the day but we had tea on the lawn and Dad and Nicole played boules because he said it was the nearest he'd get to France this summer. I packed, and Nicole made me weigh my suitcase on the bathroom scales because she was convinced it would be over and embarrass Mr and Mrs Clifford at the airport. It wasn't of course. Although even if it had been I can't imagine why anyone would be embarrassed by an overweight suitcase.'

I hadn't imagined that travel arrangements would make Nicole flustered. She had plenty of practice.

'I'd never noticed before,' Cate said. 'But she was prickly that day. And then Debbie turned up, said she'd come to see us because we were going to be away for three weeks, but she only arrived as we were leaving.' Apparently Deborah was not in favour either. 'If it hadn't been for the cassette that got stuck we would already have gone.'

'What cassette?'

'We were going to Heathrow in Nicole's BMW, and when we started up she put this Erroll Garner on, the machine chewed it up, and she threw a wobbly. So Dad took the radio – it's one of those removable ones – out of the car and sorted it out. He was a bit cross.'

'Why?' Such minor practical problems didn't usually make Stuart irascible.

'I don't know. He said that the record he'd taken it from was so scratched now that the cassette was irreplaceable.'

'Then what happened?'

'He put the radio back; he and Debbie waved us off.' She was still for a second. Her last view of him had been a literal farewell – but not a happy one. It must have been even worse for Nicole to look back on the argument that preceded the leavetaking – probably driving away feeling grumpy and glad to see the back of him, not realising that she had.

'And then?'

'We drove to Heathrow and checked in to the hotel.'

'I don't understand. I thought you flew that evening.'

'No. My flight was at six the next morning and Nicole's at six-thirty. She didn't want to get up at three to drive to the airport so she booked us this room. The Cliffords had offered to have me to stay at their place, but Nicole said sharing was as cheap for two of us in the hotel as one – and it saved me struggling to Hammersmith with my luggage.'

'Very drab, depressing places, airport hotels. You feel like you're in a vacuum.'

'That's right. It was weird. A bit like being in a film. Seeing the planes coming in and taking off from the bedroom window. But it didn't feel like London, or even Britain really. It could have been anywhere.'

'Didn't you eat? That must have reminded you.'

'Yes. But don't you think it's quite fun to have that kind of food sometimes?'

'What – succulent ocean-fresh prawns on a cool bed of iceberg lettuce sort of stuff?'

'Yes.'

'Not really. It never tastes of anything. I like junk food, but it should be genuinely cheap and tacky. No pretensions to gentility.' I thought of the kebab I had eaten the previous week. Fierce with chilli sauce, its grey meat fatty as it cooled in the pitta. I had put half of it in the bin on the street, knowing how the kitchen would smell if I dumped it indoors. But I'd liked the idea of eating it.

Cate smiled. 'I don't believe you. When was the last time you went into a McDonald's for a quarter-pounder and fries?'

'OK. I can't remember.'

'Exactly. You're talking about something you know nothing about.'

'I still like thick chips, covered in salt and doused in vinegar, wrapped in newspaper.'

'That just proves it. They don't come in newspaper these days. It's against an EC regulation or something.'

'OK OK. You win.'

'You probably hate those little sachets of instant hot chocolate as well.'

'They remind me of swimming bath vending machines. Like some perverted Proust. Show me a cup of hot chocolate and I smell chlorine.'

'We had some before we went to bed.' I could picture them, in a no-man's-land of excited anticipation; their separate holidays ahead and the burdens of family, school, exams, left behind. They probably ate up the free biscuits and chocolate by the kettle as well, leaning against the pillows, midnight feasting. But no. I had to remember; they apparently didn't like each other.

'It worked, anyway,' Cate continued. 'I slept like a log. Hardly heard the alarm call.'

A terrible moment – when the bell cut into your sleep and you staggered, zombie-like, to a strange bathroom where the over-harsh light stung your eyes, and once under the shower the shampoo took over. Rushing down to reception with the faint clamminess from drying and dressing too quickly, throat scalded by the snatched cup of coffee, the lurch in the empty stomach as you lifted off into the dawn. Why did I love it?

'So you couldn't really help the Superintendent then?'

'No. I'd told him it all the first time.'

What had Cromarty expected? That Cate would have recalled some suspicious figure hanging about as they left? Or perhaps a car in the lane that didn't belong to one of the locals. It hardly seemed likely; they had been gone for several hours before the intruders came. 'Did he ask you anything else?'

'Yes. He asked me if Daddy had any enemies that I knew about. I said it was a strange word to use. Daddy wasn't a soldier.'

It was the word Cromarty had used with me too. Perhaps policemen don't realise that normal people don't have enemies. I supposed it was easier and more interesting for them to imagine some vendetta than to trawl through endless lists of known villains, or, worse, to have to track down some unconnected unknowns with no previous form.

'Then he said, had I seen him or heard him arguing with anybody? Which I hadn't. Apart from the usual stuff with Nicole, or Mr Cuttifer, or me.' She blushed. 'Then he asked whether living here was a permanent arrangement. I said I didn't know whether it would be for any longer than the start of term.'

'It's up to you. You're welcome to stay as long as you like.' I hadn't expected to be quite so instinctively hospitable.

Cate smiled, more it seemed to herself than me. 'And he asked about the will. Who Daddy left what to.' That made me angry. He shouldn't have asked Cate – as executors Boy or I could have told him and spared her that at least. Anyhow, if Cromarty had been hoping to discover a hitherto obscure beneficiary with blood on his hands he must have been disappointed; nothing more than very close family.

The next day Danny Whitney, a friend who worked for the *Guardian*, rang and demanded that we meet for lunch.

'I might have been busy,' I said, as we sat down at a table in the Coach and Horses, more or less deserted at such an early hour, the satellite sports channel silently showing a test match, a couple of subeditors from the paper taking a hair of the dog and perusing the runners and riders at Sandown Park. 'What couldn't wait?'

'I had the police round yesterday. Ugly bastard called Cromarty. Woman sidekick – Sergeant Mirren. They wanted me to confirm that you and I spent the evening of July 31st together. It was a fraction of a second before I twigged exactly what night that was. Have you been getting up the Old Bill's nose, Alex?'

'No,' I said, shell-shocked. 'I don't think so.'

'Because, unless you're a suspect for the Alliance Building Society heist, it looks to me as if they're trying to fit you up with Stuart's murder.'

Chapter Seven

'Why would they want to do that?' he asked.

'I can't imagine. I suppose they haven't got any other suspects. He was asking Cate about the will yesterday, and if he's viewing the legatees as possibles that puts me on a shortlist of one.'

'How's that? I mean, I know the whole thing's ridiculous, but how can he rule out all the others?'

'Easy. There were only three; Deborah was tied up by the men who did it, and Nicole and Cate were asleep in the same hotel room at Heathrow airport.'

'Why men?'

'What?'

'Why did you say men? Why not just one man?'

'I don't know. It just doesn't seem the sort of thing one bloke would have done on his own. Setting out to burgle a place, putting somebody out with chloroform or some such thing, tying them up, shooting somebody else with their own shotgun . . . They couldn't fit me up, could they?'

Danny pursed his lips. 'Don't suppose so. You're not poor or stupid, you've already got a good solicitor. But plenty of innocent people get put down—'

'If you're to believe your own newspaper.'

'And the Law Lords.' He finished the last of his pint. 'Want another?'

'I think I'd like a Scotch.' I felt in need of something bracing.

'Be careful,' Danny said, as he handed me what looked suspiciously like a treble. 'I'd call your brief now, just let him know what's going on. It's bloody diabolical.'

At least he didn't seem to think it might be true. 'What exactly did you tell them?'

'The truth. That we went to the Gay Hussar with Scotch Woodcock and Simon Charteris.'

We had; I could almost taste the Hungarian garlic sausage that Simon had claimed would condemn him to the spare room. Danny and I had gone on to Ronnie Scott's to see Joe Pass. The others hadn't come, Simon because he had to catch the last train to his wife and baby in

Greenwich and Scotch, in his own words a carefree bachelor, because he had an unaccountable dislike of jazz guitar.

Danny added, 'I said we parted outside the club at about two. That was right, was it?'

'It was probably only about one.'

Danny looked at me expressionlessly over his glass. 'What's an hour between friends?'

'A mere bagatelle. I think I told them one anyway.'

'Well that's all to the good, because he pressed me on that point and I said I couldn't be one hundred per cent sure.' He thought about it. 'Still, you giving an earlier time makes you sound quite casual about the entire affair.'

'I was. I didn't even think I was being questioned at the time. Not for this reason anyway. It was just background, you know, filling in time while we waited for them to shift the body and stuff.' I had been so stunned I hadn't noticed the insidious nature of the questions. So you were on your own, were you? Oh no, I was with . . . I hadn't given addresses but I suppose I must have mentioned Danny's paper. 'It must have been a bit of a shock for you too.'

'It was,' he said. 'When I realised why they were seeking character references. I told them you were guilty of nothing worse than cuckolding the odd husband.'

I didn't react; what could he know?

'Or stealing the bread from the mouths of the working class.' He touched my wrist. 'Seriously, I'm really sorry about this, Alex.' But it was hard for him to break out of the bantering mode. 'I'd do a spot of plea bargaining and confess to the Alliance job. Very neat. Driving away a hole-in-the-wall cash machine with a JCB.'

'No good. They'd do me for not having an HGV licence as well.' I rose to leave.

'Up the revolution,' he said. I pretended to be surprised. This was an old joke. 'Consumer revolution, of course.'

Boy advised caution. 'Do nothing. If you get hot under the collar about them barking up the wrong tree, they'll only take it as proof they've found the right one and it will be harder to shake their conviction.' It was an unfortunate choice of word. I assumed he meant conviction as in belief. 'Danny's probably got it wrong anyway.'

This seemed unlikely but I carried on as normal and waited for the heavy plod of policeman's boots on the doorstep, or the heavy breathing of Cromarty's certainty at the end of the phone. Nothing happened.

I drove Cate down to Stirton to gather her things for college, and Nicole met us there. She was dressed in nautical fashion – deck shoes, white jeans, Breton striped jersey, neckerchief, navy reefer jacket. She seemed determinedly bright, optimism and practicality varnished into place. 'Will you be taking everything?' she asked Cate.

'Do I need to?'

'Well, if you don't it may have to go into storage. I've thought about it and decided to sell up. I don't feel I can live here again. I'm sorry if that's upsetting for you.'

'No,' Cate said. 'This place doesn't make any sense without Daddy.'

For a second they were in accord. Then Nicole said 'Right, we'll leave you to get on with it then, darling. Dump anything for throwing out on the landing.' She turned to me. 'There's a lot of stuff in the coach house – you know, tools and so on. I know you're not much of a DIY man but there might be some bits you want.'

We walked across. Already there was the first, faint suggestion of autumn in the air. Inside the coach house it smelt of motor oil and highly polished car, overlaid with the scent of the apples that someone, presumably Mr Cuttifer, had collected from the small orchard and packed in to cardboard boxes. Nicole saw me looking at them.

'How stupid. Why hasn't he taken them home for himself? He knows there's no one here to eat them. I suppose the green houses are full of rotting produce, too.'

'Old boy like him probably needs to be given permission.'

Nicole leaned back against the bonnet of the Jaguar. 'More fool him. Oh well, he might not be here for much longer. I'm keeping him on, on the advice of the estate agents, until the place is sold – stop it getting untidy and overgrown – but whether the new owners will want his grumpy face peering over the hedges is another matter.' She banged the car. 'You haven't taken this back.'

'No, I thought you might be using it.'

'I've never driven it, and I wouldn't want to start now. Dead man's shoes.' She turned away, shoving her hands viciously into her pockets. 'Don't waste any more of your money – or Cate's.' She blundered out. I made to go after her, and then changed my mind. She was bound to be frustrated and angry. Who could blame her if the frayed edges showed from time to time? And if she was hitting out at the wrong people, well, there was no right person to attack. I wanted to show sympathy but needed to choose the right moment.

There wasn't much on the shelves and workbenches that I could find a use for; old-fashioned storm lanterns for night fishing, several rods, and tins containing hooks and lines neatly labelled in Stuart's handwriting. More peculiarly there was a vast assortment of nails, screws, and well-maintained saws, planes, drills and the like, despite the fact that I was sure that Stuart had always got a man in whenever a household job needed doing. He must have been more of a potterer than I had thought. I was extricating the clay pigeon launcher from beneath the bench when Cuttifer came in. 'Morning,' he said cautiously.

He was standing by the motor mower, his woollen glove on its handle in a proprietorial fashion.

'Giving the lawns another trim?'

He nodded. 'Dare say it'll be the last for this year. Maybe altogether for me.'

I told him to help himself to the fruit and veg.

He pursed his lips judiciously. 'Seems a shame for them to go to waste.'

'Exactly.' Something else occurred to me. 'Do you fish?'

'A bit.'

'Why don't you have all this tackle then? Help yourself.'

'But this is worth a bob or two.'

'Well, Nicole's offered it to me but I'm not an angler. If you don't take it, it'll as like as not be thrown away or sold for virtually nothing to some house clearance merchant. I'm sure Stuart would have been happier for it to go to a good home, to someone he knew who'll look after it as well as he did himself.'

'Well, if you're sure she – Mrs Buchan – won't mind.'

'Why should she?'

He looked round warily. 'I think she blames me and the wife in some sort of way.'

'What on earth for?'

'We was on holiday, you see.'

'I don't understand. Even if you'd been here, you don't live in, do you?'

'No. We've got the cottage next to the Greyhound.'

'Then you wouldn't have been here when the . . . burglars came anyway.'

'No, but the wife would have been up in the morning. I'm glad she wasn't, mind, it would have left her in a terrible state finding Mr Buchan's body.'

'Yes, I'm sure it would. It's a blessing really that you were away, then.' I still didn't understand. 'So why do you think Nicole blames you?'

'She said Miss Deborah should have been released twelve hours earlier. Told the wife – if you'd been there like normal she wouldn't have had to spend all that time tied up.'

'But that's ridiculous.'

'The wife knows it's just the heat of the moment, like. Maybe feeling guilty she was on holiday herself. Not that she should,' he added hastily. 'I mean, how can you know something terrible like that's going to happen?'

'You can't.' I lifted the launcher, and wobbled, thrown off balance by the weight. Cuttifer offered to lend me a hand and together we carried it to the Saab.

'How's young Cate?'

'Bearing up, I think,' I puffed, aware that I did not really know.

'Poor kid. I've always had a soft spot for her.'

'And she for you.'

'For my tomatoes maybe.' He straightened quickly. 'Right, well,

I'd better get on.' He set off at a brisk march back to the coach house. Changeable old stick, I thought, and then saw that Nicole was returning.

She apologised for her rudeness, which wasn't necessary, and I told her more or less what Cuttifer had said. She blushed, and looked down. 'I didn't mean anything by it. It's just that I'd forgotten they were away, and when Debbie told me how long she'd been in that state . . .'

I put a hand out and she moved into my arms for a hug but without responsive pressure. She stood limp, head bowed, as if she felt she had to accept affection and sympathy.

'How is Deborah?'

'All right, I think. Closed up, you know.' She sniffed. 'But in the end he was only her stepfather.'

This contrasting of her daughter's position with her own closeness to Stuart seemed uncharitable, but I dutifully said: 'It must have been worse for you than anybody, of course.'

She rallied at this. 'And for you. And your father, of course.'

What about Cate?

She looked up at me with her clear grey eyes. Close to, the crow's feet were clearly visible through the membrane of make-up, but the eyes themselves would have grabbed the attention across any room, and the make-up was masterly – an actress's job. It was a shame her career had been interrupted so early. I could imagine her in seventies movies.

'I don't think anyone will ever know how Dad's taken it,' I said, thinking of his performance at the funeral. But I knew little more about anyone else's deepest feelings, senile or otherwise, just as they could not know mine. 'If you ever want to talk . . .'

'Thank you,' she said, and then broke the spell. 'What's that bit of equipment?'

'Launcher. For clays.' She must have seen it before; but probably only with someone sitting on it.

'Would you like his guns as well?' There was a horribly embarrassed pause before she said, 'Obviously not the one that—'

I agreed to take the others and, what with Cate's stuff and a couple of crates of old Buchan family papers that Stuart had stored when Dad went into the home, ended up making three trips. Cate came on the second – so that she could start clearing away at our end, she said, but I suspected it was to avoid formally leaving the house for the last time.

When I'd packed the last load I went out onto the terrace and sat at the wrought iron table. Somewhere along the valley rose ugly black smoke, reminiscent of TV terrorism but signifying stubble-burning. Nearer to home, drifting over the kitchen garden wall, were the friendlier pale grey wisps of Cuttifer's bonfire. Nicole joined me, and lit a cigarette. She had given up in '87. 'All done?'

'Yes. Guess this will be my last visit. What about you?'

'No, I'm back to see the furniture off on Monday,' she said. 'And the new landing carpet laid.'

I couldn't think of anything to say to that.

'I'm keeping it all,' she said, looking back at the house. 'I'm sure there'll be far too much for any place that I'm likely to buy, but until that happens I don't know which pieces will fit.'

'Will it be in London? Your new place?'

'I think so. I've had enough of the countryside. It was always Stuart's dream, this.' She gazed across the lawn to the trees.

'His own little bit of England,' I said.

'His kingdom.'

I was very surprised to hear Deborah's voice when I answered the phone the following evening, and more so to hear *Songs of Praise* on her TV in the background. I'd not put her down as a home worshipper or the type of habitual viewer to whom the *Epilogue* is as acceptable a wallpaper as soap opera.

'How are you?'

'Oh, OK.' She sounded rather jittery. 'Are you busy this evening?'

'No.' I could hardly believe that she was going to suggest meeting up. We never had before. 'Did you have something in mind?'

'Is Cate there?'

That made more sense. 'No, I'm afraid. She's gone to the pictures with Jane Clifford.'

'Would you like to meet for a drink? I know it's short notice but . . .'

I was far too intrigued to haver. 'When?'

'Now?'

'Where?'

She suggested a wine bar around the corner from her flat in Clapham. The last time I had been there it was dark and plush – all mahogany woodstain, burgundy velvet curtains and eighteenth-century wall maps. Now they had replaced the abbreviated menu of steaks and pies with that year's topical favourite, tapas. The smell of garlic and oil hung in the air, and Catalan scenes from the freshly whitewashed walls. Deborah was sitting at the bar, a glass of kir before her, apparently part of a small group consisting of a couple of young men in cords and crew neck sweaters, and a tall Sloane wearing the obligatory Alice band and shirt with upturned collar. Deborah herself was as always smartly dressed – for once in trousers, a type of tailored jodhpur with a contrasting metropolitan variant on the hacking jacket. Her long black hair was coiled in a tight ballet-dancer's bun.

Why she had invited me to meet these people I could not imagine but she slipped from her stool and introduced me. Johnny shook hands, Rory languidly raised the Mexican lager bottle from which he was swigging through a filter of lime segment. Fiona, the flatmate, presented a cheek to be pecked. I obliged and retreated to the edge of the group, on

Deborah's other side. The two lads were talking about rugby. 'Can I get anyone a drink?' I asked, wondering whether to order a bottle, and as Fiona was saying that another glass of kir would be lovely, Deborah, over whose head I was looking, leant back so that her body was pressed against mine and my arm, resting on the counter, was over her shoulder. I was confused and flexed against her, uncertain as to whether she was going to fall, but after a moment she moved away.

'Actually, why don't you and I go back to the flat? If that's all right?'

'OK. But let me –' I waved the ten pound note '—now I've offered.'

'Don't worry. Johnny will buy my kir,' said Fiona. 'If he knows what's good for him.'

'Sorry about all that,' said Deborah as she hurried down the street. 'Let's get inside and I'll explain.'

Her flat was half of an Edwardian house, its communal hallway empty apart from the pile of mail that no one had claimed. We went upstairs, and along a narrow landing into the living room. It was still decorated, as I guessed the entire flat had been, in developer's beige berber carpet and magnolia walls. On these hung the usual mixture of framed art posters, against them stood the usual mixture of Habitat sofa units and director's chairs. Pushed into a corner was a gateleg dining table, through an archway was a minute fitted kitchen. Deborah said 'Make yourself at home,' and I sank into a unit. 'I'm going to have some gin. What would you like?'

I tried to see unobtrusively into the fridge which she had open: cans of something – lager? coke? Lucozade? – but no obvious bottle of wine. On the table with the Gordon's was a decanter of sherry, the colour of which suggested Cyprus cream rather than fino. 'The same, thanks.'

She poured them in large tumblers with lots of ice and very little tonic which was encouraging, there being nothing worse than a G & T tasting simply of T. She only took off her jacket as she sat down and I wondered if she had a complex about the size of her bottom.

She had seen Cromarty that afternoon. He had wanted to run over various details with her, during the course of which he had happened to enquire whether she had known the contents of her stepfather's will. She had not. Was she surprised? Was her mother surprised? Back to the attacker. Had she remembered anything else about him? How tall, for instance? Yes, it was difficult to estimate heights in feet and inches. As tall as, say, your father's brother?

Deborah stared at me. I felt sick. I wanted to say, 'The bastard', but instead I said, 'And was he? About as tall as me?'

'No,' she said. 'I checked. When you came into the wine bar. You're definitely taller, and, well, harder than he was.'

'Harder?'

'Somehow bonier.'

I realised the enormity of what she had done. 'You're very brave.'

'Not really. I mean, after the police had gone I realised what they were getting at, and I was sure it couldn't have been you and . . . I thought you ought to know that they were implying it could have been. I mean, it's stupid, you're Stuart's brother, for Christ's sake. So I rang you up to tell you and then . . .' She looked away. 'I thought I should be absolutely sure. Sorry.'

Hence the wine bar with several people to hand for her test. Had that not ruled me out we would have stayed there, she would have made up some reason or other for wanting to see me, and after I had gone rung the police. Maybe.

She poured more gin.

'Thanks.'

'More tonic?'

'Just a dash. I meant, for letting me know.' I explained that Danny too thought that Cromarty was enthusiastic about me as a suspect. As we talked I grew angrier and more self-righteous. Deborah agreed to confirm to him what she had discovered. She had his phone number.

'I want to ring him now,' I said. 'Drive over and knock him and his bloody ridiculous theory on the head once and for all.'

'OK,' Deborah said, but she sounded nervous, and slurped her drink.

I finished my own. 'But of course I can't. I'm over the limit. The bastard will probably book me for drunken driving.'

So I stayed, and had another, and Deborah asked me about Stuart's childhood, and the business, and his first wife, and I found myself talking at great length. Fiona came in, sized up the situation and announced that she was going for a bath in tones of such portent that Deborah giggled. 'That means no access to the loo.' We finished the gin, and eventually she became a little tearful, and hugged me tight when the taxi came. In my inebriated haze I thought how convenient it would have been in some ways if she, not only a girl of spirit but a housetrained PR executive, was destined to work with me rather than Cate.

The next morning, of course, I felt guilty about that. When I collected the Saab from outside Deborah's flat the curtains were still drawn. Perhaps she was not that reliable a workmate. I had arranged to meet Cromarty at ten. 'I'll see if he's free,' the woman had said.

'I think you'll find he is,' I replied, certain he would not be able to resist the prospect, and I was right.

Stoneyheath police station was a square block of discoloured concrete and virulent red brick, with windows of mirror glass – an exercise in seventies' alienation that looked more like a CIA outpost than the home of the British bobby, but perhaps I was feeling particularly paranoid that morning. I had only spotted it on my second circuit of the one-way system which, like so many, managed to show the town it decongested in a very unfavourable light. The signpost as one left the motorway which announced 'Stoneyheath – Historical town', was only accurate if it meant the history of jerry-building.

I parked under a row of small windows of bottle glass that looked disturbingly like a cell block, and walked round to the front. A traditional blue lamp had been ludicrously fixed to the concrete lintel above the swing doors. I'd never been into a police station before; the nearest thing I could think of was the tax office, and then I'd had my accountant with me. I wished I had my solicitor with me now, but Boy was in Manchester for some reason.

I had imagined sitting in Cromarty's office, getting a feel for him from the photos on his desk, the calendar on his wall, the golf trophies on the filing cabinet, but I was shown into a small, windowless room, its eau-de-nil walls scuffed near the skirting board, the table with the tape recorder screwed to the floor.

Cromarty was smart as men are at the beginning of the working day – collar and cuffs still buttoned, tie knot neatly centred, shoes shiny. He introduced Sergeant Mirren, the woman Danny had met, who was attractive in a brassy, hard-nosed way. In an effort to reduce Cromarty to the level of some kind of criminal, I tried to imagine him cheating on his wife with Mirren, perhaps in the back of a striped patrol car, the siren going off when they . . .

'Just an informal chat, I assume,' he was saying, 'so we won't bother with the tape unless you want to.'

I shook my head. If it was so matey and informal, why was the Valkyrie present?

'So, what can we do for you? Have you remembered something you'd like to get off your chest?'

In the absence of anger – which hadn't returned that morning – it was difficult to work out how not to sound pompous, but he had given me an opening of sorts. 'There is something I'd like to get off my chest but it's not a memory, it's a complaint.' He gazed at me placidly. 'You have been dropping very heavy hints to at least two people that I know of, and God knows how many that I don't, that you think I shot my brother.'

'Surely, Mr Buchan, that is merely your interpretation.'

'Their interpretation. They both got the hint so clearly that they rang me up to tell me about it.'

'And who are these people?'

'If you don't know then you obviously have been spreading it around.' Cromarty looked sad, as if such a jibe was not worthy of me. His technique for winding people up was very good. 'Danny Whitney and Deborah Makepeace.' No response. 'It amounts to harassment.'

'Hardly that,' Cromarty said mildly. 'We've not asked you a single question or paid you a visit.'

'Well, it's certainly defamatory.'

'Had we accused you behind your back it might have been, but we have never said we think you did it.'

'Not in so many words. But just as clearly.' He spread out his hands, palms upwards, absolving himself. 'It's an abhorrent suggestion, and a pack of lies. Don't sit there like Pontius bloody Pilate. Do you think I murdered Stuart?'

He eased himself back in his chair. I sensed a certain tension in Mirren, who was recrossing her ankles.

'Well now, Mr Buchan. You surely cannot blame me for doing my job. A rich . . . richish . . . man is killed with his own shotgun; his stepdaughter is chloroformed and tied up. All that is taken is a negligible amount of cash. There are no signs of forced entry, and no fresh fingerprints apart from those of the deceased, his wife, daughter, stepdaughter, cleaner, and yourself. The others were all in the house on a regular basis.' I protested.

'I know. Your prints may be a perfectly legitimate consequence of your finding the body, but consider the alternatives. Of these the stepdaughter's a victim, the wife and daughter were together in a hotel bedroom at Heathrow airport, and the cleaner was holidaying with her husband on the Cornish Riviera. You can hardly blame us for checking whether your alibi . . . sorry, explanation of your whereabouts on that night was corroborated.'

His tone had taken on the sterility of a higher civil servant, not something I remembered from our previous meetings. He was a subtle man – not allowing me any moral superiority, making himself the voice of reason and me appear coarse and unhinged. 'Which it was.'

'Yes, although technically speaking it does not rule you out, timewise.'

I laughed in an attempt to release my frustration, but I think Cromarty saw it as attempted incredulity. He renewed his attack.

'This killing might have been part of a bungled burglary but the circumstances are not congruent with that; in which case we need to establish another motive. There is no evidence of any particular feud, or business problem, or sexual . . . indiscretion. It is therefore only sensible to look at who benefits financially from the death.' He hardly needed to add that this left the same small circle as the fingerprint evidence, minus Mrs Cuttifer – unless she was a psychic prepared to kill for a crate of Cox's Orange Pippins and a couple of second-hand fishing rods.

'The only witness you have is Deborah,' I said. He didn't challenge this statement. 'And her recollection is hazy. Nothing more than the size and density of her attacker.'

Cromarty had adopted a poker face but the minute shifting of Mirren in her seat indicated that it was true, and that she disliked their prime suspect knowing how little evidence they possessed.

'But not so hazy that she was unable to rule me out.'

A flicker of the eye indicated that Cromarty's attention was fully engaged. 'What do you mean?'

'Ring her and find out. She'll explain. But under the circumstances I must ask you to cross me off your list and stop blackguarding me to my friends.' I felt lightheaded, triumphant, vindicated. I stood up.

Mirren opened the door, with what I imagined was stoicism. Cromarty shuffled a couple of papers. 'Well, thanks for letting us know,' he said conversationally.

'I wish you luck,' I said. 'In finding the actual killer.'

'Appreciated. Of course,' he looked up, 'if there was more than one killer then the accomplice was never seen by Deborah. Goodbye.' And he bent his head to the files.

I couldn't fault his logic. I too instinctively imagined that there must have been more than one murderer. If he wanted to keep me at the top of his list he could; and he seemed as disinclined to believe in burglars as I was in fairies.

Chapter Eight

I was at a party in my parents' old house in Watford, sharing a drink and a natter with the chat show host Jerry Churchill, the beautiful international model and rock star's wife Divine McAlpine, and the one-eared painter Vincent Van Gogh, who my mother was tempting to another slice of Battenburg, when the fire brigade arrived.

The floral Vymura became the darkened wall of my bedroom and the tender's alarm bell the ringing of my telephone. The clock said three-thirty a.m. The voice of the girl at the end of the line was crackly, and echoey enough to be coming from the interior of an empty museum. Having warily established my identity, wavering over whether Alex or Mr Buchan was a more suitable title, she said: 'It's Emma Woodhouse, I don't know whether you remember me—'

'Yes, of course.' How could I not remember the absurdly literary name of Cate's college room-mate? I was about to ask what she wanted when, as my thought processes warmed up, I realised there was only one thing she could want. 'Is something the matter with Cate?'

'Yes . . . well, not really, she's asleep now.' Relief, but then . . . 'The thing is, it was our college ball tonight, and Cate had invited this third year, Phil Higgins.'

The story rambled a little – I assumed Emma was not entirely sober herself – but the bare bones seemed to be that during the evening Cate had become fairly drunk, at one point disappearing for fifteen minutes to the lavatory. While she was gone Phil had been approached by an old flame and they had danced. Cate had returned to find them locked in an embrace, their tongues exploring each other's dentition. Presumably in deference to my advanced age Emma had described this delicately as 'sort of French kissing'. Cate, having taken stock, eschewed diplomacy in favour of a rather more direct response, and hit Phil over the head with a wine bottle from the nearest table.

At this point the pips went and Emma fumbled for more money.

'Number, give me your number,' I shouted.

'Hang on, it's, shit, someone's scribbled it out—' The line went dead.

Left sitting in the darkness this suddenly seemed more frightening than a black comedy of adolescent betrayal. What if Phil had an eggshell skull and Cate had been arrested for manslaughter? What if he had hit her in return and she was bruised and broken in hospital? Not knowing whether Emma was going to ring back I found the mobile and got a number for the college from Directory Enquiries but it was simply linked to an answerphone message detailing the opening hours of the Bursar's office.

While I was getting dressed and drinking tea – both precursors to any kind of action – she did call again.

The boy had been knocked out, and an ambulance sent for. By the time it had arrived he was conscious, but bleeding copiously, and had been removed to the casualty department of the city infirmary. The other woman, and a fair proportion of the over-excited dancers – high on alcohol, Ecstasy, romance, or just the end of term, were hysterical. The senior tutor had asked Emma to take Cate to their room, where she had visited them later to reassure herself that Cate was not likely to do anything more stupid, nor suffering from a potentially fatal overdose. Satisfied on both counts Ms Boscawen had left Emma in charge until the morning – and as soon as she had gone to her bed and Cate to the arms of Morpheus, Emma had called me.

'I don't know why exactly. I just thought someone should know and you're the nearest, well, the only . . .'

'Were the police called?'

'No, not then, but I suppose they might be in the morning.'

'Shall I come up?' She did not reply. 'I'd better come up.'

Driving across London at night can be soothing – deserted streets, little traffic, the soft orange glow of street lights. Driving up the motorway is downright spooky – those vast expanses of darkness in which the occasional set of tail lights sears the eyeball, the sense of emptiness and solitude which can so quickly become soporific. I decided to take the A1 instead, where the route would be broken by roundabouts and roadside settlements. The drizzle south of the Watford Gap became freezing fog beyond Grantham, and I gloomily contemplated snow and ice before Scotch Corner. It was a mild December in the south but winter came earlier and harder in the north east.

I had made this journey twice in the last two months, first to deliver Cate at the start of term. She had been quiet until I told her how nervous I had felt on the train to Durham at the beginning of my time there, wondering whether the other passengers of my age were headed for the same destination but unable to ask, whether I would make any friends, and what it would be like to live away from home, unable quite to comprehend the freedom of not having to explain to anyone where you were going and why, of being able to decide which meals to eat and how much of them without the wastage becoming a moral issue, of having a space to truly call your own.

Then she had told me how she had resisted Nicole's suggestion, made immediately after the wedding, that she should join Deborah at boarding school, marshalling arguments about academic upheaval when really she was just frightened of leaving home. It was understandable: losing your mother at nine and half-losing your father to another woman at twelve would make you want to hang on to what you'd got. Benenden must have looked like banishment.

And now she wanted to call my house home. Rather tentatively she had asked, a week before her scheduled departure, whether it was all right for her to return at Christmas, which we both knew meant for every vacation of the next three years. To my surprise it didn't feel like an obligation at all – I was pleased, but it raised one problem, and I had to explain about Saro. She looked confused, obviously feeling that she should say something more than, 'Oh I see,' but unsure what. I changed the subject.

Arriving at St Catherine's College that first delivery day had made me realise that, whatever the diminishing statistical importance of the traditional nuclear family, it was alive and well and settling its daughters into higher education. Fathers, rendered over-hearty or over-quiet by the overwhelming femaleness of the situation, traipsed backwards and forwards with cardboard boxes; mothers, perhaps recalling their own salad days, waved hockey sticks and badminton rackets in gung-ho fashion; younger siblings got dangerously in the way of the squadrons of sensible saloons and estates that nipped and tucked amongst the parking bays; the girls themselves furtively eyed one another as they queued for room keys, wondering whether they had dressed correctly and whether they would be sharing. Had I been Cate I would have been horrified to discover that I was one of those for whom a room-mate had been arbitrarily chosen, but she seemed relieved.

When we had giggled at the name – Woodhouse, Emma – and located the landing, we found the parents responsible for this appelation already in possession. I scrutinised them for traces of irony, but they were stolid products of the Edinburgh middle class. Perhaps Austen was too English to have been taught in their schools.

The Woodhouse luggage was all in the middle of the floor. 'We haven't started to unpack, because Emma wouldn't choose a bed,' said her father. At that moment Emma arrived with one of the two stereo systems the room was destined to contain, and after a stilted conversation in which both insisted on the other taking first pick, Mrs Woodhouse mercifully agreed to my suggestion that we leave them to sort it out alone, and we went for a cup of tea in the dining hall where they attempted to conceal their disappointment that Cate and I were not real Scots.

By the time of my next visit, to deliver the Mazda, it was clear that Cate and Emma had become real friends rather than forced intimates. Cate wanted to show off Emma to me as much as her new car to Emma, and it was only with difficulty that I persuaded her that, exhilarating as my drive had been, four hours in the Mazda was enough, and if they wanted to take it out for a spin they would have to do so alone.

Cate had rung a couple of times since, never forgetting to ask politely, 'How's Saro?' to which I invariably replied, 'Very well.' This awkward little ritual had been worse until I asked her not to call Saro 'Mrs Beaumont', which made her sound like either an old lady or a society courtesan.

I had been wrong about the snow – the car park of Cathy's, as I had discovered the inmates referred to their *alma mater*, was puddled by rain, but the morning sky was so dark it might as well still have been night. The college, which had been under construction when I had graduated in 1973, was built of purplish brick to a design based on the honeycomb. Polygonal rooms clustered around polygonal landings within polygonal buildings. For the safety of the undergraduettes the structures that made up the hive were all linked by tubular glass walkways in the manner of a molecular model.

I sat in the Saab and lit a cigarette, drawing strength from it along with the smoke. The figures criss-crossing the walkways seemed like extras on a film-set. I waited for the clock on the dashboard to reach nine a.m. before I scurried across to the entrance hall. The porter's desk, also of brick, was unmanned. I stood on the stone-tiled floor by the pond in which fat koi carp swam amongst the lilies and smelt the bacon from the dining hall. Through its open doors I had a clear view of the breakfasters below a high glass ceiling supported by intricate beams of matt black ornamental scaffolding. One or two had men in tow but it seemed that by a process of self-segregation they had congregated at one end. Many of the eaters were still in dressing gowns, an informality encouraged by the architecture and what Cate had described as 'aggressively matey single sexdom'.

Previously I had wandered up to Cate's room without a second thought, but the dressing gowns made that seem impolite – like going upstairs in someone's house without being invited to. I hovered for a minute or two until it became obvious there would be no official with whom I could register my arrival or gain tacit permission for my invasion of the staircases, and I set off.

One of the many defects of the honeycomb design theme was that there were no long corridors or sharp left and right turns. You entered and left successive small polygons at oblique angles, very quickly losing all sense of direction and, if unlucky, yourself. Rumour had it that there were still women who had taken their degrees years ago searching for a way out. At one point I emerged onto a glass walkway and could see my car below and the cathedral in the distance, but within seconds I was back on a seven-sided landing, staring at another set of doors, some bureaucratically marked only by their number (B17), some with an additional blu-tacked scrap of paper bearing the occupant's name (Jane Greenwood, Dramsoc Sec), and others with Paddington Bear memo boards bearing messages such as 'Why aren't you in?', 'Come for coffee S&M' and the odd drawing of a smiley face. Nothing much here had changed since my day. You knew that beyond the Paddington doors would lie soft toys on pillows and Snoopy calendars on walls.

Two dressing gowns, a comfortable lemon candlewick and a racy short kimono, emerged from their hutches. Defeating stereotype, it was the kimono that asked frostily if I was lost. Her gaze fell on the suit I had decided would be most likely to impress upon the authorities my suitability as a responsible guardian. It made me feel more like an unwelcome commercial traveller or a bailiff.

'If she's not in, will you be able to find your way back?' asked the kimono, having given directions. Jokes about minotaurs seemed ill-advised so I simply nodded my thanks.

'Bring a ball of string next time,' said the candlewick. 'That's what the hooks on the porter's desk are for.'

Cate's door now boasted their surnames in Letraset Gothic. I knocked. No reply. Again. 'Who is it?' A soft Scottish burr.

'Alex.'

'Hang on.' A certain amount of muttering and scurrying, and then the door was opened by Emma, who had evidently pulled on sweat pants and a jumper over her night shirt. The brown hair that I had only ever seen in a pony tail hung around her long, thin face. Traces of eye make-up were the only other indication that she had fallen into bed at a late hour. She ushered me in. I stepped over a crumpled black dress on the floor.

Cate was sitting up against her pillow, holding her duvet around her, her face scarcely darker than her baggy white tee-shirt. Inside the panda rings of mascara her eyes were bloodshot, and there was a bruise on her right cheekbone.

'I didn't know you were coming.' She ran a hand through her short hair.

'How are you feeling?'

'Terrible. There's some Nurofen by the sink. Could I have a couple?'

Emma brought her tablets and a mug of water. There was a short silence. 'I'm going to have a shower,' Emma said and, gathering a towel and some clothes, she left the room.

'I'm sorry you had to drive all this way,' Cate said politely. 'She shouldn't have rung you.'

'She was right to.' She hadn't said she was sorry for what she had done the night before. 'Do you remember what happened at the ball?'

'Of course. I wish I didn't.' Still calm, if edgy. 'What do you think will happen?'

'I don't know.' I was finding it hard to have this conversation. I wanted to hug her, or slap her. I wasn't sure which. 'Why don't you have a shower too? I'll make some tea, and then we can decide what to do.'

'It will have to be Nescafe. We don't keep milk in here.' She swung her long white legs out of bed. For the first time I noticed the scar on her left knee.

When Emma returned I checked the name of the boy Cate had brained and rang the hospital. They expected him to be discharged that morning, once the registrar had done his rounds. His scalp wound had needed twelve stitches.

'Poor Phil,' Cate said flatly. 'I didn't mean to.'

'So what was it? You were pissed and you just saw red?'

Cate nodded, and looked away.

Their tutor had made no arrangement to see Cate, so rather than waiting in dread I suggested she took the bull by the horns and went to apologise. I offered to go with her, and she accepted. The air was fresh enough to bring a spot of colour to her cheeks. When we got to the door she said, 'Perhaps I'd better go in on my own. I don't want her to think I'm hiding behind you.'

'OK. But tell her I'm here. Good luck.'

The tiny smile. She knocked on the door. I leant against the wall opposite, wanting a cigarette but feeling it might give the wrong impression. After ten minutes or so the door opened and Cate came out, followed by a middle-aged woman in a Chinese quilted jacket who introduced herself as Jane Boscawen. 'We are going to see the Principal, Mr Buchan. Would you care to come?'

'Of course,' I said.

The Principal's residence was across the lawn, behind a low box hedge. As we approached, with Ms Boscawen saying, 'Terribly long journey, you must be very tired,' there was a flutter of movement at the picture window and the door opened.

The Principal had salt-and-pepper hair and a large collection of cased butterflies on the wall. Her delicate watercolours of hedgerow flowers and reproduction furniture looked uncomfortable in the uncompromisingly modern house. She offered us coffee which she poured from a thermos, and lit up a Senior Service. I felt positively virtuous dragging on a low tar Silk Cut.

It was clear that she had been thoroughly briefed as there were no preliminary explanations. 'What you did, Cate, was inexcusable, and I have to say that under normal circumstances I would have considered asking you to leave, particularly as the attack was physically unprovoked – moral turpitude is no justification. However, I know what you have been through this last year, and as there have been no other adverse reports about you I am prepared to give you a second chance.'

She paused. For a moment I thought Cate was going to miss her cue but in the nick of time she said, 'Thank you very much.'

'However,' continued the Principal. 'Any future misdemeanour, and I will have no hesitation in changing my mind, which would obviously put your degree and entire future in jeopardy. Do you understand?'

'Yes,' Cate said. 'I'm sorry, Mrs Thompson.'

That was one hurdle. I voiced a worry I had had all morning. 'So the police won't be brought in to this?'

'Not by me, Mr Buchan. We don't encourage the constabulary to enter college premises unless it's absolutely necessary, and last night's incident hardly constituted a public order problem. As far as I'm aware the casualty department have the same policy. But I cannot speak for Mr Higgins. I imagine he would be within his rights to make a complaint, should he so wish.'

We left shortly after, returning to Cate's room, and while she brought Emma up to date I rang the hospital again. Phil Higgins had been discharged and was on his way back to his college – Palmerston, where I had been an undergraduate twenty years before.

'I don't suppose he'll want to see me,' Cate said.

'He might see me,' said Emma doubtfully.

'Perhaps it would be easier if I tried,' I suggested. 'What's his room number?'

Palmerston was named after the Victorian advocate of gunboat diplomacy but had been built in the 1950s in the style of a council estate in one of the Greater London overspill towns. The corridor walls still had that speckled paintwork reminiscent of municipal toilets, and chipped turquoise linoleum, presumably to enhance the masculine ambience created by the smells of damp games kit and athlete's foot powder, and the sound of heavy rock from behind grey doors. On Higgins' door was a note saying 'In bar'.

The bar was bound to be crowded before Sunday lunch; it had not been designed to accommodate more than twenty per cent of the inmates, but many more would be anxious for a pint to precede their cardboard roast meat and stodgy fruit crumble. The stale beer smell out by the pigeon holes became the heady sweetness of Newcastle Brown as I reached the entranceway and peered through the smoke of a hundred cigarettes at the assembled company of sweatshirted hearties and rather fewer self-conscious arties. It was all very familiar, but the glances thrown in my direction proved that I looked far too old to be even a mature student.

Standing by the counter was a tall boy with the dark line of stitching clearly visible on his forehead and a black eye.

'Phil?'

His gaze barely shifted from the upturned glass of Exhibition at his lips, but eventually he drained it. "Four pints, Barney. You've got the wrong man. I'm Gary.'

His companions, who had feigned disinterest in my arrival, studiously concentrating on Gary's drinking feat, watched our conversation as closely as they could without blowing their cool. I explained the reason for my mistaken identification.

'He's in the corner,' Gary said. 'The one with the lumberjack outfit and the bandage.' He was sitting at a table with a pair of leather-jacketed companions.

I thought I'd get a drink before I went across. 'Will they serve me?' I asked Gary, remembering the rules.

'As you're my guest,' he said, grinning. I wanted a glass of wine but that seemed unlikely, so I asked for a bottle of Pils. 'Southerner,' Gary said.

I gave him a fiver. 'Get a round in. It's a pleasure to drink at prices like these.'

Phil was a clean-cut Latin matinee idol – more male model than man. Not hard to see why Cate had fallen for him. I explained who I was. He looked suspicious. 'I just wanted a chat. If you've got a moment. I don't want to keep you from your lunch.'

'If you'd eaten here,' he said laconically in a surprising Bradford accent, 'you wouldn't worry about that. You're doing me a favour.' His mates laughed.

'I have eaten here. Often. Doesn't sound as if the cooking's improved one jot.'

That helped to get us off on the right foot. The acolytes went off to their food, the bar emptied and I bought us each another and some cheese and onion crisps before it closed. I asked how he was feeling.

'OK, apart from a slight headache, and the beer's sorting that out. Wish it could make the hair grow back on the shaved patch.'

'I know Cate's very worried about you and very sorry for what happened,' I said. 'But she was afraid you wouldn't want to see her.'

Phil snorted. 'She's right. Look, I'm sorry to say this but she's mad. We were all, you know, a bit merry, and Trish, who I used to go out with, was just giving me a snog, nothing more. Nothing to go berserk about.'

'Perhaps it doesn't look like that if you're berserk about someone. I mean, I'm not trying to excuse her . . .' although that was, of course, exactly what I was doing.

'I don't know what she's said but there wasn't really anything between us. We weren't a couple. She asked me to the ball and I accepted in spite of . . .' He laughed. 'We'd barely kissed.'

'Perhaps she wanted more.'

He gave me a look that was half withering contempt, half mutual male suffering. 'I'd tried. We'd been out a couple of times but it was "I just want to be friends". You know.'

I did, but hardly thought agreement was guardian-like behaviour. I nodded minutely.

'I mean even if you think someone's entitled to ownership rights, no-one could say she had them.'

I needed to use my trump. I explained about Stuart. Phil hadn't known, and was immediately more forgiving. I broached the question of the police. 'Wouldn't have thought of it,' he said. 'People have enough hassles without that.' I couldn't have agreed with him more. I didn't chance asking him whether he'd reconsider seeing Cate.

'I don't want to see him,' Cate said. We were walking down to the river. 'I've been so stupid.' She scuffed up the fallen leaves on the footpath with her shoes.

'You must have been fond of him.' I was intrigued by the discrepancy between his account of their acquaintance and that suggested by what she had done.

'I don't think that's the right word,' she said. We came out from under the last of the dead elms on to the bridge over the Wear.

'I'm sure it's not,' I said. 'What is?'

She leant against the parapet and looked down in to the water, which danced with the skeletal reflections of the trees. Beyond her the cathedral loomed darkly. The setting was so Gothic it would have been quite easy to mistake the two teenagers in parkas on the opposite bank for hooded monks. 'I f— sort of fell in love with him.'

What was the f word? Fancied? Fantasised? 'I can see why. He's very handsome.'

'I fell in love with him,' she said, 'and he betrayed me. At least, that's what it felt like.'

Strong feelings to have kept hidden, but then all hers seemed to be. Had she been too shy or too frightened to give in to them or even express them to Phil? 'I'm sorry,' I said.

She was crying. I leant next to her and put my arm across her shoulders. Our voices condensed into smoke in the chill air and mingled as they floated away.

'I've spoilt everything.' She buried her head against me.

'Of course you haven't. We've fixed what can be fixed. It'll blow over.'

She sobbed again. 'And now I know I didn't love him at all.'

I found a tissue and lifted her face to wipe her eyes. 'Term's nearly over. I'm sure they'd let you take off a couple of days early under the circumstances. You could come back with me tonight.'

'Miss Boscawen suggested that.'

I sensed a reluctance. 'Do you want to?'

'Of course I do . . . but I can't. I've got to stick it out. Otherwise I won't come back to Durham at all.'

I felt proud. 'I think you're right. It's cold. Shall we go and have a drink to warm up?'

'Are you going to read the riot act?'

'I think we can take that as read, don't you?'

'Thanks.' She straightened up. 'I couldn't face a pub. The smell would make me heave.'

'The demon hangover. I was thinking more of tea.' I took her arm, and we went like tourists to the Undercroft in the cathedral cloisters, where sombre Norman grandeur had been tamed with vases of flowers and a choice of Lapsang or Earl Grey to go with the cream and scones, and the nice old ladies and the nice young clerics. Very reassuring.

Chapter Nine

We did a lot of walking that Christmas. On the day itself we stopped off at Stirton Ash on our way down to lunch with my father in Eastbourne. We'd brought some flowers to put on Stuart's grave and we laid them out to the accompaniment of 'Hark the Herald', sung by what sounded like a substantial and enthusiastic congregation inside St Mark's. I asked Cate whether she wanted to join them but she shook her head. 'Can we walk up the lane to the house?'

It was a grey day, cold but with none of the sparkle that accompanies snow or frost. The sky was so dark that there was scarcely a horizon where it met the dank ploughed earth of the field opposite the Hall. The gates were shut, but we could just see over. The new owners had put fairy lights in the pine by the coach house and an alarm box high on the gable. Had they known about the murder? A child was riding a gleaming scooter around the circular drive.

In the dining room where we had held Stuart's wake, the ritualistic sideways shuffle with occasional genuflection of a bowed head signified a woman laying the table.

After a moment, as if this diversion had been my idea, Cate said, 'Come on. We don't want to be late for Grandad.'

The car was by the lych gate. As I was unlocking it, she leaned over the churchyard wall and looked back at the bouquet. 'They're such a bright red.'

I wondered if anyone ever visited Angela's grave. It hadn't occurred to me to suggest it. As if she had read my thoughts Cate said, 'The ones I put on Mummy's were yellow. I remember that as her favourite colour, although Daddy said he wasn't sure.'

'Did you usually go together?'

'We used to go the Sunday before Christmas, always. Then last year Nicole had organised this lunch party and he said the wreath would have to wait, that he'd pop and do it after work on Monday.'

There didn't seem anything to say about this minor betrayal, so I concentrated on the road.

'I made a bit of a fuss about it. Said I was going anyway. Missed lunch. Actually it was awful. The cemetery's nowhere near a tube and you know what Sunday buses are like. Took me all day.'

I could see her, poor kid, catching the train to Victoria, trudging across London with her wilting bundle of hothouse lilies to Acton or some such place, counting out the grids of the municipal burial ground until she found the intersection where Angela's tombstone stood, possibly with the remains of the previous year's tribute, a twist of wire, a frond of evergreen, still at its base.

'I went back on the Tuesday evening to check. There was nothing else there apart from mine.'

I tried to think back to last December to provide him with an alibi, but couldn't. 'If he said he was going, then I'm sure he did. Awful though it is, someone could have taken the flowers he left. It happens.'

'I suppose it does.'

'Or he might not have taken anything. If he was too late leaving the office to get to the florist's. It's the visit that counts, isn't it? And if he said he was going to do that, he would have done. I know it.'

She had nodded acknowledgement and smiled her tight little smile, and to lighten the mood I began to speculate about all the different types of Christmas that might be going on behind the front doors of the villages through which we passed.

In all honesty I hadn't been looking forward enormously to our own, the arrangement of which had been something of a diplomatic trial. Ever since Stuart and Nicole had moved to Stirton Hall, I had spent the day with them and my father had stayed with them for anything up to a week, but this year, obviously, the pattern would have to be broken. In November, on one of my fortnightly visits, I had suggested to the old man that I collected him on the 24th and returned him from Camberwell to Matron's tender care on the 27th. He was dubious, chiefly because of his unswerving conviction that men could not cook, but agreed to consider the proposition.

In the mean time I had tentatively asked Cate what she might be doing, half expecting her to be going to Nicole's in some latterday version of the wartime truce in the trenches, but she simply said she hadn't arranged anything. I was glad, but concerned that this might leave her stepmother alone. Without telling Cate I rang Nicole and the two of us conducted a cagey conversation in which it eventually became clear that we both felt under obligation to invite the other but need not. Relieved, Nicole offered her drinks party on the 26th and I lunch at Rules on the 22nd.

I had then spent a week in vague contemplation of poulterers' windows, eyeing up boxes of dates in Sainsbury's, wondering whether a bottle of green ginger wine was an essential addition to the drinks tray, when the old man dropped his bombshell.

'I don't want to be any trouble, and I'm sure the dinner here at Seaview will be perfectly all right. After all, I take all of my other meals here.'

I argued, cajoled and eventually wheedled but he would not be moved. Even when I pandered to his prejudices and said that, although I could not be expected to manage anything more than the pork pie for supper,

Cate would be with us and the guarantor of our gastronomic wellbeing, he would not be moved. Which is why, as the result of an eleventh hour compromise, the three of us were eating at the Grand Hotel.

The old boy was full of beans, spruced up in a new cardigan beneath the jacket of his best suit, looking forward to everything from the sherry and cheese straws in the bar beforehand to the promise of liqueurs and petit fours in the lounge afterwards. We exchanged presents, but his had been bought on an off day and he gave me a seasonally-wrapped carton of Benson and Hedges, a brand of cigarette that I had never smoked, and Cate a one pound record token and a Cadbury's selection box. She kept a straight face throughout the unwrapping, kissed him on the cheek and showed him the bag that I had bought her.

It wasn't until I had started to think about something for Cate that I had realised that we were in a no-man's-land between acquaintanceship and intimacy which ruled out so many potential gifts. Clothes were too personal, contained too many messages, books and tapes alone too anonymous, household objects unnecessary and money plain patronising. Seeing her gazing at the enormous soft leather sack in the window of Liberty's was a boon. I had filled it with bits and pieces from the Body Shop, a large bottle of what seemed to be her favourite perfume, a couple of hardback novels as she only ever bought herself paperbacks, and a pile of CDs.

'It's just like a real stocking,' she had said. 'Thank you.'

I had been unable to stop myself from laughing. 'You're so polite, and very good at concealing your . . . surprise.'

'What do you mean?'

'You haven't got a CD player.'

'No,' she said, found out but rallying admirably, 'but I can listen to them here.'

At which point I suggested she have a look in the studio, where the requisite hardware sat in its box, surrounded by foam chips which could have doubled as pre-prandial snacks at the Grand Hotel.

She was telling Dad this story as we drank our vegetable soup, although I could see that he hadn't the faintest idea what a CD was. During the smoked trout he embarked on a long anecdote about tinned sardines which moved effortlessly into games of sardines at Christmas in Saltcoats before the war. By the time the turkey had been demolished I was flagging, having long since passed anything which might have been called my alcohol allowance, but Cate was positively bubbling and the old man was riding a crest of reminiscence. I ordered them a half-bottle of dessert wine, knowing it would appeal to his sweet tooth, and he cheerfully followed his pudding, rum sauce and brandy butter with a couple of mince pies. Finally setting down his spoon he asked, 'Dare say you two will be off skiing as usual?'

There was a short pause. 'I've never skiied, Dad.'

'You've always loved it though, haven't you?' He refocused on Cate.

'Can't think why you married him really. Lovely girl like you. Still, you've kept him on the straight and narrow, Angela. Pity his brother never found himself a wife. Can't you introduce him to anybody suitable?'

Cate had her napkin to her face, her cheeks above it flushed. She rose. 'I'll . . . keep an eye out,' she mumbled. 'Excuse me for a second.'

I topped up Dad's glass. 'I'll just sort out the coffee,' I said somewhat wildly, 'have a cigar,' and I followed her.

She was in the corridor, leaning against the wall, with the crumpled linen still pressed to her mouth. I lifted her head, her eyes were brimming. 'I'm sorry,' I said. 'He can't help it.'

She removed the napkin and with it came a snort of laughter. 'Pity about his brother,' she gasped, before another paroxysm of giggles.

By the time we had seen him up the front steps of Seaview, into the welcoming arms of matron who, noticing how tipsy he was, faked censoriousness, it was dark. But with the traditional, puritanical British view that a spot of fresh air would do us good, we set off along the promenade towards the model village. I remembered that walk, when I was a boy, being a major expedition that had taken the best part of a morning, so I was somewhat shocked to discover us past the bowling greens and before the gaily-painted entrance after no more than ten or fifteen minutes.

'How old were you?' Cate asked. 'Well, no wonder. You were a toddler, probably only about two feet high. How sweet.'

'But a bore to walk with.'

And then she asked about the holidays we had spent there, and I found myself comparing the relative merits of Hastings – amusement arcades, the constant aroma of candy floss and fish and chips – Eastbourne – boating lake and theatre as well as the ubiquitous model village – and the appalling Bexhill with its Stalinist blocks of shuttered flats and a front whose unimaginative wastes of pavement and flowerbeds were more like a giant war memorial than a place for enjoyment.

Hers had been very different: camp sites in southern France, ski resorts in the winter; she had never been on a pier. We looked back along the beach at the shadowy bulk of Eastbourne's, its legs gartered with frills of white foam. The sea was not particularly rough but the breakers were crashing with Tchaikovsky-like enthusiasm, each thump punctuated by the sucking of a thousand straws in almost empty beakers.

'Let's walk back along the beach,' Cate said. 'I want to be closer to the sea.' And she limboed lithely beneath the railing and dropped from the concrete esplanade to the pebbles. Progress was slow; walking across stones is like wading through treacle, and the sharper ones jabbed at my feet through the thin soles of my suede loafers. Cate, imperviously air-cushioned in sturdy Doc Martens, ploughed ahead, creating small avalanches on the shelving slopes. The wind pulled at her coat and drove the deliciously pungent smell of seaweed up my nostrils.

She sat on a breakwater and gazed out across the water in a way that suggested introspection, so I hung back and, as if in a timewarp, found myself attempting ducks and drakes with some flat pebbles. The first couple were useless, one bounce each, but the third skipped across the water as if designed by Barnes Wallis.

'Five,' Cate said. I hadn't even noticed her approach. 'Why is it boys are so much better at that than girls?'

'Probably because it's completely pointless.'

'It's been a really nice day.'

'Good.'

'I wish we didn't have to go to Nicole's tomorrow.'

We did, of course; and I was just explaining why when the surf engulfed my shoes and Cate's resistance was swept away on a tide of giggling sympathy.

Any time from six Nicole had said, so I had planned to order a taxi for about half past, but when the time came there was no sign of Cate, who had disappeared to get ready more than an hour before. I gave her the grace of another five pages of my book and then called her. There was a long gap before she shouted, 'OK, I'll be out before he rings the bell.'

I didn't think my expression could have changed, but she was so acutely tuned to reactions that she said, 'What's the matter?' as soon as she came into the room.

'Nothing,' I said, and I meant it. I was just surprised. She had changed out of the relatively smart clothes of the day into an old pair of jeans and a baggy jumper in a nondescript colour.

'I don't see why I should have to dress up.'

'No. Whatever you're comfortable in.'

We were both thinking of the cocktail dresses, the Thai silk trousers, the costume jewellery, that were likely to be on display.

She sat heavily on the sofa. 'It's just . . . I tried on everything and none of it seemed right.' She kicked an angry leg at the empty air. The doorbell rang. She stood and looked at herself in the big gilt mirror over the fireplace. 'I can't go like this.' Her face, scrubbed after her bath, was devoid of make-up. I was frightened she might be about to cry.

I tried to think what I had seen her in. 'What about those baggy striped trousers?' Rather like fifties bohemian curtain material. 'And your black lycra top?'

'Do you think?' At least she was intrigued that I had an opinion. 'What about a jacket or something?'

'I'll just pop down and tell the taxi to wait. Why not try them?'

On the stairs I remembered a monkey jacket, bought second-hand in the seventies, never yet teamed with the bow-tie and wing collars that it had been designed for; I had worn it with frayed Levis and, embarrassingly, an embroidered kurta. Never mind. It was, as far as I recalled, in pristine condition. I scrabbled about among the hangers in the attic until I found it. Cate hovered on the landing awaiting approval. The jacket found favour, a very heavy brooch pinned to its lapel.

'Have I got time to do my make-up?'

'I think you'd better now you're partied up.'

'What about the driver? Will he wait?'

I smiled. 'I think so.'

'What did you tell him?' She applied mascara vigorously.

'Nothing really. I was just terribly sexist, raised my eyebrows and said "women" in a downtrodden way.'

She caught my eye in the mirror, grinned, and smudged a lash.

'Sorry,' I said.

Sitting in the warm dark taxi she thanked me. 'It does look OK?'

'Wonderful. And nothing like what Nicole or Deborah will be wearing. So no competition tonight.' And, more to the point, no loser. I wouldn't have dared saying that in the light but my guess was right because all she said was no.

Nicole's new home turned out to be a flat – the upper two floors of an early-nineteenth-century house in Primrose Hill. There was a view of Regent's Park from the back bedroom window, or so she said. The atmosphere of schizophrenia was no doubt due to the mismatch of her furniture with the previous owner's decor. I recognised one or two pieces from Stirton Hall, which suddenly made me glad that she had moved. A party without Stuart, or reference to Stuart, in Stuart's house would have been unbearable.

Equally I had feared that the air would be heavy with the sound of people not mentioning his name, but the early frenetic gaiety settled into the contented buzz of guests at ease with themselves and their ritual confessions of over-indulgence. The only person who did refer to him in my hearing was Bill Starling, Deborah's Merlin and Nicole's seemingly steadfast companion in adversity. After we had exchanged politenesses about his pick of the year's new plays which had appeared in that Sunday's *Observer*, he suddenly asked, 'Have the police made any progress with their investigation?'

'No – unless they've told Nicole anything new since the 22nd when we had lunch.' It had been a constrained affair until I had forced our unspoken memories into the open over coffee, and was largely responsible for my apprehension of this evening.

Starling, eating canapés, fingered his beard in the way that some people dab on a napkin, and I peered surreptitiously for traces of egg or olive in its tuft, but there was nothing other than a sheen which might have been grease. He said, 'Not as far as I know, but then I don't like to bring the subject up.'

No, I bet you don't, I thought. We both looked at Nicole, in full conversational flight by the window. The traces of rural gentry that she had acquired with Stirton had already vanished, giving way not to the speech mannerisms of the legal secretary that I had first met, but to the budding actress of her youth, and her sentences were peppered with darlings. 'How does she seem to you?' I asked.

'She's been very brave, of course. In her heart she's an old trouper, show must go on, that sort of thing, and most people are convinced, but I can tell she's hurting terribly underneath.'

Uncharitably I wondered whether Starling's claim to a special insight was based on his own rejection – he had not been able to worm his way into her bed yet and therefore . . . alternatively it might just be his courtier mentality, constantly needing to imply that he knew her better than any other acolyte. Then again, maybe he did have a special insight, other people's sexual attractions are often mysterious. The half of my brain not engaged in this distasteful speculation thrust and parried in a duel over the role of the Arts Council, a subject he must have debated so often I assumed he was also on automatic pilot.

'Alex.' It was Deborah, resplendent in a glittering frock carefully designed to draw attention to her cleavage while disguising her posterior. Starling paid attention from the corner of his eye. 'Excuse me, Bill,' she said, propelling me by the elbow, 'but there's something I must discuss with Alex, and Mummy's charged me with forcing people to circulate so you must keep moving.' She was flirtatious enough to get away with it.

'What is it?' I asked, as she handed me another glass of sparkling burgundy.

'Nothing. Just returning your favour at the funeral. Thought you'd been stuck with him quite long enough.' Starling was gravitating towards Nicole by shuffling from the camouflage of one group to another. It was rather like watching a crane; you never saw it move but if you so much as blinked it would be balanced on the other leg by the time you looked again.

'How's Cate getting on?' Deborah said, after a while.

'All right, I think. What does she say?'

'Not much. She's never been very fond of me. Or of Mummy it would seem,' she added provocatively.

I shrugged.

'I suppose I could have understood it a few years back. That woman, my mother, replacing her mother.'

'And taking away a big slice of her father's love and affection perhaps. She'd got used to it being just the two of them.'

'But you'd have thought she'd have got over it by now. I mean, before Stuart . . .'

'Is it hurtful for Nicole, Cate living . . . staying with me?'

'The strange thing is, she doesn't seem to mind—' Deborah abruptly changed the subject as Nicole and Starling moved within earshot and we were discussing property prices when the lights went out.

There were several gasps and half-screams, immediately replaced by exaggerated jocularity as cigarette lighters were used to illuminate the progress of Nicole and a number of helpful men to the fusebox. Starling, without permission, so perhaps his feet were well under the table if not the duvet, lit the ornamental candles on the mantlepiece, and I could see that Deborah looked stunned. Her hand was still gripping mine, long nails quite sharply clamped into the base of my thumb.

'Are you all right?'

'Yes, it's just. . . .' She lapsed into silence.

'What? What's the matter?'

She shook her head. 'It's nothing, stupid, but that first moment after the lights went out was just like being in the bathroom that night at Stirton.'

'Just the dark, and the surprise, I expect.'

'No, more.' She was insistent now. 'It was exactly the same feeling.'

'How the same?'

She struggled to clarify but gave up, shaking her head. 'I don't know.' The lights came back on, breaking the mood, and revealed Cate hovering a couple of feet away.

'How are you doing?' I said.

'OK. Are you all right, Debs?'

'Yes, fine. I could do with another drink, though.' I volunteered to get them and went in search of a bottle, glad to free my brain from the burden of conversation while I mulled over what Deborah had said.

Exactly the same feeling meant what, in the sight-deprived dark? No one was touching her, she wasn't eating or drinking, so it had to be a sound or a smell, or both. It was hard to imagine a similarity between the normal smells of a bathroom – antiseptic, toothpaste – and this smoky atmosphere, and bathrooms were usually silent. So – caused by what?

A presence. The killer's presence. Announced by some characteristic scent or noise – aftershave, tobacco, BO, nasal breathing, a grunt – in the fraction of a second before he grabbed at her out of the dark, and which Deborah had experienced again just now.

I didn't have a complete picture of those in our vicinity at the moment of revelation but I knew who had been standing directly behind her; Nicole had been chatting away to Bill Starling.

Chapter Ten

When I bumped into Starling in the kitchen, a spurt of hatred so strong ran through me that I had to retreat to the bathroom and splash cold water over my face.

Part of me said the idea of Merlin as murderer was absurd but in other ways it was surprisingly easy to imagine him doing it, his motive Nicole, revenging himself on the man whom she had chosen in preference to him after the departure of Charlie Makepeace. This wasn't entirely rational; after all, Makepeace had left four years before Nicole remarried and, according to Deborah, Starling had been on the scene for all of that time, but then a man besotted is not rational. He may have believed that he was on the verge of a breakthrough with his object of desire and that Stuart had somehow cheated him of his just reward. Thereafter every slight marital discord that he had observed or heard about would have stoked up his conviction that Nicole needed saving from this fate worse than Stuart's death and that, in the fullness of time, the relieved widow would fall into his arms. After all, he must have favourably reviewed misplaced obsessions of this sort many times over the years.

It would have been easy for him to inveigle from Nicole that, with her and Cate away on holiday, Stuart would be home alone – bad luck that he had found Deborah in residence. Whatever physical appearances suggested, Merlin's social behaviour and career marked him as a man of ambition and tenacity, not given to panic. He would have coped with this unexpected eventuality. Admittedly, it was harder to see him as a shooter, but then you wouldn't need much expertise to hit a man in the chest from a couple of yards.

Whatever my suspicions, I did not see how I could test them further except by finding another opportunity to discuss the murder with Deborah and release more of her memories, and that would have to be handled very delicately. Any thought of contacting Cromarty I quickly dismissed. He had explicitly said that there were no unidentified fingerprints at the house, and it seemed unlikely that any more fragile forensic evidence remained after the advent of the new owners. In the absence of that it would seem as if I was accusing someone else with no more proof than Cromarty had held against me or, if he still suspected me, that I was simply trying to muddy the waters. I had not heard from him since my visit to the police station and this did not seem the best reason for renewing our acquaintance.

The next day the whole business seemed so unreal I knew I couldn't talk to anybody about it, and in any case I was preoccupied by a different set of complications, arising from our having contracted to see in the New Year with Boy and Molly Chippenham. Each year they assembled a different party at their Devon farmhouse; my turn had last come three years before. Molly had extended this invitation to Cate who, somewhat to my surprise, had accepted. I had asked who else would be there but the list was incomplete, so it was only afterwards that I discovered that the Beaumonts – Saro, Henry and the three boys – would be there also.

'Can either of us get out of it?' Saro had asked.

'I don't see how.' I knew that she meant me – changing the holiday arrangements of her family was like turning an oil-tanker. 'I mean, I could invent an excuse but Boy is involved enough with my business affairs to stand a chance of finding out in the future, which would be awful.'

'I'm sorry,' she said, 'it was unfair of me to ask.'

Cate, who had always contrived to stay out of the way when Saro came to the Camberwell Road, said nothing until we had arrived at Longacre and been shown to our accommodation, in the flat above the garage. Molly was apologetic: 'I know there's only one bedroom, but the sofa bed is very comfortable, and it was either you or the Beaumont boys out here and we thought Saro might like them under slightly closer supervision.'

'Don't worry,' I said, 'it's fine.' It was. The garage had been converted from a small deconsecrated chapel by the gate; upstairs we had a large sitting room with a cooker and fridge in one corner, a bedroom, and a shower room with WC.

'How are you going to manage?' Cate asked once Molly had left.

'Well, thanks for assuming I'd be sleeping on the couch, but you're right, I'm a chivalrous chap and I will. As the lady said, I'm sure—'

'I don't mean that, I mean you and Saro. It's not exactly an Edwardian country house party, is it, with people creeping along corridors in their dressing gowns and everyone happily back in their own rooms before the maid brings early morning tea.'

I laughed, but she was very tense.

'I mean, I suppose she sleeps with Henry, so if you do . . . it will be here.' She turned away.

'Don't worry, nothing will happen. It's agreed. So you don't have to stay out of the way or invent alibis for us. I wouldn't put you through that. I wouldn't put myself through that. I mean, I'm sorry, because I have put you in a position where you might have to watch your tongue, but you shouldn't have to lie because literally nobody knows so no one can ask you any potentially incriminating questions.'

She lightened. 'I can be discreet.'

When I had finished hanging my clothes in the wardrobe in her room I returned to find her gazing, absorbed, out of the dormer window in the sitting room. It held the best view of the L-shaped, thatched farmhouse, with glimpses of the stone barns and stabling behind. I joined her. It was raining thickly; the glass ran with it and the cobbled drive was dark and glistening. The Beaumonts' blue Mercedes had just pulled up by the front door, rear wiper still beating. The car doors opened cautiously as Molly appeared in the glass porch, unfurling an umbrella.

The boys spilled out: James at eight, all bounce and enthusiasm; Harry, eleven, gangling and pushy; Hugo, thirteen, awkwardly diffident, hoping to appear cool. Henry, their father, was heavy in an Aran sweater, his rosy bald patch clearly visible beneath the drift of greying hair combed back from his high forehead. He waved away Molly's umbrella so that she hovered functionless as the brothers hauled down the luggage from the roofrack and Saro, enveloped in a large Barbour, her features hidden from us beneath a checked slouch hat, released Fletcher, their golden Labrador, from the estate's rear.

Faint curses and instructions floated up to us as Fletcher ran excitedly through a puddle, barked at the suitcases and jumped up at Molly, marking her butcher's apron and the Jaeger dress beneath with muddy pawprints.

'Control that brute, Saro,' Henry demanded, as Molly protested that there was no harm done, and at a cross word from his mistress the chastened animal came to heel. Fletcher was very much Saro's dog, trained, in so far as he was trained, by her and named by me after the other half of the seventeenth century playwrights Beaumont and Fletcher. He had visited Camberwell Road several times, and one of my anxieties over the keeping of our secret during this trip had been that his enthusiastic recognition of a man he was supposed never to have met would strike Henry as untoward. I was relieved, then, that his affection, as demonstrated on Molly, seemed indiscriminate.

Down on the drive she, apparently discussing the state of the garden despite the gradual reduction of her guests to drowned rats, turned to point out the ivy growing on the chapel walls, and saw us at the window. I just resisted the temptation to pull guiltily back, which would have confirmed me as the peeping tom I now felt like, and therefore was obliged to exchange embarrassed waves with my lover and her cuckolded husband while Molly exaggeratedly mouthed, 'Tea in ten minutes', and then juggled the umbrella in order to display her ten fingers in case we had failed to get the message.

Cate said in a small voice, 'I wish I hadn't come.'

'Too late for that,' I said. 'It'll be fine, anyway.' I scarcely persuaded myself but it was more fun than I had expected.

I had told Cate that the Chippenhams' daughter Abigail, more or less her age, would be at home but it turned out that she had gone skiing, so the nearest adult to Cate in years was Saro at thirty-five. Cate adapted to the situation beautifully, so that after a day or so any subconscious talking-down to her, or attempts to find special topics of conversation for her at dinner, had ceased.

'Absolute credit to Stuart, that girl,' said David Frobisher who, with his wife Claire, made up the party.

Hugo Beaumont was just old enough to be painfully self-conscious in her presence and Cate had not developed the grace to deal with it so, wisely, Molly placed them apart at meals thereafter, but her relations with his brothers were straightforward enough – Harry magisterially ignored her and James got on with her like a house on fire.

He was extremely impressed by her Mazda, in which we had driven down, and became our regular travelling companion on trips to the coast or Exmoor, bouncing in apparent comfort on the half-seat behind us. His brothers were of course equally impressed but could not afford to show it; the adults had assumed at first that the car was mine and I had come in for much good-natured joshing about the male menopause during which Saro had given me the trace of a wink.

Until New Year's Eve that was the only private sign I received from her, but in a strange way that made our proximity a pleasure rather than pain. I was seeing her now as I never had before, in a different kind of intimate detail, domestic and familial, Saro the wife and mother, walker of dogs and setter of bedtimes, maker of scones and doer of crosswords.

By tradition the Chippenhams dressed for dinner on New Year's Eve, and there was some discreet female jockeying for position by the fire in the draughty sitting room – Cate's black top had sleeves but only of Lycra and her flared mini-skirt was of thin taffeta; Claire Frobisher, after a muffled exchange, despatched David to bring her a shawl; Saro's bare shoulders looked as cold as marble. They were glad when we moved to the warm kitchen for dinner, and the boot was on the other foot. Dinner jackets were hung over chair-backs, bow ties loosened and sleeves rolled up as midnight drew nearer and the last bottle of claret washed down the cheese. Molly switched on the radio to catch the chimes of Big Ben, and Boy opened a couple of bottles of champagne to drink a toast.

We stood and raised our glasses, 'Happy New Year', and embraced the person next to us. In my case that was Saro, and as our lips met for fractionally longer than was strictly necessary her fingers pressed my wrist and her pelvis momentarily touched mine as she looked hard in to my eyes. I was suffused by a warm glow and then she was gone, moving on to David Frobisher, and I was circulating in the opposite direction – a noisy peck on the cheek from Claire, a slap on the back from Boy, a giggly squeeze from Molly, a crisp handshake from Henry, and a limp one from a scarlet Hugo who had just been through agonies of indecision over precisely how to kiss Cate and, owing to mutual misinterpretation of intent, had ended up planting one on the end of her nose.

When I reached Cate we hugged tightly and she treated my 'Happy New Year' seriously, saying 'Thank you, I hope so.' I kissed her forehead and we joined the circle to sing 'Auld Lang Syne' in the sort of directionless way that loses heart somewhere in the second verse and drifts to a stumbling halt that can only be covered by the pouring of more large drinks.

The next morning, inevitably, I had the hangover depression and desire to be somewhere else, which paracetamol and liver salts only partially fixed. As I sat nursing a mug of tea at the window of the flat, the sight of Boy, apparently full of beans, hauling his clay pigeon launcher across the yard, reminded me that this morning had been set aside for shooting. I had been worried about the effect this might have on Cate, but when I broached the subject she had said, 'Well, I've never really done it before, but I'll have a go.'

For a second I thought she had missed my point; then she said, 'It would be silly never to touch a shotgun again because of what happened to Daddy; I mean, you wouldn't refuse to drive if someone had been killed in a car crash, would you?'

I agreed with her; the analogy that I had used myself was that of getting back on a horse after being thrown. Nevertheless I felt more peculiar than last night's alcohol warranted as we assembled in Boy's five-acre field. The idea was simply to give those of us who had shot before some much-needed practice before we went rough shooting in the woods that afternoon, and for those who had no intention of pursuing game to have some fun and rudimentary instruction in how to hold and point a gun. Boy sent up some simple targets, floating away towards the hedgerow, and we had five shots each. Henry, using one of an immaculate pair of Purdeys, took each of his five before they had been in the air more than a couple of seconds. Claire missed her first two and, gradually finding her eye, winged the third before blowing the last two to smithereens. Hugo, proudly toting his father's other Purdey, missed his first but dusted his second, at which point his brothers' hoots of derision became cries of fluke. Studiously as he tried to ignore these, they must have made him tense for he failed to hit the others. As I loaded my barrels, I could hear Saro giving James and Henry Junior a sound ticking off.

I had already called, 'Pull' when I saw the movement behind the hedgerow. I lowered the gun and broke it open as the clay span safely over the hedge and fell away out of sight. Boy was mouthing at me as I pulled out an ear-plug, '. . . Forget to take the safety off, you silly bugger?'

I explained. 'Touch of the DTs,' laughed David Frobisher but Molly said, 'What about Basin's bull? I mean, it shouldn't be out now but . . .?'

'I'll take a look,' I said, and set off across grass hard with cold. There was nothing in the next field but more grass, although a rook took off as

I approached, and a piece of orange baler twine fluttered from a twig. I turned to call that it was all right. Molly was pouring coffee from a thermos, Claire and Boy were smoking, and Cate had a shotgun to her shoulder, its barrels pointing straight at me.

I froze. One of the first rules of clay shooting is that you never point an unbroken gun at anybody, even if you are sure it's not loaded, because you may be wrong and even if you're not, the person you're pointing it at doesn't know that.

I didn't, and the fact that Henry was by her side, obviously expounding some of the finer points of technique, didn't make me any happier. It would be all too easy, once she had me lined up, for him to say, 'and then you squeeze the trigger gently' and for her to do it. At this distance the spread of shot was unlikely to be fatal unless I was unlucky, but I wasn't feeling so lucky. I stood still and opened my mouth to shout, and as I did so Boy happened to look round.

'Put that bloody gun down,' he bawled, and Cate dropped it. There was no bang.

By the time I reached the others Boy was apologising for having shouted, but reiterating that Henry should have known better, Henry was shrugging in a sheepish way and Cate, red in the face, was on the verge of tears. Saro, tight-lipped, which with her lips meant very tight indeed, was obviously angry with Henry, and Molly with Boy. Cate clearly expected me to be angry with her. 'I'm sorry,' she said, 'I didn't think.'

'It's all right,' I said. 'You knew it wasn't loaded.'

'I didn't actually. I didn't look.'

I didn't let Henry begin the apology he felt obliged to make but considered damned silly.

Cate was subdued for the rest of the morning, reluctantly taking her turn but hitting very little. As we filed back for lunch, steak-and-kidney pie and bottled Guinness, I said, 'You're not still brooding about this morning's little fiasco?'

'No. I'm just freezing,' she said, a little too insistently.

'Good. Anyway, I can't imagine old Henry not checking whether there's one up the spout. Probably ingested that with his mother's milk.'

'No, he didn't check.'

'Oh well, no harm done. What will you do this afternoon?'

'Have a lie down, I think. I'm not even sure I can face lunch.'

'Feeling a bit fragile?' asked Boy, drawing alongside. 'Large sherry should put you right. Always works wonders for Molly.'

'What about you?' Cate raised a smile.

Boy pulled a battered hip-flask from his pocket. 'I've already had my hair of the dog.'

'Just the one or a whole headful?'

'She's sharp,' Boy chuckled.

'But blunted by hospitality, I think,' I said.

'Absolutely,' she yawned.

Inevitably it was only Boy, David, Henry and I who went into the woods that afternoon. The sky was clear and bright, but the temperature was already falling again and the puddles on the rutted track were still iced over, cracking underfoot. Where the shadow of the tall pines had prevented the penetration of direct sunlight, the frost of the night before clung tenaciously to the boughs of trees and the fronds of ferns beneath. We put up a couple of snipe, both missed, and a cock pheasant which Boy bagged and his springer spaniel, Nelson, triumphantly retrieved, but the place had such a mysterious lustre I would scarcely have been surprised had I glimpsed a pterodactyl swooping across a clearing or a hobgoblin scuttling for cover. There was no conversation and my mind wandered through the land that time forgot and half-remembered Grimm's fairy tales. The light retreated and the cold slipped through sweaters and beneath the skin.

'Perhaps we should call it a day,' Boy said.

'Not just yet,' Henry said, quickly. 'I heard another couple of pheasants calling, and you know it's a good time for them. We might even get a duck or two heading for the lake. Let's give it another half hour, unless Alex wants to get back to the ladies.'

I shook my head, and by silent consent we continued. What had he meant by that? Why single me out unless he knew something? Had he picked up the vibes from Saro's embrace the previous night? It was subtle but perhaps a husband had extra-sensory powers of perception. Had Fletcher put his head on my knee once too often, or Saro mumbled in her sleep?

If he knew, he had not said anything to Saro or she would have told me. If he was uncertain, maybe this sly innuendo would be it, an attempt at provoking a revealing reaction. If so I had done the best thing by outwardly ignoring it.

I had never before thought of Henry in terms of complaisant husband; he was competitive even outside of work, and fortunes these days were not built and maintained without determination. Surely aggressive, acquisitive bankers never surrendered without a fight and never ever gave up something for nothing. Even if he suspected, he would have a strategy, a plan of action. I would myself.

What could be better than disposing of your rival – solution and revenge in one fell swoop? I thought of his guiding Cate that morning – 'aim for the centre of the body' – a fatal accident and his finger wasn't even on the trigger. But it hadn't happened . . . so the fallback was a lowering dusk and four hair-triggered hunters filing through the undergrowth. A flapping of wings in the gloaming, quite likely, well attested by the others, and bang. He had, after all, vetoed the idea of light stopping play.

Despite the creeping cold I felt the prickle of sweat beneath my shoulder blades. I was in front and the last time I had looked Henry had been directly behind me, perfectly positioned. I wanted to turn round but couldn't. I moved a little to the left, hoping to catch a glimpse from the very periphery of my vision. There he was, no more than a silhouette now but marching implacably along. The best thing was to get behind him. For a wild moment I contemplated stopping to retie a shoelace, but I was wearing the ubiquitous green wellington. There was a squawk, and a flicker of movement to our right. I dropped, swivelling, to my knees to get Henry into view and below the spread from his 'misfire', instinctively raising the gun to my shoulder as I did so. The dark shape of a pheasant zig-zagged upwards along the path that we would have taken, and reflexively I squeezed the trigger. Without earplugs the noise was deafening. For a second the bird appeared to speed up, carried by the impact, and then it fell. Nelson charged forward. No one else had fired.

'Well,' said Henry. 'Good shot. Most unorthodox stance, though.'

Except it wasn't Henry, it was Boy. Henry had somehow drifted to the back.

Luckily the dusk concealed my surprise and embarrassment. 'I just wanted to give you blokes a clear shot once it rose.'

'Encouraging someone to fire a twelve bore over your head. You must have a death wish,' the real Henry said.

On our way back to the farmhouse Boy, having separated us from David and Henry by engaging me in a pseudo-business conversation and then dawdling until they had politely moved ahead, said, 'Don't take what old Henry said to heart. Tactless, I know, but just a slip of the tongue. Nobody could blame you for being a bit paranoid under the circumstances. I think you've done jolly well going out with the guns at all after Stuart . . .'

He was right of course; my flight of fancy would not have happened without the background of the murder, and the fact that I could jump to ridiculous conclusions so easily made me doubt even more my suspicions of Bill Starling, but when I heard Cate inviting Saro and Henry to dinner I thought my persecution complex might be grounded in at least a little reality.

Chapter Eleven

'. . . before I go back to college.'

'It would be lovely,' Saro attempted to refuse gracefully, 'but Henry's very busy and . . .'

'What am I too busy for?' His antennae had unfortunately twitched as mine had. It was explained and of course he accepted.

Later Cate apologised. 'I thought New Year had gone so well that you wouldn't have any worries, and that it would sort of normalise Saro dropping round at the house. And I like them, especially her. I'd like to get to know her better. But I'll cancel it if you're not a hundred per cent.'

'No,' I said, 'don't do that. It'll be fine.'

It was arranged for the day before Cate went back to Durham, which in itself surprised me, an odd choice of companions for your last night in London, your uncle's mistress and her husband. Perhaps I was just peeved that she had not wanted to spend it with me alone, but in an odd way she seemed to have set this up for me.

We planned a menu – smoked mackerel pate, boeuf bourguignon and chocolate profiteroles – but the supposed advantage of not marooning anyone in the kitchen seemed like less of one as our guests' arrival drew near. I'd have been quite glad to have left Cate to make pre-prandial conversation while I made patterns of sculpted vegetables or drew Japanese heiroglyphics with one sauce in another, except that I couldn't be sure she wouldn't drop a clanger. Imagine walking back into the room to find the cat inadvertently out of the bag.

At least Cate's angst over the pudding – only her second attempt at it – had been in private. I opened wine and emptied pistachios and olives into bowls. I smoked.

In the event it wasn't too bad. I had one rocky moment when, after Saro had commented on a picture that we had bought together, Cate offered to show her round the house, but she accepted sweetly and they went off, leaving Henry and me alone. I buried him in a discussion about the state of the economy, which lasted safely until we sat down to eat.

At the dining table I managed to banish my memories of previous occasions when Saro had sat in the same chair under the same low light, but afterwards, when she was reclining on the sofa with a glass of Cointreau, it was less easy to forget that she had been sprawled there naked, with the cushions disarranged around her.

Henry, rising, asked: 'Which way the WC?'

'Down,' said Cate, the hostess in command. 'Do you think, on your way back, you could collect the coffee? It should be ready.'

When he returned he said, 'Interesting collection of books.'

Soon afterwards they called a taxi.

'Wasn't it a clever idea of mine,' said Cate as we stacked the dishwasher, 'to take Saro round the house? It made it perfectly legit for her to know where everything was and to have seen, you know, the bedrooms and everything.'

I had to laugh. 'What a schemer you are.'

'Was my chocolate sauce all right? I was afraid it was too thick.'

She went off the next morning, her bags stacked about her, and the place felt very empty. I mooched about until I could stand it no longer, and then went for a walk in the park.

Immediately behind the house was an Edwardian arrangement of flower-beds and walkways, with a recently restored bandstand its centrepiece. Beyond that were several hard tennis courts, on whose pink surfaces laboured plump middle-aged professionals from the square, covertly comparing themselves with the occasional younger and fitter bands of medical students from the teaching hospital down the road. Beyond them, as if civilisation was slowly petering out, there now stretched an expanse of unkempt grass and straggly bushes, peopled by blank-faced joggers with their walkmans, and thoughtful dogwalkers. On all sides the park was bounded by busy roads, not, with the exception of my street, obviously arterial but offering the rat-runs beloved of Londoners who always know a special way to get from obscure point A to obscure point B.

I walked to the far road where, in the depression that was probably a bomb crater, or the hollowed-out foundations of some demolished factory, the council had erected an adventure playground, the course for some gigantic game of pirates. Huge timber bulwarks supported tyres on ropes, creaking and swinging a little in the wind. In the summer this might have been a place of joyful noise but now, empty apart from a couple of bored black kids scuffing at the dirt, it prompted the obvious comparison with a multiple gibbet where public executions could be watched from the concrete balconies of the high-rise blocks of flats in the distance.

The kids who used it would come from the flats via the underpass that had been driven beneath the road after a spate of fatal traffic accidents. On their side of the road, between the flats and the underpass, was an even more barren expanse of open space – acres of tawdry grass, with no football pitch marked out or any attempt at landscaping, as if the authorities had accepted the need for an area to contain the increased leisure-time of workers and unemployed alike but had lost enthusiasm before they had done anything useful with it.

Why they had not put the adventure playground there was hard to imagine. Perhaps, accepting that for the architects, barristers, and medicos who lived in the square, the road constituted a border their children were not permitted to cross, the council had been attempting to encourage mixing, but if so the experiment had failed. The playground was clearly an outpost territory of the dispossessed.

I could hardly afford to be holier than thou about this. I'd never ventured through the underpass myself. I just couldn't see the point.

On the way home I bought a packet of crumpets; comfort-eating seemed in order. I was halfway through one when the phone rang.

'It's Saro.'

'Hello. Henry out?'

'No. I told him I had to make this call.'

A discordant note which I tried to ignore. 'To say thank you for last night?'

Her voice always had a cracked, emotional timbre – now it had an extra sibilance. 'No. He knows about us.'

Henry finding out had been so much on my mind that I felt a kind of excitement along with the surprise. This was the crunch. 'How?'

'In the taxi last night he was very tense. I asked if he was all right and he said: "I didn't know I had a namesake who was a playwright."'

I remembered Henry coming back a little flushed – from alcohol, I thought – and remarking on the interesting book collection. I also remembered the second-hand copy of Beaumont and Fletcher, a present from Saro with love from her inscribed on the flyleaf, that was part of that collection.

'I knew at once that he knew,' Saro was saying, 'but he didn't say anything else until we got home because of the driver.'

I could imagine the sickening lurch of her stomach in the darkened taxi and the waiting for the journey to be over. 'Then what?'

'What do you think?' She sounded weary.

'Are you all right?' I was suddenly suspicious of the hissing.

'I'll live.'

'He's beaten you up. What's he done?'

'I hit him back. I've got a big bruise on my cheek and a broken tooth. He's got some scratches on his face and very sore balls.'

'Is he there? I'll come for you now. I won't be long.'

'No, Alex. You haven't understood. It's all over. I'm sorry.'

I couldn't absorb this. After a while I managed to say, 'Why?'

'The children, for one thing. If I left he'd stop me seeing them.'

'He couldn't do that.'

'He said he would use every means at his disposal to restrict my access. I couldn't bear it.'

'We'd fight him. No court would let him get away with it.'

'It's not just legal. They're boys. He'd turn them against me, poison their minds. Some judge might force them to see me, but they'd hate me for destroying their parents' marriage. I'd just be a tart to them. You know, from madonna to slag in one fell swoop.'

It sounded harsh, even for kids brought up with the single-sex boarding school ethos. 'I'm sure they would understand. Please don't stay with that blackmailing bastard just because—'

'Alex it's not just . . . you can never say just anything when it's your child, and it's not just the boys. I don't want to leave him.'

I couldn't think of anything to say.

'Henry just wanted me to sever all connection without a word but I explained to him that wouldn't work so he agreed to this phone-call as long as it was final. But we can never speak again now. For my sake, and yours . . . I don't mean he would harm you but that you'll hurt yourself . . . don't call me, or come round, or anything. If we meet by accident sometime, and I'll try and make sure we don't, try and pretend it never happened.' Her voice was gentle, reasonable, persuasive.

'Is that it, then?'

'That's it.'

I swallowed hard. 'Saro, it can't be. I . . . We never said this before but I . . . I love you. I should have said it.'

'It wouldn't have made any difference, Alex.' A pause. 'Don't torture yourself by thinking that anything you could have done would have given this a different ending. It was good though.' Finally she sniffed, once, 'Goodbye', and she was gone.

I turned that conversation over and over for evidence that she had made it under physical duress, but there was none. If anything there had been a strange note of something approaching triumph when she had described the injuries that she and Henry had inflicted on one another.

I went around the house looking for something personal that she might have left – I wanted something with her smell on it to hold while I drank myself to unconsciousness, but there was nothing. She never had left any clothes, put off, I supposed, by Cate's moving in so there was only the picture and that bloody book.

I pulled it down from the shelf. What had made Henry look in it? From what he said in the taxi he clearly had no knowledge of seventeenth-century dramatists, and hidden among the hundreds of volumes in the kitchen/diner, I'd forgotten it myself.

She had given it to me three years before, picked it up in a bookshop in Hay-on-Wye not long after I had suggested calling the dog Fletcher . . . That must have been it. Idly waiting for the coffee Henry had glanced along the shelves nearest the kitchen end and come across a spine with – what a peculiar coincidence – not only his but his dog's name joined together. What more natural than to pick it up. What bad luck.

I've never been any good at solitary drinking, or at least not good enough to get seriously smashed. I gave it up as a bad job, and went to bed in the hope of boring myself to sleep with late-night TV.

The most ironic thing about the next few weeks was that people around me at work, friends, acquaintances, probably noticed no difference. None of them had known about Saro, so how could they be expected to guess that she had abandoned me . . . been forced to abandon me . . . and what was the point of blowing the gaff at this late stage; it would only embarrass everybody and cause further dislocation.

So what people saw, I supposed, was me absorbed in my work, perhaps staying late more often than usual, but then we were busy, appearing a little distracted and low-key at the dinner table or in the pub but that had happened before . . . Boy confided that Molly thought the full weight of Stuart's death had only now hit me. I reassured him. 'I'll perk up in the spring,' I said.

I hoped it was going to be as easy as that. Despite what Saro had said I had rung the house at Campden Hill Square several times on that first Monday; during the day an answerphone relentlessly clicked on and I replaced the receiver without leaving a message. When I tried at seven Henry crisply said, 'Eight three four two' and, knowing that cutting the line would immediately identify me, I engaged in an absurd attempt to avoid that by saying, 'Sorry, wrong number,' in what I hoped was an Australian accent.

On Tuesday evening I drove round there, or at least almost there. I parked the car on Campden Hill Road and went into a dark and smoky pub called the Warwick Castle which Henry referred to as his local, although I suspected that meant a jar on a Sunday lunchtime or a quiet summer's evening. I certainly wasn't expecting to see him there amongst the old top drawer eccentrics quietly supping their pre-supper pints, or the young bloods of Holland Park knocking back draught Bass and sausages, while their girls, Saro twenty years before, sipped spritzers and decided which film they would chatter through.

I don't know what I was expecting, really. Saro had told me to stay away and the answerphone suggested she doubted my self-restraint and was determined to avoid speaking to me. I told myself I was worried about her, that Henry might be beating her up, but I only half believed it. I also had a niggling feeling that she and Henry had reached a very satisfactory accommodation in which I was an irrelevance, a has-been, the boys an excuse to fob me off, but I couldn't leave it alone.

After a couple of pints I walked down to the square. There was a lovely warm glow in the ground-floor window of their house, criss-crossing layers of light thrown by standard and table lamps. I stood in the shadows across the street and watched but no one came into the room, even to draw the curtains. Despite the fact that it was uninhabited it managed to convey an atmosphere of cosy domesticity. There were other lights on, behind blinds in the upper storeys. I wondered which was their bedroom. I don't know how long I might have stayed there if I hadn't become aware of the dog walker, a pair of cashmere-coated dachshunds by her side, gravely regarding me from her gateway. She looked like a member of the neighbourhood watch and I half-expected her to whip out a mobile phone, if not a walkie-talkie, and call up the local police at once. As casually as possible I walked away.

After another couple of days I knew that I had to see Saro again, not even talk to her, just see her, to prove that she was still real, alive, there. I borrowed one of the company cars that she would not recognise – an anonymous Vauxhall – and parked so that I could see her front door in my rear-view mirror. It was eleven a.m., early enough, I hoped, to catch her either coming home for or going out to lunch, but not, I prayed, the sort of time at which the dog-woman would be on the streets.

There was nothing to do except sit and smoke. I had the radio on and the despatches of foreign correspondents gave way to the overly-optimistic presenters of a consumer affairs programme. I wound down the window to let out the fug and the interminable anecdotes of the *My Music* panellists, and suddenly she was there on the top step. Instinctively I wound the window up again, as if she might smell me.

She wore a fitted overcoat, a fur hat, and dark glasses. To hide what? A fresh black eye? The ravages of continual crying? When she reached the pavement and paused, as if uncertain of her route, she took them off. She was more heavily made-up, to hide the bruising I guessed, but her eyes were clear, bright, calm. A picture of serenity. She headed in my direction and I slid lower in my seat. As she approached the car I lost her face in the rear-view mirror, instead watching her midriff expanding in the wing mirror. Then her slender ankles and muscular calves were passing the passenger window, shimmering in their ten denier Dior, and finally the outline of her hips through her coat as she bent to the lock of her Golf, parked further down the road.

Once she had driven off I knew that was that. I wouldn't watch again. It didn't stop me thinking about her but slowly the whole affair became more dreamlike – places that we had been together bathed in soft-focus so that when I went to them in real life their jarring angles and imperfections were shocking. A knock-on effect was that everything else apart from the business began to seem unreal too. My imagining Henry's murderous intent at New Year, disproved by the victorious real-politik of his actual approach, seemed much the same as my theory of Merlin as killer – a flight of fantasy.

When Nicole told me, after an unsatisfactory conversation with Superintendent Cromarty, that she was convinced the police were scaling down their hunt I was hardly surprised. They would only solve the crime now by accident, when the burglars were caught at some other country house and the records were scanned for similar break-ins. Cromarty had obviously suffered from a touch of the Agatha Christie's in suspecting me, and so had I in my turn with Bill Starling. I was glad that Nicole did not ask me to kick up a fuss, demand that the Chief Constable keep the file in his pending tray, complain to the newspapers. She too had obviously seen the light.

I didn't see Cate until a couple of weeks before the end of her term, when I had to visit a client in Newcastle and stopped off to buy her dinner on the way back. She had offered to meet my train at the station and I had declined, on the grounds that the timetable was too erratic. 'I'll see you in the bar of the Royal County,' I said.

I was surprised, then, when, as I stood at the station entrance, breathing in the frozen soot in the air and taking the returnee's affectionate look at the castle and cathedral, spotlit in the distance, I was flashed by the headlights of her car. I walked across to it – she had pushed the door ajar.

'This isn't what we agreed,' I said, 'but very nice nonetheless. It's bloody cold out there.' I leant across to kiss her cheek. Given the air temperature her skin was very warm, and the smell of freshly applied perfume strong. 'Is that why you came?'

'No,' she said slowly, and my heart jumped. What? Sent down? Pregnant? She was looking straight out through the windscreen. I waited. Finally she blurted: 'I couldn't meet you in that public place without knowing.'

'What?'

'Have you forgiven me? For Saro?'

'Of course,' I said, with a rush of relief. 'Of course.'

Afterwards, when I was southbound on the Intercity 125, I thought that wasn't true. I hadn't forgiven her, until that moment. From the time it had happened I had cursed her for inviting them round, but I hadn't thought that she would be brooding about it to the same extent. I had been vindictively pleased when she had asked, as always, 'How's Saro?' and, after I'd told her, fallen silent, completing the conversation in a little girl's voice. Neither of us, of course, had referred to her helping hand, and I almost immediately dismissed the unworthy sentiment. I could see now that our subsequent telephone conversations had been subdued, but I had been somewhat preoccupied.

When we had reached the bright foyer of the Royal County I had been shocked by her appearance. It wasn't the clothes or the strident make-up, lent an extra tartiness by the way in which the strawberry blonde had grown away from her roots, but the tired stain beneath her eyes, and the couple of disguised spots on her chin. I'd never seen her so run down. Over dinner she had become increasingly animated, but in a way that rang offkey, until I asked her whether there was anything else upsetting her – work, people at college, a bloke – and she laughed and said she was just jaded and looking forward to getting home, and what about our company.

I told her then about the MJB project. This low-profile corporation, of which most Britons knew no more than the initials, had made extensive purchases within the European chemicals industry, hitherto dominated by the Germans, and was belatedly intent on making a song and dance about it. Its first step was a lavish annual report, which we were to produce, with the dangling carrot of redesigning MJB's logo and mounting a major advertising campaign if this initial assignment went well.

To this end I was being taken on a sightseeing trip of its European sites, returning a couple of days before Cate's term ended.

The tour was, inevitably, a demanding whistlestop, despite the luxury in which it was draped. For the first leg I was accompanied by MJB's deceptively jolly chairman, Kenneth 'call me Ken for God's sake' Crawshaw, a one-off dynamo who, although a working class lad made good, neither clung publicly to his roots nor attempted to assimilate into the landed gentry. We flew to Paris and then northern Germany in his private jet. Ken's corporate communications director, Tony Groombridge, a clubbable smoothie who knew everyone you had ever met, waved his boss off at the small airport, and then vanished for a meeting in Munich, having assured me that he was leaving me in extremely capable hands.

I knew that for once he was telling the truth. Dervla McKenna was one of his assistants, an efficient, patient, friendly, multi-lingual Dubliner in her late twenties. Like all successful business people I knew there must be a certain amount of steel in her soul – how else could she have avoided the stiletto in the shoulderblades, let alone managed to deliver the occasional telling blow necessary for a rise to the corporate cream – but I had never glimpsed it, and I had seen plenty of her as she was my initial contact at MJB.

She was short and rounded, with a sweet smile, soft hazel eyes and long black hair, the style of which she altered at least a couple of times a day. When we sat in the Mercedes that the managers of MJB's German subsidiary had sent to collect us, and she ran considerately down the list of the local dignitaries I was destined to meet over dinner, the hair was in one long plait. By the time we met them at the restaurant it was piled above her head.

Our hosts were, to a man, kitted out with gunmetal grey suits and gunmetal grey cars. They commended to us, with no apparent irony, the local leather-shorted brass ensemble, whose sub-Wagnerian laments accompanied our first course of local white asparagus. The same lack of irony was demonstrated the next day by the non-smoking production director who proudly detailed the environmental improvements achieved at a plant which turned out half of Europe's cigarette filters.

That evening we moved on to Milan and a hotel which pointed up the cultural dividing line across which we had flown. Where the German mini-bar had bulged with bottles of orange juice and mineral water, the Italian was full of champagne, Campari and grappa. Where the German bathroom had sported a notice pointing out the energy waste involved in laundering unused towels, the Italian offered a shelf full of complimentary colognes, beneath which were a couple of ashtrays, in case you forgot to take one of the fifteen or so in the bedroom into the shower with you.

Dervla and I were treated to another gourmet meal and the Italians practiced their considerable charm upon us both until leaving us at our hotel at about eleven, promising to collect us at eight for a tour of the pharmaceuticals factory.

We stood in the foyer, waiting for our room keys.

Despite covering her mouth, Dervla failed to disguise a yawn.

'Suffering from hospitality fatigue?' I asked.

'I couldn't absorb another fact or another figure. Or another compliment.' She grinned.

'How about a nightcap? And a winding down sort of conversation. Without any sort of praise whatsoever.'

'OK.'

So we sat in the hotel bar and drank cognac and coffee, until we realised it was two and the next instalment of our grand industrial tour was creeping closer. But a precedent had been set. The next night, in Athens, we waved the triumvirate of Greek packagers off as if we were about to retire to bed, and then slipped out down the hill to a pavement café where we sat gazing at the Acropolis and I found myself telling her about Stuart's death, and Cate, and so on.

It wasn't a thing I would normally have done, but being in Athens had reminded me of my journey to Spetse as the bearer of the bad tidings, and the nature of this trip, the sense of it being time out of the real world, had telescoped normal proprieties.

The next evening, our last, we were in Barcelona and, bolder still, told our blazered companions that we would make our own way back to our hotel as we felt like a breath of air. We strolled, without conscious aim, until we came to the huge stalactite towers of Gaudi's church of the Holy Family. Surreality, in the form of fire-eaters, fat prostitutes, anorexic junkies, sad-eyed dancers and musicians, was all around. Dervla told me about her love/hate relationship with Ireland. 'How different to grow up a Catholic in a place like this.'

We drifted down to the waterfront, drank coffee, contemplated walking up to examine the site of the Olympic village but, as Dervla said, prosaically, 'Wrong shoes.' Still we were reluctant to let the day close, and we sipped Fundador in the hotel bar for another hour. Finally, as we parted at the lift, she caught my hand and gave me not so much a kiss as a glancing blow on the cheek. I lay on my bed and looked at my watch. It was three. I liked her – she seemed, convent upbringing apart, fairly uncomplicated fun. Possibilities blossomed, but it wasn't a good idea to sleep with your clients, and anyway I had missed the moment. Tomorrow we were returning to England, pausing only to take in a petro-cracking plant at Tarragona.

That in itself was unearthly – floating in cool, air-conditioned splendour through the hot, dusty countryside with a hot, dusty tongue from the brandy and cigarettes of the night before, just becoming accustomed to the white-walled, red-roofed villages, when suddenly we were on a desolate plain of giant metal storage tanks and pipe-bedecked towers, criss-crossed by grubby railway trucks and heavy lorries, the sky hazy with smog smudging the orange flares flickering from tall chimneys.

In hard hats and overalls we were walked around this industrial gulag, the subject of incurious scrutiny from the few uniformed worker bees that we passed. We finished up in the computer rooms where the whole operation was monitored by a handful of technicians in white jackets, in front of them screens of the constantly changing data that would give the first indication of a potentially explosive deviation from normal working, behind them walls of the usual pin-ups; footballers and film stars above lunchboxes, denim jackets and newspapers.

My attention wandered from lack of sleep. I glanced at Dervla. Having spent six days with her I could tell that she had risen in a hurry this morning. Her hair, for the first time, was hanging straight – neither pinned, plaited or clipped – and she was having to flick it behind her ears every few minutes. She wore no make-up other than a quick dash of mascara, an omission she repaired in the cloakroom of the restaurant where we were taken for lunch.

We sat at a large table, looking out across a road, a strip of shingle and a flat, grey sea that reminded me of Eastbourne. From the smiles of the plant's MD and his chairman this was clearly expected to be the culinary *pièce de résistance* of our trip. The waiters brought enormous iced pyramids of seafood – lobster, gambas, oysters, mussels, seaslugs. I caught Dervla's eye as she returned from the restroom, her face refreshed, and we exchanged a flicker of sympathy. But after the first glass of bubbly, things seemed a lot more palatable. They knew it was our swansong and were determined to give us a good send-off. We ate calamari and swordfish, and sweet liqueur-soaked cake. We talked of the difficulties of lobbying in Brussels and the fortunes of Manchester United. Toasts were drunk. We were returned to the airport in a haze as consistent as that hanging above the plant. In-flight it seemed only sensible to preserve this buoyancy with more champagne. At Heathrow we agreed that public transport would be unbearable and shared a taxi. When it stopped outside my house I said, 'Want to come in for a coffee? We can easily get a cab to run you on to Bromley later.'

'OK,' she said and we unloaded the luggage, paid the driver and climbed the stairs to my drawing room. I switched on a lamp and some music. We decide to have not coffee but one last glass for the road, for old times, although six days is hardly a lifetime. We drank a toast to new friends and subsided on to the sofa. I leant back into the corner cushions and she leaned with me. We kissed. Her body was soft and heavy. As the kiss continued her knee came round mine and I was stroking the back of her leg, the rasp of her tights against my finger and the drift of her hair across my cheek.

When I saw the door opening I must have gripped Dervla harder, which she mistook as a signal to press herself against me more firmly and her tongue probed my mouth more insistently. Cate burst in to the room saying, 'Surprise,' assessed the situation in one frozen moment, and then slammed out again, the door bouncing on its hinges behind her.

Chapter Twelve

Unsurprisingly, Dervla jumped and her eyes opened. 'My niece,' I explained as we disentangled ourselves, although of course it wasn't an explanation for the furious exit. I went out onto the landing in time to hear the front door bang below. Back in the drawing room I parted the curtain to see the Mazda roar away from the kerb, only to be halted almost immediately by a red light on the pelican crossing outside Iceland. That at least afforded me some grim amusement – it might teach her not to be such a drama queen.

'Sorry about that,' I said. 'She must be upset about something.' But why would that make her flounce out?

'Is she . . . young for her age?' Behind that question I presumed Dervla meant, is she childish, a spoilt brat?

'I wouldn't have said so, until now.' I thought of the bottling at the college ball. Perhaps she was more of a wild child than I imagined. 'She'll be back.' I tried to sound relaxed about it. There wasn't anything I could do until she did return. 'Forget her. Have another drink.'

'I'd better not. What I had better do is get a taxi home.' Could I detect a wariness now in her eyes where before there had been only abandon, something more than the puncturing of the mood warranted. We sat waiting for the taxi, chatting to cover the undercurrent of embarrassment. In the end we had the drink, more to occupy our uncomfortable mouths than anything else.

Lying in bed, with the first stirrings of a hangover and the last stirrings of lust, I consoled myself with the thought that Cate's intervention had saved me from the mistake of mixing business and pleasure. I resolutely didn't worry about where she could have gone – she had a car and money; it wasn't as if she was walking the streets. I read her the riot act in a couple of satisfying ways before I fell asleep.

In the morning I pushed open the door of her room, half expecting, hoping, that she would be asleep beneath the duvet, but there was nothing but tidiness and the smell of furniture polish.

I wondered who to ring. The police? Report her as a missing person? That seemed a little excessive and anyway, as I thought I knew from numerous detective series, the kindly sergeant would only say, 'She's over eighteen. There's nothing we can do for the moment, sir.' Ring the hospital, check at least that she hadn't had an accident. If her racing start had been anything to go by she would have been driving recklessly. But which hospital? I could start with King's College and Guy's, but then where?

Instead I went in to work, and as I got nearer the office I began to think that she would be there, waiting to apologise, dishevelled from having spent the night in the car, Dorothy clucking over her.

She wasn't.

I held a budget meeting, rehearsed a presentation, put in a call to Dervla who was 'in conference'. Then I shut myself away with a sandwich and a jug of coffee, announced to Lynn and Dorothy that I did not wish to be disturbed, and tried to consider it logically. After fifteen hours she must have gone somewhere. I couldn't make an exhaustive list but I could at least check the obvious ones.

I started by ringing Nicole. I wouldn't worry her by telling her what had happened. If she had seen Cate it was sure to come out in conversation. Nobody home. Throwing caution to the winds I left a message on the answerphone asking her to call me urgently.

Next the Cliffords. Joan answered. I introduced myself, uncomfortably aware of the last time we had spoken, at the villa on Spetse. I knew from her slightly puzzled response that Cate could not be there, but I could hardly hang up. 'I'm sorry to bother you, but I've forgotten who Cate said she was meeting today, and I just thought it might be Jane.'

'But Jane's still down in Exeter. Her term's not over until next week.' And, of course, neither was Cate's. Joan Clifford was chuntering on. 'I thought ten weeks was short enough . . .'

Absentmindedly I agreed that the holidays were excessive, and that it would make more sense for them to take their degrees in two years and start on a career. Presumably Joan had never been a student. Eventually I excused myself and rang the payphone on Cate's landing at St Catherine's.

I looked at my watch. Half past one. There should be a fair chance of catching someone going to or from lunch. It rang, and rang. I let it, remembering that often it was only the irritation factor, not public-spiritedness, that made someone pick it up. On the seventy-eighth ring, someone did.

She reported that there was no one in their room. I asked her to leave a message for Cate or Emma to call me.

About four o'clock Emma did. 'She's not here. She left for London yesterday.'

I explained. Somehow it was much easier to tell the story, slightly doctored, to her than it would have been to tell Nicole. Was that age, or just that I thought the burden of worry that I was imposing would be less? 'So can you imagine where she might go? Is there anywhere she's talked about?'

'Not really . . . Well, not realistically.'

'What do you mean by that?'

'Well, she couldn't go there, not just like that.'

'Where?'

'Well, she was talking about this villa, in Corsica. It belongs to her stepmother.'

'I know of it. What was she saying about it?'

'Just how beautiful it was, and how it was hardly ever used . . . a waste. She was saying we could go there in the summer, she just had to square it with the wicked stepmother – oh, I'm sorry, I didn't mean . . . it's just that's what Cate calls her . . . you know, for a joke,' she tailed off unconvincingly.

'It's all right. Anything else?'

'Not really. I mean, she has been talking about it a lot, but I mean, she wouldn't just have taken off there, surely.'

I couldn't see why not. She was angry and impulsive, there were planes and she had a credit card, and her luggage with her. Obviously this was not sufficient for a sensible Scot. 'I mean,' Emma added, 'she said that her stepmother would probably turn her down anyway out of spite.'

'How has she been, in the last few days, weeks?' I thought how ill she had looked the last time but one I had seen her. I hadn't registered details of her appearance the previous evening.

'A bit down.'

'Do you know why?'

'No. I mean, I guessed her dad and stuff.'

'Is that what she said?'

'No. She said, just everything. Then, in the last few days, she said that it would all be all right.'

'What would?'

'Everything. She would make everything all right.'

'How?'

'I don't know.'

Would Nicole have to be asked for Cate to go to Corsica? I rang Deborah. I could hardly find out what I wanted without telling her something of the story.

'No, she could get the keys from the woman at the village shop. But she might have asked Mummy anyway. I know she'd heard from Cate. Why don't you ask Mummy herself?'

'She's not in. She's not away or anything?'

'Not as far as I know. But then we don't live in one another's pockets.' She sounded peeved.

'How is she?' It was a ritual inquiry; I got more of a response than I expected. Nicole was edgy, withdrawn, unresponsive. Deborah sounded on something of a knife-edge herself. I sympathised, promised to meet for a drink after work one evening.

Lynn came in with a bunch of letters to find me muttering, 'Like walking on bloody eggshells,' and removed the remains of my lunch in silence.

I spent the afternoon working on my MJB report – no return call from Dervla, or anyone else for that matter. Once again, on my way home, I imagined that Cate would be waiting when I opened the door, in fact I sensed it so strongly I was certain for a second that she was standing at the foot of the stairs in the half-dark, just as she had that day she had cut off her hair . . . but it was nothing.

I tried Nicole again with no more success and then dialled the number of the villa in Corsica that Deborah had given me. As that long ring fuzzed down the line I remembered listening to the same connection with Cromarty watching, his little eyes fixed on mine, the additional handset pressed so hard against his ear that the trapped blood had turned it red. The ringing stopped, replaced by a silence so strong that I thought at first I had been cut off. Then I could distinguish something extra in the hissing; someone taking short, shallow breaths. 'Hello? . . . Cate, is that you? . . . It's Alex . . . Say something if it is you . . . please . . .' Then the connection was broken. I dialled again, but this time no one answered.

I knew it was her – the sound of the breathing had made her so close I was only surprised that I had not felt its soft heat against my lobe. I knew also what I had to do.

I rang the firm's travel agent and told him I wanted the first flight he could get me on to Corsica.

'Which bit of the island?'

'South. Near Sartene. I didn't even know there was more than one airport. Thought it was Ajaccio or nothing.'

'There's one the charters use at Figari which is a little closer. Hold on.' I could hear him tapping away at his terminal. 'Yep. I can get you on a flight to Figari from Gatwick at seven-thirty Friday, tomorrow morning, providing you don't mind roughing it with the year's first crop of tourists.'

There weren't many of them. As it was only March, I was surprised there were any at all. I accepted my complimentary glass of sparkling wine and, as they chattered enthusiastically about the holiday to come, wondered for the first time, my certainty until then having been sustained by the making of arrangements, whether I was on a wild goose chase.

I had asked Lynn to postpone my scheduled client meeting on the grounds that I had food poisoning. As I was not in the habit of making this excuse or any other I knew it would be believed by the client – Lynn would have to think what she liked. All I told her was that 'something urgent had come up' and that I would call in. I had told her to get Cate's number if she 'happened to call' and rung Emma with the same instruction. I hadn't believed that she would, unless it was from the villa. Touching down at Figari, for which the term airport was something of an exaggeration, I was not so sure.

There was one dusty runway surrounded by scrubland, a stubby control tower which looked about as lively as the similarly-shaped water storage tanks that hang about on the outskirts of French villages, and a terminal building scarcely more than a Nissen hut. A sleepy gendarme, his submachine gun hung carelessly over his shoulder, gave our passports a cursory glance as we passed through what I imagine counted as immigration and customs formalities.

My fellow travellers were rounded up by their courier and shepherded to their coach while I looked for the car-hire desk. There were four plastic counters, none of them manned, but one had a small Hertz sign on it. I waited by it for a while, until the coach had driven off, but no one came. Even the patron of the café had vanished. In some frustration I leant over the counter to see if there was any relevant instruction or a bell to ring – there wasn't but, tucked beneath the shelf, there was a bulky white envelope with 'Mr Buxon' written on it. Under the circumstances it seemed unlikely that they were expecting another customer with so similar a name.

Out in the carpark I found the little Peugeot that matched the key and in its glove compartment a small road map of the island. Unfortunately it showed the airport as a dot near the N196, so when I reached a signpostless fork in the road I had mentally to toss a coin. I went left, which was a mistake, as I discovered when I finally found a hamlet with a bar to ask in. I turned around.

Under other circumstances the drive would have been fun, the N196 affording one unspoilt upland panorama after another, the sky bright, the sun warm through the windscreen without making me sweat. Occasionally the tight bends did that, particularly when my wandering attention was brought to heel by meeting a speeding Citroën or careering military truck. The presence of so many earnest servicemen was explained, I guessed, by the Corsican nationalist movement, whose crudely daubed blue graffiti adorned remote roadside rocks. As the road began to drop towards the sea I saw, to my right, the ancient grey stone terraces of Sartene, where, owing to the inadequacy of the map, I needed to ask further directions.

The town's main square was crowded; it was market day. I left the car in a side street and wandered through the hubbub, looking for a tourist information office or a shop that could sell me a better map.

It could have been anywhere in rural southern France, except for the sprinkling of handsome ebony faces of the indigenous Corsicans, a reminder of the nearness to North Africa and medieval Moorish incursions. The melée was further confused by some sort of religious procession – a priest at the head followed by adolescent acolytes carrying banners and the plaster effigy of some sort of saint atop a long wooden pole. Bringing up the rear were the usual gaggle of black-scarved old women. Why did this sort of religion always seem to miss out the middle-aged?

The spectacle drew a small crowd, good naturedly calling out encouragement to the faithful. As it was Lent perhaps they were on some sort of penance; it couldn't have been a Feast Day.

I decided my best chance of asking directions lay in the relative quiet of a bar. The waiter brought me coffee and explained that if I turned left at the river there was only one coast road, I could not miss it. Waiting for the scalding brew to cool sufficiently to drink, I was gazing idly across the square when I saw a familiar silhouette.

She was a hundred yards away by the church wall, her back to me as she watched the disciples return to base, but I had that jolt of instant recognition. The trouble was, it wasn't who I had been expecting. It wasn't Cate. For a second or two, as the waiter chattered on, I struggled to name the template, and then, as my mind began to settle for some other explanation – déjà vu, looks like a woman from the office or the supermarket – she turned and I realised it was Nicole.

I scrabbled for some money as I stood, and thrust a note into the disgruntled waiter's hand, trying not to take my eyes off her. Crossing to the door, its frame put her out of my sight for a second and once in the sunlight I thought I had lost her. Then I spotted the jaunty Breton-striped jersey disappearing down one of the streets behind the church. I dodged between the stalls, occasionally elbowing a recalcitrant shopper aside, finally surfacing to see nothing in that street but a man in dungarees unloading a vegetable truck, and a couple of kids playing some sort of hopscotch on a flight of steps. I ran past them, my heart banging as loudly as my shoes on the cobbles.

At the bottom was a T-junction; I glanced left and saw the very last trace of her turning the next corner, hardly more than the wake of her passing on the air – had I glanced right and then left I would have missed her entirely. For the first time I called out, but she did not return. Cursing myself for having paused, I ran after her. Round the next bend was another street of the same high grey stone terraces, more carved than built, this one shuttered, silent and sloping down the hill.

I skittered down it, wondering whether she had gone right or left, but when I got to the bottom there was no choice, just a courtyard of blind apartments, and no quarry. I stood in the middle of it and turned full circle, regarding the high walls pitted by time and weather, and then explored the dark entranceways to dead-end alleys and the echoing stairwells. The lady had vanished.

I sat on a cold, granite step, and remembered something Stuart had told me about Sartene. This old quarter, mostly inhabited by the *noirs*, was a warren of passages, not only from street to street but from house to house. Buildings with separate entrances were very often joined at the attic level, or by rooftop bridges. Looking back I could see one further up the hill, arching above the street a level or two above the laundry lines.

I forgot why the architectural style was as it was, smuggling of some sort, but I recalled to what use it had been put in the Second World War when the city was occupied by German troops. A soldier, pursuing a curfew breaker, would find himself alone in a court like this, his target having disappeared. The remainder of his patrol, hot on his heels, would find him with his throat cut and not even a house-to-house would produce a culprit, the assassin having slipped away into the night and out of town along one of these medieval rat-runs which had become perfect conduits for the partisans. Eventually the Germans would only brave these streets in formation, and preferably in armoured cars. Effectively the *quartier* was no-go area.

Even in the afternoon it was easy enough to picture; the dark figure sliding from a doorway and his knife sliding between your shoulderblades. When a man came out of the stairwell opposite and looked at me curiously I felt intimidated, an unwanted intruder, but he got on his Lambretta and buzzed noisily off, and the sound shook me out of my reverie. Why Nicole should have been skulking here I could not imagine, but presumably she would be going back to the villa at some point. I would wait for her there.

The hire car had been boxed in. To move I either had to shift a baker's van or demolish the corner of a house. After a fruitless wait, hoping that it was only making a delivery, I went in search of the nearest boulangerie. Madame Boulangère was very sympathetic but her husband had gone out with a friend and his keys – until he returned there was nothing she could do.

When would that be? She regretted not until the middle of the afternoon. I checked my watch. One o'clock. 'You mean about three?' I asked hopefully. Her shrug suggested the hope might well be in vain. I thanked her and returned to the car to consider my options, which were limited.

As far as I could make out the villa was about twenty miles away, along a road broken only by hamlets too small to be shown on a car-hire company's map. There might be a bus service but it was unlikely to be frequent. There might equally be taxis for hire, or another car, but was it worth it seeking one out to save a couple of hours, less than a couple by the time I had made arrangements?

Earlier that day I might have said yes, but now that I knew Nicole was here I wasn't so sure. Her behaviour had not necessarily been odd, she might just have not heard me. After all, she would hardly be expecting to see me. Anyway, she was either on her way to the villa, in which case she would be with Cate soon, or had already been there and spoken to her. In other words, Cate was taken care of. Unless, of course, my intuition had been wrong and it was Nicole who had answered the phone at the villa last night. In which case Cate could be anywhere, including back in London.

The irony of this almost raised a smile. I went into a *tabac*, bought a phone card and rang the villa again. No reply. Then my house, with the same result. At least someone answered in the Buccaneer office, but they had not heard from Cate, and I did not feel in any position to return the call from Dervla McKenna.

The calls had used up about half an hour and ruled out looking for alternative transport. Instead I went into a restaurant and ordered a rabbit casserole and a small carafe of Corsican rosé, as dry and full-bodied as any red. I smoked a couple of cigarettes and drank a couple of coffees and, with very little fretting, I had willed the hands of my watch to three o'clock.

The baker's van had not moved but unfortunately the baker's wife had. Their shop was shuttered and there was no reply to my knocking. There was nothing I could do, except sit in the car and reflect on the fact that I would not be cut out for the life of a gumshoe. I hated the periods of inactivity, and then when something did happen my reactions were far too slow, plus I was useless at fathoming the significance of what was going on. Why hadn't Deborah known her mother was going to be in Corsica? Did that mean Cate was here, or the reverse? Or were they simply unconnected? If Cate wasn't here, where was she? I thought almost longingly of the MJB report.

The baker, a fittingly plump fellow, released me from my parking trap at about four-thirty and, in a dwindling light as the sun faded over the water, I crossed the river and followed the narrow road that aped the stuttering coastline.

The village was too small for a proper square, just a straggle of houses running up from the beach and over a headland where a shop, a church, a hotel and a bar-restaurant looked down on a cemetery and a tiny natural harbour in which a few small fishing boats bobbed. I stopped the car to get my bearings. The reality reminded me of Stuart's holiday snaps and, judging by those Kodak views from the villa, it had to be on the wooded hillside beyond the hotel. I followed a track which ran into the trees, passing an unoccupied chalet bungalow, and rounding a corner, knew that I had arrived.

The apricot walls, biscuit-coloured roman roof tiles, and peeling deep-green shutters were the unmistakeable background to snapshots of barbecues and bikinis passed around at Stirton Hall in years gone by. The house was more attractive than they had suggested, its scruffiness, which Nicole had not allowed Stuart to dispense with, more in keeping with the surroundings than their nearest neighbour's suburban chic.

There was a car outside, another little Peugeot like mine, but no other sign of life except the sound of an engine running somewhere up the hill.

I peered through the window at a kitchen. It was empty, but on the table were a couple of bottles and some glasses, so someone, more than one person, had been here.

I opened the front door. I don't know why I didn't call out, perhaps because I had in that backstreet and she hadn't responded. There was a beaded curtain to my right which I guessed led into the living room. I parted it and paused on the threshold, letting my eyes adjust to the mass of shadows which was all the room seemed to consist of. When one of them lurched forward I simply blinked, assuming some optical illusion, and then it had coalesced into a moving, screaming person and I was diving to one side. The consequence of this was that she tripped over my ankles and sprawled her length. The curtain shook and rattled like so many snakes. I sat up, slightly groggy from the glancing contact my head had made with a chair, and caught her leg as she scrabbled across the floor, trying to reach the kitchen knife which had been knocked from her hand by her fall. 'Cate, stop. What's the matter? It's me.'

For a split second more she struggled, and then suddenly went limp and tipped towards me, like some rag doll waiting to be put back in the toybox. Her white T-shirt was hanging over one shoulder, and both it and her trousers seemed smeared with dirt or grease. Her hair was damp with sweat. 'Have you seen her?' she asked.

'Nicole?'

She nodded.

'Yes, I—'

She leapt up, her stare in that half-light still as startling as the gape of a jack-in-the-box.

I caught her. 'Not here. In Sartene.' She stared harder, apparently torn between me and the door.

'Hours ago,' I said. 'Is that who you thought I was?'

She nodded. I looked at the knife, a long Sabatier blade that could have severed an artery or punctured a lung without any significant pressure, let alone the lunging of a frightened girl. The beginnings of several long questions formulated themselves in my head, but all I eventually said was, 'Why?'

Cate looked at me for a second. 'Because she killed Daddy.'

Chapter Thirteen

'Why?' I asked.

Cate shook her bowed head.

'How?' I asked.

Cate had found the evidence in the bureau. She handed me the form. It was a copy of a car hire agreement, torn at the bottom, but with the hirer's name – N.D. Makepeace – clearly visible at the top. I had to absorb the separate pieces of information slowly. Nicole was still using her maiden name on her credit cards. The car, an Austin Montego, not a brand she would normally have been seen in, had been hired at Heathrow on 31st July 1990 – the night Nicole and Cate were staying there in readiness for their holiday flights the next morning, the night of Stuart's death.

'When she realised I'd seen it and understood,' Cate said, 'she didn't even try to deny it. Just broke down and told me everything.'

It had been the perfect opportunity. Stuart, as Nicole thought, in the house alone, and her with a cast-iron alibi. Once Cate, more than a little tipsy, was fast asleep and sure to stay that way thanks to the sleeping tablets in her hot chocolate, Nicole had collected the Montego and driven to Stirton, parking it on the main road and taking the public footpath across the fields to the front gate. The Hall was in darkness. She had let herself in and taken a shotgun from the cabinet in the study, unlocking it with the key kept in Stuart's desk. She had crept up the stairs and, pausing on the landing to look out of the window, seen Deborah's car in the coachhouse. Until that moment she had assumed her daughter had left. She went back downstairs and sat in the dark in the kitchen until she had calmed down and decided what to do. Under the sink was a bottle of chloroform that Stuart had used for killing butterflies when, in his first and most passionate country gentleman incarnation, he had wanted to line his study with glass-casefuls of the things. When Deborah went to the bathroom Nicole was waiting behind the door. Taller, stronger, and with surprise on her side, she had held the chloroformed pad over Deborah's mouth and nose for long enough to render her unconscious, then tied her to the bathroom chair with some washing line and gagged her with a scarf and a J cloth. She had intended shooting Stuart as he slept in bed, but he had surprised her on the landing. She had dropped the gun in the back garden, but in her confusion had forgotten to mess up the house as much as she intended to make it look like burglary, although luckily she had taken the cash from the desk when getting the key for the shotgun cabinet. She retraced her steps to the car, arriving back in her hotel room with two hours to spare before the early morning call.

Cate told this story with a deadpan delivery at odds with her dilated pupils and the tear tracks on her cheeks.

'Why?' I asked. Cate seemed bewildered. 'Did she do it?' I added.

'I . . . don't know. She hated him.'

'I didn't know that. Did you?'

She didn't even notice my question. 'She just kept repeating it. Over and over again. I hated him. I hated him.'

'Where is she now?'

'Gone. We screamed and shouted and she ran out and got in her car and drove off.'

'So why the knife?' I picked it up from the floorboards.

'I thought she might come back and kill me. Regret having confessed and want to get rid of the evidence.' She shivered.

I put my arm around her. That seemed ridiculous but if Nicole had killed once . . .

'It's all right,' Cate said, a statement which under the circumstances seemed about as far from the truth as it was possible to be. 'I'm just cold. Not frightened now you're here.'

'How long has she been gone?'

She thought. It was preternaturally calm. I noticed the goose bumps on her pale forearms. 'Half an hour, maybe three quarters, before you came.'

'Do you think she's gone to the airport?'

'I don't know. She must have passed you on the road.'

'I don't think so.'

'She was driving a Lada jeep. There are loads of them about. You wouldn't necessarily have noticed.'

'I would have done. There was so little traffic about I was aware of it all.' Besides which, I was looking out for Nicole, not wanting to lose her again. I scanned my memory. 'A man in a Renault 25, a van, a BMW that overtook me. That's all.'

'But she must have passed you. It takes half an hour to get to the main road at Sartene.' She sounded alarmed.

'Perhaps she went the other way.'

'There is no other way.'

'What do you mean? The road goes on past this little turn–off.' I gestured at the dirt track outside.

'Only for about a quarter of a mile or something. It stops on the headland. By the Greek chapel.'

I knew I hadn't missed Nicole. I tried to think what to do. Was she dangerous, or just a danger to herself? Should we get the hell out and find a policeman, or look for her?

Despite what I had been told it was hard to change my image of Nicole, hard to take it in. 'Let's just drive down there and have a look.'

Cate stared at me.

'I'll take you up to the bar in the village first if you like. But you can't stay here on your own.'

'No. Let's stick together.'

I had a worrying thought. 'You don't keep a gun here, do you?'

Cate said nothing but nodded slowly. Then she stood up and went to a cupboard. Inside was a rack with a hunting rifle and a couple of shotguns.

'Jesus. It's a fucking armoury.'

'It's OK,' Cate said. 'They're all here.'

'Let's . . .' I looked for a diplomatic phrase '. . . take them with us.'

Outside it was twilight. I threw the hunting rifle and one of the twelve bores into the boot and locked it. The other I loaded and put behind the driver's seat with the safety on. I could hardly believe what I was doing. Cate watched wordlessly, casting, as I did, the occasional furtive glance around, hoping not to see anything in the shadows.

A couple of birds calling in the gloaming and the occasional rustle of wind were the only sounds, apart from the chugging of that diesel engine I had noticed when I arrived.

Cate was settling herself in the car.

'Have you got your own generator?'

She looked at me as if I was crazy. 'I don't think so. Why do you want one?'

'I meant is that what that noise is – the generator running your electricity?'

'No, it sounds . . .'

'Like a car. Ticking over.'

I took her hand and the twelve bore and we followed the track up through the woods to a clearing where they used to have picnics.

The Lada was parked there, overlooking the headland and the last faint outline of the chapel and its cross against the sea. Its engine chuckled reliably on, pumping the exhaust along the hosepipe wedged in through the driver's window. I dropped the gun, ashamed of having it, and wrenched the door open, coughing as the escaping fog invaded my nostrils and lungs. Nicole's head lolled to one side but she sat up in her seat and I scrabbled to feel her pulse . . . then, unable to find it, her heart. Nothing. Dead eyes, dead woman. I let her go and she stayed straight, having committed suicide in her seatbelt.

Feeling the heat from the exhaust against my feet, at which the hose now benignly laid, I belatedly turned off the engine. Cate was standing back from the car, trailing the twelve bore from one hand, and I went to her. 'Is she . . . definitely . . . dead?' I nodded and, as the enormity of what had happened flooded through me, tears burst.

The gun slipped away and her hands gripped mine, squeezing very hard, and our cheeks touched, hot and wet. We stood for a long while in the cool and quiet. I could feel Cate's heart banging away, frenzied at first, then slowing gradually to a more normal rhythm, but still so strong. Not like Nicole. Poor demented Nicole. Calculating murderess Nicole. Choking out her last over what must have been a favourite view. How strongly she must have wanted to die not to have ripped open the door and revived herself with lungfuls of sea air.

I gathered myself. We had to do something. Call someone in authority. I drew back enough to dab the runnels from Cate's cheeks and then, with a sniff, she took the handkerchief and dried mine. 'Let's go back to the villa and ring the police.' I began to lead her down the path.

'Alex,' she said tentatively, 'do we have to tell them? That Nicole . . . did what she did.'

I stopped.

'I mean, we know what happened, but if we tell the police then Debbie has to know too.'

We looked at one another. Cate was extraordinary. To be able, so soon after her own discovery and terror, to consider protecting Deborah from the awful legacy of her mother being a killer. As if she could read my thoughts she said, 'It's not just for her sake but for mine. The press would be all over us. I've seen stories like it in the papers. Journalists shouting through the letterbox. Taking pictures with telephoto lenses. Raking up any old—' I thought for a second she was going to say scandal '– shit about Daddy. And Mummy.'

Was there any? About Stuart? Not that I could recall. About Angela, blamelessly laid to rest after that fatal final run in Gstaad? Impossible.

Then I remembered the cameras clicking at the church before Stuart's funeral. They probably didn't need anything real to get them started, in fact without anything real they would become maddened like hornets, stinging anything that moved within the environs of the family. And Nicole's first husband was a film star. 'Hollywood gangster's ex blows away hubby number two.' 'Fatal attraction: ad man was drawn to killer divorcee after first love martyred on ski slopes.' 'Orphaned heiresses Deborah and Catriona bravely bit back the tears today as . . .'

Why put Deborah through the heartbreak? What did it matter if the murder was never officially solved as long as we knew? On the other hand . . . 'It's a crime, withholding information from the police.'

'I know,' Cate said quietly. 'But not a very big one.'

Not a very big one. Perjury. Not by comparison with shooting someone.

'It's not harming anybody,' she added.

Quite the reverse, in fact. She looked up at me, pained, vulnerable, imploring.

'It's not going to be easy. There'll be lots of questions. Why did Nicole kill herself?'

'She was in pain. Grief-stricken. I mean, she was, really, in a way.'

'What were you doing here? What was – am – I doing here?' We hadn't discussed that at all.

'Yes, I'm sorry about that, I just needed to see you and when there was someone else there I . . . well, I just wanted to be on my own, you know. I'm sorry I frightened you.'

A sudden doubt struck me. 'It was you on the phone, wasn't it?'

'Yes.'

'Why didn't you say something then, for God's sake?'

'I don't know. I'd just found that car-hire docket and sort of worked out what had happened. I was a bit shocked and, well, scared, I suppose.'

'Why didn't you tell me about it?'

'I don't know. It was hard to know where to start. I suppose I hoped you'd come out after me.'

'Which I did.'

'Thank you. Although when Nicole turned up I thought you hadn't. She didn't say anything about having seen you on the plane, and I didn't see how you could have missed each other.'

Nicole had presumably been on the scheduled service to Ajaccio. I explained about the charter flight to Figari. This was a surreal conversation to be having under the circumstances.

My head whirled but I knew I had taken the decision. 'Let's get inside and talk it through. We haven't got much time.' How could we explain that having found a dead relative we had left her body in the woods for an hour before we informed the gendarmes? Practicality asserted itself. I retrieved the abandoned gun – 'I do not understand why you felt it necessary to take that on a search for your missing sister-in-law, monsieur' – and returned it, with the pair in the boot, to the wall cupboard while Cate changed her grubby sweatshirt. Then we set about getting our stories straight.

Chapter Fourteen

The language barrier was our greatest ally in the hours that followed. We affected to understand only rudimentary French which, as the first policemen on the scene had no English other than 'Hello', allowed us to translate and discuss their questions before replying. When, eventually, an interpreter arrived, we retained the advantage of the thinking time allowed by his translation.

They left us in the villa, having taken our passports with the apology, 'We are compelled. Until the facts are verified', but by the next morning they were apologetic and relaxed. They had been in contact with London and verified not only the story that we had told them but also that Nicole was the divorced wife of a Hollywood film actor. This, it seemed, made suicide without a note more easily comprehensible, a gesture of inconsolable passion that spoke for itself.

I had worried that if our expressions did not reveal that we understood more French than we claimed then Deborah, when she arrived, would question the mysterious linguistic regression of a stepsister who had been fluent from the age of eleven. More seriously, I thought Deborah might cast doubt on Nicole's presumed motive, spurring the satisfied gendarmes on to further investigation.

But when the taxi delivered her from the airport, she was quiet and resigned. She accepted the presence of the interpreter and answered the sympathetic questions without animation. No, of course she hadn't expected her mother to commit suicide, otherwise she would have tried to prevent her, but her mother had been very withdrawn lately. Depressed? Yes, that must have been what it was. She had a photograph of the view across the chapel to the water in her bedroom. Yes, and here her voice trembled a little, as far as she knew Nicole's relationship with Stuart had been a happy one. She had missed him. Her mother had certainly used sleeping tablets in the past – she didn't know whether she had been taking them recently. She did drink socially, sometimes spirits, yes, vodka occasionally.

The post-mortem had revealed a powerful mixture of recently ingested drink and drugs in Nicole's stomach. Enough, it seemed, to have made her drowsy before she sat in the car and taking further hold as each minute passed. That helped explain why she hadn't, at the last, resisted suffocation.

The pill bottle was found in her bag, empty, and, on the kitchen table, two empty wine bottles and a bottle of Smirnoff with no more than an inch remaining. Cate said Nicole had been drinking 'quite a bit' that afternoon but she wasn't sure whether the vodka bottle had been full. She didn't know anything about the Temazepam.

When framing our story for the gendarmes we had thought it safest not to embellish the truth, simply leave most of it out. So Cate had confined herself to telling them when Nicole had arrived, saying only that she hadn't been expecting her. It was Deborah who, unwittingly, offered an explanation for her mother's arrival.

Deborah had spoken to Nicole at about five on Thursday evening, telling her, in the course of conversation, that Cate was missing and that I thought she might have gone to Corsica. My urgent answerphone message, which Nicole never returned, then spoke for itself.

The only possible reason for her not having destroyed the incriminating car-hire docket at the time of the murder was that she had forgotten it. Whether she had subsequently remembered it, lying there in the bureau, but assumed that she would be the next, probably the only visitor to the villa, and could dispose of it then, or whether she was reminded of it for the first time by Deborah's phone call, was impossible to know. Either way, she must have been panic-stricken. She had to get to it before Cate, the person most likely to understand immediately its meaning.

Without calling the villa she had no way of knowing if Cate was already there, and she probably could not bring herself to do that. After all, even if the phone was unanswered, it did not prove that Cate wasn't on her way. Nicole's only course of action was to take the first flight. If she was lucky, Cate was safely occupied in Scotland or Spain or Sussex. If not she could only hope that the girl would not go poking around in the bureau.

Her heart must have sunk when, in the Lada jeep she always hired from the dealer in Sartene, she arrived at the village shop and found the keys to the villa had been taken by the mademoiselle. Had she noticed, when she let herself into the villa, her stepdaughter's wariness, fear having overcome Cate's fury?

Presumably not because, according to Cate, they sat at the kitchen table for a couple of hours, drinking wine, keeping a conversation going, the one trying to discern whether the other knew anything, the other pretending she didn't. Eventually, unable to bear the suspense, Cate said she was going to the loo, ran up the stairs, and waited on the landing. Seconds later she heard the rustle of the bead curtain as Nicole went into the living room, and crept down again, to find her stepmother searching through the papers. Cate said she could not remember what she had said then. It was either, 'Are you looking for this?' or, 'Don't bother,

I've already found it.' Whichever cinematic cliché she had employed, it was enough to crack Nicole's façade, and unleash an hour of tearful confession and hatred before Nicole charged out of the house. Cate thought there had been a gap before the Lada drove away, which tied in with Nicole collecting the hosepipe from the garage, but she had felt too weak to go and look and then, as the shadows lengthened, too frightened. Increasingly convinced that Nicole would regret her frankness and return, Cate had collected a knife from the kitchen and crouched down in the comfortingly small gap between the sofa and the bureau, from where she had charged at me.

When the police took Deborah to identify her mother's body, I offered to accompany her and Cate, understandably, said she did not want to remain in the villa alone. But the three of us were returned there that evening and we made an uncomfortable house party, so although we had the wherewithal to make a meal I suggested we went out.

The small restaurant in the village was, so early in the season, less than half full and most of the diners were local. Consequently the place fell silent as we entered, with the exception of a party of German windsurfers who continued joshing one another in the noisy way that I normally would have found extremely irritating. On this occasion, however, I was profoundly grateful. The banter reminded the locals of their manners and within seconds a host of forced conversations had broken out. A couple of times, looking up to attract the waiter, I caught the hastily averted gaze of curious eyes and thereafter studiously confined my field of vision to our check-clothed table. It was a curious way to be discovering the drawbacks of celebrity.

Being on public view affected our choice of food. The lobster looked delicious but somehow smacked too much of gaiety for a bereaved family, so I ordered an unchallengeable steak and *frites*. Deborah had a pizza from which she abstractedly scraped the topping in minute pieces and Cate had a squid dish which appeared to consist of three or four joke rubber tentacles in a beige sauce.

'What are they stuffed with?' I asked, as Deborah left us in search of the lavatory. Cate had been chewing with the bored application of a ruminant cow.

'Sand, I should think,' she said, poking at her plate in a disconsolate way.

'Let's get you something else. Lobster salad?' I knew she liked it.

'Oh no, that would be too much like fun.' A tiny flicker of a smile.

I smiled back. 'Snap.'

'Why did you make us come out? It's like being in a zoo.'

'I know. But at least it gave us all an excuse to have baths, get changed, do our make-up. Used up some time and got us out of that gloomy villa. Stops Deborah from brooding.'

'You're right.' She topped up my glass from the modest carafe. 'Can I have one of your chips?' Her eyes flickered beyond my head and her face reset into stolid endurance. A few seconds later Deborah resumed her seat.

We didn't linger – no puddings or coffee – and both women went up to bed as soon as we returned to the villa. I wasn't sleepy, and after ten minutes in the rocking chair I couldn't face staying in the dank, stuffy house, so I put on a sweater and went for a walk, taking one of the Scotch bottles for company and warmth. The moon was bright behind scudding clouds and the breeze blowing through the pines was cold.

Not really knowing where else to go I followed the track towards the clearing where we had found the car. Before the first bend I paused and looked back at the house. At one of the bedroom windows, framed between the peeling green shutters, was a figure in a white robe, apparently watching me. At this distance against a dark background the face and hair were not distinct enough for me to identify which of the girls it was. I waited, expecting a wave or some other sign of recognition, but there was no movement. I turned away, and when I looked again she was gone.

Reaching the vantage point over the chapel I sat against the trunk of a tree and took a swig from the bottle. I had not, for a moment, thought the ghostly figure at the window might be an apparition, or that the robe might be a shroud rather than a Marks and Spencer nightshirt. Did that mean that I had kept my commonsense in the face of the extreme provocation of unreal events, or that I suffered a deep lack of imagination?

The car was gone, removed by the gendarmes to their laboratory in Sartene, but the ruts remained, and a small oil spillage on the sandy soil. I stood above it and looked out as she must have done. What could have made her kill Stuart, not in a fury but with carefully plotted premeditation, and then have such a fit of remorse that she was driven to take her own life?

Perhaps he had been such a bastard . . . But how? I had never seen any sign of infidelity or violence, the daughters seemed not to know of any major rift, Stuart had never indicated to me that he disliked Nicole, let alone abused her. OK, some men clearly were consummate concealers of domestic intimidation but I could not see my brother as one of them. If not, though, what was the alternative?

Either Nicole had done it for money or she had done it for love. Although the capital sum she had acquired was substantial, it would hardly have provided her with more income than she would have had access to through Stuart's continued earnings. Maybe he didn't give her much from those earnings? Her clothes, car, holidays and pursuits suggested otherwise and she had had sufficient financial independence to have purchased this villa. Love, then?

If so she had concealed her Romeo very well, or at least from me or any of the mutual acquaintances who might have mentioned 'Nicole's new man' in delicately probing tones. I thought back to the parties, the wake, even the occasion when Cate and I had seen her outside a Soho restaurant, trying to picture a face in common but no one came to mind except . . . For a moment I considered Bill Starling, invariably and eagerly hovering around the throne. Had Merlin cast his spell on her? I couldn't see it somehow. I knew women were supposed to be less susceptible to good looks than men but with Charlie Makepeace and, admittedly to a lesser extent, Stuart, Nicole had demonstrated her taste for the handsome. Startling simply wasn't in the same bracket nor, as far as I could tell, did he make up for it in wit or wisdom. As Deborah had once said, he could bore for England. In any case, if one of those two was in the other's thrall it was Starling who worshipped Nicole, not the other way round.

Scuffing the sand underfoot I picked my way through the undergrowth to the chapel, which turned out to be scarcely more than garage-sized, its crumbled stonework repaired with breezeblocks and corrugated iron. Inside, a light glowed. I pushed open the door. A couple of red-glassed oil lamps burnt on the altar, throwing flickering shadows across walls decorated with gold leaf and mosaic. The strong smell of incense and, unexpectedly, cooking, hung about the hard wooden chairs. I sat down and closed my eyes. For some reason I was more aware of the sound of the sea in here than I had been on the cliff. It was peaceful.

I waited for something to come, prayer or revelation. But nothing did, just the dull, rhythmic thump of the waves below and the faster side-drum of my heart. Goodbye, I thought. In the end there's nothing else to say but goodbye. I'm sorry you came to such a sad end. Had I known sooner that you killed my brother I would have been angry, but it's too late for that.

The incense was choking me. I pushed back the chair with a loud scrape. On my way out I noticed, behind the door, the drum of vegetable oil that presumably fed the lamps and explained the odour of frying tonight.

Outside the air was salty and fresh. I breathed deeply as I followed the path down to the beach. It was like stepping into the type of thickly textured abstract that covers the entire wall of a Stuttgart art gallery. The sand was soft and pale, the surf a spurt of titanium white between it and the thick dark grey sea, the sky above thinned with white spirit. I sat down in the sand and took another slug of Scotch.

The back of my neck insisted strongly that someone was watching me from the jumble of rocks and scrub that fringed the beach. I resisted the temptation to turn round, hoping that they would go away believing themselves undetected. Whoever it was, it could hardly be a mugger in this remote place; it wasn't statistically possible for there to be two acts of violence so close together. As it occurred to me that I had been applying this kind of logic just before we found Nicole's body, I was aware of movement at the periphery of my vision. I gripped the neck of the bottle, knowing only that it wasn't Cate.

Then Deborah coalesced from the darkness. 'Can I join you?'

'Pull up a dune.' I offered her the bottle and she took it, unselfconsciously but rudely wiping the neck on the sleeve of her sweater. The gleam of a white cuff showed below.

'The chapel's magical at night, isn't it?'

I nodded.

'Pity when you go in the daylight you can see that the gold and silver is from cigarette packets, the mosaics are bits of broken crockery and the stained glass is done with sheets of coloured polythene. It's pathetic really.'

'I don't know,' I said, sidetracking. 'Just using what's available and affordable.' I was hit by a sudden, sharp memory of my brother, bent over the dining room table back in Watford, working on a cardboard terrace for the train layout in the loft, sticking translucent Quality Street wrappers in the windows. Deborah seemed poised to say something of import. I had a disturbing presentiment that she was going to embark on some debate about the illusion of religion, using that poor undersized chapel as a metaphor, and I didn't feel up to it. It would just make us both more depressed.

'Why did she do it, Alex?'

For one terrible moment I thought she was asking about the murder, then realised she could only mean the suicide. 'I don't know. Couldn't face it any more? Nothing to look forward to? She must have been bottling up a huge amount of grief.'

'I suppose. But why now? I mean, nine months after,' she asked, as if it would have been more appropriate on an anniversary.

Nine months; the length of a pregnancy. The gestation of guilt, the first contractions as Nicole realised that Cate might find the evidence of that guilt, her mad dash to the villa, but too late: it could no longer be contained and was delivered, screaming into the world as a suicide.

'I should have been there for her. To get it off her chest. But . . .'

'What?' That sounded harsh, accusative, which I hadn't meant but I was having trouble keeping this double-layered conversation going.

'But . . . I couldn't really talk to her about it. Him. And she seemed so cold about it that I thought she was trying to forget. Or had forgotten.' There was a note of disparagement amongst the distressed chords of her voice. 'I mean, she sold the house, dropped the friends she'd made in Stirton, took up where she left off.'

Not where she'd left off, surely? Where she'd left off was as a divorced legal secretary with an adolescent daughter to keep at boarding school. Where she'd taken up was as a rich but relatively young widow, a merry widow. If she had been merry. Presumably not. She had confessed to Cate as if she was relieved, when she could have resisted, argued, at least attempted to get away with it.

What had she been doing wandering through the market square in

Sartene? We knew she had taken a taxi from the airport, but why did she not go straight to the villa? Even if, through force of habit, she had wanted to hire a jeep, why hadn't she got the cab to drop her at the Lada dealer?

Had she heard me calling her and hidden in those old tenements? Or was she following some circuitous route to the dealer, putting off, now that she was so close, the moment of truth, taking a last look around, having a last coffee or a glass of wine in a place that she loved, so wrapped up in her own contradictions and sense of impending doom that she had heard nothing?

'Do you still think about him often?'

Deborah's question pulled me back from this dizzying welter of speculation.

'Stuart? Of course, but less than I did, I suppose. It will be the same for you and Nicole. In time. Whether that's a good thing, a desirable thing, I don't know.'

'I wasn't thinking about Mummy. I meant Stuart.'

I was shocked. Why wasn't she thinking about her mother? But, I supposed, it was too close. She hadn't had enough time for the perspective of reminiscence. However, it was clear that she still thought about Stuart, and wanted to share the pain with me. I was surprised that she did think about him much. After all, he was a stepfather she had known for only six years, most of which time she was away, either at boarding school or living in her own flat in London. It seemed to me she could not have an enormous stock of memories to draw on.

I felt I could hardly share my recent thoughts about Stuart. Wondering whether, as he took that final fatal walk down the corridor, he was frightened. Had he heard something, a suspicious noise, or was he just following some late-night routine, setting clocks, checking windows, except that he wouldn't have left the kitchen window open, would he? He hadn't been in bed anyway, because the sheets were unruffled. Perhaps he was going to the bathroom? But he had one *en suite*, and anyway, the bathroom was engaged. Deborah was tied up in the bathroom.

Was that what she thought about? When she thought of Stuart? Coming to, with a thick head, unable to speak through the gag, unable to move her arms and legs. Unconscious, she wouldn't even have heard the shot. For some time, particularly after it was light, she must have expected to be found. After all, even if Stuart did not normally use that bathroom he would have sought her out to offer breakfast or say goodbye on his way to work. And then, when he hadn't come, had she banked on the arrival of Mrs Cuttifer and her multi-surface cleaner, or had she known the Cuttifers were on holiday? At what point had despair set in? She had known her mother and stepsister were away for a fortnight. Who else could there be?

For her to know that her mother was a murderer who had put her through that would be too much. Cate had been quickly, instinctively right.

I suddenly remembered the party at Nicole's where Deborah had said, after the lights went out, how strongly she had been reminded of the bathroom and that pounce in the dark, and how I had thought, if it was anything more than imagination, that it must have been the smell of Bill Starling that she half-remembered. But it wasn't. It was the proximity of her own mother. And she hadn't suspected. Well, how could she? It was unthinkable.

Had Stuart known? He was shot from the front so he must have confronted his murderer. Had he recognised his wife? She must have been disguised, if only to avoid any chance of being identified arriving or leaving. But how? A stocking mask? A balaclava? Would he have had time to spot, amongst the burglar's apparel, some familiar detail? I hoped not.

Deborah passed me the bottle from which she had taken another swig. 'What are you thinking about?'

'It wasn't anything very happy. I was just thinking about the night he got shot.'

'What about it?' she said guardedly, and who could blame her, waiting for me to force her to relive that experience. She stared out to sea.

'I was just trying to picture where Stuart had been when—' I remembered just in time '– they broke in. What he was doing?'

'He was in bed,' she said, 'wasn't he?'

'No. I mean, he hadn't been in bed.'

'How do you know?' she asked sharply.

'Sheets weren't disturbed. But he was ready for bed. He must have been pottering around, I suppose.'

'I suppose so.'

'You didn't hear him?'

'No,' she said, 'I'd been asleep, quite deeply I think, for a couple of hours or so before I got up to go to the bathroom.'

'I wonder how they didn't bump into him before you.'

'I don't know. It was dark.'

It obviously had been when she woke up; perhaps Stuart had turned the last lights off a couple of minutes before. But no. Nicole had told Cate that the Hall was in darkness when she arrived, and she had been there long enough to collect the shotgun and the cash, climb the stairs, spot Deborah's car in the coach house, return to the kitchen, find the chloroform, reclimb the stairs, hide in the bathroom . . . If Stuart had been roaming round the house at the same time without bumping into her it must have been like some Hollywood comedy thriller, him turning the corner as she entered the corridor from the other end, the sound of him closing one door exactly masking that of her opening another. It was ridiculous. He must have been shut away in his bedroom. But doing what? Dozing in a chair? Surely when you fell asleep in a chair it was with the light on?

I shook my head. No answer.

There was something else about the scenario that didn't fit, some way in which the pieces were wrongly positioned, but I couldn't put my finger on it. I gave up trying. 'It's getting colder,' I said. 'Let's go back, shall we?'

'All right,' Deborah said.

We scuffed our way back across the sand and up to the villa. As we turned the last bend and the shutters came into view I asked, 'Was it you watching me from the window?'

'Yes,' Deborah said. 'Sorry, did I frighten you?'

'No,' I said, 'as long as it was one of you and not a hallucination.'

'Or a ghost,' she said.

'I don't believe in those,' I said firmly.

'Neither do I.'

I opened the door. The room was empty but Cate was there, her proximity as insistent as if she was holding my hand or slapping my face. I crossed to the stairs and turned. 'Good night,' I said to Deborah, who was rummaging in the fridge, and as I swung back I expected to see Cate's face above the banisters or the flicker of her stepping back into the shadows, so strong was my feeling that she was watching me. But there was nothing. I walked up the stairs and along the corridor to her bedroom. The door was shut. I paused outside, listening intently. No sound. I was half-tempted to open it, to see whether she was asleep or awake, but I heard Deborah's footfall on the stair and moved on to my own room.

Was it just a projection of my thoughts on the beach – the elusive figure, always just out of sight, as it was in films, as Nicole had been in the streets of Sartene? I stared at the wall separating my room and Cate's. I didn't think so. Ever since I had been here I had been very conscious of her, sensitive to her slightest movement. Even now, through the plaster-skinned breezeblock, I was aware of her as a fuzzy, ill-defined form emitting Cateness like the heat detected by an infra-red sensor.

It was, I thought as I fretted myself to sleep, the conspiracy factor, binding us together.

The police had said that we were free to return to the UK whenever we wished, and although we had offered to stay with Deborah she had said she would prefer a day to sort through the effects on her own, so I rang Ajaccio airport. It was a Sunday morning so I expected a long wait but not to be told, when the phone was finally answered, that our earliest flight was midday Monday.

The thought of another day at the villa was clearly as depressing to Cate and she suggested driving to Bonifacio, a port on the southern tip of the island, for lunch. I half-expected Deborah to decline in order to make a start on sorting the villa's contents but, without enthusiasm, she said she would come too, as if she had to have us out of the country before she could settle to anything.

It was a gloomy meal, the desultory conversation only relieved by surroundings interesting enough to watch in silence; the leprous façades of the narrow harbourside houses, the yachts negotiating the channel to the open sea.

After we had finished we drove across the headland to a sandy beach beyond salt flats which, under the heavy grey sky, was desolate enough to reinforce our mood. Nevertheless we stayed, walking and paddling, killing time, and we stayed together despite having little to say. It was as if we were scared to be alone with our thoughts or how they might be voiced in a pair as opposed to an uncomfortable trio.

And all the time I could feel the tension in Cate, gliding through the water from her ankles to mine, boring into my shoulders as she sat behind me in the car.

The next morning as we packed our things, still offering all the while to stay if Deborah wanted us to, the tension was as strong as ever. It was there as we drove in convoy, shut in our separate rented Peugeots which had to be delivered to the airport. When my arm brushed hers at the check-in desk she recoiled as if bruised. On the flight we could hardly speak, the tight, light conversation spluttering and dying in fitful, infrequent bursts. In the taxi from Heathrow, with the unreal mundanity of roadworks, traffic and English drizzle beyond its windows, we both slumped with studied casualness in our separate corners, bags between us. At one point our eyes met accidentally and we looked away, as if from strong sunlight, as if any longer contact would have given the game away. On the doorstep I fumbled with the keys and eventually we stumbled into the shady hallway, clawing the luggage in behind us. I leant back on the door, pushing it closed. I felt almost dizzy with relief.

'We made it,' I said. And Cate fell against me and suddenly we were kissing as if our lives depended on it.

Chapter Fifteen

It was a spontaneous combustion.

We said nothing. Cate's arms locked around my neck, her fingers occasionally stretching up to pull at my hair. I could feel the movement of her shoulderblades through the soft cashmere of her sweater; the silk lining of her suede jacket brushed against the backs of my hands.

Eventually she opened her eyes and moved far enough back to allow her scurrying fingers to pick at my shirt without our mouths losing contact. I pushed the jacket off her strong shoulders and she wriggled out of the sleeves, her pelvis banging against mine, and then she was leaning into me again, her breasts cushioning the collision of our ribcages, her hand bumping my groin and I realised she was struggling with the brass fly-fastening of her jeans.

We subsided to the floor, writhing like snakes to lose jeans, shoes and socks, and as she grabbed at my buttocks my burrowing hand found her surprisingly silky tussock of pubic hair and the soft wetness beneath. She took a gasp of breath and I said, with the tiny amount of self-possession I had left, 'We need—'

I was sure there were some in my bedside drawer; if not I think desire would have driven me down the street for them but Cate said, 'In my handbag,' and scrabbled across the carpet for it, swinging it high and upending it so that wallet, purse, lipsticks, Lil-lets and keys cascaded around us. She tore at the faded packaging of the single condom and then, with bizarre formality, handed it to me to put on.

The whole sequence hardly broke the pace or rhythm of a fast and furious coupling. Cate pulled me into her, grunting and gasping and, at the finish, arching her back as she groaned. Spent, we collapsed in an untidy heap and, as my heartrate slowed and my brain re-established normal thought processes, I propped myself up on my elbows. She looked up at me, mascara smudged around wet eyes as if their deep black pupils had leaked.

'Are you all right?' I asked.

'Oh yes,' she said, smearing her hand across her face, 'thank you.' And she gave me the tentative, complicitous smile.

I underwent a final, involuntary spasm of longing, answered by her vaginal muscles, but I was shrinking fast. I withdrew, the condom crinkling from lack of internal support. I hoisted myself up saying absurdly, as one does on such occasions, 'Don't move, I'll be back.'

In the basement lavatory the redundant rubber, unbeaten by the flush, bobbed jauntily on the aquamarine surface of the bowl, and the outside world slyly and shockingly intruded with the thought that it must be removed before Betty next came to clean.

I ran back up the stairs. The discarded clothes, the contents of Cate's handbag and our luggage still littered the floor but she was not there. I don't know why this panicked me because, although I had only been gone a couple of minutes, very few people would choose to lie alone and half-naked on the hall carpet. But it did and, having glanced in the kitchen, I chased to the top of the house; the drawing room, her room and my bedroom were all empty. As I was about to try the door connecting my room and the bathroom she opened its other door to the landing.

'What's the matter?' she asked nervously. In the patch of shadow between the attic stairs and the landing window her long legs looked very white and, bare beneath the moss green sweater, strangely vulnerable, despite the strong calf muscles. Perhaps it was the way the soft inner thighs pressed gently against each other.

'I don't know,' I said, but I did. 'Oh Cate, what have we done?'

She stared at me. 'Don't you . . . want me?'

'Oh yes,' I said, immediately giving in to the plaintive call of my heart. 'But . . . is this what you—?'

She looked down at her feet. 'It's what I've wanted most of all. Exactly what I wanted. I just didn't know if it ever would until—' She swayed slightly, and caught the banister rail for support. 'I'm a bit wobbly for some reason. But,' she continued as I put my arms around her, 'I'm really happy.'

And so it was easy to block out the black clouds swirling round the edges of my thoughts with the next eruption of longing, this time a leisurely drift of kisses and caresses, their swell carrying us into the evening until it was too dark to see each other and we lay watching the play of lights from the Camberwell Road on the ceiling.

'I'm thirsty,' Cate said. She giggled. 'And sweaty.'

I stroked her spine. 'Do you want tea or booze, a bath or a shower?'

She stretched. 'Booze and a bath. I'm too bubbly for tea and too lazy for a shower.'

I opened a bottle of chablis, poked around in the cupboard under the sink for the long-neglected ice bucket and attempted to make a reasonably professional job of draping a white teatowel around the thing. When I returned to the bedroom Cate was lying on her back, arms clasped behind her head, cover tucked up under her chin. I poured her a glass and went to check on the bath.

'It's ready,' I said, dropping down beside her on the mattress.

'Oh, OK. Thanks.' As if suddenly embarrassed by her nakedness she felt by the side of the bed for a T-shirt but there were only a bra and sweater, neither appropriate for a walk to the bathroom. She got up somewhat self-consciously, moving as quickly as she thought acceptable between the screening provided by the duvet and that of the bathroom door, which she pushed almost shut behind her.

I could still see her, reflected in the mirror, cautiously lowering herself into the hot water, but it seemed fairer not to look. Sex is not the most intimate context for nudity; to be relaxed without clothes with a lover in other domestic situations takes time. I accepted that, but I was sorry because I did not want to be left on my own.

'Are you hungry?' I asked, pulling on chinos and a denim shirt.

'Yes.'

'What do you want to eat then?'

'What have we got?'

The 'we' leapt out of the sentence at me. It was a natural thing for her to say – she had lived here on and off since last August; it was, as much as anywhere else, her home – and she had probably said it many times but never with the resonance it had tonight. I realised how disappointed I would have been had she said 'What have you got?'

'I'm sure there's stuff in the fridge and freezer. But we can get almost anything from a takeaway, so you choose.'

'Oh, don't go out,' she said quickly, and I was glad, because I did not want to leave the cocoon of the house and she didn't want me to leave her alone.

I looked in the mirror, now steaming up, and she was safely hidden beneath a mountain range of foam, so I took the bucket in to her and refilled our glasses. 'Pot luck, then.'

Under artificial light the mess on the hall carpet looked depraved – more the result of ransacking than lovemaking. I guessed if it embarrassed me it would embarrass Cate so I tidied it up, stacking the jeans and shoes neatly near the cases, putting every last ticket stub and mint packet back into the Mulberry sack I had given her last Christmas.

In the kitchen the answerphone's messages-waiting light flashed angrily but I ignored it. The outside world was on hold. I cobbled together a sauce for pasta with pesto and tinned tomatoes, set the water to boil and, feeling unable to settle, took the luggage upstairs. There was a light on in Cate's room. For a second I hesitated and then rapped on the door, calling out, 'I've got your stuff here.'

'Oh, er, come in.'

She had dressed as if she were going out, and was putting on her make-up. For a second I wondered if this was a way of re-erecting barriers, but then she said, 'I didn't know whether to, you know, er, get dressed er, properly or—' She gestured helplessly with her mascara brush in one hand and the bottle in the other.

My heart leapt. 'You look beautiful.'

We ate in the drawing room, plates balanced on the captain's chest, deliberately talking about impersonal things – books we were reading, a film Cate had seen – until we had finished the wine. She had refused coffee and yawned but made no move. When I stood up to gather the plates and glasses her expectant gaze followed.

'I guess,' I said, 'I'd better ask. Do you want to sleep with me tonight?' I tried to laugh. 'No obligation.'

Relieved, she attempted insouciance herself. 'It's no obligation.'

Cate fell asleep in the traditional manner, her head on my shoulder, one arm draped across my stomach, but it didn't last. After half an hour or so she rolled onto her back, her lips parted, fingers slackly spread, breasts lolling on her ribs. Only the hush of escaping breath and the flickering beneath her eyelids confirmed brain activity. Slowly, and as delicately as I could, I extricated my hand trapped beneath her and rubbed it until the nerves fizzed painfully back to life.

When, after another hour, I had rotated through 360 degrees, made a mental checklist of things to do (urgent) at the office, run through the stations on all three Kent coast lines out of Charing Cross and visited every service station on the M1 without sleep seeming any less elusive, I got up.

There was not enough milk for Horlicks or cocoa and it seemed perverse to ingest the stimulating caffeine of tea or coffee, so I settled for a glass of carbonated water and a cigarette at the drawing room window.

Whole legs of lamb and triple chocolate gateau were on special offer at the freezer centre. The usual mix of tired Austin Montegos and Ford Sierras on the car lot advertised their not so special features – tinted windows, central locking, radio/cassette – in the matey yellow-and-red script of their windscreen stickers. Easy terms were still, apparently, available.

I wished.

The wet road reflected the underripe orange of the streetlights. A night bus cruised past, its bright upper deck peopled by black office cleaners, mostly contemplative, and white revellers, mostly still exuberant, gesticulating, chorusing laughter at the evening's outrageous events. On the back seat a boy, no older than Cate, slept under his Russian hat.

Cate. Upstairs asleep in my bed, our relationship irrevocably changed. She couldn't just move back to the spare room as if nothing had happened, go back to being my niece. I didn't want her to. But.

Incest. I supposed that was what it was. I had once heard or read the ecclesiastical law listing all types of complicated forbidden relationships and I didn't remember niece being on it, but I doubted whether it was a grey area, like certain sorts of cousin. We were blood relatives. We had broken a taboo.

How would it look to others? How did it look to me? A seedy, middle-aged man, Uncle Alex, corrupting an innocent little girl. I might as well wear a plastic mac and carry a bag of sherbet pips.

Of course I knew it wasn't really like that. I wasn't some old lecher, pressing my paunch and unwelcome attentions on an unwilling nymphette. I was only thirty-something, in decent nick, and she wasn't a pubescent waif. She was five feet ten and as strong as an ox with a vote, an income and a mind of her own. She carried a condom in her handbag (although, a small voice insisted, it looked as if it had been waiting in there a long time) and she had made her mind up to use it with me.

But that didn't stop the nauseating waves of guilt and dread. She was young enough to be my daughter. Had I exerted undue influence from my position as unofficial guardian and front-line provider of various goodies like sports cars, CD players and even, for God's sake, the bag the condom came from? Had I, however subtly, coerced her?

How could I have done? I hadn't seen this coming until it knocked me flat. Even on the way home from Corsica I had ascribed the crackle to conspiracy and not sexual electricity.

'Alex?' She was in the doorway, swamped by an enormous T-shirt on which the more than lifesize head of Hilda Ogden, all curlers and knowing eyes, leered at me. 'Are you all right?'

'Yes. No.'

'What's the matter?' She put a tentative hand on my shoulder. 'Can I . . . can I help?'

'You're the matter, Cate—'

'Why?' She sounded frightened. 'What have I done?' Her hand dropped away.

I took hold of it but I couldn't look at her. I watched a punk bounce along the pavement, eating a bag of chips. Where had he bought those at this time of night?

'I shouldn't have let what happened happen. I know, you've said, you wanted it too, but I feel like I've betrayed a trust. What's that phrase? *In loco parentis*?'

'Don't say that. You're not. I'm not a child and I made up my own mind.' Her hand tightened against mine. There was a pause as if she was considering the points one by one. 'You haven't betrayed my trust, which is what matters, isn't it?' She hurried on, evidently wanting this question to remain rhetorical. 'I know you have looked after me, protected me, this last year, but lovers can do that, can't they? I don't think of you as family, I don't want to think of you as family.' She snatched her hand away in frustration. 'I wish you weren't family.' She moved away and sat on the sofa, talking in a low voice, almost as if to herself. 'It's so stupid. When I had a family I hardly knew you. I didn't really know you at all until I came here and by then I was an adult without a family and you were my friend not, not my bloody uncle.'

I remembered her saying on that Greek harbour the previous summer, 'I've never thought of you as an uncle', and then a bit later, 'You're not an uncle uncle.' I certainly wasn't any more.

'Surely it's only how we feel that matters, isn't it?' she demanded. 'Not anybody else. They can't know what it's like. It's none of their business.'

'Maybe not,' I said bleakly. 'But that's not really how society works.'

'Fuck society. Anyway, how are they going to find out? As long as we don't tell them.'

I thought of how difficult it would be, not to betray in one unguarded moment, by a single gesture, the true feeling between us, how, in the end, it was bound to come out. I felt weary, and patronising, and defeatist.

Cate looked straight at me. 'Alex, please, please don't give me up now.'

And the idea of secrecy as an impossible burden, skulking behind net curtains, crumbled. It was the alternative, Catelessness, that was unthinkable.

'I can't give you up,' I said, smiling. 'You're right. Fuck society.'

She threw herself at me and we hugged until we were breathless. 'It's cold,' Cate said, finally. 'Shall we go back to bed?'

Our first morning, after she had drunk some tea, Cate lay still, as if expecting more sleep, but I was aware of her half-closed eyes following my progress from bathroom to dressing room. 'What are you going to do today?' I asked, as I knotted my tie.

'I don't know,' she said, and then, as if that might sound feckless, given that I was going to work, she added, 'I've got revision to do, for prelims. Are you in tonight?'

'Yes, not until eightish, though.'

'Shall I cook?' she asked diffidently.

The doorbell rang, and Cate sprang guiltily from the bed, as if the caller might be able to see where she had been lying.

'It's probably just the postman,' I said. 'If you look out of the furthest window you can just about see who's on the step.'

She did so, pulling the T-shirt over head. There was a short silence before the bell rang again. Cate was transfixed at the glass.

'Well,' I said. 'Who is it? Meter reader? Bailiffs?'

She backed away from the window slowly, as if a sudden movement might attract the visitor's attention. 'It's Superintendent Cromarty,' she said quietly.

Chapter Sixteen

'I was very sorry to hear about Mrs Buchan,' Cromarty said, almost as if she was my wife rather than my sister-in-law. 'Very sorry, and very shocked.'

His little eyes were flicking back and forth around the kitchen. I knew that he had seen it before, when he came to interview Cate, so what was he doing? Simply refreshing his memory or looking for alterations, clues to wider changes?

'Yes,' I said. 'It was terrible. Thank you for your condolences.' There could hardly have been anybody I less wished to see, but I had thought that to half-open the front door and keep him on the doorstep would have been to invite suspicion in even the most dense plod. Having ushered him in, however, I did not want him to settle for a cosy chat, so we stood awkwardly by the unit separating cooker and sink from the dining area. Or rather I did. Despite not having been offered a seat Cromarty managed to look comfortable, at home.

'I'd make some coffee, but as you can see I'm on my way to work.' I gestured loosely at my suit and tie. 'A meeting at nine,' I added, knowing that behind my head the kitchen clock read 8.35.

'Oh, don't worry,' he said. 'I was just passing. On my way to Southwark Crown Court.'

We both knew that the most direct route from Stoneyheath was straight up the A2 to the Elephant and Castle, so that he was at least a mile out of his way.

'Yes,' he said. 'It must be hard, keeping a business running at times of family crisis. Having to fly out to Greece or Corsica or wherever.'

This was provocatively rude in a way that was impossible to answer. 'You make it sound as if it was a weekly occurrence,' I said, 'whereas even if I did resent it, the fact is that I've only lost two working days.'

'I had no inkling that something like this might happen,' he said. 'Did you?'

'No. I had no idea.'

'But . . . you hadn't been intending to fly out to the villa on Friday?'

'No.' Knowing that Cromarty would not mind his own business I had to decide at what point to switch from giving him polite but minimal answers and tell him our version of the truth. 'I went because when I spoke to Cate on the phone she was upset.'

'That her stepmother was suicidal?'

'No, she was suffering from the usual student anxieties and depression, I think, but being at the villa, with its memories of her father, had made them worse.'

'Well,' Cromarty said, 'I admire you for responding so quickly to your niece's, um, discomfort. But didn't you think Mrs Buchan could sort her out when she arrived?'

'I didn't know that Mrs Buchan was going to be there.'

'So her visit was also unplanned.'

'Not necessarily,' I said. 'But I didn't know about it.'

'An odd coincidence then,' he said, emphasising the weakness of our story as if to himself, guessing that I couldn't let it rest.

'All I can tell you,' I said, 'is that Deborah spoke to her mother on Thursday afternoon and thought she sounded depressed. She thinks she may have told Nicole that I thought Cate had gone to Corsica, and that I was worried about her. She doesn't think that Nicole made any mention of going to Corsica herself, but she may have. Who knows, perhaps her hearing that Cate was going made her think that she would like to be there herself. Or perhaps she became worried about her, thought the place might get to her. It obviously got to her when she arrived.' As a piece of irrefutable but inconclusive padding, cotton wool between Cromarty and the truth, I thought this was quite good.

He considered it for a moment or two and then ignored the flannel, going straight for the fact I thought would be better heard from me than from anyone else. 'So, you were worried about Cate before the phone call?'

'Yes, like I said, the usual stuff but' – I shrugged my shoulders diffidently – 'I haven't had much practice with adolescent girls.'

Under the circumstances that could have been better phrased. He didn't go for the obvious laugh line but the effort of not doing so seemed to put him off his stroke for a second or two. Then, back on song, he asked, 'So, you were half-expecting Cate's call from Corsica?'

Perhaps I was overestimating both his powers of deduction and the availability of French telephone records but I wasn't going to risk falling into a trap. 'No,' I said, 'I rang her.'

He looked like a man wanting to ask another, if not several more questions. When was Cate's trip planned; if it wasn't, how did I know where to call her; how even did I know she wasn't still in Durham; then why had she left my house so abruptly? Perhaps I was being paranoid or perhaps he knew that any more at this stage would be overstepping the mark, laying him open to the accusation of harassment of the bereaved, prying into something only tangentially connected with a British police case. In any case he offered the apparently anodyne remark: 'Cate's a lucky girl.' And then he dropped his gaze, as if mulling it all over and added, 'Or at least, lucky to have you looking out for her.'

Was it just my guilt that made everything he said seem so deliberately ambiguous? Surely 'looking out for' someone meant watching their back, more a description of alibi-making than simple caring?

'How is she?' Cromarty asked.

'About as well as can be expected,' I said, attempting a wry smile.

'Still living here then?'

'When she's not at university,' I said.

'Is she in at the moment?' A question casually put.

'Yes,' I said, 'but in the bath I think, unless it's a poltergeist splashing about in there. Can I give her a message?' I added, to establish that there was no possibility of his seeing her.

'No,' he said. 'No matter. I just thought I'd pay my respects.'

Another strange phrase. I decided I'd co-operated enough. Anything more would be suspicious in itself, given my professed hurry. 'Thank you. I'll tell her. And now,' I looked at my watch, 'I must be off.'

Cromarty played one last masterly shot, presumably more for the sake of calling my bluff than from any expectation of benefit.

'I'll walk with you to your car,' he said, in a friendly way.

'It's all right,' I said, rubbing salt in the wound. 'I'm running so late now I'd better make a couple of phone calls before I leave.'

'Sorry to have held you up, Mr Buchan,' he said, back on the doorstep. 'I'll be in touch.' And even that farewell sounded like a threat. As he walked down the steps he glanced up and I wondered whether he was looking for another glimpse of Cate at the bedroom window, whether he'd known all along that she was not in the bath when he arrived.

He wouldn't have got one because we had decided the bath was the safest place for her until I gave her the all-clear.

I rapped on the bathroom door and she opened it, wrapped in a bathsheet, her hair turbanned in another towel. I gave her the gist of the conversation.

'I'm sure he knows there's something fishy going on, but he's not sure what. I can't see him leaving it alone, he just doesn't feel able to ask me any more at the moment. But he's bound to pop in on Deborah when she gets back.'

'I don't see what good that will do him. She doesn't know anything. He'll just have to accept that it was coincidence.'

She was right. She was certain there were no other pieces of evidence at the villa for Deborah to find, so presuming that Nicole had confessed to no one else, which seemed likely, all we had to do was remain silent.

What was more we were doing good, so why did I feel so guilty? Because, I reflected as I walked round to the square to collect the car, Cate and I had another secret.

The Saab wasn't there. For a moment or two, during which righteous indignation pushed my blood pressure far higher than the interview with

Cromarty, I thought it had been stolen. Then I remembered; it was in the car park at Gatwick airport. Laughing, I let myself back into the house, explained to Cate, and asked to borrow the Mazda.

She giggled. 'You can, on one condition.'

'Anything,' I said.

'That you pick it up from Heathrow. I was in such a state when we came through yesterday I completely forgot about it. And that's your fault.' She gave me the coy, complicitous smile.

'I haven't got the time,' I said heartlessly. 'I'll get a cab.'

'And I have, I suppose?' She put her hands on her hips in imitation of a Hull fishwife. Dressed as she was in a sweater and a pair of yellow socks it was ridiculously endearing.

'You,' I said, 'are an idle student and I, remember, have a company to run to keep you in the style to which you are accustomed.'

'Our company,' she said, in the manner of one who knew she was being greatly daring, not sure how far the joke would go. 'Make sure you take good care of it. Increased profits or yields or whatever they are. Or there'll be hell to pay at the annual general meeting.'

'Have you been reading the *Financial Times*?'

'No.'

'Sure?'

'Yes.'

As I was closing the front door she said: 'Just the business bit of the *Guardian*.'

By the time I returned both cars were back in the square, the dinner table was laid and the smell of casserole escaped from the oven.

'You went to Gatwick and Heathrow by public transport?' She nodded. 'And all this?' I waved my arm around the room, taking in the napkins, candles, and fruitbowl piled high with grapes and imported peaches. She nodded again, unable to prevent a small smirk of selfless satisfaction. 'What about your revision, young lady?' And I grabbed her around the waist as she hit me with a sofa cushion, closing her mouth before the third 'bastard'.

The next night she went out. She had announced her intention with just a hint of the interrogative, as if I might have a valid objection, but I had ignored it. 'Have a good time.'

I went to bed about midnight, leaving a light on in the kitchen. I had expected to fall asleep quickly but my mind skittered about a problem with our catering client, and after ten minutes I realised half my attention was on the traffic noise from the Camberwell Road. I knew she hadn't taken her car so it was only the growl of buses and the chug of ticking-over taxis that attracted me.

She must have had a mini-cab or a lift because her key in the door was a complete surprise. She came up the stairs straight away and I heard her stop on the landing below and go into her room. Through my half-open door, the stairwell ceiling was stained by the light from beneath her bedroom door. I closed my eyes and listened to her moving about, preparing for bed. Sensible and considerate.

Then, after a few minutes, her footfall on the stair. I kept my eyes closed, my head averted. She slipped into the bathroom through the landing door and cleaned her teeth – faint scrubbing noise – with none of the fumbling or banging into things that one might have expected from someone in the dark. She must have night sight as good as a cat's.

The bathroom's bedroom door opened – a habitual squeak – and then she was easing back the duvet and lowering herself delicately onto the mattress. Only when she had listened to the regular sound of my breathing for several minutes did she rest her hand against my hip. I was happy.

I was happy all the time I was with her. Operating by some instinct very few women I had known possessed, she never put a foot wrong, walking the tightrope between cloying and offhand, passionate and funny, yielding and aggressive, demonstrative and discreet. Her only wobble was the first time she came into Buccaneer when, standing by the window behind my chair, chatting about her day, she leant over and wrapped her arms around me, nuzzling my ear as the door swung open and Dorothy said, mother-hen-like, 'I'd expect you'd like some coffee, Cate.'

'Do you think she saw?' Cate asked, after the door had closed behind her.

'No,' I said. 'By the time she'd stopped concentrating on not spilling the stuff into the saucers you were safely upright, I think.' I'd known Dorothy for long enough to know that had she seen and interpreted that gesture as anything untoward she would have been incapable of keeping the disapproval off her face. 'But it was a close shave.' Below the level of the desk I squeezed her hand. 'This place isn't safe, even if we think everyone's gone.'

'Sorry,' she said and, touching her lips with her finger, placed it, just for a second, on my cheek.

I was happy when I was with her, and happy that business was holding up rather better than the gloomy prognostications of the trade papers and, increasingly, the national press. Even the MJB project was back on course, after one uncomfortable meeting with Dervla McKenna, in which, feeling a prize hypocrite, I had to apologise again for the childish antics of my niece. I also felt obliged to suggest dinner some time soon, but at Simpsons where I thought the formality should distance it as much as possible from our abortive grope. Anyway, as luck would have it, we were both busy enough for some time to remain just that.

But things could not be hectic enough, or happy enough, to entirely eradicate those times when, alone in the car or the early hours, I felt that Cate and I were doomed to tragedy.

We could not carry on like this, in secret, for very long and we certainly couldn't in public. Either would blight her life. I couldn't talk to Cate about it, she got too upset, but I consoled myself – some bleak consolation – with the thought that on April 21 she would be returning to Durham and that somehow nine weeks apart might make a difference. She might meet someone else, decide to spend the summer with them, travel overland to India or wherever the modern student equivalent was, and come the autumn our infatuation would be a distant memory, painful but past.

Nicole's funeral was set for April 15, it having taken some time to get the body released and organise the service. This, for no obvious reason, although I suspected the hand of Bill Starling, was to take place at St Brides, Fleet Street.

I walked down from the office through a persistent drizzle, alone because Cate had without warning announced that she could not, would not come. I had tried persuading her, first on the grounds of sheer politeness, second that it would upset Deborah and was at odds with the concern that had produced our conspiracy, and eventually that her absence would create suspicion we could do without. Eventually she had buried her head under the duvet and I left with the last weary blast of the frustrated: 'Ah well, it's up to you.'

I had cut it fine, not wanting to hang around outside the church with mourners who, until the service is over, can think of nothing to say, and as I scuttled up the alley separating St Brides from the pub, the organ was already playing. An impatient verger ushered me through the archway, and I slipped as unobtrusively as possible into the back row of the choir stalls which ran the length of the nave, the church's only pews.

The place was surprisingly full considering it was two o'clock on a Monday afternoon. It was hard to imagine an advertising executive getting this kind of turnout but, I reminded myself, she had mixed with theatricals and hacks, both professions keen on a good memorial service.

Across the aisle, nearest the altar and the flower-bedecked coffin that stood on trestles before it, was the family. Men did not seem to play a large part in the Leadbetter clan, whose name Nicole had borne before marriage made her a Makepeace. In the back row were two women easily identifiable as her sisters, one of whom had a husband and two daughters in tow, the adolescent girls carrying a heavy dose of the Leadbetter features. Strong genes, passed down by the dominant woman in front of them who had to be Nicole's mother, but not strong enough to impose their will on the Makepeace genes that had fashioned Deborah. She stood, her veil an unsettling echo of Nicole's own at Stuart's funeral, between her tall, pale grandmother and her shorter, dark father but there was nothing in her looks to suggest that she was related to anyone there other than Charlie.

His costume was as impeccably that of an upper-class Englishman as the dignified set of his jaw, but entirely at odds with the heavy

Californian tan that accentuated his naturally sallow complexion. He sang the hymns without reference to his songsheet, prayed with the quiet intensity of a monk, delivered his reading with the haunting resonance that had made him the critics' Hamlet of his generation. I wondered what Mrs Leadbetter thought of the leading role given to the man who had abandoned her daughter for Hollywood and a succession of American bimbettes.

As the service progressed I discreetly studied the rest of the congregation. A couple of places along from Charlie, presumably as close to the family centre of events as he thought he could get, stood Bill Starling, bald crown glowing, grey hair catching on his collar, wispy goatee groomed to a point, eyes shining behind his glasses. For a second I felt a pang of sympathy; he must have loved her.

Further along, among the odd mixture of vaguely recognizable TV bit-parters and horsy types from Stirton Ash, I spotted Molly and Boy Chippenham and Saro and Henry Beaumont. It was the first time I had seen Saro since the day I had sat outside her house, hoping for just a glimpse to alleviate my cold turkey. My heart skipped a beat. Was this vision all I needed to readdict me, or was it just the shock of recognition, the panic about what we could possibly say to each other when we met on our way out or at the wake?

I forced myself to look away and there, tucked in the far corner, was the answer to my question. Wearing that same baggy black blazer, head bowed over her hymn book, was Cate. Love burned through me like raw spirit. It was all I could do not to cross over to her there and then.

'Don't think I changed my mind about it,' she said, when we were standing together, watching the small family party embark for their journey to the crematorium at Kensal Rise. 'I only came for you.'

I squeezed her upper arm, trying to convey how pleased I was. It must have been painful but she didn't flinch. 'That's all right,' she said.

A small, blonde woman approached. 'Biddy Armitage. I don't know if you've been told, there's a small gathering back at my club. The family will join us as soon as they can. I do hope you can come.'

'I can't, I'm afraid,' Cate said decisively. 'But I'm sure Alex . . .'

'Of course,' I said, to remove the exaggerated expression of disappointment from Biddy's face.

She explained how to get there – 'Walkable on a nice day, but in this weather I should think there'll be plenty of people sharing taxis' – and moved on to the next group.

'Sorry,' Cate said, 'but I really couldn't face that.'

'I won't stay long.'

'It doesn't matter. I'm going over to the Cliffords'. I thought I might stay the night. I knew you'd want to do the right thing.' She glanced round almost nervously. 'I'm going to go before people start trying to persuade me otherwise.' She kissed me on the cheek and was gone, diving out of the side entrance into the rain.

I turned round, looking where she had looked. By the main doors the Chippenhams and the Beaumonts were bobbing backwards and forwards in unmistakeable farewell ritual. I slipped back into the body of the church, not up to a confrontation with Saro or Henry, and studied the memorial plaques.

'Are you all right, old man?' It was Boy.

I nodded.

'I shan't want to attend another of these things for a while,' he said, tapping his furled umbrella against his shoe. 'Are you going to this do?'

'Are you?'

'Oh yes. Thought we'd better. As much a mark of respect as the religious bit really. The Beaumonts can't make it, unfortunately. Got a load of bankers for dinner or some such thing.' His disapproval was evident. 'Where's young Cate?'

I made her excuses.

'Better share a cab with us then. Let's find Molly.'

The Terrano Club had an inauspicious entrance, a steel door in a Dickensian passage behind the Coliseum, but from it a narrow, panelled staircase opened into a suite of rooms resembling a neglected Edwardian country house. Log fires burned beneath oak mantles, the floors were covered with faded Turkey carpets and the walls with an engaging mixture of hunting prints and fifties abstracts. Through the windows the roar of traffic in Trafalgar Square was just audible. Relaxed young waiters dispensed drinks and finger food, presided over by Biddy Armitage, her black dress as suitable for a club manager as it was for a funeral. The men, on the other hand, once the context for their dark suits and black ties was removed, resembled nothing so much as a convention of chauffeurs.

'It's not at all seedy,' Molly was saying to Boy. 'I expect the entrance of El Vino's would smell of urine if it was in a tiny alleyway like this.'

'What's happened to Bill Starling?' I asked. 'I'm surprised he isn't here.'

'Perhaps he's actually got to write something for his paper,' Boy said disparagingly.

'Don't be silly,' Molly said, 'he's a theatre critic. He only works in the evenings. No, he went to the crematorium. In the second car, along with Nicole's sister, Jeanette.'

The family party arrived awkwardly, as if aware that they were spoiling the atmosphere of a convivial get-together. Grandmother was installed at a corner table, and surrounded herself with a protective wall of sons-in-law and granddaughters. Deborah clung to her father's arm, circulating with him from group to group, and as they moved on I heard the swell of Charlie's enticing voice, recounting anecdotes, raising laughter and the tempo of the event.

Bill Starling bustled hither and thither, getting in Biddy's way as he needlessly duplicated her instructions, but she could see as I could, perhaps we all could, that it was displacement activity to distract him from his grief. As I was returning from the bar with another Scotch – for some reason it seemed the most appropriate drink on this gloomy afternoon – he literally bumped into me.

'So sorry, Alex, it is Alex, isn't it?'

'Yes. Don't apologise.'

'Thank you for coming. Deborah says you were such a help in Corsica.'

It didn't seem his place to be offering thanks on behalf of anyone so I ignored that and said, 'There wasn't much I could do.'

'It must have been terrible,' he invited me to expand. His little reddened eyes were almost pleading with me for more information. He hadn't had the opportunity to speak to Cate and, knowing Deborah's opinion of him, I doubt whether she had told him much, merely felt unable to refuse his help in organising the funeral.

'It was. And such a shock.'

'I know.' He looked away for a couple of seconds, blinking. 'I only saw her the day before and she said nothing about going to Corsica. I just don't understand it. I mean, I'd grown pretty used to being a confidant, you know, I thought she told me most things.' He took a quick swallow at his wine. 'I blame myself.'

'What for?'

'Oh, for not understanding how depressed she was, but honestly she just seemed a bit down, you know I put it down as much to the time of year as anything, thought she'd perk up in the spring proper. We'd talked about going to Italy, you know, Florence, Venice, all that. In fact we even talked about it that day, I dropped in on her for tea, and she was laughing about the time she went to Siena to see that horse race and the place was so packed they couldn't get within a hundred yards of the Campo . . .'

He tapered off, lost in reminiscence. I shifted my weight from one foot to the other, prepared to take my leave.

'I just didn't attach any significance to the phone call at the time.'

'What phone call? From Deborah?' I couldn't help myself being interested now that I was getting an eye-witness acount of Nicole's realisation that she could be found out.

'She just came back and she was very quiet and I asked her if she was all right, was it bad news, and she just said, "I don't know, Bill. My stepdaughter. A mysterious little madam." But she didn't say anything about Corsica and, well, the conversation just petered out. I didn't really mind because I'd said I'd be back in the office by four-thirty.'

'And that was the last time you spoke to her?' It was a heartless question but it occurred to me that he might have rung her later that evening.

Starling nodded, and then brought himself back to the realm of general tributes. 'It was such a tragic waste. She was such a wonderful woman.'

I didn't agree with him but it was not the time to say so. Instead I gave a sad, contemplative nod and he wandered off. I found myself a stool by the bar and settled down to mull over what Merlin had said and his place in the scheme of things. He seemed to have been very frank, and to have no idea of what she had done. Maybe, but then he saw himself as her confidant and many others agreed. Could he have not known of her hatred of Stuart, and not seen her pleasure at his demise?

It was hard to imagine Nicole committing the murder – despite her confession I could not get a clear picture of that night in my head – but it was even harder to imagine her planning it and executing it alone. Everything about her outburst to Cate suggested a woman driven by passionate hatred and then overcome with remorse, both incompatible with the detailed plot she had followed. And there was still no obvious motive.

Had Merlin not just known but provided motive and plan? It was surprisingly easy to imagine a conversation along the lines of, 'Who will rid me of this turbulent priest?' with him, pretender to the throne, furnishing the details, perhaps participating on the night. Then Nicole, gradually regretting what she had done but unable to talk to her fellow conspirator about it, bound to him forever by their shared guilt. Perhaps suicide was a relief.

'Penny for your thoughts,' Boy said, leaning against the counter beside me.

'Not worth it,' I said as he refilled my glass. Grandmother was gathering herself to leave, and I realised the party had thinned substantially with more abandoned glasses and plates than remaining revellers. I looked for Deborah, whom I had not yet spoken to. She was extricating Charlie from a group by the window, still fastened to his arm. Then she caught my eye and they headed in our direction.

'Alex, thank you for coming.' I offered the usual anodyne commiserations. 'Have you met my father?'

'No,' I said, offering my hand to be firmly gripped by Charlie. His signet ring was cold. 'But I have, of course, seen him before.'

'This is Alex, Daddy, Stuart's brother.'

His eyes, slightly widening, perfectly indicated increased interest. How could you ever have an intimate relationship with an actor? You would have even less idea of whether they meant it than an ordinary person. I reminded myself that, although she had never practiced her craft, Nicole had only met Charlie because she too was an actress.

Deborah's Aunt Jeanette tapped her on the shoulder. 'We're ready to go back to Edgware. Will you come with us or make your own way?'

Deborah hesitated for a moment until, unseen by Jeanette, Charlie made a minute shooing movement against her arm. 'I'll come with you, if that's all right. I'm sorry Alex, Boy,' she added once Jeanette had moved out of earshot, 'but it was a compromise. Family dinner at Aunt Marion's in return for holding a thing for the friends here.' She turned to her father. 'I wish you'd come.'

Charlie raised an eyebrow to me. 'I can't see me and your grandma breaking bread at the same table somehow. Come on, I'll see you out.'

We watched them walk to the head of the stairs, Charlie's arm lightly across her shoulders.

'She obviously adores her daddy still,' Boy said, 'despite the old bugger deserting her.'

'He's the only one she's got.' A thought struck me. 'Are you Nicole's executor as well?'

'Yes, for my sins. But it's not a very complex job. Everything goes to the girl. She had a will before she married Stuart, in which she left her flat to her sister Marion, the only one living in London, to be sold for Deborah's upkeep. Not that it was worth very much, it had been bought with a big mortgage, but of course as property prices rose there was an increasing surplus. Anyway, she left her will like that until she'd been married to Stuart for about three years, despite the fact that the flat had been sold and she'd bought that bloody villa in Corsica. I suppose she was waiting until Deborah was eighteen. Obviously I hadn't drawn up the original will, hadn't even known Nicole at the time, but she came to me and said she wanted to sort it out. I thought she was going to make provision for Stuart but she didn't, just left everything to the girl.'

'Which must be quite a bit.'

'Well, Nicole didn't have much in her own right until Stuart died apart from the villa and one or two bits and pieces, but now there's also the flat in Primrose Hill worth maybe £150,000, the rest of the proceeds of Stirton Hall, another £300,000, the investments which, together with the ones Stuart left Deborah herself, must give the girl an income of about forty thou a year, and a good £200,000 in cash which Nicole got on Stuart's life insurance and which she hadn't reinvested, despite my best efforts. Of course under the circumstances Nicole's own life insurance policy is worthless.'

'Of course.'

'Nevertheless, Deborah's a very wealthy young lady. I just hope she doesn't squander it.' Boy was back on his hobbyhorse of women's potential for falling prey to fortune hunters. 'Oddly enough,' he added, as Molly arrived with the air of a woman intent on hearth and home, 'I thought she was going to do something about that, not long after Stuart died. At any rate she rang me and said she wanted to alter her will . . .'

I waited but he seemed to have stopped. 'And?'

'And what?' Molly asked.

'Oh, nothing,' her husband said, and then, over her head to me, 'she missed one appointment and then cancelled another. I presumed she'd changed her mind. Perhaps she thought Deborah was mature enough to cope.' And he shook his head at such folly.

'How do I put up with it?' Molly asked me, although whether she meant Boy's attitude to women in general or his dismissive treatment of her in particular was unclear. 'Are you staying, Alex, or can we give you a lift anywhere?'

As Boy was pointing out that they hadn't got the car and Molly was explaining patiently that she meant the sharing of a taxi, Charlie Makepeace, who had returned to the bar, said quietly, 'Have a drink with me, if you've got nothing more pressing to do.'

I accepted, and bade Molly and Boy farewell. Charlie was ordering large Scotches, and a couple of beers to go with them. 'I'm not in London often,' he said, 'and I thought I'd want to look up some old acquaintances tonight, but I find now I'm not in the mood for a rumbustious evening at Langan's.'

'I'm not surprised.'

'Oh, I'm very resilient. Not one to be knocked out by a small thing like the death of an ex-wife.'

I thought that for some reason he was trying to shock. 'It wasn't so much the funeral,' I said, 'more that Langan's at any time is pretty appalling. Unless you're desperate to be noticed. And I would have thought you'd passed that.'

He laughed. 'You're never past that if you're an actor. Not really.' He rubbed his cleanshaven chin reflectively and I remembered that the last time I had seen him on TV he had had a beard. 'Have you been married?' he asked.

Unusual to assume it was over, unless he knew from Deborah that I lived alone, or unless you had been divorced as often as Charlie. 'No,' I said, 'but an unconfirmed bachelor.'

'Be careful if you try it. It's habit-forming. I seem to be about to tie the knot for the fourth time.'

'Didn't, er—'

'Staten,' he interjected helpfully.

'—Staten come with you?' I suddenly remembered Deborah saying last year that when she had had dinner with Charlie, he had been acompanied by this seventeen-year-old rather than his third wife, Dory. For a second I wondered if he had, now that he was committed to Staten, brought her eventual successor across the pond, but that seemed an ingenue too far even for him.

'No, she's giving my credit cards a pasting back home in Beverley Hills.' He seemed resigned to his fate.

Bill Starling trotted past saying, 'Ah, Charlie, I must ring the paper and then we can have a proper chat.'

Charlie nodded, smiling and then drained his glasses. 'Fancy continuing elsewhere? It's just that the thought of an hour with gloomy old Bill makes even Langan's a scintillating prospect.'

Without much knowing why I followed him down the stairs, into a taxi, and into the American bar at the Savoy.

'I'd much prefer a smoky old pub,' he said, 'but we'd be plagued by autograph hunters.' He laughed his rich throaty chuckle. 'I should hope. One of the penalties of fame, you have to drink somewhere expensive enough to keep out the masses.' He raised his glass, this time a family-size vodka martini. 'Here's to Merlin.'

'He was very fond of Nicole,' I said. 'And very . . . loyal.'

'And you wonder if she ever let him inside her knickers?'

'Don't beat about the bush, Charlie.'

'I'm sure he never beat about hers. Oh, I know, we can never imagine our women entertaining lesser men, but I'm certain about Nicole. She likes . . . liked . . . her blokes headstrong, like me and, I guess, like your brother. Merlin's too prissy. Too afraid to ask for what he wanted, let alone take it.'

So this was Charlie Makepeace, the sexual highwayman, red in tooth and claw, and that was another nail in the coffin of the Starling theory. Charlie talked a lot about Nicole that evening but none of it helped clear the muddied waters: if anything it stirred them up. Unwittingly he sank the notion that she might have killed Stuart for being unfaithful. Nicole was spirited but a sport, he averred: the worst she had dealt out in punishment for his various affairs was the occasional black eye, delivered in the heat of the moment, often by the agency of a saucepan or other kitchen implement. A far cry from premeditated murder.

In any case, if Stuart had had a mistress, who was she, where was she and why had I never come across her?

So, I asked Charlie, when we had seen off another pitcher, toyed with the idea of eating and abandoned it as too complicated, did he find the age gap a problem?

'No,' he chuckled. 'Better bodies. More pliable, or do I mean friable?'

'Easily persuaded or apt to crumble?'

He threw back his head and laughed. 'I think I mean both. Built-in obsolescence. But I don't have a problem with that, and neither have they until their friability is fried. They can't take it.'

'It must be difficult,' I said, 'to accept that your usefulness is at an end just because you've got a couple of crow's feet.' None of Charlie's wives had had the chance to do any serious ageing. 'After all, where would we be if the same standards were applied to us?'

'Too true. Absolutely nowhere. But it's funny, they've all been able to put up with me being an absolute bastard, particularly Nicole. Even when Ali got pregnant, I don't think Nicole would have chucked me out if only they'd been more of an age. She would have thrown a few things and then considered it in a civilised fashion. It was just the fact that she was thirty and Ali was eighteen that made it impossible for her to accept. Silly, really.'

'Well,' I said, unable to agree but unwilling to argue, 'better luck next time.' And soon after that I took a taxi home. All in all I had learnt very little of use about the whys and wherefores of Stuart's murder or about the one subject, acting aside, in which Charlie Makepeace could claim world-class experience – conducting relationships with women half his age. Somehow I didn't see him as a great rôle model.

The only bright spot was that Superintendent Cromarty, who seemed to make a habit of hanging around funerals, had not been in evidence. I fervently hoped that, Deborah being the sole beneficiary of the will, he would stop sniffing around Nicole's suicide as if hoping to unearth some illicit gain. There wasn't one and he couldn't stumble on the solution to Stuart's murder, no matter how much he truffled away, but it would be less wearing for Cate and me and our secret life if he wasn't trying.

Chapter Seventeen

It was hard getting used to Cate not being around. I had known her for eight months and we had been lovers for less than five weeks. But that, I told myself, had to be that. No good could come of it.

Obviously I didn't tell her so. I knew she would disagree, and I would be secretly glad that she disagreed. Instead I remained affectionate but not always available, helped by a distance of two hundred and eighty-five miles, and the fact that she only had a phone on the next but one college landing.

At first she rang every evening; I took to leaving the answerphone on every other evening even if I was in. She played her hand well, careful not to ask directly where I had been, gradually adapting her calls to match their success rate.

After a fortnight she said that she had thought she might come down for the weekend. I said it was a shame I had to go to Dublin to see a client.

'Oh.' The silence carried a dead weight of disappointment and I resisted the impulse to offer to drive up the next weekend. She brightened: 'Couldn't I come with you? After all, I am an employee. I've got a salary and a car to prove it.'

'It would mean four days off for you. Not a very good idea with your exams coming up, is it?'

'Not if I met you there. I'm sure I could fly from Newcastle or somewhere.'

'And anyway,' I continued, as if these two excuses were part of the same sentence, 'the thing's at a very early stage. I'm not sure if Costelloe would be happy to have anyone else around.'

'I could just hang around in the hotel until . . . no, forget it, I'm sorry, I'm being stupid. It would be nice if you could come up here some time though. You know, like you did last term.'

Had Cate accompanied me to Dublin she would have seen that my business with Eamon Costelloe could have been accomplished in one hour on any weekday afternoon. True, he took me to Shelbourne Park on the Saturday night to watch one of his latest acquisitions win an ugly little trophy and a hundred quid, and on to one of the basement night clubs in Leesom Street afterwards, but I was only one of a triumphant party of eleven. We had made free with the Guinness and Jameson chasers at the track, and after Eamon's dog had crossed the line moved on to champagne by way of Black Velvet.

'Do yourself a favour, Alex,' he told me for the third time that night. 'Put a grand on the Mighty Atom in the Derby. I have a feeling in my water that this year is going to be my year.'

Eamon had had that feeling for ten years, during the course of which, it was rumoured, he had spent a million pounds on Greyhound Derby prospects, so far without success.

'Are you sure that feeling is not the collision of whisky and Veuve Cliquot?'

'You're a sanctimonious old Presbyterian at heart, Alex,' he roared, and clapped me on the back, soaking my shirt.

I took my cue. 'I am, and as it's three o'clock I'm away to my bed. Thanks for a great night out.'

'It's been a pleasure doing business with you, as always, Mr Buchan. And don't forget, accept nothing less than fifty-to-one.'

It was a cold night, but bright, so I walked back along the canal to Ballsbridge, where I was staying. The lights on the water reminded me of Christmas night in Eastbourne, when I had played ducks and drakes and got my feet wet with Cate sitting on the breakwater watching.

I stopped on the lock gates and smoked a cigarette. Back the way I had come occasional taxis cruised across the bridge, and the wind brought the calls of a band of revellers, homeward bound, but down here it was quiet, the houses curtained and mostly in darkness. I leaned over the railing and stared down into the tarry depths of the canal, and it reminded me of the winter's day Cate and I had stood on Prebends Bridge in Durham, her in tears, me comforting her.

Back in my hotel room I poured the mini-bar's three miniatures of Black Bush into my tooth glass and dialled the college pay phone. Fifty-four rings before someone answered, an improvement on the last time I had tried it. Considering the hour they were surprisingly civil.

'I'm sorry to disturb you. I need to speak to Cate Buchan. She's in J3.'

'Is it an emergency? I mean, it's quarter to four.'

'It is, rather.'

'OK. I'll see if she's there.' After a long pause, during which I fancied I could hear the sounds of snoring muffled by an inadequate breezeblock bedroom wall, there came the unmistakeable delayed slam of a swing door. 'No answer. Do you want to leave a message or something.'

'No, no message.'

'Are you sure, I mean, if it's urgent?' My Good Samaritan was obviously waking and warming to her task, but when I demurred again she took umbrage and more or less slammed the phone down.

For a moment or two, long-forgotten emotions surged around my system. Not in at four in the morning? What was she doing and who was she doing it with? A remarkably graphic mental picture of her doing it with somebody far younger and more athletic than myself was extremely hard to blot out. I had another whiskey and composed myself. She was a student, for God's sake. Staying out till four in the morning was one of the points of going to university, it was something you did as a matter of course, it didn't necessarily imply that you were lying naked in the arms of another . . . And, I reminded myself, even if she was then that, surely, was what I wanted, wasn't it? Then I could get back to normal life.

By breakfast time I had got as far as admitting unconditionally that it wasn't what I wanted but that it was bound to happen anyway, eventually, so I might as well help the process along. After all, like removing a plaster, the longer it took, the more it would hurt.

Another week passed, another three telephone conversations in which I filled up the time talking about the business, places I had been, people I had seen, and Cate answered questions about her revision and her social life in monosyllables. She sounded tired and irritable. Then, on the Sunday evening, when I was telling her about a prospective client in Edinburgh, she said, 'Can you stop off here on your way up or down, it doesn't matter which? Please?' There was no attempt to disguise the desperation in that last plea.

I steeled myself. 'The thing is,' I said, 'you're so close to your exams now, you need all that time for revision.'

'How am I supposed to revise when I'm worrying about you?'

'About me? There's nothing to worry about with me.'

'Of course there is.' Her voice rushed down the line. 'What you're thinking about me, why you won't see me, that you don't . . . well . . . care for me any more.'

I sensed her skirting round the word love, not wanting to introduce it into the conversation in case it was dismissed. I took a deep breath.

'If you don't come,' she said quietly, 'I'm going to fail anyway, I can't concentrate on it. Please come. Please.'

'Of course I will,' I said before I could stop myself. 'As long as you promise to work in the meantime.'

A strategy so easily destroyed by a couple of sentences had to be fundamentally flawed. The future would have to take care of itself. As soon as I accepted that, unalloyed pleasure at the prospect of seeing Cate again flooded in. I deferred it until after my Edinburgh meeting, telling her that I would catch an early train south to Durham on the Saturday morning. In the event the dinner I had expected to have with the client failed to materialize, but despite the pall this cast over the prospects of our getting his business, I was in a state of happy anticipation. I wandered through Princes Gardens in the early evening sunshine, amongst homeward-bound office workers. The benches were occupied not only by little old ladies and loudly-checked American tourists, but also by besuited men incongruously munching on ice cream cornets.

I went into a place at the east end of the gardens, an uneasy cross between a brasserie and a cocktail bar, with greeters whose designer silk ties and deferential manner could not disguise their muscle power or true function. It was hard to imagine the polite, middle-class crowd inside getting into fights so perhaps the bouncers' job was to keep out the winos hanging around outside the National Gallery. I sat at a window table, looking up at the grey silhouette of the castle on its mound, alone but subsumed into the collective buzz of there being a whole free, hot, weekend ahead. After a beer I walked up to the castle where the stands were being erected for the annual Military Tattoo, and sat watching the hustle and bustle far below on Princes Street. The trains pulling out of Waverley Station, passing absurdly through the centre of the gardens with their bandstands and gaily coloured flower beds, made me think of Cate, fourteen hours away. Too restless to eat immediately I wandered down the Royal Mile and the streets between the castle and the Grassmarket, studying menus, unsually unable to get excited about wild salmon or haggis, eventually settling on an American diner, its walls covered with old gasoline signs and baseball pennants, where I munched a chilliburger to the accompaniment of a Madonna in concert video. She looked nothing like Cate but it didn't take much, just the half-similarity of her peroxide mop to Cate's strawberry blonde, to start the replay of edited highlights of our relationship.

The next morning, sitting on the train, slicing through Northumbria, on time, I tried to imagine what she would be doing. Waking as I passed through Berwick, unlocking her car as I left Newcastle, parking at the station as Chester-le-Street shot past. As the 125 slowed into Durham, I looked for her on the platform. She was about halfway down, her pale cotton trousers and loose, sleeveless top blowing in the breeze, the edge of her thumb resting against her teeth as she watched the train pull in. For some reason first class is always at the front so my carriage rolled past her, but when I got out she was still facing away from me, scanning the few passengers alighting from the rear of the train. I walked up behind her and touched her lightly on the shoulder. She twitched and squeaked with surprise and then she had slammed herself into my arms and her head into my neck.

After about five minutes, when the train had left for London and I finally had a free mouth, I said, 'Well, we've got this place to ourselves . . . now . . . but I take it you don't just want to stay here until the next train comes and then wave me onto it.'

She laughed. 'No. Shall we go and have some coffee?'

'Where?'

'My room, of course. I don't want to share you with anyone just yet.'

In the car I surreptitiously studied her as she drove. She looked exhausted. Her eyes were animated but a little bloodshot, and beneath them grey stains defied her uncharacteristic foundation. The scarring of a couple of spots on her chin, viciously annihilated that morning I guessed, reminded me of the last time she had met me from the station. Like a mindreader she said, 'You look well.'

I toyed with the idea of lying to her, but it was such a clichéd insincerity I didn't. 'You don't.'

She took her eyes off the road and searched mine for reassurance. 'Beautiful,' I said, 'but not well.'

Relieved, she said, 'Not beautiful. Too many chips. Too much chocolate.'

In the college car park she picked up my overnight bag. 'No,' I said, 'lock it in the boot. I don't want them thinking I'm staying.'

She smiled. 'I don't suppose the porter would care.'

'Really? I bet he worries more about you young ladies and your moral welfare than any of the tutors.'

As we passed him at the desk, a squat Geordie in his sixties with a sleeveless pullover and surprising, captain of industry half-moon spectacles, she sang out 'Hello Albert' and he grunted in reply. As soon as the swing door had put him out of earshot she giggled. 'I think you're right. He gave you a very old-fashioned look.'

We climbed the stairs in silence. Cate's landing was empty, the only sign of life the muted sound of a Smiths album from one of the study bedrooms. She unlocked her door, pushed it open, ushered me in.

The curtains were drawn, so it was in deep brown Victorian semi-darkness. The beds were neatly made, the air was heavy with the smell of perfume, talc and washing, feminine smells. 'Sit down,' she said and gestured to one of the beds – hers, I recognised the alarm clock. I sat somewhat self-consciously on it while she filled the kettle at the sink and, when she thought I wasn't looking, swept away a couple of pairs of knickers drying on the radiator.

'How's Emma?' I said.

'OK.' She started to tell me about Emma's part in a college revue while fussing with the cups.

I stood up and walked to the window, wary of the small gaps between the furniture, feeling too big for the room. I parted the curtains a sliver.

'Don't open them,' she said immediately.

'All right.' I let the thin material drop.

'I don't want them spying on us.'

I supposed she had a point. The rooms were arranged around polygonal yards so small that it was almost possible to pass cups of sugar from window to window. I returned to the bed and she came and sat next to me, putting the coffee on the bedside table.

'Are you staying?' she said. 'I don't mean here but at the County or somewhere.'

'I don't think so,' I said. 'I'll catch the last train tonight.' She looked crestfallen. I put an arm round her. 'You really do need the time. But I promise I'll see you as soon as your exams are over.'

She kissed me, and then let herself go so that she subsided onto the mattress, pulling me down on top of her. 'I've missed you,' she mumbled.

'Ditto.'

She started to unbutton my shirt.

'What about Emma?'

'Promised to be out all day.' She smirked. 'You don't think I really asked you back for coffee, did you? And I haven't got any etchings to show you. My motives are entirely dishonourable. Albert would be shocked.'

'What a smooth operator you are. No wonder you wanted the curtains drawn.'

She wriggled and started to unbutton her own top.

'It's all right,' I said, 'I'll do that.'

It was strange at first, rolling around on a college bed again, but as I entered Cate not only did the complications slip away but also the years, until I was twenty and we were at one, free to do whatever we wanted.

'Yes,' she said.

It was like moving underwater, in summer air thick with heat and the weak light seeping from beyond the curtains and beneath the door, the surfaces of our world.

'Yes,' she said.

I felt the sweat prickling between my shoulderblades and a runnel at the base of my spine. Strands of Cate's hair were sticking to her forehead.

'Yes, yes,' she said quietly but with concentration, squeezing the words out.

The knock at the door might as well have been a cattle prod. We jerked convulsively and then froze, me as if at the uppermost point of a press-up, Cate with one arm gripping the bedhead, one knee raised and the other foot hooked over my shoulder.

'Emma? Cate?' the voice said softly – as if they might be asleep – but insistently – as if determined to wake them in the most considerate way possible.

We gazed at each other, shocked.

'Bugger,' said the voice. 'Why haven't you got a message board, you silly people?'

My left arm quivered and the bed creaked. Cate's eyes flickered with amusement.

There followed the unmistakeable sounds of someone dropping a bag and rummaging through it, presumably looking for pencil and paper. 'I don't know why I'm bothering to leave a note really,' the voice mused. 'You'll probably say you're too busy to come.'

Cate stuffed her free hand into her mouth to stifle a giggle.

A piece of paper, with a Snoopy motif, slid under the door and footsteps retreated across the landing. Several moments too soon Cate let out a hoot of laughter and I subsided on her, half-expecting the voice to make an irate return.

'Shhhhh. Who was that?'

'Oh, just Anna. Probably a meeting about the end-of-term revue. Trust her to butt in at precisely the wrong time. You don't think she realized we were in here, do you?'

'Who knows? That snorting great laugh of yours could probably be heard three landings away.' I had an unwelcome, fleeting vision of opening the door to meet the accusing eyes of a gaggle of college tutors, including those of the principal who had so reasonably given Cate one last chance in December.

Cate's concerns seemed somewhat different. 'You don't . . . you don't think she was listening at the keyhole before she knocked, do you?'

'No,' I said. 'If you heard two people at it, any normal person would just creep away, surely?'

'Yes,' she said, suddenly sombre. 'I suppose you're right . . . Aaaaaahhhh!' She sat bolt upright.

'What's the matter?'

'Cramp . . . aaagggghhh . . . in my foot.'

And by the time I had rubbed it better it seemed sensible, or at least imperative, to finish what had been so rudely interrupted.

Eventually Cate lifted her head from its resting place on my chest and reached for her mug. 'Eeuurgh, it's stone cold.'

'Well, what do you expect,' I said, glancing at the clock. 'You made it an hour ago.'

'I'm thirsty. Do you want another coffee?'

'A coffee full stop, you mean. Yes please, or we could go out and get a glass of wine or something somewhere if you like.'

'Not just yet.'

I watched her as, naked, she crossed the room to the kettle and then it suddenly occurred to her that I was doing this. She swung her bottom away from me, pressed her thighs together and wrapped her arms across her midriff, which made it hard to bend and switch the plug on. 'Don't look at me,' she said. 'I've put on half a stone.'

It was true, she had; her belly was more rounded and there was a touch extra wadding on buttocks and thighs, presumably a result of the chips and chocolate she had mentioned in the car. But she was no less beautiful, and at her age a week of constructive exam panic would take the weight off again. I was about to dismiss it when I thought it would sound too much like a forced compliment. Instead I rolled on to my front and said, 'So you won't be wanting any lunch or dinner before I go then.'

She dropped on me, knocking the breath from my body, and straddled my back. 'Don't tease me.'

I tried to turn my head around but with her strong arms she pushed it face down into the pillow. 'And don't look at me.'

'Apart from the fact that I like looking at you,' I spluttered, 'not being able to would make our relationship very difficult.'

'You can once I've been on a diet – which will start tomorrow when you leave me all alone with my revision,' she said, but she sounded quite happy about it, even when she added: 'Flab's so horrible.'

'But all the better to crush me with,' I mumbled through the tickling feathers threatening my nostrils.

She bit my ear.

'What big teeth you have, Grandma.'

I got the message that Cate was 'back to normal weight, and desperate to be looked at, oh, and guess what, I've passed the dreaded Prelims so I won't be hanging around the office for the next two years, more's the pity', when I arrived home from some charity ball, rumpled and sticky from six hours in a dinner jacket. I wanted to ring her there and then to congratulate her but it was too late, or perhaps I just didn't want to risk finding her out like last time. Instead I decided to pay a surprise visit the next day.

I had resolved never again to lie on Cate's college bed, regardless of Emma's guaranteed absence, so I took a taxi from the station to the Royal County Hotel and dumped my overnight bag there before setting off for St Catherine's.

The oldest part of Durham is built on a peninsula formed by a kink in the River Wear, which I crossed for the first time by Elvet Bridge, looking down on the holidaymakers hiring rowing boats below, and then turned left along the Bailey, past a smattering of pubs, shops and cafés, far more touristy than when I had been an undergraduate. I caught a glimpse of the dark bulk of the cathedral up a cobbled side street, and passed the Assembly Rooms where the operatic society were mounting a production of *The Cunning Little Vixen*, then the entrance to the cathedral close, of paler, honeyed stone, and the blistered sash windows and institutional drainpipes of the older colleges, St Chad's and St John's, their open doors emitting tantalising whiffs of cool, echoing interiors as churchlike as the cathedral itself. Then I was heading down again towards my second Wear crossing; one last bend, one last neo-gothic arch and I was above the densely wooded river bank, not so much a riot of colour as a rich exercise in minimalism, twenty different shades of green occasionally made gaudy by the direct hit of sunlight. The overpowering scent of wild garlic hung heavy in the still, midday air. I descended to Prebends Bridge, catching the first breeze since Elvet, and leant, as so often before, over the parapet. A couple of rowing boats drifted lazily downstream and a sculling pair, working against the current, cut between them, disturbing the perfect reflection of trees and clouds.

On the bank which I had just left, a student picnic party had settled on the expanse of grass between the towpath and the water, just as we had done in summers past and, Durham never having been at the forefront of fashion and the heat being a great leveller, they looked much as my generation might have done: Hoorays and Sloanes, theologians and engineers alike wearing bright T-shirts and sundresses. What was different was the spread, laid out on white tablecloths. My memories were of pasties from the bakers and dry cider, but here there were bottles of rosé, elaborate dishes of Mediterranean vegetables, chicken legs and what looked suspiciously like a pile of quail's eggs.

Strangely it was Emma that I recognised first, head thrown back, laughing at the joke of a boy in baggy shorts and a vest which informed us that he had been to the British Virgin Islands. Then I spotted Cate, rolling over to reach for a peach, returning to a conversation with a circle sitting crosslegged like a class outing. I fixed on the back of her head, wondering whether I could prove the theory that someone being watched eventually senses it, but I was beaten by one of her companions who nudged her and nodded in my direction. They all stared, so I raised a hand and then Cate was scrambling to her feet, running towards me, hitting me with a whirlwind of flailing limbs and exclamations. Her compatriots looked on with undisguised curiosity until it was obvious that Emma had offered an explanation of my presence. I wondered precisely what that was.

'So now what?' I asked as we leant against the parapet, her initial surprise, my congratulations, our endearments spent.

'Take me away from all this,' she said.

'If you like,' I said. 'But it's very pretty and you were in the middle of lunch.'

'Not this, not now.' She waved her arm around. 'This is lovely and you can come and meet everybody.'

'If you're sure,' I said, 'but what am I?'

'My friend,' she said, shooting me one of those complicitous little grins. 'That should do.'

'As long as it matches what Emma's told them.'

'Don't worry about her. She won't spill the beans.'

So she knew then. This raised all sorts of questions but now was evidently not the time to ask them.

'Anyway, you're changing the subject.'

'OK. Take you away from all what when then?'

'I just thought,' she said, stroking my hand, 'that we might both deserve a holiday.'

'And where might we go?'

'Well, you can choose, of course, but I quite fancy Thailand.'
'I see.'
She grinned cheekily. 'You mustn't worry about the money. I'll pay. I'm a woman of independent means, you know.'

Chapter Eighteen

When we left Heathrow we were both excited but, business class notwithstanding, a fifteen-hour flight takes it out of you and somehow we had contrived to arrive at Bangkok at nine in the morning. We passed from the nippy air conditioning of the plane to the chilly air conditioning of the terminal and then the positively arctic interior of our taxi, the cold emphasised by two intervening blasts of tropical humidity. The taxi eased itself into the slowly moving queue of traffic pushing into the city.

As in countless other airport approaches international brandnames coupled with unfamiliar local advertising slogans shouted at us from billboards, grey office blocks were randomly scattered about the roadside scrub – only the palm trees held the promise of anything exotic or interesting. I wished it was the middle of the night – not only would this tedious drive have been a mysterious blur of neon and shadows but the prospect of a long sleep would have soothed our scratchy tempers.

Cate had pulled her jacket around her shoulders and snuggled against my shoulder, certain there would be nothing worth looking at. The buildings slowly crowded in, taller, more colourful; then there were pavements and people; open shopfronts with vegetables or motor cycle parts; heavy power cables slung across the road at seemingly little more than lorry height; street sellers cooking satay over braziers; and suddenly we were swinging up a ramp and the driver was saying 'Royal River.'

Before the Honda had drawn to a halt my door was opened by an admiral of the Thai fleet – gold buttons and braid competing with his crisp whiter-than-whites to dazzle us. Only the lack of campaign medals gave him away as the commissionaire. His white-gloved hands plucked our luggage from the boot and as I fumbled with the unfamiliar currency, Cate stumbled after the swinging tassels of his epaulettes through the smoked glass entrance of the hotel. Having delivered us to the reception desk he touched the glistening peak of his cap and resumed his watch in the hot sun.

With smiles the receptionist entrusted us to the bell captain and with a snap of his fingers he summoned two minions – one to show us to our room and another to bring our luggage, considered unworthy to travel in the same lift. Less than five minutes after stepping from the taxi we were alone in our enormous room. Had it not been for the gigantic bed with elborately carved teak head and silk spread, the floor area could have induced agrophobia. The desk and television set huddled for comfort against the far wall, the armchairs and coffee table sat, embarrassed, in a sea of beige carpet which intensified the vaguely fungoid smell.

'Wow,' Cate said, sliding one of the built–in wardrobe doors. 'I don't think we've brought enough clothes.' She sniffed. 'What is that smell? It was in the corridor as well.'

'Rotting, I should think. It must be so humid that the carpets are disintegrating from the moment they're laid.' I opened the blinds and we blinked in the brilliant light. Beyond the net curtains were glass doors and a balcony with wrought-iron table and a climbing plant.

I stepped outside. Ten floors below lapped the rusty, muddy waters of the Chao Phraya River, a quarter of a mile wide, teeming with life. Strings of industrial barges plodded, elephantine, in mid-stream; ferries criss-crossed from landing stage to landing stage, the first wave of passengers leaping with great aplomb across the narrowing gap to the jetty at each stop. Around the larger vessels tiny canoes, peddling fruit or drinks, danced attendance, so fragile they seemed threatened by every bow wash, let alone the bows themselves.

Beyond the far bank, under a haze of exhaust fumes trapped in the still air, was the sprawl of Bangkok with, away to the right, the glinting golden roofs of the Royal Palace and accompanying pagodas. The view reinvigorated me. 'What do you want to do now?'

Cate flapped her shirt, reminding me of how grimy I felt. 'I'm going to unpack,' she said, with a certain relish. I had noticed how she had enjoyed filling the suitcases in Camberwell, deliberately mingling our clothes for the first time.

'OK, I'll have a shower then.' I stood under the jets for a long time, purging my body of the journey and the last shreds of fatigue, looking forward to stepping out into the city. But when I came out of the bathroom the bedroom was once again in semi-darkness, the silk bedspread draped across a chair and Cate, fully dressed, fast asleep. Quietly I got myself a beer from the fridge and went to sit on the balcony.

That afternoon we did the obvious thing and visited the Royal Palace. In one of its pungent temples we stood for a long time before the heavy golden Buddha, until the incense overpowered me and I retreated outside, waiting for Cate among the mirrored mosaic pillars, taking too many photos, as one does. When she finally emerged she seemed preoccupied, a mood that persisted as we walked back through a maze of narrow streets to the ferry.

'What's the matter?'

She leaned her head against mine for a fraction of a second, and then turned to look out at the water, easily taller than most of the Thais between her and the deck rail. 'Don't take this the wrong way,' she said, 'but I'd like to get a ring.'

I knew immediately what she meant. Perhaps I was paranoid but I thought I had detected a second's puzzlement from the woman at the reception desk when we checked in. Our passports showed that we had the same name and we were sharing a room but there was no wedding ring on the appropriate finger. I suppose it could have been worse, her passport photo depicting her as an idiot child; in fact it was an uncomfortable sixteen-year-old scowling in the picture.

'It's a good idea,' I said, shoving the symbolism as far back as it would go, which wasn't very far. 'It will save any embarrassment.'

She squeezed my hand. 'I knew you'd understand. I promise I won't wear it anywhere else but here.'

We went into one of the city's cavernous shopping blocks where, amongst the windows full of beaten brassware, carved ivory, bolts of silk and serried ranks of the local, pointy-headed version of Buddha, we found a jeweller's.

'What about something like this?' I said, pointing at a tray of intricately-wrought pale rings in the generic style of many of her earrings.

'No,' she said, 'it has to be a bog-standard gold band, otherwise people will keep asking questions about it.' Once again I could see she was right; people did examine engagement rings at parties but who were we likely to meet here? 'But they are beautiful.' And so it was that Cate ended up with the plain band on the third finger of her left hand and the other on the third finger of her right.

And of course we did meet people. Not in the Royal River, which like most international hotels was as easy to disappear in as a jungle but when, after a couple of days, we decided we had had enough of the capital and would go up country. We hired an air-conditioned car and ventured out onto roads which, as soon as the Bangkok gridlock was passed, became a terrifying free-for-all. A Dutchman we met one night explained that he had been told it was a consequence of religious observance – if you looked over your shoulder before pulling out you might glimpse Buddha – but, as Cate said, that hardly explained the kamikaze three-wheelers coming straight for you on the wrong side of a deserted road. As he and I talked desultorily of the changes containerisation had wrought on the great European ports – I had a shipping client and he worked in Rotterdam – I heard his wife ask Cate how long we had been married.

'Oh, hardly any time at all,' she replied with a becoming awkwardness that the Dutchwoman clearly perceived as shyness.

'Ahh,' she exclaimed, 'so it is your honeymoon.' And her husband gave me one of those 'you old dog' looks and ordered, despite our good-natured protests, a bottle of champagne.

'I'm sorry about that,' Cate said, as soon as we were back in our room. 'But we'll never see them again.'

'No,' I said. 'Anyway, it's quite exciting leading a double life, isn't it?'

'You should know, you did it for years,' she said, and immediately bit her lip. 'I'm sorry, I didn't mean to be bitchy . . . it's just, I mean I draw the line at having to describe our wedding—'

'Very quiet.' I echoed what she had said in the hotel bar.

'—but, well, I mean it is our first holiday together so it is a sort of honeymoon, isn't it?'

And although I lay awake that night worrying about the blurring of fact and fantasy, she was right about that too. It was a sort of honeymoon. We took too many photographs of each other among the red ruins of Ayutthaya, against the sunset spires at Sukhothai, with the temple monkeys and fighting kites.

We rode elephants through the hills to a camp in a clearing of stilted huts where, after a barbecue, we sat on our verandah listening to the cacophony of frogs and crickets from beyond the treeline drowning out the hissing of our hurricane lamp, drinking the spicy local whisky and watching the ghostly white-coated retainers picking their way from hut to hut along paths marked by flaming brands.

Abandoning our car we took a noisy long-tailed boat, a canoe powered by a truck engine, up river; we bought hand-painted umbrellas, fake watches and an elephant carved out of a block of teak in Chiang Mai and then, chauffeur-driven in a midget mini-bus, sealed behind tinted windows, we entered the Golden Triangle where, for the first time in ten days, I thought of Stuart. We had heard from our guide that the poppy problem was much exaggerated these days, that the Thai government had the situation under control, that the heroin supplied to the west was much more likely to come from Burma or Laos. We had stood overlooking the apparently uninhabited jungle of both of those countries across the Mekong River, along the turbulent brown waters of which a dilapidated tramp steamer ploughed its lonely furrow. We had even sampled the officially sanctioned delights of the opium pipe in one of the village's souvenir shops and were on our way back to Chiang Rai when, rounding a corner, we came across a small collection of bungalows. Not Asian bungalows, but of the type that might be found in one of England's south-coast resorts where the buyers of architect-designed retirement homes have a penchant for exotic detailing to complement the red brick and alpine plants. So, a corner of a foreign field that was, to all intents and purposes, England, until around the corner of one of the bungalows – from about where the car port would have been had there been any necessity for a car port – came two men with submachine guns; guards who were clearly no more policemen than the bungalows were those of public officials. They gave us on the road a casual, dismissive glance – more tourists getting a vicarious kick out of their glimpse of the home life of the drug barons – which made one wonder whether there might be other areas of endeavour unofficially officially sanctioned on a strictly local basis. And suddenly this mixture of the deadly and the banal, Eastbourne as war zone, brought Stuart to mind and I felt uncomfortably cold, in a way that could not be attributed to the air conditioning, until we reached the hotel.

It was an isolated outbreak. The next day we flew south, the reflection of our Fokker perfectly mirrored in the paddy fields, back to Bangkok but it seemed stifling after the expanse of the country and within twenty-four hours we were on the move again, looking for somewhere to unwind and unravel the tangled memories of our whistlestop tour.

We took a small villa within a resort complex outside Hua Hin. Only a couple of palm trees and a low wall separated us from the beach of white sand and the crashing rollers beyond. Behind us, through a cordon sanitaire of manicured gardens, were the hotel's bars, restaurants and pools. During the day we mostly lay on loungers on the deck, reading, rubbing suntan lotion into each other's skins, petting the tame baby elephants that wandered the poolside, taking the occasional swim or Singha beer to cool off. In the evenings we mostly ate in one of the restaurants, walking slowly back by the deserted pool, its surface an electric, melancholy blue beneath the floodlights, slipping into the warm shadows of the trees, the soft lamplight of our room, and the hypnotic glow of the next embrace.

The pictures show Cate, heavily freckled, in her austere black swimming costume, and smiling from behind an enormous steamed river fish, but not Cate leaning back against the trunk of a palm, her sarong parting to reveal a tanned thigh, or Cate rolling over in the cold midnight sand and saying, 'Let's just stay out here', which we did until one of the inquisitive beach dogs gatecrashed the party.

We were happy and so contented that I worried what effect the strictures of England would have, but Cate adjusted very well. She took to coming into the office every day, working hard to learn about the business. She was quick, bright and, as far as I could tell, popular with Buccaneer's employees and those clients to whom I introduced her. She was the soul of physical discretion everywhere except our house and seemed without a care in the world.

After a couple of weeks she announced that she had to go up to Durham for a few days. This seemed such an odd thing for a student to do in the middle of their summer vacation that I couldn't help asking why.

'None of your business,' she said with as much cod mystery as she could muster. 'All will be revealed in good time.'

'Don't tell me – you didn't pass your exams after all. You've got to do retakes.'

'What a preposterous suggestion. Are you accusing me of being stupid?'

'No,' I said. I went to the stove to tend the vegetables.

'You're not going to sulk until I tell you, are you?'

'No, it's beneath my dignity. I just won't give you any of this asparagus.'

I thought that patience would bring its own reward, but when she returned no explanation of her trip was forthcoming. I thought that deliberately ignoring her second absence, to the point of not even asking her if she had had a good time, would draw her into the open, but no. Every so often businesslike envelopes of varying thicknesses arrived for her and were spirited away to the privacy of her room. When she announced her third disappearance I felt my hackles rising but bit my tongue. The worst thing was, it was a Thursday and I particularly resented her being away at the weekend, but on Friday evening she rang. 'Can you come up on the early train, it's desperately important?'

'Christ, you're not in trouble, are you?'

'Why do you always assume that?' she demanded petulantly.

'I can't imagine.'

'Oh, don't be like that. I promise, you'll be really pleased.'

'I suppose that's better than being really mystified. Give me a clue.'

'No.'

'In that case . . .'

Cate changed tack. 'Oh please, please come. If you do we can do anything you like with the rest of the weekend.'

'Anything?'

'Absolutely anything. I'll be your slave.'

'Well—'

'Oh thank you.'

'—of course there won't be much of the weekend left by the time I've plodded three hundred miles and back—'

She shrieked with exasperation.

'See you at eleven,' I said with more *sangfroid* than I felt. 'Collect me from the station.'

She was there, but when we reached the car park there was no sign of the Mazda. 'Don't worry,' Cate said. 'It's not very far.'

We walked down the hill and across the roundabout at the top of North Road more or less in silence while I worked through a range of possibilities. When we set off between the Victorian terraces of Atherton Street, still within the shadow of the railway viaduct, a suspicion began to solidify. The 'Sold subject to contract' sign set it. 'What have you done?'

Cate, who had been almost skipping with excitement, stopped before the last house in the street which, like all the others, had a front door that opened directly onto the pavement and the distinctive Durham first-floor bay. 'I've got a place of my own.' She brandished a key. 'Don't slag it off until you've seen inside.'

I had no intention of doing so. I was, after all, hardly the best person to complain about buying rented property in an unlikely location.

'Of course,' she said ironically after she had shown me around the small front parlour, tiny garden room, the kitchen, scullery, two bedrooms and a bathroom, 'I'm only doing it for your benefit.'

'And how do you make that out?'

'Well, you made it very clear that you wouldn't sleep with me in college again and I was worried that you would be sex-starved once the autumn term started, whereas now . . .'

'Whereas now I am supposed to spend every weekend decorating this slum property.'

'No, you shan't see it again until it's finished. I just wanted to make you fully appreciate the before and after effect.'

She gazed fondly on the small concrete yard, complete with coal bunker and battered dustbin. 'Shall we go and have a toastie at the Elm Tree?' she asked and, when I nodded assent, added: 'By the way, I'm going to need a bit of time off work,' before running into the hall.

I was proud of her. She had paid a good price and, beyond the high brick wall at the end of her yard, were Oliver's, the long-established delicatessen, and the Colpitts pub. There were many worse locations in Durham. She even organized her renovations so that she was in the office three days a week. Life, with the exception of the enduring worry of the recession which, luckily, meant lost sleep rather than lost business, was good.

It was her voice that I expected to hear when the telephone rang on the first Wednesday in September, so before I answered it I switched off the water into which I had been about to drop the pasta, anticipating a long conversation.

'Oh Alex, thank goodness you're there.'

It was Deborah. I felt an immediate flush of guilt for not having rung her, hardly having given her a thought in more than a month. 'How are you?' I asked too effusively, missing, in my embarrassment, her tone of voice.

'Oh . . . er . . . all right. Look, I've had Superintendent Cromarty on the phone.'

What could he have found out? New evidence from the Corsican police? Something missed in translation spotted by a new recruit to the Stoneyheath CID? I felt sick. 'What did he want?'

'He says he thinks they've caught the men that did it. He wants me to attend an identity parade.'

Chapter Nineteen

Working in the advertising and design business provides plenty of practice in the art of responding calmly and circumspectly to any statement, no matter how shocking or ridiculous. 'That's unbelievable,' I said.

Which it was, although apparently not to the Kent constabulary. But then they didn't know that the real perpetrator of the crime had been reduced to ashes by the municipal oven at Kensal Rise and deposited . . . where? In a casket on Deborah's own mantelpiece? It seemed unlikely. Perhaps scattered to the four winds from the top of Primrose Hill; at any rate beyond the long arm of the law.

Unlike this unhappy pair, caught after trying to fence some items stolen from an opulent oasthouse conversion in the Kentish Weald. That was more or less all Deborah had been told before agreeing to go to Stoneyheath the next morning. Understandably she was nervous, thinking that she might confront the villain who had chloroformed her and tied her to the chair in the bathroom, and she wanted me to go with her. I, of course, agreed.

By the time I had put the phone down my mind was racing. The police had clearly made a mistake – whatever else these men had done they had not shot Stuart and taken the petty cash from his desk – and Cromarty would have to be told. But what? For a few minutes I trawled hopelessly for a plausible alternative, then accepted that nothing could explain our certainty that they were innocent other than the full story of Nicole's confession and the inevitable question – why didn't you tell us at the time? Perhaps we could be charged ourselves, although I wasn't sure with what. Withholding evidence, wasting police time, conspiracy to pervert the course of justice? And on top of that, worse than that, Deborah would find out the awful truth about her mother.

I tried to imagine a scenario in which I told Cromarty on some sort of man-to-man, confidential basis but it wouldn't play. Apart from my sense of his suppressed animosity he was a career policeman with an unsolved murder on his record. He could hardly be expected to leave it there, blocking his chance of eventually becoming Deputy Chief Constable and Master of his local Masonic Lodge.

I felt like a schoolboy again, protected by a web of deception that, no matter how frantically I spun more lies, half-truths, circumlocutions or economies, was about to be torn down. The sense of impending doom reminded me of the night before examinations, a realisation that the good impression created by bullshit in the seminar and blatant plagiarism in essays was about to be exposed, and that it was far too late to do anything about it.

Cate rang and, as gently as I could, I explained the situation to her.

'I'll come back now,' she said.

'You'll be driving half the night.'

'So? I seem to remember you doing that for me once.'

I didn't argue, but I knew she wouldn't be back before about three, so I went to bed to try and get a couple of hours' sleep. Inevitably I tossed and turned in the dark, with the chattering radio merely taking the edge off my thoughts, until the examinations analogy gave me a sudden spurt of hope. Sometimes when you turned over the paper the questions were not as bad as you thought, did not, miraculously, require any of the difficult answers. What if this was the same? Deborah had not known what the case was against these men; what if there was some incontrovertible evidence linking them to the Stirton Hall murder, and the identification parade was simply to add ballast to the case? What if they had done it, and Nicole's confession was the imagining of a woman driven over the edge by grief, guilt, depression, a story to spite her unloved stepdaughter?

Trying to convince myself of this I drifted off, to be woken by Cate sliding into bed beside me.

'Sorry, I was trying not to wake you.'

'It's all right, I wasn't really asleep.'

'You were sparked out.' She cuddled up against me.

I asked her about the journey and then, because it was dark, I tried out my theory on her.

Several beats of her quickening heart. 'You might be right . . .' She stopped, the heart slowed, speeded up, slowed again. 'No,' she said, 'that's not right. I wish it was but . . . it's not. Why would she have made up such a story, and even if she was deluded do you think she could have made up details like that?'

'But that's not the issue,' I said. 'She had to be capable of devising the plot – the only question is whether she carried it out or whether she thought of it after the event and made it fit the facts. I would have thought the second was easier.'

'OK. I take your point but I think that's what it is . . . a debating point.'

'You're right,' I said wearily. 'I was just desperate for some way out of this. The only thing we can do is keep you out of it.'

'How?'

'Say it was me that she confessed to. We'd have to readjust the times a bit but otherwise it would work. The motive for keeping it a secret is just the same, only instead of us doing it to protect Deborah, it was me doing it to protect you and Deborah.'

She lay silent for a moment and then lifted herself on an elbow, her face close to mine. I could smell the long drive's chocolate and cigarettes on her breath. 'That's very . . . gallant.' She kissed me, grazing the side of my mouth with her lips, and I thought she was patronizing me until she put her head back on my chest and I felt the wetness of her tears. 'But it won't work. When she sat at the table with me in the villa and told me about . . . about it . . . you were in Sartene, waiting for that baker to come back and move his van. If the Corsican police check it out they'll probably find loads of people who saw you. Mrs Baker for a start.'

'Perhaps they won't check it out.'

'But they might, and then we'd be caught out again.'

'OK, let's say that Nicole confessed to me when I saw her in Sartene. I know I didn't even speak to her but nobody can prove that. After she confessed she ran off, and I couldn't chase her to the villa because my car was blocked in.'

Eventually Cate said thoughtfully, 'Even worse. Where are you going to say you and she had this very complicated, long conversation? Potential witnesses behind the windows on every part of the route. And the time. We don't know where she was coming from or where she went. She might have just left one person when you saw her in the market square and gone straight to another when she gave you the slip. Then there physically wouldn't have been time for her to tell you the half of it.'

'If these people do exist, then why didn't they come forward at the time?'

'Why didn't we? Who can guess at their reasons?'

'They would have been unearthed.'

'Not necessarily. It wasn't a murder investigation.' She sighed. 'It won't work. There are just too many imponderables.'

Frustrated though I was that she was right I was impressed by her ability to think coolly and analytically in a crisis. She would be a great asset to the business if we still had one after all this.

'Anyway,' she said as if telepathic, 'must remember they can't charge me, us, with anything serious.' And then, almost as an afterthought and much more the little girl: 'Can they?'

'No,' I said, 'I suppose not.'

'The thing is,' she said a little later, 'there is a way out.'

'Which is?'

'Well, we know they didn't do it so there can't be any evidence against them. So they can't be convicted. So we can stay quiet.'

'You have a touching faith in the English legal system. What about the Guildford Four and the Birmingham Six?'

'I know, I know. But these men aren't Irish terrorists.'

'Neither were they, as it turned out.'

'You know what I mean.'

'Well, yes and no. I mean, I can see that you think the Irish dimension adds something to it, but what about the Carl Bridgwater case, or that boy who lived with Christie at 10, Rillington Place?'

If she didn't know these cases she didn't say so. Instead she asked, 'Tomorrow's just an identify parade though, isn't it?'

I nodded.

'And Debbie can't identify anybody because there will be no one on parade who was actually there. So no harm can be done by saying nothing,' Cate said. 'But you might be able to find out more. You know, how strong their case is. If there's nothing to it then we're safe. They might get them for this other job but that's not our problem.'

'But if they do decide to prosecute for Stuart's murder, we really are in trouble.'

'If it looks like going any further then I'll tell them about the confession. We can say that I never told you about Nicole and that you didn't tell me about the identity parade because you didn't want me upset until there was anything definite, so I won't get into any more trouble than now. And you're off the hook.'

I tried to examine the best and worst paths of this strategy.

'Let's just find out more before we decide to say anything,' Cate pleaded. 'Not just for me or for you but for Debbie. Please.'

If revelations were necessary I had no intention of letting Cate carry the can, but this was not the right time to argue that through. Despite my scepticism of the justice system, there was more to gain than to lose by waiting to see how things stood. 'All right,' I said.

Deborah picked me up at nine the next morning and we drove down to Stoneyheath in her sporty little Peugeot hatchback. She drove aggressively, as most owners of souped-up small cars do, Napoleon complexes with four wheels, but jerkily, for which she apologised as part of a spasmodic monologue.

'I'm a bit on edge. Isn't it silly? It's so good of you to come with me. I couldn't think who else to ask. I mean, I've got plenty of friends but it didn't seem suitable somehow to ask them to an identity parade. What's the etiquette? I mean, I couldn't think what to wear.'

I'd opted for a dark suit and tie, what I hoped was the respectable citizen look, although probably all gangsters dress like that when visiting their local nick. Deborah had decided on a high-necked, baggy woollen dress. I had noticed before that she was self-conscious about the size of her seat but this was something different – an attempt to disguise her entire body shape, a protective covering against the eyes of the intruder.

If Superintendent Cromarty was surprised to see me he didn't say so. He introduced a detective inspector from one of the Medway towns, and Sergeant Mirren.

'We've already met,' I said to the sergeant, as hands were shaken with the uncomfortable bonhomie of businessmen assembling for a tricky meeting.

She merely nodded but Cromarty said, 'Of course. I'd forgotten this wasn't your first visit.' And he gave me what seemed, in my hypersensitive state, an unpleasant smirk.

After he had explained what was to happen, we were ushered into a viewing gallery, no more than a dimly-lit expanse of blue linoleum on which several orange plastic stackable chairs had been abandoned. The long window looked out onto a whitewashed room with an unvarnished woodblock floor which only needed the line markings to double as a squash court, and there the line-up assembled under the bright and unforgiving fluorescent lights.

Whether it was the unhealthy pallor it gave their complexions, or the fact that they were holding numbered cards, all these men looked like hardened recidivists. Dressed in dark sweaters, jeans and trainers they faced the window, some attempting a laboured insouciance, as if they just happened to be passing or were waiting for a bus, others staring at us with a glum intensity. Although we had been told that all they could see were their own reflections it was hard to believe.

One of the suspects was clearly a small, ferretlike man as there were four of those, while his companion had been taller, as there were also four approaching six feet.

'OK, take your time and have a good look,' Cromarty said diffidently, but you could feel the expectancy, the willing her to succeed, in the air. At first Deborah simply stood, her arms hugging her chest, but then, as she became absorbed by her task, she began to pace slowly backwards and forwards, ending with her nose more or less pressed against the glass, her gaze fixed somewhere in the middle of the line-up. Out of the corner of my eye I tried to monitor the officers' reactions as the tension increased. Had she, for whatever reason, settled on one of the guilty men?

Maybe half a minute passed and then, just as Cromarty stirred towards her, Deborah turned and said, 'It's no good. Can I go out there, closer to them?'

The bubble burst and someone sighed but Cromarty, apparently unruffled, said, 'Of course, if you feel up to it.'

She nodded. Once again I thought how brave she was – she knew that she needed smell or presence to remind her. The moment at Nicole's party when the dark and a particular scent had triggered her memory came back to me. Of course, what she had smelt was her own mother, but some block had prevented her from recognising it.

A uniformed sergeant escorted Deborah from the gallery and moments later she reappeared by the line-up. Once again there was a breathless hush in the close. Caught up by it I studied the faces again. Number one might have appeared in any TV cop show as a petty villain, number two could have been a regular in any betting shop but number three, there was something familiar about number three. I was sure I had seen his stubbly double chin and creased cheeks somewhere, perhaps in the Greyhound at Stirton Ash, perhaps that was what had linked the Wealden suspects to Stuart – it was, after all, a local man.

I shook my head. What was I doing? I knew the truth but some seductive doublethink and, more important, the charged atmosphere had made even me want to pin the tail on the donkey. What must it be like for Deborah? I prayed she didn't convince herself that she recognized one of these numbers.

She had stopped in front of number four, so close to him and at such an angle that for a moment I thought she was going to do what she had done with me in the wine bar and lean back against him to see whether he might have grasped her from behind. His face strained with the effort of not being drawn into returning her gaze. He was a chubby man, his torso soft beneath his sweater. Was that what was attracting her? She had said that I was 'too hard' to have been her assailant – was this fat man the closest that she could get to the reality of Nicole's breasts, probably camouflaged by several layers of clothing, pressed against her as the chloroform took effect.

Then it was all over. Deborah was shaking her head, the line-up flickered with relief, the inspector mumbled and kicked a chair before glancing guiltily around to see whether his petulance had been noticed.

'Was he one of your suspects?'

'You must know I can't tell you that,' Cromarty said.

Deborah returned. She looked flushed. 'I'm sorry,' she said. 'I'm not saying it wasn't one of them, two of them I mean, but I can't say it was.'

'But something stirred,' Cromarty said. 'Didn't it?'

'It was – well, it just brought it all back to me.' Deborah sat down abruptly and heavily on one of the orange seats, pushed forward by Sergeant Mirren, and blew her nose.

'More clearly than before?' the inspector asked, and Cromarty flicked a silencing glance at him.

We all waited. Deborah looked up, finally aware that she had not said enough. 'Nothing new, I'm afraid.' She looked around for Mirren. 'I'd like to . . . could you show me where the Ladies' is?'

As if she had uttered some magic spell the rest of us remained in a state of suspended animation until the door closed. Then the inspector and the uniformed sergeant fell into mumbled conversation, leaving Cromarty and me to our own devices.

'Well, that's a disappointment,' I said, having settled on the strategy that any relative would hope for a conviction.

Cromarty nodded.

'Have you got enough evidence to charge them anyway?'

'They've already been charged with . . . with offences unrelated to your brother's murder, and we shall, of course, as always, be endeavouring to bring to book those responsible for that particular tragedy.' He gave me a searching look, as if trying to decide whether I was, surprisingly, a closet vigilante. 'Between you and me we have nothing to link this pair with Stirton Ash other than the similarity of the type of house, its relative proximity to the place they turned over, and the fact that they have carried a shotgun.'

'But I thought it was Stuart's own gun that shot him?'

'Quite right,' he said. 'Although it didn't pull its own trigger.' He smiled a ghost of a smile, presumably seeing in my phrasing the unconscious liberal at work – only the gun was guilty. 'The thing is, their success with the shotgun at Stirton Ash may have encouraged them to get one of their own for next time. It's a possibility.' He smiled again, but without humour. 'A faint one. Look, Mr Buchan, the identity parade was a long-shot; now it has produced nothing I wouldn't necessarily expect a positive outcome here. After all,' he added wryly, 'we can hardly expect a couple of cons facing at worst armed robbery to lie down and confess to a murder, can we? It's not logical.' He scratched his ear and looked me straight in the eye. 'Of course, if it was the other way round it would be a very different matter.'

We were interrupted by Deborah's return and she and I were in the car park before I analysed that last remark. The only sensible explanation, given the emphasis, was that he was taunting me, letting me know that the identity parade had had two purposes, the more important of which was to put the frighteners on the suspects. Faced with the prospect of being stitched up for murder, who wouldn't admit a lesser offence for which other evidence, however circumstantial, existed? Cromarty, the master of the quick conviction.

This was, in one way, a relief: it meant, in all probability, that there would be no need to tell the truth about Nicole. But, although Cromarty had couched what he said in such a way as to be deniable, it seemed to me that he wouldn't have spoken to me with that kind of hostile intimacy unless he was sure that I was less than pure. Cromarty was still convinced there was a skeleton in my cupboard.

We were crossing Blackheath, beneath the largest wraparound sky London offers, full, that morning, of cumulus piles of Biblical proportions, and I was watching the perennial kiteflyers and thinking of their Thai equivalents when Deborah said, 'Do you know, it was very strange. I was dreading that parade, but when it happened I was fine. I tried very hard to remember that night, really let myself go and concentrated on it, but when I did, all of a sudden I found myself thinking about Mummy instead.'

It was a good job I wasn't driving the car, otherwise we would have swerved into the motorists drinking tea by the caravan-café. As it was, I merely gripped the door handle and swallowed hard, but she didn't seem to notice.

'It's silly, isn't it, but for the first time I just had this notion of her . . . well . . . up there . . . out there somewhere' – she made a sweeping circular motion with her arm – 'protecting me.'

Chapter Twenty

Once again, as the days passed and there was no further communication from Cromarty, or from Deborah who had gone to Portugal with a group of friends, the whole affair resumed its background place, always there but mostly out of sight, as if on a high shelf.

Cate continued to work at Buccaneer, happy to be assigned to one department after another for a fortnight at a time, to plough through the files that made up the company history, to go for the occasional drink after the office with her colleagues. It was on one such evening that I was meeting Danny Whitney, Simon Charteris, and Scotch Woodcock of the *Guardian*.

'If my thing peters out,' she asked, 'can I come along and join you?'

I was surprised. She'd never suggested anything like that before and the cautious, compartmentalised part of me warned me off but the other bit, that took pleasure in watching people discover how attractive a person she was, overruled it. After all, the likelihood was that her quick drink would turn into a meal or a film or just a long drink and the next time I would see her would be curled up in bed.

Given that journalists can never be sure when they are going to have finished for the evening, our starting point was usually a little backstreet pub called the Gunmaker's where you could sit over a pint for an hour, undisturbed by landlord or loud music, until the entire party had assembled. When I arrived that night only Scotch was there, a large gin and ginger ale on the table before him, a large cigar in the corner of his mouth and, when he saw me, a large grin on his face. 'My dear chap,' he clapped me on the shoulder, 'how in Beelzebub's name are you? A Stella, isn't it?' Scotch never forgot a man's poison. He turned to summon the barman. 'I say, matey.'

Scotch was no more than a couple of years older than the rest of us, but it was sometimes hard to remember that. He was old-style Fleet Street, a news editor who wore braces, elasticated metal armbands to keep his cuffs clear of the now non-existent ink and, outside the office, a stained Burberry and racehorse-owner's brown trilby.

I had known Danny since college and Simon since he and Danny had first worked together at *Chemical Month*, but Scotch was a much more recent acquaintance, and on the only previous occasions we had been alone we had talked about jazz or his other passion, fell walking. So it was again – he had spent a weekend in the Brecon Beacons and I had bought yet another Erroll Garner album. This lasted us twenty minutes and another round before he said, 'No progress in your brother's business, then?'

For one inadequate, younger-sibling second I thought he meant Buccaneer, and then I realised that as far as he was concerned Buccaneer was my business. I shook my head.

'The groundhog still in charge of the case, then?'

'Cromarty, you mean?' I smiled; the mixture of pushy and piggy was spot-on. He nodded. 'Where did you hear that name for him? I didn't see it in any of the cuttings.'

'I coined it, I think. Or at least I was there when it was coined.'

'In Stoneyheath?'

'I was on the local paper, the *Chronicle*, from 1978 to 1982. For a while I thought I was stuck there for life. Terrifying. Not a decent hill for two hundred miles.'

'Only twenty miles from Fleet Street, though.'

'Quite. So near and yet so far.' He took another sip at his gin.

'He couldn't have been a superintendent then?'

'No, detective sergeant. Smart, ambitious. A pain in the neck if you were a reporter. He'd have liked to have had me for withholding information.'

I disguised my surprise with a large swig of my own. 'What sort of case?'

He looked slightly sheepish. 'Oh, that was a murder too. I just happened to know all the people involved.'

'What happened?'

'Oh, he couldn't get me for anything. It was my salvation, really. After my conflict of interest was cleared up I got several pieces about the bloody business, and it was a bloody business, in the *Telegraph* and thence a job in Manchester.'

Conflict of interest? How bloody? I was just about to ask when Danny arrived, full of indignation that his front page story had been demoted, and Scotch was up and off to the bar, ordering more drinks. When Simon turned up with more *Guardian* gossip and some Square Mile rumours about my client MJB, the subject of the earlier Stoneyheath murder was firmly dead and buried.

If Cate had been five minutes later she would have missed us. The early warning of her arrival was that both Simon and Danny instinctively looked up as the door opened, and their gazes lingered longer than they would have had the entrant been another old hack sloping in for a mid-evening snifter. Then the perfumed breeze by my cheek, the circumspect peck of her lips and, 'Hello, Alex. I thought you might be gone.' Introductions all round, the boys obviously having trouble reconciling the young woman, smart in a linen business suit, with their previous mental pictures of my niece.

As we walked to a local Italian shortly after Danny confirmed this. 'Beautiful girl,' he said. 'Not cocky, but not lacking in self-confidence.' Ten yards ahead Cate was in animated conversation between Simon and Scotch, both of their heads slightly inclined towards hers. 'Not what, I may say, you had led me to expect.'

'And what was that?' I asked when it was clear I was meant to fill the silence.

'Sulky schoolgirl in bovver boots with a bad peroxide hairdo and attitude.'

'I guess she was like that, a bit. She still wears the boots sometimes.' But that was about all. Gradually, over the summer, the hair had changed shape and colour; now it was shorter, with a subtler mixture of copper and gold threaded through the natural brown, its maintenance a matter for monthly attention from a man in Kensington. Her room in Camberwell was the depository for an expanding collection of clothes, individualistic but chosen only to make her stand out acceptably within the confines of the area of the business she was exploring.

'I suppose if you're related,' Danny mused, 'you can't see her in quite the same way?'

'And what's that?'

'Quite a catch.' He laughed. 'And living under your own roof. What a tragic waste.'

Cate was a palpable hit that evening; inevitably the centre of attention at first but never awkwardly so and soon putting herself further out, always a part of the conversation but never its focus. It was a very grown-up performance, and I was about to tell her, not that of course, but how proud I was of her when she closed my mouth with a heavy-duty kiss. The taxi driver rather ostentatiously closed his dividing window and I wondered how the night sight of the gentlemen of the press was, they being huddled on the pavement not fifty yards behind the traffic lights at which we had stopped.

'Scotch is really sweet,' Cate said. 'I mean normally someone kissing your hand would be really creepy but not him, somehow.'

'He's a remarkable man,' I said.

'But why's he called Scotch? He doesn't drink it and he's from Carlisle?'

'Scotch Woodcock. His surname's Woodcock.'

'Yes?'

'It's a savoury, anchovies on toast I think, served at the end of Edwardian dinners.'

'That's quite appropriate. He's got that air about him; fruity, historical. Did you call him that?'

'No, he's always been Scotch, ever since I've known him.'

'I was just thinking of the soup and fish.'

'I'm lost.'

'Same era, I suppose. You know, the first day I came to our house, and you said how appropriate the hunting prints were for putting on your soup and fish in the green room.'

So there we were. A couple with shared memories – we even had a photograph album of our holiday in Thailand. I had seen it in the luggage Cate was assembling to take back to Durham.

I had promised to go with her, a couple of days before the start of term, to help her settle into the house whose decorating she had been up and down supervising. As the time drew near her buzz of anticipation grew almost audible. 'Anyone would think you were looking forward to leaving me,' I complained, hamming it up enough, I hoped, to make it clear that I didn't mean what I was saying.

'Oh, don't say that.'

'All right then, I'm looking forward to the peace and quiet and a decent amount of space in my own bed.'

'You pig. Anyway, if you're not up every weekend sharing mine I'll want to know why.'

The day before we left Cate wanted to be special – well, so did I – and I had an invitation to a reception at the Café Royale. 'Let's go,' she said. 'I've never been there and we can go on and eat afterwards.'

She looked stunning in a dark blue silk number which shimmered under the lights like diffused moonlight across a night sea, and I was aware of heads turning to look at her as we negotiated the crowded salon; I turned to look at her several times myself. We drank champagne, mostly refused the canapés on the grounds that we didn't want to spoil our appetites, and I introduced her to various business acquaintances whom she charmed. Then, casting around again for the nearest ashtray, I caught sight of another guest looking in our direction. Only this one wasn't captivated so much as angered. It was Henry Beaumont.

As soon as he realised I had seen him he turned away, but I was aware of his eyes raking the room and I knew instinctively that he was searching for Saro to keep her out of my way. There was an unstable weight, like loosely bagged oranges, in the pit of my stomach. I should have guessed they would be here. I looked at Cate, safe enough with Barbara Springett and the Atkinsons, and with the traditional lavatory-goer's cry of, 'Back in a mo', made for the cloakroom.

I washed my hands at the row of basins and then splashed cold water over my face, which immediately made me feel better. As I was blinking and wiping my eyes a rich voice said, 'Keeping you up, is she, Alex old boy?' It was Bartleby Coles, PR man to the new gentry of the investment houses.

'Hello Barty. What are you talking about?'

'The new tottie. Lovely. Like a . . .' he gave it a second's thought '. . . like a young foal.'

'Barty, you're treading on very thin ice.'

'Why, not married are you?' He chuckled. 'I'd snap her up if I were you. Or at least take out an option. See if she rises like the sap—'

'Barty, she is my business partner—'

'Bloody hell—'

'And more importantly my brother's daughter.'

'Sorry, old boy. No offence.'

'None taken, I'm not so sure,' I said, walked out into the corridor and ran slap bang into Saro.

She grabbed at my sleeve and said, with the authority of an ex-lover, 'Come with me.' I followed her round a corner and down a flight of deeply-carpeted stairs into another reception on the floor below. She thrust a glass into my hand.

'Do you know any of these people?' I asked, reading the words *Romantic Novelists' Association* spelt out on the pegboard by the door.

'Of course not, but it's less risky than having a conversation outside the Gents' or being caught on the fire escape.'

'I'm sorry, I didn't come expecting to see . . . how are you?' She looked as well as ever, perhaps a touch browner from the last summer holiday. The tooth was mended but I wondered whether I could detect a tiny scar on the top lip.

'Oh, all right. Getting on with being a good wife and mother. And how are you?'

'Oh, you know, plodding on . . .'

'Is Cate a good lover?'

There seemed no point in pretending with Saro. 'Jesus Christ, is it that obvious? I thought we were doing a good job of being discreet but even Bartleby fucking Coles asked me about it in the bog just now.'

'Barty? He wouldn't know a scandal if it knelt down and gave him a blow job. He just can't imagine anyone not screwing available – what does he call it? Crackling?'

'Tottie. So it's not common knowledge.'

'Not as far as I know. But it will be if you admit it as readily as you did to me. Why worry anyway, it's not incest. God, you weren't even sure about that, were you? On second thoughts, you're right to keep it hush-hush. It would seem a bit squalid. Very bad for business, I should think. It's a good job you established an alibi for not having a girlfriend while you were with me, isn't it? Otherwise tongues would start to wag, however discreet you were.'

'I know,' I said, feeling weary but defiant, and recognising that here, for the moment, was the one person I could say this to. 'But in answer to your earlier question, Cate is very good, for me. I am in love with her and please don't accuse me of cradlesnatching because it really wasn't like that.'

'No,' she said, her voice suddenly tender, 'I'm sure it wasn't.' She paused, looked down at the floor. 'Alex, there's something you should know about . . .'

I waited with a sense of impending doom, although I could not imagine what she was going to say.

She looked up at me. 'You're happy, aren't you?'

I nodded.

'Then, just take care. I must go.' She smiled, a quick grimace. 'And keep practising that discretion. Don't follow me back up the stairs or there'll be hell to pay.'

I went down to the ground floor and, as an alibi, bought some cigarettes in the cocktail bar, throwing my old packet into a wastepaper bin by the lift. Re-entering the fray I saw Henry at once, Saro safely gathered in to his conversational group, but he was still casting wary glances around the room. Cate scarcely seemed to have noticed that I had gone missing but as we were walking up Dean Street to our restaurant she said casually, 'Did you talk to Saro or Henry?'

'Yes,' I said, knowing honesty was the best policy, up to a point. 'I bumped into her outside the cloakroom.'

We walked on, Cate gazing lazily into windows. 'How was she?' she asked eventually.

'Oh, all right.'

'Good,' she said as I opened the door of Soho Soho, and then, lifting her voice as she smiled at the receptionist: 'I hope they've got duck.'

They had but it didn't seem to make her happy. Our conversation throughout the meal was lacklustre, any jollity forced. For a while I dismissed it as the let-down that can result from having built up an occasion to be something special, but that didn't explain the wary glances Cate was giving me, the look of someone waiting to be hit.

As we took refuge in our pudding menus I could bear it no longer. 'What's the matter?' I took her hand. 'It can't just be the lack of *crème brûlée*.'

She twisted my fingers in her own. 'What exactly did Saro say to you?'

So, she was insecure in the face of my ex-lover. 'Well, she knows about us.'

'Yes.'

So, she didn't find it remarkable that Saro had guessed but she still seemed poised for some blow. 'She wasn't critical. She was pleased that I was happy.'

'That's all?'

'Yes.' Was that so strange? It was, after all, Saro who had left me. She had no claim on me. 'Actually, that wasn't quite all. Before she asked if I was happy she said there was something I should know, then she changed her mind. I don't suppose it was anything to do with you.' But the change in Cate's expression indicated that it was. 'What is it?'

She stared at the tablecloth. 'I left that book out where Henry could see it.'

That explained how he had found out. 'Hoping that it would break me and Saro up? I can't believe it.'

'I didn't believe it myself. I mean, I didn't think he would notice really. It was just an impulse, a wicked impulse and part of me's felt guilty ever since, but then in another way I'm not sorry because it means I've got you now. Except that I haven't unless you can forgive me. Can you?'

'It could have had the opposite effect, did you think of that?'

'It was a risk, I suppose, but then I didn't really think there would be any consequence, one way or the other.' She swallowed. 'Can you forgive me?' She fixed me with a pleading stare.

'Let's go,' I said, averting my eyes. 'I can't think here.'

Meekly she gathered her handbag and went to the lavatory while I paid the bill.

'Can we walk for a bit?' I asked, once we were on the pavement. She nodded and we set off down Shaftesbury Avenue towards Piccadilly, Cate silent at my elbow.

I was disturbed by this new imperfection in Cate but then, she hadn't meant to do actual harm, had she? She had been driven by love to do something stupid and I could hardly complain about the results.

She had put Saro in a position where Saro had to choose, and Saro had chosen Henry over me. OK, the children came into it, but I was convinced now that she would have chosen Henry anyway – Henry and the house in Campden Hill Square, Henry and his superior wealth, Henry and their hereditary circle. I was, in the end, no more than the bit on the side.

Whereas Cate . . . Cate loved me with a passion, would do, it was clear, almost anything for me. And I felt the same about her.

There was no alternative. I took her arm. 'Of course I forgive you.'

Chapter Twenty-One

I wasn't quite sure what I had expected – perhaps that Cate with her first place would have kicked over the traces and painted it black or lined the walls with sheets of tabloid newspaper, although her choice of car and clothes hardly suggested either. In any case the little house in Atherton Street was a model of tasteful conversion. The bathroom and the kitchen were entirely white, with the exception of a banana yellow carpet in the one and sisal matting in the other, while the remaining rooms were painted in varying tints of white peach in the dining room, aqua in the front parlour, rose in the study, apple in the hall and on the landing, primrose in the lodger's bedroom – and all were carpeted in what I had always thought of as builder's berber beige with flecks of brown and grey. 'It sort of pulls the whole thing together, don't you think?' Cate said proudly as we stood admiring the pristine newness of it all. 'Particularly as the rooms are so small and the doors will be open a lot of the time.'

We had driven up in convoy, both cars loaded down with books, clothes and appliances but Cate would not, could not start unpacking until we had properly savoured the splendour. So we sat on the sitting room's striped sofa and drew the Persian-influenced curtain that separated the study from the french window and the backyard. We opened the kitchen's drawers and cupboards, fiddled with the central heating controls and ran the bathtaps and the separately powered shower. Only then did she show me her *pièce de résistance*.

Her bedroom was a Chinese lacquer red with a black japanned wardrobe, chest of drawers and bed. The windows were draped with a rich pattern of birds and heiroglyphics; even the berber was effectively hidden beneath silk rugs. The rest of the house was as yet without personality, but this room was finished down to the duvet cover and the pair of kimonos hanging behind the door. In the faded light of a grey autumn afternoon the effect was overwhelmingly rich and . . . not cosy but welcoming, warmly absorbent.

Cate waited with bated breath for my reaction.

'You bottled it all up until you'd climbed the stairs then.' I paused.

'Well?'

'Beautiful.'

She blushed and shrugged her shoulders as a polite disclaimer. 'But do you feel at home here?'

'Absolutely,' I said and dropped onto the bed.

Emma was to be her lodger and had been told all about us. 'And does she approve?' I had asked.

'She wouldn't be living in my house if she didn't,' Cate had replied immediately, and then added: 'Well, she was dubious at first but now I think she's convinced. Enough, anyway, to tell a little white lie. If anyone notices we have the same name or asks how we met, Emma and I say you're a distant cousin. You don't mind, do you? The thing is that sounds vaguely aristocratic whereas . . .'

'I know, whereas uncle isn't at all respectable. Good idea.'

Cate had giggled. 'I toyed with the idea of simply saying you were my guardian, it's so wonderfully Gothic, but as Emma said you couldn't help wanting to ask loads more questions if you were told that.'

We had one night at the house before Emma arrived with her parents. As their Volvo estate pulled up three feet from the sitting room window a terrible notion hit me. 'Jesus, Mr and Mrs Woodhouse don't know about us, do they?'

'Of course not,' Cate said blithely, waving to Emma and heading for the door.

I hared up the stairs and into the front bedroom. I knew that Cate wouldn't be able to resist a grand tour and had visions of Fiona spying the rumpled bedclothes and my intimate garments scattered about the carpet, the dawning recognition, the hissed explanation to Hamish, the accusation, the damning moral verdict, the tears, and Emma being dragged away to see if a last minute place was still available at St Catherine's before their year had even begun.

But the room was innocent. All my things were tidied away into my holdall, the bed a board of virginal calm. It still didn't explain where I had slept, as the mattress destined for Emma was encased in plastic on its pine base. I hoped they would assume I had roughed it there in a sleeping bag, so considerate of their daughter's feelings that I had endured the rustle of polythene all night rather than sully her quarters.

I felt such a fraud standing in the kitchen with Hamish, making the tea, with him saying he understood that I came by on business every now and then and it was a relief to him, but Fiona particularly, that I would be able to keep an eye on the girls. When we returned to the sitting room with the tray Cate, clearly finishing the tour, was talking about how she had found curtain fabric to match the striped sofa.

'Yes, it's an unusual blue,' Fiona said.

'Mmmm, but I particularly wanted it,' said Cate, pulling off cushions, 'because it's so easy to do this.' And with a flourish she conjured a metal-framed bed from its depths. She gazed expressionlessly at me. 'Very useful for when we have the odd friend to stay – or even relatives.'

And her beam suggested that the Woodhouses might well be included on a list of prospective users.

After they had gone Emma went to unpack in earnest, which involved a lot of trips up and down stairs with kitchen implements – like every shared house they had a surplus of garlic crushers, cork screws and potato peelers – and, having washed up the lunch things and hung some more pictures, we eventually made another pot of tea and Cate called her down. The three of us sat for half an hour or so over it, chatting a little politely for I hardly knew Emma, and then she announced that she would go to her room. 'Give me a shout when you're ready to do something about supper,' she said and disappeared. After we had heard her door firmly shut I said, 'We can't have this.'

'What?' Cate said, although she knew perfectly well.

'Well, it's your place, but I presume you would expect Emma to have the run of it, otherwise why bother having a lodger?'

'Of course.'

'Then she mustn't feel confined to her room just because I'm here, or that she has to tiptoe around us. It will be awful.'

'I know, it's just a bit awkward.'

'For her or for you?'

'For all of us.'

'Not for me,' I said, 'I've done this before, remember. Only rules are bedrooms are private and no sex, even prolonged snogging, elsewhere unless the house is completely empty. After all, it'll be the same for her when she has blokes round, won't it?'

'Yes,' Cate said doubtfully, although at the time I wasn't sure whether she doubted Emma's aptitude for bedding blokes or her own tolerance. I had intended to stay for supper before heading back but it was clear that they would be better for having their first evening alone together so, despite Cate's protestations, I gave it an hour to avoid Emma thinking she had driven me out and then called out a casual goodbye.

I had intended to go up for the weekend a fortnight later but, as if we hadn't had enough death in the family, my father passed away. 'Very peacefully,' the matron said, and although I guessed she said that to everyone, even the relatives of those who had been riddled agonisingly with cancer, in Dad's case I could believe her. A massive heart attack at three a.m. might have caused a few moments panic or distress but little more.

I felt very little pain. This might have been familiarity breeding contempt, my emotions being cauterized against further bereavement, but I suspected was more to do with the fact that Dad had hardly been part of the real world for some time. He had lived in a refurbished past where the exploits of his youth were inextricably entangled with things he had read in history books, and Stuart, Angela and my mother, were resurrected at the whim of his confused mind. His corporeal self was no longer of much use to him.

The funeral was complicated by the fact that none of the family, even the distant relations, any longer lived near Watford, which was where Mum was buried and the space for Dad remained. As a result, after a plan of campaign and troop movements of D-Day-like complexity, I got Eastbourne inmates, Ayrshire cousins, Berkhampstead workmates, and other geographically disparate bit-part players in Buchan history first to a red-brick neo-Byzantine church and then to a red brick neo-Tudor roadhouse where we were compelled to hold the wake.

The surroundings may have been drab and dispiriting but it was a surprisingly lively affair. The workmates, some of whom appeared only to stay in contact via the network of 'In Memoriam' announcements in the local paper, regaled each other with anecdotes of production lines past and long-obsolete stores procedures, when if you had your own brown coat and a pocketful of ballpoint pens you were somebody. The inmates were just happy to be let off the leash, exchanging the soporific TV set and south-coast gentility for a bottle of brown ale and, nod nod wink wink don't tell Matron, a whisky chaser. The Scottish contingent were on the whole too calvinistic to enjoy that aspect of the proceedings, but ate heartily and basked in the sanctity of their close blood relationship to the deceased. After a while, seeing that the waitresses were doing their job and that no one would miss us, Boy Chippenham and I slipped away from the function room to the lounge bar.

'It's very good of you to come,' I said, 'especially as I hardly remember inviting you.'

'Oh, you didn't,' he said, 'but I'm the family solicitor. My attendance goes without saying.'

'You weren't Dad's solicitor,' I said, wishing that he had been.

'No, but funerals are a habit that's hard to break,' Boy said complacently, brushing vol-au-vent crumbs from his waistcoat.

Cate's head popped over the top of the mahogany bench on which he was sitting. 'There you are,' she said. 'Bunking off.'

'I came for a conversation. All anyone in there feels it safe to say to me is how sorry they are and what a marvellous old boy he was – they save the interesting anecdotes until I'm out of earshot.'

'It's just as bad for me,' she said. 'The great-aunts keep telling me how much I've grown, which is very rude as since they last saw me I've been too old to grow up, so all they can mean is I'm looking fatter.'

'Not at all true,' Boy said with easy gallantry.

When I dropped Cate off at Watford station – she had only come for the day – I offered to visit that weekend. 'Don't,' she said. 'I'll come down. I'd like it to be just us, wouldn't you?'

As she had a lecture at five on a Friday I knew she wouldn't be in until about ten, so I suggested she meet me in the office. I had a lot of paperwork to shift and that evening, with clients safely switched off for the week, seemed an ideal opportunity. When the time came, of course, I had other preoccupations.

Ever since the funeral I had been brooding about the possibility of afterlife. Under normal circumstances, like any sceptical agnostic, I didn't give it a thought – you rotted back into the earth and that was that. No such thing as the independent spirit . . . probably. But that meant any real life was better than none, even Dad's mixed-up, chair-bound musings. The only possible reason for wanting death was intolerable physical pain which for some reason drugs had been unable to alleviate. Or mental pain – where you couldn't continue to co-exist with the inside of your head.

This brought me back to Nicole: she hadn't been able to live with hers. Well, OK, she had shot her husband and, admittedly by force of unexpected circumstance, subjected her daughter to eighteen hours of terror so maybe she had grounds for wanting to obliterate everything, but why had she done those awful things? It was not a spur of the moment crime of passion, no one had suggested she was a schizophrenic or sociopath, but on the other hand there was insufficient financial gain to brand it a commercial crime. Reluctantly, I was drawn again to the conclusion that Stuart must have done something to inspire his own murder. But no one, not least the daughters had dropped any clues, and I could hardly bring up the subject any less elliptically than I had done with either Deborah or outsiders without alerting them to my disbelief in the burglar hypothesis.

I didn't know if I really wanted to find anything but I could think of one other place to look. I had had enough experience of accountants, the Inland Revenue and VAT inspectors to know that you could discover a lot more about someone's activities from a combination of appointments diaries, receipts and credit card statements than might at first seem plain. So on that Friday afternoon, before she went home, I asked Dorothy to put all of the relevant documents that covered the year from July 31st, 1989, on the table in the so-called boardroom next to my office.

She, of course, recognised the period as the year preceding Stuart's death and I thought for a moment she was going to warn me off, but she merely pursed her lips and did as she was asked. However, she locked the boardroom's outer door behind her and, before leaving the building, rapped on my door. 'I'm off now.'

'OK, have a nice weekend.'

'And you. Alex . . .'

'Yes?'

'It doesn't always help to go raking over the past.'

I wondered why she thought I was doing it. Surely she couldn't suspect my real motive?

She hovered. I could see it had cost her an effort to say what she had.

'No,' I said in an attempt to placate her. 'What's gone is gone. I just need to check a couple of things.'

'Right then.' Still she lingered.

'Bye-bye, Dorothy.'

'If you need any help, I'm quite familiar with all the files, or I could just keep you going with tea and sandwiches if you're going to be here late.'

'Dorothy, I'll be fine. Thanks.'

And reluctantly she retreated, pulling on her headscarf and brandishing her brolly with the duck's head handle against the autumn drizzle pattering on the window.

Was she protecting his memory? Or was I just being paranoid? It wasn't sandwiches she was offering with the tea but sympathy.

Chapter Twenty-Two

Although the diary entries were cryptic many of them were immediately recognisable – denoting meetings with clients who at that time were no more than a name, a briefly-glimpsed face or an anecdote but who, in Stuart's unavoidable absence, I now toiled to see in Birmingham or Crawley.

Some brought back memories of business pitched for and never won or rearguard actions to retain business that ended in failure. Long-forgotten evenings at the drawingboard and the overhead projector swam past, some full of acrimonious discussion, others as quiet and solitary as this one, the office empty and still, the world ending where, beyond my door, the shadows overpowered the desk-lamp.

Some of his trips simply reminded me of how I had been inconvenienced by his absence – 'Glasgow: Stevenson' was a late phone call from one of his other clients necessitating a panicky taxi ride to Shaftesbury Avenue and missing the first ten minutes of a Noel Coward revival; 'Fete Committee meeting 7.30' a missed opportunity for a late-afternoon tryst with Saro.

My life was there – holidays, birthday, provincial jaunts, and the repeated, at first inexplicable phrase, 'Alex: ECA'. Not a client's initials, or if so one I had forgotten despite apparently regular appointments. Then, checking my own diary, I realised that he had been recording my secret meetings with Saro.

A strange feeling, discovering the progress of one's own affair mapped out in someone else's journal. And why ECA? Ten minutes' effort, until it occurred to me that I had been sidetracked, produced only one possibility – Extra Curricular Activity – but of course I could never know whether that was the right answer.

What it proved was that, if my brother had recorded my secrets then, albeit heavily disguised, he would have done the same with his own.

I had been working resolutely through a month at a time – diary entries first, noting any that I couldn't understand, and then crosschecking with his expenses. As I had expected, for he was a methodical man, there were no discrepancies. Every restaurant bill, train ticket, and plane ticket corresponded to engagements. There were a couple of taxi fares that seemed too large for the journeys suggested by the appointments, but only a couple, and an apparently suspicious receipt for lingerie and nightwear dovetailed with a shoot for a duvet manufacturer.

That had taken me to the end of January 1990, halfway through the last year of Stuart's life. I made myself a pot of coffee and had a small Jameson's. I was hungry but I had promised to have supper with Cate when she arrived, so I ignored this and smoked another cigarette instead.

The first of the Porter entries was in late February, along with a King's Road restaurant receipt, and although Porter meant nothing to me I didn't think too much of it – it could have been an old friend or a slight contact – until, in the first and second weeks of March, there were two more mentions – no times but on both days bills from restaurants within a mile of Sloane Square.

We had two clients and three suppliers from this neck of the woods but none of them, as far as I knew, employed a Mr or Ms Porter. I flicked forwards through the diary. Even a cursory glance showed a spattering of Porters, once a week all the way through to July, through to the end. I crosschecked with the client and supplier files to see whether I was wrong about Porters on the job but I wasn't. I crosschecked with my own diary to see if my own engagements on the first few Porter days sparked any useful memories but they didn't because I had been out of the office and wouldn't have seen Stuart.

Abandoning any other line of inquiry I set about tracking each Porter entry, my halfhearted belief that Porter might be a legitimate Stirton Ash or social connection fading. Only very special friends, or mistresses, warrant that many appointments. Not all of them were lunches, or at least not lunches with receipts; on a couple of the relevant days there were winebar receipts from Battersea Rise, and on one of those and on two others without such tabs there were recorded taxi fares of £12. From our office that was an unusually high fare without being anything like high enough to have got you to Heathrow but it sounded about right for Clapham Common, which was where Battersea Rise was.

So Porter was probably someone who worked near Sloane Square and lived in Clapham, or somewhere in that direction. A glance at the residential phone directory showed nearly four columns of Porters – at least 400 – and even within the 'A's there were four or five that could have comfortably used a wine bar on Battersea Rise.

There were few other clues. Porter may have liked the theatre: on a couple of her, and I had now convinced myself it was a her, days it was noted that Stuart had been to the National Theatre – but that could have been with Nicole. Once there was an otherwise unexplained train ticket to Bristol and there were a couple of petrol receipts from Wiltshire and West Sussex. The one thing I was sure of was that she liked mussels, lobster and langoustines because they appeared on several of the costings of their meals together and Stuart never ate shellfish – he was allergic to it. But that wasn't much to go on.

I went back to the diary, looking to see how Porter related to other elements of Stuart's life but she appeared so often it seemed, after a while, more fruitful to look at her absences. The only weeks after her initial appearance in which she did not crop up were the third week of March and the second week of June.

At the beginning of the third week of March Stuart had written 'N skiing with Gibsons'. After Angela's death he had not skiied again himself, but had not presumed upon his second wife to follow his example, although I had occasionally wondered how he coped with the thought of Nicole flying down the piste, aware of the ease with which a fatal accident can fall out of a cold but clear blue sky.

I turned the page to the fourth week and, sure enough, there was a flight number and time indicating Nicole's return. But this was odd. If Porter was a mistress why had Stuart not taken advantage of his spouse's absence to see even more of her?

Maybe, unfortunate coincidence for the star-crossed lovers, she had already booked a holiday of her own that week. It was, after all, only a couple of weeks after the start of the liason. Unless, the penny dropped, with Nicole away the mice could play at home. No need for appointments if Stuart and Porter were rendezvousing each night at Stirton Hall.

Cate's presence presented an immediate objection to this theory but further scrutiny of the diary revealed, on the Tuesday of that week, only a day after Nicole's departure, the message 'School trip'. Not conclusive but conceivable that Cate had conveniently been despatched on a tour of the battlefields of the English Civil War or the landscapes of Thomas Hardy or some such thing.

I poured myself another Jameson's. Could he have risked it, even so? A village, even a commuter-belt village, is a small and observant place. Repeated comings and goings by Porter would have attracted some attention, and she could hardly have holed up in the Hall without being noticed by Mrs Cuttifer, who could scarcely have been so disloyal to her mistress as to not mention the visit of her master's.

I turned to the second week of June but there was no mention there of Nicole being away. Nothing apparently in common with the third week of March at all, apart from the absence of Porter. Looking for another angle I searched for Nicole's recorded trips. There was one in early February, a long weekend in Yorkshire, no given purpose, but that was a couple of weeks before Porter. The only other began on July 31st: 'N & C to Heathrow' it said. Which was where it had all finished, or started.

There were a few advance entries for events after his death. On August 1st 'N to Corsica' and 'C to Greece' had been crossed out, superseded by Nicole's murderous decision to take Cate to the airport the night before. On August 15th, the diary, undone by events beyond its control, confidently claimed 'N returns'. In between there were several business appointments but, once again, no Porter.

I looked at my watch. Nine-thirty. Cate should be here soon. Should I tell her what I had been doing? Would she see it as muckraking, sullying her dead father's reputation, or would she approve of efforts to find out why he had died? If I wasn't going to tell her then I had to clear away some of this stuff spread all over the table and across the carpet.

She must have wondered why her stepmother had hated him so much, but perhaps I should wait until I was certain. After all, it wasn't as if I had a positive identity for Porter or could confirm that she was definitely his mistress and therefore a motive for murder. But I couldn't see an easy or discreet way to take this further.

I wandered into the outer office with the coffee pot and, passing her desk, thought of Dorothy. She, having access to Stuart's diary, must have been given some explanation for Porter and although it almost certainly would have been incorrect it might contain a clue to the truth. I sat in her swivel chair and rang her house in Orpington but there was no reply, so despite her offer to help me she must have made some arrangements for this evening.

I twirled round in her chair, far faster than she ever did. The fact that she had been prepared to forego her drink, or film, or bridge made her offer doubly touching. The cylorama went door, pot plant, filing cabinet, window, shelves, door, desk-lamp, cork board with postcards – a mosaic of postcards because Dorothy kept adding to her collection from the first news of Paris in the spring to the last rays of autumn sun in Tenerife. She not only collected the cards sent by employees to 'everyone at Buccaneer' but also those sent to me by old and friendly clients, which were removed from my desk with the same efficiency as other correspondence was removed for filing.

The postcards were only taken down when Dorothy had assembled sufficient Christmas cards to replace them. It was quite possible that a postcard from Porter, feelings for Stuart hidden by an innocuous message that had meant nothing to Dorothy, anxious to expand her holiday art gallery, had graced this board for months, from that second week in June, through his death and mourning and funeral until, in the second week of December, it had been discarded in favour of Yuletide greetings from Speedy Couriers or Run-of-the-Mill Reprographics.

If only I had begun this quest earlier I might have caught this vital evidence before it hit the waste paper bin. I twirled again. Door, potplant, filing cabinet . . . Filing. Could Dorothy, that assiduous keeper of the company's records, possibly hold an archive of beach communications? For a second I thought nobody could be that anally retentive and then, what the hell, it would only take a minute, started looking in the logical places – P for Post and C for Cards. Nothing there but perhaps she had filed them according to their source where known so I tried M for Miscellaneous and H for Holidays and then, as a pointer, the personnel files to see if cards from employees at least had been retained. No joy.

Then I remembered that once credit-card slips had been tallied with receipts Accounts kept them in large manila envelopes, one for each month, in one of Trudi's desk drawers. I tried Dorothy's desk drawers but they were locked.

The key was blu-tacked to the underside of her desk, and the postcards were in the bottom drawer beneath a copy of Woman's Weekly, one manila envelope for each of the last five years, so perhaps that was their shelf-life.

I tore open the 1990 envelope and something like a hundred cards spilt out. Trudi had been to Marbella, Dorothy herself to the Isle of Skye. I read my own embarrassingly hearty hailing from Florence in May. There were only two cards from the second week of June: 'the gang' had been sent a shot of art deco architecture in Florida by Alan, a junior designer, and Mr S Buchan had been sent a view of boats in the harbour at Paxos.

On the back, in a rounded hand, in black ink, it said simply, 'Having a lovely time but wish you were here. Debs'

So here she was, Debs, Porter D, easily traceable in the phone book, Debs, Deborah, odd coincidence, no, no coincidence, this was just a postcard from Deborah to her stepfather. Damn.

Deborah. Deborah who lived in Clapham and worked where? . . . for Platform PR in SW1? SW3? I looked them up. Elizabeth Street; a stone's throw from Sloane Square. Shit. No coincidence then. Deborah and Porter had to be the same person – porters on platforms, presumably some sort of family joke – and I had spent two hours puffing down the wrong track. Bugger. Shunted into the sidings by the false signals of a nickname. Very disappointed, and in an effort to shake myself out of a seemingly endless sequence of poor railway metaphors suggesting themselves as appropriate to my predicament, I went back to the boardroom and shuffled the papers around a bit, but I had run out of steam. Fuck.

I buried my head in my hands, feeling tired, old and stupid. Outside, I heard a taxi's diesel echo against the tall buildings and the sharp slam of its door. I waited, hoping to hear the ringing, metal catching on brick, of our front door opening and the hum and subdued thuds of our lift, but there was nothing. Not Cate then. I let a comforting vision of her, tousled and vulnerable in her baggy green jumper, legs bare, be replaced by another of her in windblown sarong and blue vest, feet in the silver sand, against a tropic moon but there was something hovering at the edges of that one – another night, another beach and Deborah in her baggy sweater pulled over a white nightshirt to ward off the sea breeze. I felt the tingle of cold air brushing the hairs on my wrists fractionally before the faint smell of Arabian nights that was one of her perfumes, and then Cate said, 'God, you look as if you've had a bad day.'

She was leaning against the door jamb in jeans and an expensive, shiny aubergine version of the old mod's parka looking bright, beautiful and fresh despite her train journey. 'I'm sorry, I didn't mean to startle you. Well, actually I did but you look as though you've seen a ghost.'

'No,' I said, and pulled her onto my lap. 'Just an angel.'

'You haven't been at those Mills and Boons again, have you?'

'If I could get inside your coat,' I said, popping a couple of studs, 'I'd rip your bodice and then it would be another story.'

'Promises, promises. So what have you been up to?'

I told her. 'And I thought with the mysterious Porter I'd found the explanation for his death.' I looked up at her. She was very still, her eyes fixed intently on mine. I smiled ruefully, encouragingly. 'But then Porter turned out to be Deborah so—'

Her gaze flickered and settled on a point somewhere beyond the venetian blinds. No surprise, no relief. Her face was suddenly so pale I felt I was seeing a ghost. Or ghosts. I shivered. It seemed there was to be no 'so'. Cate moved to the window and stared resolutely out towards the dome of St Paul's. Realisation burst within me, dead and cold and spreading.

'So now you know,' Cate said savagely. 'My dad was screwing my stepsister.'

Chapter Twenty-Three

Cate had come home from school one lunchtime in early May because her English teacher was sick and she thought she would get more A-level revision done there than in the school library, with its distractions of friends and gossip. She had walked from the station, across the main road, down the lane to the bridge and then across the water meadows to the church. It was hot and, having too many bags to carry her blazer, she was sticky and afraid that her armpits smelt. She was going to buy an icecream from the post office but it must have been a Wednesday because it was shut. When she crossed the gravel drive she was thinking about having a nice cold shower instead. She didn't remember noticing any cars particularly, perhaps they were all in the coach-house. She got her key out because she knew Nicole had gone to Salisbury for the day with Marjorie Naylor, but the back door was unlocked. Presuming her stepmother had returned early or that for some reason Mrs Cuttifer was still around – perhaps they had a big dinner party on – she dumped her bags on the kitchen table, kicked off her shoes and switched on the kettle before going out into the sunny passage. She wasn't, she said, particularly aware of being quiet but I knew how silently Cate could move through a building. She was at the base of the Victorian stairs when she heard the unmistakeable grunts and gasps of sexual congress.

She didn't know what to do so she just stood there, curling her toes in the thick pile of the pink carpet. The only people likely and with any right to be in the house were Nicole and Mrs Cuttifer.

Even when you used her christian name – Mabel – it was impossible to imagine Mrs Cuttifer having sex, even with Mr Cuttifer, and if it was them why were they doing it here rather than in their own cottage? But Cate couldn't really imagine her dad and Nicole having sex either, and in any case he was at work. And, likewise, her mind shying away from the possibility of having stumbled upon them, if it was them why weren't they in their own bedroom on the other landing?

It was just possible to imagine Nicole, not in the throes of passion but in some soft-focus seduction scene – Cate had seen her in a glamorous nightdress last Christmas morning. Perhaps she had taken a lover, the bitch. That would explain why she was using one of the other bedrooms.

Cate could see that making any sort of noise would let the lovers know they were discovered and, while their panic would be well deserved, it would be hideously embarrassing if they confronted her. Her only alternative was to leave the house immediately and return when she was expected.

She was poised to do this when a short female laugh brought back her doubts that this could be her stepmother. Perhaps she should check – if it was Nicole she would creep away as before and decide later what use to make of the knowledge; if not, if it was some intruder, she would ring the police or something. She tiptoed up the stairs.

All the doors on the landing were shut with the exception of Deborah's, which was a couple of inches ajar. On hands and knees Cate crept forward until she could see through the gap and there – very logical really, it was her room – was Deborah, on the bed, her back to Cate, astride a pair of hairy, male legs. Her head was thrown back and she was moving it slowly from side to side so that her long, black hair brushed the tops of her plump white buttocks, their width accentuated by the lilac camisole caught on her prominent hip bones.

Cate, despite a certain shame at her status as peeping tom, was intrigued. What was Debbie doing here? Having an affair with a man from the village, or were they both Londoners, just passing and so crazed with lust that they had to make an emergency sex stop and thought this would be more comfortable than the back seat of the car?

Deborah was becoming more agitated, rocking backwards and forwards and mumbling, among the 'ohs', something that sounded to Cate like 'S'you' or possibly 'Phew'. But then she arched in triumph and, as she fell forward, an unmistakeable much deeper voice said, 'Oh baby, baby.'

That, it seemed, was what affected Cate most as she recounted the tale to me, sitting on the edge of the boardroom table, for a couple of tears jostled down her cheeks at that point. I wanted to comfort her but she was fiercely alone, so I said, 'What did you do?'

'I felt sort of paralysed, and they were panting and squelching – and then I suddenly remembered the kettle which was about to boil and it lets off this horrible buzzing sound and then they'd have known someone was there so I slid to the stairs and scuttled down them and caught it just in time but there was steam in the kitchen so I opened a window and tried to fan it out. Then I heard someone in the bathroom above and I was frightened the other one might be coming down so I slipped into my shoes and picked up my bags and crept along the back of the house against the wall to keep out of sight of the windows until I was round the corner and then I ran across the lawn and through the gate into the kitchen garden and shut myself in the greenhouse. I knew I'd be safe there because no one goes in the greenhouses when Mr Cuttifer's working and he'd whitewashed the glass so nobody would see me even if they came down the lawn.' She shrugged. 'And I stayed there till quarter past five when I would have got home if I'd caught the 4.30 from Victoria. And then I climbed over the wall and came back in through the front gate.'

Cate stood up and jammed her hands in her pockets. 'And do you know, I thought that one or both of them might have gone, but when I went in they were both sitting in the drawing room having tea with Nicole as if nothing had happened. She was as pleased as punch, of course, to have her precious daughter there, persuading her to stay for dinner, stay the night. I don't know how she didn't guess, there and then. Debbie was glowing with it, she could hardly keep the smug, satisfied smile off her face.'

'When did Nicole find out, do you know?'

Cate shrugged.

'Did you ever see any more evidence of—' I was going to say 'their affair' but it seemed inappropriate '—it?'

'Not really.'

'Rows about it, references to it?'

Cate shook her head.

'But you think Nicole did find out, and she killed Stuart because of it?' There was nothing like stating the obvious.

Cate nodded.

'You could have told me before,' I said intending sympathy but probably sounding querulous.

'I couldn't. I couldn't.' She looked at me for the first time. 'I wish I hadn't now, really.'

'You didn't have any choice,' I said, to comfort. 'Anyway, sometimes things are better shared.'

'Not this,' she said.

'Shall we go home?'

She nodded. 'Can I get drunk?'

Cate claimed not to be hungry – I wasn't myself any longer – but I rang the pizza place and they delivered, and as she sat watching an old Woody Allen movie and polishing off a bottle of Chablis I saw her hand reach out absentmindedly and stuff a slice into her mouth.

I sat in the chair opposite with my own bottle – of St Estephe – and let my numbed and increasingly befuddled brain fit her revelation to previously puzzling facts. The position of Stuart's body was no longer a mystery – he had been coming from Deborah's room, which was why his own bed was unruffled.

I remembered what Cate had told me about their departure for the airport – Nicole uncharacteristically fussing and then Deborah arriving unexpectedly just before they left. 'If it hadn't been for the cassette that got stuck we would already have gone,' she had said. This family farewell was now cast in a rather different light – Stuart irritated not by the ruin of his jazz recording but by the fact that his mistress would arrive before his wife left and, when she did, both wife and daughter waving goodbye believing that the pair left standing on the gravel drive would be in bed together before they were on the M25.

In bed, enclosed by Deborah's blood-red walls, wrapped in her blood-red duvet . . . no, that was poetic licence. I could clearly remember, the day I brought Cate back from Greece, thinking how much like a room set in a furniture store Deborah's lair looked with its crimson walls and jazzy black and white duvet. But the contrary picture niggled, unwilling to be displaced, until a context established itself. I had untied Deborah in the bathroom and she had gone to her room to clean up. As she pulled the door closed I had distinctly glimpsed red bedclothes. Odd because she had left the house in an ambulance and not returned before . . . perhaps Mrs Cuttifer or Nicole had changed them but Mrs C was on holiday and Nicole was not accustomed to changing the beds, had done no other work around the house, had barely stayed there a couple of hours . . .

Deborah had not only been cleaning up herself in the five minutes she was behind that door. Under the cover of the running taps she had been stripping the sex-stained sheets, evidence from which the police might deduce her illicit relationship with her stepfather if they combed the house for clues. Presumably there was a laundry basket in her room and she guessed that they wouldn't go to the lengths of trawling through the family's dirty washing. I pictured her as she came out onto the landing and now I could see, if I concentrated, the monochrome behind the summer frock and the big Mulberry bag – the Mulberry bag which had presumably contained the empty champagne bottle Cromarty had noticed in the kitchen and which hadn't been there when I passed through on my way to finding the body.

Extraordinary presence of mind – whatever her suspicions during the long hours bound alone in that bathroom it must have been a profound shock to Deborah to find out that her lover was dead, and yet within ten minutes she was working quickly and competently to ensure that that love remained a secret.

She might have simply wanted to conceal it from the authorities, but that seemed less likely than her wanting to conceal from her mother the fact that she had stolen her husband.

So Nicole could not have confronted Deborah – or Stuart. She had somehow discovered what was going on and decided that the only way to resolve it was to kill him.

Why hadn't she tried fury, scorn, tantrums, threats, ultimatums? Perhaps she was afraid that they would fail and she would have to leave her house, her way of life, humiliated, unable to look her erstwhile friends in the eye. If that was it then it had backfired: after the murder she had sold the house and shut out most of the county set, but, I supposed, at least she had done it as a plucky widow and not as the subject of appalled speculation. Imagine, my dear, she was such a bad wife her husband preferred her daughter.

Imagine. Imagine finding out that your partner had turned from you to the nubile charms of your own flesh and blood. It wasn't the first time that Nicole had seen her husband attracted to younger bodies – Charlie Makepeace had left her for an eighteen-year-old, or, rather, she had not been able to forgive him that dalliance as she had forgiven those with women of her own age. Nicole must have begun to see it as inevitable – men will move from older to younger at the first opportunity. Perhaps that had been the only reason Charlie had ever found her attractive – she was young and willing – and Stuart, who she had thought was different, had only taken her until something younger came along. Her self-esteem must have been at an all-time low.

She had been subject to the ultimate betrayal and, understandably, may have felt she could never forgive Stuart, but hadn't she been equally betrayed by Deborah? And yet, far from wreaking the same vengeance on her, Nicole had seemed oddly protective. Yes, she had bound and gagged her but she hadn't intended her to stay like that any longer than the next morning. I could hear Mr Cuttifer telling me, 'I think she blames me and the wife . . . told the wife – if you'd been there like normal she wouldn't have had to spend all that time tied up.'

In the midst of all her planning, confronted with the surprise of Deborah being there, Nicole had forgotten the Cuttifers were in Great Yarmouth. The thought of what might have happened if I hadn't come along must have haunted her. OK, eventually she could plausibly have rung the office, ostensibly inquiring about Stuart, asked me to pop round, but by that time Deborah might have died from some all-too-imaginable combination of asphyxiation, terror and dehydration. She must have been sitting on tenterhooks in Corsica, wondering why, all that long Wednesday, no one had rung to tell her of the tragic death of her husband in a burglary.

So she had loved her daughter, despite everything. Perhaps, then, the reason she had committed murder rather than talk to Deborah was that she could not risk Deborah even knowing that she knew. The humiliation and guilt would shatter their relationship and Stuart had died to protect that relationship. On that front Nicole had been, I supposed, more successful. Deborah apparently had no suspicions of what her mother knew or had done. But that hadn't stopped Nicole taking her own life.

Having drifted into the realms of pure speculation I tried to drag myself back to one or two unresolved physical details. Deborah had arrived at Stirton as Nicole left for the airport, so why had Nicole told Cate, before her suicide, that she was surprised to find Deborah there when she returned to kill Stuart? Surely she would have expected her to be there, in the arms of her husband. Had she instead believed Deborah's claim that she had only popped down to say goodbye because it had been backed with some convincing evening engagement back in town, or had Nicole only claimed to be surprised for Cate's benefit, putting her off the scent, not wanting her to know the truth about her father? Again, I would never find out.

Neither would I solve the conundrum of Stuart's pyjamas and dressing gown. He had been in bed with his mistress; it seemed unlikely that he would have slept in his pyjamas. So what had happened? She had gone to the bathroom. Had he woken and found her missing, waited a while, and then dressed to investigate? Or had he been awake when she left, easing herself from his embrace, giving him a sleepy kiss? When she didn't come back surely his first instinct would have been to call out? 'Debs, are you all right?' Had he heard a scuffling in the quiet house, something that didn't quite fit the movements of someone having a nocturnal pee? And if he called, how was he answered? By a disturbing, beckoning silence? Or by a soft voice, calling his name? After all, to fulfill her plan Nicole had to shoot him away from Deborah's bedroom. Were those pyjamas and dressing gown a pathetic attempt at propriety from a man who had heard his wife's voice outside? Had he come out, reached for the light and seen her at the end of the passage, walked towards her, mouthing excuses? Or had he stumbled out onto the dark landing, his first light the flash of the gun?

'Have you had enough of this pizza?' Cate asked, brandishing the plate. As far as I was aware I hadn't had any, so she had made a good meal. There was only one slice remaining.

'Yes thanks.' The Woody Allen video had finished and the set had reverted to junk late-night TV. Both wine bottles were empty.

'I'm going up. Are you coming?'

I wavered, uncomfortable. She wasn't looking directly at me but I sensed a plea for company and support. 'Yes, I'll just run these things downstairs.'

In the kitchen the red light on the answerphone was flashing. I hit playback. Rory Cleaver wondering if I wanted to see a band at the Mean Fiddler on Monday, a photographer I hadn't used in ages suggesting a drink, and Boy Chippenham offering lunch. From Boy it was but a small mental leap to wills. No speculation now as to why Stuart had altered his will, transferring half his share portfolio to Deborah, the April before he died. I went upstairs.

Usually, if Cate went up first, she left the bedside lamp on, but tonight the bedroom was in darkness so I let myself into the bathroom from the landing and, having cleaned my teeth, switched its light off before passing into the bedroom. I dropped my clothes on the floor and slid beneath the duvet. Her hand felt for mine and gripped it tightly.

'I'm sorry,' she said. 'At least I've known for a while. It must be even worse for you.'

Worse? Accepting that your brother is a . . . a what? I ran through a number of words like shit, bastard, worthless two-timing louse, but none of them seemed appropriate or sufficient.

Worse accepting that your brother is a whatever than that your father is a whatever?

Impossible to answer. We were both equally close blood relatives. We had both respected him. Still did. This affair wasn't, after all, the whole of the man. Could it be described as a tragic flaw, not just sordid but an error driven and dignified by love?

Why was I trying to excuse him? Was it because I could see uncomfortable parallels between his situation and mine? Was my seduction of Cate, part of the family, a young girl in my charge, so different from his of Deborah? All right, I wasn't married, still less to her mother, but then Deborah was older, independent, able to make up her own mind whereas Cate was a bereaved schoolgirl living under my roof.

All of my old doubts about us, carefully suppressed, came back with a vengeance, given an extra, terrible spin by this comparison. Don't blame me, Stuart, for screwing your daughter, as in business I'm just following your example, a man after your own heart.

I must have squirmed uncomfortably because Cate rolled over and laid a calming hand on my stomach and her head on my chest. I tensed and registered her minute answering retraction. There was a pause before she said: 'Don't.'

'What?'

'Push me away.'

'Cate, I'm sorry—'

'I knew this would happen. What he did is making you feel guilty. I'm not stupid. I can see how some arsehole psychiatrist could make them look the same but they're not. They couldn't be more different. You're not betraying anybody. You couldn't. Family isn't relevant to us, it's just an obstacle . . . a fucking awful coincidence. Don't say anything. I know we met because I was your niece but I didn't really know you until my close family, my real family, were dead. We are different. We're two people who . . . well, I fell in love with you as a . . . as an individual. Not a Buchan. We're not family, we're us and family's just . . . an inconvenient memory, not even the same memories. Even our memories of our family are completely separate. We've got to forget it, shut it out, or we're finished.'

Was she saying that to me or to herself?

She levered herself up onto her elbow and looked me in the face. 'That's all over. Now, it's just us. Isn't it? Alex, I love you, you can't leave me. You can't.' And she subsided. 'What will I do? I don't want anything else. You can't. Please.'

'I know,' I said. 'I can't.'

Chapter Twenty-Four

On Sunday, after I had dropped Cate at the station, I went into the office and tidied all the papers away. Cate was right. That was what had to be done with the entire affair, but could it? Now I knew I found it impossible to imagine that no one else had known. Mr and Mrs Cuttifer? Deborah's flatmate? Dorothy?

I waited, on the Monday morning, for her to ask me how I had got on but she said nothing, behaved absolutely normally. Every time she brought me a cup of coffee, or put a call through, I expected some sign of complicity or suspicion but, when she was leaving at six and popped her head round my door for the last time, all she said was, 'How's Cate? Is she well?'

And as I breathed a sigh of relief I lied. 'Oh yes, thanks, she's fine.'

It had been an exhausting weekend. On Saturday morning we were tense with the effort of not talking about the night before, about Stuart or about us. We sat in the kitchen, Cate concentrating fiercely on a set text, so fiercely that she rarely turned the page, and I ostentatiously rustled the *Guardian*. We offered each other toast and butter and tea in a dreadful parody of a long-married couple. The radio chuntered in the background, the hands of the clock crept stealthily on.

Eventually I asked, 'Do you want to do anything this weekend? I mean go anywhere, see something?'

She shook her head. 'I just want it to be over. I mean, I just wish it hadn't started.'

'I had to find out some time.'

'Did you?' She sighed. 'What's going to happen to us?'

'I don't know.' I felt stifled, as if the air was thick and tropical, not autumn-thin. I jumped up. 'Let's go for a walk.'

We let ourselves out of the little door in the garden wall and into the park. Since I had last been there the council had established a corral of carved wooden animals, elephants standing side by side with buffaloes, dark with last night's rain, forlorn without children to ride them. The flower beds were empty, the tennis courts occupied by a lonely doctor with a pile of tennis balls, practising his serve. Where was his partner? It was too late for him to be on holiday. Perhaps, fatigued, coming to the end of a 24-hour shift at the hospital, or maybe even in theatre, performing an emergency operation. Panicky but too tired to react properly. That was how I felt. We mooched on, past the gallows of the adventure playground and through the subway, where our voices would have echoed if we'd been talking. We kept a foot or so apart, hands in pockets. Eventually we stood on a manmade hillock, looking down at the manmade lake, around which a bunch of disconsolate anglers sat in parkas and woolly hats like street-credible urban gnomes.

'Do you love me?' Cate said.

'Yes.'

'Then nothing else matters.'

'It does.'

'Not to me. I don't want you to protect me from yourself. It's unnecessary, I'm not fragile, you can't break me . . . except by rejecting me.' She gripped my wrist, compacting the flesh. 'See, I'm tough.' She held on but looked steadfastly at the water. 'Let's go back and make . . . fuck. I want to fuck. If we don't do it now we never will again, will we?'

The awful truth of that skewered my disorganised thoughts. A decision had to be made, and there was no time for analysis. I felt a rush of elation loosen my tight muscles. 'You mean,' I said, 'that you want me to take you home and take you.'

She smiled. 'Anywhere, any position.'

'OK,' I said, 'let's run.'

'Not too fast,' she panted as we clattered through the subway. 'We need enough energy to give each other a good seeing-to.' Her words pounded a middle-aged man with a chihuahua, whose head jerked up in shock, only to be hastily averted when confronted by Cate's full-throated laugh.

Afterwards, of course, we hadn't solved anything, but we had given ourselves more time, a breathing space.

'Heavy breathing space,' Cate said.

I explained that it was simply age, not cynicism, that made me doubt the future. At thirty-nine I could clearly remember all of the forevers of nineteen, my own, broken quite quickly, others, couples who had managed five or ten years, none together still.

There was no arguing this point but Cate refused to acknowledge the complications of the age gap. Then I asked her what she thought would happen when she left university.

'I'll work with you,' she said innocently, happily.

'But if you're there all the time, how long do you think it will be before people realise we are lovers? It's not possible to conceal it every moment of every day. Nobody would want to.'

'They'll have to accept it.'

'Maybe they will. It may sour the atmosphere a little, though.' Rather more than a little. 'You'll have to put up with that.'

'I'll manage.'

'And outside of work? It's acceptable for you to live here now because you're a student but it will seem very odd to people if you don't move out when you've got a job and a very good salary.'

'I've got a good income now.'

'It's not the real income. It's people's perceptions. They will gossip, and with foundation. What I'm saying is we can't have a normal social life. It's not just a question of going to parties and pretending, although that would be awful enough. People will find out and then we'll be pariahs.'

'Well, we'll get some new friends.' Easy to say at nineteen. Then, she added: 'Anyway, who are these people who are going to ostracise us?'

I started to list them.

'But they're all your friends, people who knew Stuart.' For the first time I was aware she hadn't called him Daddy.

'You're right.' It was selfish. 'But I've known them a long time.'

'I'm sorry. I can see why it would be difficult for them in particular to accept us.'

'What they'll think of me.'

'They might not.'

'No.'

'Anyway, we've got a couple of years before it's a problem, if it's legit for me to stay here so long as I'm a student.'

Her brow was furrowed; I wanted to smooth it. 'Perhaps you could do a PhD.' And I was rewarded by smile lines instead.

Later, in bed, she said, 'I'm sorry. I don't want to take your past away.'

'Don't worry,' I said, 'no one can do that.'

Later still I said, 'The other thing is . . .'

'Surely,' she said, dozy, comfortable, 'there can't be any more disadvantages.'

'This is a big one. You won't be able to have any children.'

'Oh, that's all right.' She burrowed her head into my armpit. 'I don't want any.'

And her assurance was so blithe, her happy conviction so total that, rather than being reassured, I was immediately reminded of the student girls I had known who had said this, confident of their careers, now worrying about their kids' careers. Even Julia, who had shared this house with me, was apparently dragging a couple of toddlers around the supermarkets of Leicester.

But that, too, was as yet a non-problem. Might never be one, either because Cate would stick to her guns or because by the time she recanted she would be living with someone else. I slept, she slept, we got up late, ate and then she was on the train, leaning worriedly out of the window saying, 'So, is it all right?' and then, 'Come soon' and then, 'I love you' and then I was in the office tidying away those fateful records.

I knew that I could not put away my interior records so easily, but as the week wore on I was sure these images of death would not begin to fade until I was certain the crime would not return to haunt me in some more physical way. For me it was solved but for Superintendent Cromarty it was not and, as Scotch had confirmed, he was a tenacious bastard. I did not want to be subject to another of his little surprises; I needed to find out whether he had anything else up his sleeve.

Scotch knew that I had at one time been a suspect and sympathised with that and my desire as family of the victim to know where the investigation, apparently stalled, had got to. And, of course, he was a journalist and naturally curious. 'I've still got a couple of acquaintances in that neck of the woods. I'll see what I can winkle out.'

I was reconciled to the fact that there were many things I could never know but there was one other source of information as yet untapped – Deborah. I knew that talking about it would probably be extremely painful, as well as embarrassing, for her but I persuaded myself that it might also be cathartic and I invited her for supper in Camberwell, it being too cold for an outside meeting, too private for a restaurant, and a subject better suited to lamplight than daylight.

She had sounded pleased, if surprised, and arrived by taxi, clutching a bottle of wine, dressed for a dinner party.

As I took her coat and ushered her up the stairs I saw her eyes flicker through the open door of the kitchen to the dining table laid for two, but all she said was, 'Something smells good.'

I poured her a very large gin and tonic. She registered the size but there was no mock moue.

'So how are you?' she asked, once we were settled with our drinks and the captain's chest between us. Did she think that this was a purely social occasion?

'Well, OK,' I said, wondering if I should leave the subject until we sat down to eat, and then deciding that I couldn't in case she caught me off guard by asking outright what was going on.

'The thing is,' I said, 'I've been sorting out some of Stuart's things . . .'

Her expression set but, 'Yes?' she said brightly as if I might have come across an additional bequest.

'So, I'm afraid I know about you and him.'

She literally rocked, as if buffeted by a high wind, recovered, stared into her lap, bit her lip. 'Oh.'

I wasn't sure what to say next. I let the silence sit for a while and then she broke it, still without looking up. 'Does anyone else know?'

'Not from me.' I had avoided even the white lie of 'Not as far as I know.'

'How did you find out? I didn't send him any love letters or anything.'

'Nothing as intimate. Receipts, appointments, that sort of thing.'

She nodded, assuming that she had admitted guilt where before there had been only circumstantial evidence. 'So now I've confirmed it, can I go?'

'You can if you like, but I thought it might help to talk about it.'

'Help who?'

'Me, perhaps.'

She stared at me. 'Why would it help you?' Then her face, curiously destructured by shock, tautened. 'Oh I see, to save his reputation. You want me to be the little scrubber who tempted him off the straight and narrow. Well, all right.'

'Not necessarily. I just want to know the truth.'

She took a large swallow at her drink. 'I'm telling you it.' She stood up abruptly. 'I'm sorry, I need your loo.'

When she came back she said, 'Can I have one of your cigarettes? Thanks.' A drag, a gulp. 'It wasn't quite like I said. I didn't exactly make a play for him but then he wasn't angling for me either. It just sort of happened. I know. It's unbelievable. How can anyone just happen to have sex with their mother's husband?'

She had never, she said, thought of Stuart as a father or he of her as a daughter. 'You have to remember I was sixteen when he and Mummy got together and away at boarding school most of the time. Right from the start he treated me as an adult, which when you're that age is unusual and quite nice.'

In February 1990 Deborah had rung Stuart and invited him to have lunch with her, wanting to pick his brains over her possible promotion at Platform PR. They had enjoyed the meal and he had returned the invitation. In March 1990, as I knew from the diary, Nicole had gone skiing with the Gibsons, and Cate on a school trip. At their third lunch Stuart mentioned to Deborah that he wasn't looking forward to his weekend alone at Stirton. Deborah, who had temporarily fallen out with her flatmate over the omnipresence of her boyfriend, thought she could do with a break and tentatively suggested she might come down. On the Saturday evening they went to a party in a large house outside Sevenoaks where there was proper dancing. They had danced together once. They had arranged to leave at ten because Stuart did not like drinking and driving, but couldn't abide staying at a party too long on tonic water. When they got home Deborah, who had enjoyed herself much more than she expected and left reluctantly, said she couldn't imagine when she would get another chance to dance, which was a shame, she loved it. Stuart got out some records. Old, slow ones. She was wearing a very slinky black dress. They drank. One thing led to another.

'It was a terrible thing to do to Mummy, I know, I've felt guilty ever since, and I know it's no excuse but he and she weren't getting on, there were rows, and she was always on at him, and she was always on at me and then, once it was done I was hooked. I couldn't stop and neither could he. Secret lunches, snatched afternoons, occasionally at Stirton, sometimes in a hotel which was very odd, booking in for a couple of hours. I even went to meet him when he was away on business once or twice. Four times, actually. I don't know what would have happened, how it would have turned out, if he hadn't been shot.' She was poking at her eyes with a handkerchief, not a tissue but the sort of lace-edged variety that I thought only old ladies carried these days. 'Sometimes I think it was a judgment on us.'

I could feel my heart going into overdrive.

'Sorry, I know that's silly. But why didn't they kill me too? What I mean is, why didn't they treat us both the same? Why didn't they just tie him up? I suppose he must have put up a fight or something.' She slumped back against the cushions. 'Now I'm just glad she never found out. She missed him enough to kill herself, didn't she?'

It was a question but she had convinced herself that was true.

She talked on, drifting increasingly out of control as the evening progressed. At one point, very drunk and armed with coffee and an enormous, self-poured Cointreau, she said, 'Do you know, when you asked me round tonight and there was no one else here I thought for a minute that you were going to propo . . . proposition me as well. Here we go again.' She laughed, giving no indication of whether she would have accepted. 'Christ, you'd better call me a taxi.'

As I helped her into her coat she said softly, 'Don't worry. He was no Humbert Humbert to my Lolita.'

At the door she gave me a stumbled kiss on the cheek, turned to go and then stopped as if she had forgotten something. 'By the way, how's my stepsister, Cinderella?'

As I loaded the dishwasher I thought she must see Cate as a fraud, playing on her status as orphan, but then it occurred to me that Deborah might now see herself as an Ugly Sister.

Chapter Twenty-Five

Dorothy said it: 'Christmas comes but once a year, so why does it seem like every six months?' Suddenly the post was full of unwanted snow scenes from suppliers we could hardly remember, cheerily signed by Caroles and Daves who presumably had no more idea who we were, the diary was full of overlong lunches rounded off with 'just the one' glass of port, and my evenings were full of drinks parties where I sipped cheap champagne and nibbled unwanted miniature mince pies.

So when Scotch rang me to say he had some news of Cromarty's casework I promised to stop by the Coach and Horses on my way to King's Cross on a Friday afternoon. He was sitting on a stool at the bar, puffing on one of his large cigars and chatting to the landlady about, inevitably, her Christmas arrangements. I bought him another gin and ginger ale and we repaired to a corner table.

'I've had a word with an old desk sergeant at Stoneyheath and the word is – now you mustn't take this badly, frankly I'm not at all surprised, after this amount of time – that unofficially they've given up.'

I tried to disguise my relief under a grumble of protest.

'Oh, Cromarty's extremely pissed off himself but there's no suspects left in the frame and no forensic that might tie in villains caught doing something else.'

'What about the two Deborah and I went to see?'

'There may be an element of hindsight about this but the story is that Cromarty was never convinced they had anything to do with it. Another CID suggested it so he questioned them and had an ID parade to cover himself. And that, they say, convinced him that he'll never get a positive ID out of Deborah anyway so little point in trying her again.'

I wanted to be sure. 'So he has nothing, no theories of his own?'

Scotch looked slightly uncomfortable and stalled by sipping his gin.

'Come on,' I said. 'I already know he suspected me – it can't be worse than that.'

'Right from the start, Ted said, Cromarty was unconvinced by the burglary idea. There were other things they could have taken and traces they should have left. He was sure the burglary was a cover for the murder so he looked for a motive. He looked at your business but there was nothing there.' Scotch smiled. 'After a couple of weeks he was heard to say "Too bloody effete to employ hitmen, that lot, let alone do it themselves." He trawled for scandalous gossip around the villages but there was nothing there. Which left the will. Four people, one also a victim of the crime, two who gave each other an alibi and you. You stood to gain a lot of money and you found the body. But there was no usable forensic and we gave you a pretty decent alibi.'

'Thanks.'

'Not at all, my dear chap. Perhaps you'll do the same for me one day. Another drink? No, that wasn't really a question. Of course you'll have another, but what'll it be? Same again?'

While he was at the bar the phone rang for him and I thought he was being called back to the paper, but after a terse conversation with someone about a missing photograph he returned.

'And after me?' I prompted.

'Oh, he tried all permutations. He couldn't realistically see how Nicole or Cate could have done it other than in league so that was tested out but apart from the fact they both benefited from Stuart's death he couldn't see any community of interest, particularly after she came to live with you, and he couldn't believe that Deborah wouldn't have recognised them or that her mother would have left her tied up like that for so long. So that was out.'

He had come very, very close.

'Then, by a perverted sort of logic, he concluded that only Deborah herself would have consented to be trussed up all that time so he wondered about her and an accomplice but of course she had no real motive. Not left enough, he thought.'

Scotch looked at me curiously so I nodded to confirm that fact.

'His last throw was that all three of them had done it – you know, the killing a tyrannical father bit – but that never got off the drawing board because, of course, there was no evidence that Stuart was, and the circumstances weren't psychologically right.'

'What do you mean?' I asked, adding hastily, 'I mean, I know they weren't but what are the right circumstances, psychologically speaking?'

'Oh, I suppose isolated family, wife and daughters trapped with no one to turn to. Clearly not the case here – Deborah living away, Nicole in a second marriage by choice, knowing she can support herself if she chooses to leave, all of them intelligent, articulate, assertive. No mileage in that one, even for an obsesssive like Cromarty. He may be determined but he's not stupid.'

No. 'So that was that then?'

'Not quite. When Nicole committed suicide he got very excited, called it very fishy.' Scotch shrugged, embarrassed. 'Particularly you and Cate being around, you finding the body again. He wanted to fly out there but his boss put his foot down, said he'd have to make do with transcripts unless he turned up something concrete.'

'But there was nothing to turn up,' I said.

'Well, of course not,' Scotch said, 'but he was desperate to solve the case. The fact that there was no note only put him into more of a lather. I don't think the Corsicans paid much attention to him. Being decent chaps with human feelings they could understand that grief and depression might drive somebody to pump their car full of exhaust fumes. Outside Cromarty's fevered imagination it's not a popular murder method. Anyway, what finally dashed his hopes was the will. Ted thinks he'd vaguely been hoping that it would turn out to leave everything to Cate, thereby giving her a motive, but of course it left everything to Deborah who was safely in England when Nicole died.'

'The whole thing seems to have driven him demented,' I said. 'I almost feel sorry for him.'

'Oh, don't do that.'

'No, I didn't mean it. A bit worried by him, though. If he's that unbalanced he might do anything.'

'Oh, I don't think so. He knows when to cut his losses. Doesn't want his superiors thinking he's a paranoid fantasist. He's already overexposed on this case. Nothing short of an unsolicited full confession would bring him back to it now.'

On the train to Durham I was positively light-headed. Another threat over and a strangely nostalgic weekend ahead. I was going to see Cate in a seasonal student production of Ayckbourn's *Absurd Person Singular* at the Assembly Rooms, where I had appeared in a couple of plays myself.

It had hardly changed – the same dinner-jacketed boys playing at front of house management, the same dusty red, creaky tip-up seats, the same self-conscious audience, standing up in the front rows to scan the auditorium for friends and acquaintances, acknowledged with waves, halloos or exaggeratedly blown kisses. The only substantial improvement had been in the programmes – in my day these were poorly roneoed efforts but these were clearly reproduced in full colour. I wondered whether the Buccaneer photocopiers and Apple Macs had played any part.

The production had its faults – the set changes were too demanding and took thirty minutes which lost the momentum, and when you're out of the age group it's hard to be convinced by a twenty-year-old playing a middle-aged bank manager, but Cate, who spent the second act silently attempting to kill herself while the other characters continued under the delusion that she was simply attemting to get on with her housework, was excellent and the show got a prolonged standing ovation from a merry end-of-term audience.

Consequently the cast were in high spirits as we trotted along Hallgarth Street to the last night party, held in the flat of the director, Beth Turner.

She was a postgraduate, not only older than the others but very tall and dark, and so looked up to literally and metaphorically. Her place reminded me of what student accommodation should be like – the fusty, faintly grubby smell; the walls and even an old coffee table covered in a collage of posters and images cut from magazines; the battered, third-hand furniture.

The music and the conversation fought each other in an ever louder spiral and within minutes the heavy smell of dope was stoking up the natural euphoria. I don't know if Beth felt I needed rescuing, or if it was simply a sense of responsibility to the only person present older than herself, but after a while she gravitated towards me and we fell into a conversation that became too complex, if not too deep, to be satisfactorily conducted against the foreground – something that thick could scarcely be called background – noise level.

'Shall we go next door?' she shouted.

I nodded and she grabbed a wine bottle along with her roll-ups. The room was in darkness but it faced onto the street, the curtains were open, and a street lamp was directly outside the window.

'Oh look,' she said, 'it's snowing.' And it was, in that lazy way where fat flakes take their time about coming down, bobbing gently about on delicate cross-currents. We watched it as we talked, standing in the enhanced glow it had given the street light, so close to the window I could feel the cold from the glass. When the wine ran out she said, 'Shit, I guess we should hurl ourselves back into the fray.'

'Yes, I'm sorry, I've dragged you away from your own celebration.'

'I think it's still there,' she said wryly, nodding towards the din. 'And I don't suppose they'll have missed me.'

That seemed to be true, as she melted seamlessly back into the scrummage. I stood still, looking for Cate, and when I spotted her, just inside the kitchen, it seemed to me that she had been watching me, averting her gaze just before it would have met mine. By the time I had picked my way across the room she had disappeared into the bathroom which, as in so many conversions, was beyond the kitchen. By the time I did get to speak to her her voice was slurred with drink and she seemed curiously distant, but I put that down to cannabis.

She showed no desire to leave so I sat on, chatting, until, eventually, we and Jenny, the props girl, were the only remaining guests and Beth sensibly said, 'Right, I must go to bed, so I'll get your coats' and she disappeared into the front room. Taking our cue we shuffled out onto the street, the pavements now under a couple of inches of snow. We walked with Jenny as far as the Library, where she turned up the hill to her college and we ploughed on towards the roundabout. Despite the silent beauty of the night it was bitterly cold and, feeling the wet soaking through my shoes, I began to wish we had called a taxi.

Cate had slipped a couple of times and I put my arm out to support her but she shook it off saying, irritably, 'I'm all right.' I wasn't hurt – I recognised the resentment that any drunk feels when it is implied that they are incapable of walking in a straight line. She negotiated the downward slopes of Pimlico and South Street without too much trouble, ignoring the pretty high houses to her left and the dramatic towers across the river, humming to herself, but on the steep upward incline of Crossgate, treacherous cobbles beneath the white carpet, she lost her footing and fell face down.

I laughed, and went to pull her up.

'Get off,' she shouted, and scrambling to her feet, stumbled away towards Atherton Street and home.

I caught her up quite easily. 'Cate, Cate, what is the matter?'

She carried on, moving, spitting the words back at me. 'I know, I know she's attractive but did you have to go off with her like that?'

Beth? 'Cate, we just went to talk away from the noise.'

'Alone, in the dark, in her bedroom for nearly an hour.'

'Forty minutes,' I said before I could stop myself.

'Oh, so you noticed how long it took then.'

This was absurd. I had barely noticed it was a bedroom, then. The bed was in the shadows, its shape disguised by a mound of leather jackets and duffel coats.

'Cate, this is silly. I'm not a teenager, going off for a quick grope.'

'And I am, that's all I am. It must be hard to resist someone older, more sophisticated.'

We had reached her front door now and she was ramming the key into the lock. For a moment I thought she was going to shut me out but she simply stormed through into the kitchen swinging the door ineffectually back towards me. I followed. She was at the fridge, pouring herself another glass of wine.

I bit back the temptation to say, 'Don't you think you've had enough?' For some reason Beth had given her an inferiority complex. I said, 'I wouldn't describe you as unsophisticated.'

'Don't change the subject,' she barked, slamming the fridge shut.

I leant back against the tiled wall. 'Cate, this is stupid. If you were suspicious then I'm sorry . . .' I meant sorry that you should suspect me but it seemed better to leave it ambiguous, '. . . but if you were why didn't you check it out?'

'Oh yeah, burst in on you, barge into Beth's bedroom with everybody watching?'

I nearly said, remembering Dervla, 'You don't normally have a problem charging into rooms without knocking' but I stopped, remembering that perhaps she had more right than most to be scared of what she might find when she looked round a bedroom door. I tried to lighten the mood. 'It would have taken us forty minutes to have moved the coats off the bed. Anyway, you said yourself it was dark in there and you know I prefer the lights on.'

'Don't patronise me,' she screeched.

'Then don't make ridiculous accusations when you're pissed.'

That was when she threw her glass at me. Or rather, at where her blurred vision thought I was. It flew across the room, displaced wine arcing from it like the tail of a comet, and smashed against the wall about six inches from my head. There was a searing pain below my right eye, and wet on my cheek which I thought must be chablis until it reached my lips and it was hot and bitter and thick.

'Oh God, oh God,' she cried, 'I'm sorry, I'm sorry. I didn't mean it.' She hung onto me, pressing her face against mine, her fruity breath as powerful as an automatic hand-dryer, her cheeks picking up smears of my blood like a child in the aftermath of a chocolate frenzy. 'I could have blinded you.'

'But you didn't,' I said, catching at her scrabbling paws. 'Now, for God's sake let's try and stop me bleeding to death.'

Chapter Twenty-Six

After that I was justifiably nervous about Cate at the Buccaneer Christmas party but she was a model of good behaviour, charming with the clients, sober and stunning in her dark blue silk. The vogue for exotic locations and extravagant entertainment had faded in the recession – clients preferred its cost to be deducted from their bills – so we had simply invited them to the offices and hired caterers to produce a buffet.

Although the invitations were for 6.30 which, in the etiquette of these dos, implies a mid-evening finish, there are always one or two clients who hang around until shown an overwhelming example. The caterers were dismissed, leaving the remnants of the food and the rubbish for the morning and eventually I told the staff, whose own party was the next day, to make themselves scarce. At five to midnight I closed the last taxi door on Sir John Palmer, the refuse disposal magnate and, as I had discovered tonight, at length, Euro-enthusiast.

I wandered back up to the boardroom where Cate was pouring us a well-earned glass of champagne. We had kept the lights low in here and the blinds open to give the assembled throng the benefit of our almost perfect view of the immense, illuminated dome of St Pauls.

'Thanks,' I said. 'You were very, very good tonight.'

'I know,' she said, 'but when I am bad, I am horrid.' And she touched the scar which we had explained, apart from in casualty, as a slipped knife, stupidly used to cut through packaging towards me.

I played with her short fringe. 'It's no use, that curl will not stay in the middle of your forehead.'

She ran her finger across my lips and onto my chin. 'Is it any wonder I'm jealous, though. You look very sexy tonight.'

'Well, there's a coincidence.'

'I've found it very hard to keep my hands off you.' She moved closer to my ear. 'Let's do it now.'

'What, in here?'

'Isn't it every good capitalist's fantasy to screw his assistant on the boardroom table?' She leaned back against it, which drew her hem significantly further up the shiny navy stockings.

'Technically speaking,' I said, 'my assistant's Pete McColl.'

Her eyes glinted in the lamplight, which had made moons on the highly polished surface of her shoes.

'You don't even have to take my frock off,' she said, smirking, and lay amid the wreckage of the buffet.

As I pushed back the heavy silk I thought what an aptitude for staging Cate had. The lighting, the backdrop . . . even when, some time later, her hand moving backwards and forwards over the linen tablecloth caught at a stray item of food. Had it been a mushroom vol-au-vent the atmosphere might have been impaired, but it wasn't. What she grasped, and then squeezed so that the white spread over the raw pink and into her palm, was a bagel with cream cheese and lox.

'Shall we turn over?' she panted, sweeping several plates onto the floor with her other arm to clear a space for me to roll onto.

Amazingly we perfected this tricky manouevre without a break, and she knelt above me, licking her fingers, gazing dreamily into space.

'Nice view?' I puffed sarcastically.

'I've never had an orgasm while looking at a cathedral.'

Now Dad was dead I had no reason to spend Christmas in London and Cate was very keen to have it in her own house, so she went up to prepare on the 23rd and I followed on the morning of the 24th. Caught in heavy traffic on the A1 I wished that I had not agreed – I made this trip often enough out of necessity in termtime; why again? But as I got out of the car in Atherton Street I knew I had been wrong. Coal smoke drifted up from the chimneys and its smell hung in the damp air. Through the window I could see a tree, laden with gold baubles and chains and surrounded by parcels in tartan paper, and Cate's head, bent over the page in the Good Housekeeping cookery book which explains how to cook a turkey.

She wanted to do the whole thing in traditional fashion, so the cupboards exploded with delicacies that we would never eat and we went to midnight mass in the cathedral, the first time I had been to church at that time since I was an adolescent and it was something to be done after the pubs closed.

Lying in bed on Christmas morning, the torn wrappings of our first – but only our first because 'the others have to be opened after our walk and before lunch' – presents scattered across the duvet, Cate said, 'If I twisted that mirror, do you think it would reflect the cathedral?'

'I doubt it.'

'Then you'll have to take me down to the river bank.'

'Why? You saw it, you were in it, last night.'

'To continue my series, cathedrals and climaxes.'

'If you think I'm screwing on the towpath in the middle of winter you've got another think coming.'

'Apparently not, unless I can persuade you to change your mind.' She kissed my nose. 'We could road-test it round the country. Is Salisbury more erotic than York Minster? Do you find breast-shaped domes more satisfying while I respond to phallic towers?'

'Does size matter? In steeples, that is.'

'We could do a coffee-table book.'

'But probably not a television series.'

It was hard, on the 27th, to think about going back to London.

'Well, let's stay another day. If we go back to London I won't have you, you'll be in the office.'

'There are one or two things I've got to organise.'

'Well, do it from here. And don't say you haven't got your stuff because I know you never go anywhere without your briefcase. I saw you sneaking it in when you arrived. It's in the study under my desk.'

When I had, without much reluctance, conceded defeat she said, 'You can have the house to yourself for the whole morning as long as you devote the afternoon to me.'

'Where will you go?'

'Oh, I don't know, the library.'

'It's not open out of term, is it?'

'I'm not sure. Well, if it's shut I'll go to the sales in Newcastle or something. Don't you worry about me.'

She was as good as her word. At nine, while I was still in the bath, she put her head round the door and announced: 'I'm off. No slacking while I'm gone.'

But, fragrant with bath oil and wrapped in a thick, warm towel from the airing cupboard, motivation was difficult. I lay on her bed, looking at the rails of clothes in her open wardrobe. At the house in Camberwell, where she kept most of her smarter, Buccaneerish stuff, I would sometimes go and sit in her room when I was missing her. It was comforting to sniff her smell in a jumper or a dress, to take one of her vast shoe collection from the rack on the back of the door and run my hand over its smooth contours and spiky heel, sometimes to spray a little of her perfume into the air and stand on the edge of its pungent mist – essence of Cate. Here, with her so recently departed, there was no need to do that. Her scent was still detectable, her own towel still damp on the bedspread, her yesterday's socks and knickers discarded on the carpet.

I got up, put on a clean shirt and trousers. Odd that she should have left her own stuff lying around but put my cufflinks, a present from her, away. I searched along the mantelpiece and scanned the surface of the dressing table. Then I opened the big, carved wooden box from Thailand in which she kept her jewellery but it was such a tangled morass of earrings, bangles and necklaces that I had no hope of finding a couple of discreet silver cufflinks by poking about. I turned it upside down and shook the contents onto the bed. Sifting through it I came across her . . . our . . . mock-wedding ring, on a gold chain, but no cufflinks. The box's lining, a sheet of card covered in black velvet, had also fallen out, and, presumably from beneath it, some cards. I picked them up to put them back. The first was an American Express card in the name of N.D. Makepeace. An odd memento to keep of your stepmother. I turned over the second. It was an international student travel card and the photograph was of Cate, taken a couple of years ago, but the full name given was Nicole Deborah Makepeace and the date of birth was 3.7.68, not, as Cate's was, 14.6.72.

I stared at them, as if by looking hard I could make sense of them. Why were all these dates and names jumbled up in one composite person? Why had she been created? Why had she been hidden away?

The phone rang, and I wandered downstairs to answer it, the cards still in my hand. It was Dorothy. We went through the ritual exchange as to whether we had had a good Christmas and then she continued: 'I got your message. I've cancelled your lunch with Terry and Pete's taking care of the Hegarty arrangements. Now, there are one or two messages . . .' She ran through them; I dutifully told her what needed to be done and noted any numbers I would have to ring. 'That's about it, then.'

'Dorothy, can you remember Stuart's wife's full name?'

'Of course, Alex, it was Angela Catherine, maiden name Winterton.'

'Goodness, you've got a good memory. No, I meant Nicole.'

'As a matter of fact I can, although I know she hated her second name, didn't like any reference made to it, although I've always thought it was a perfectly nice name myself . . .'

'And it was?'

'Daphne. Lovely, and classical. And of course her maiden name was Leadbetter and then Makepeace after her first husband, that actor, Deborah's father . . .'

Without being sure why I didn't want Dorothy to remember this conversation as anything out of the ordinary so I attempted to turn my sneaking suspicion into a game. 'I bet you can't remember Deborah's full name.'

She sounded slightly affronted. 'That's a trick question because it's not Deborah anything. She's got the same initials and first name as her mother – she's Nicole Deborah Makepeace.'

'Well spotted,' I said heartily. 'And for your bonus, what's her date of birth?'

For the first time she hesitated. 'It's some time at the beginning of July . . . not the 1st I know . . .'

'The 3rd?'

'Yes.' She was almost tetchy. 'I'd have got there, you know.'

'Year?' I asked, to give her a consolation prize.

'1968, of course.'

'The year of the student riots in Paris.'

'The year I moved to Orpington.'

Really? I thought she'd been born and raised in Orpington but I didn't want to go into that now. 'That's right,' I agreed.

'Is that it then?' She was jovial but curious. 'No more questions?'

'No more. Cate and I were, you know, talking about the family as you do at Christmas and we just had a couple of disagreements on birthdays, that sort of thing.'

'Oh,' meaning, that was all right then. 'Who won?'

'Oh, Cate, of course.'

'Of course,' Dorothy said happily. 'She's a clever girl.'

I sat at the clever girl's desk and wondered what sort of game she had been playing here. To obtain a travel card in her stepsister's name she would have needed some other form of ID . . . not a passport because that would have had a picture of the real Deborah . . . a birth certificate. Would she have needed Deborah's co-operation? Not necessarily, because although Deborah did not live at home birth certificates are often kept by mother in a file in the bureau, easily accessible to anyone who lives in the house.

I tried to think how you came by credit cards. Absurd: I'd got several but couldn't recall exactly how I'd acquired them. By asking for them I supposed, and then I remembered the cascade of unsolicited mail on the doorstep every morning. I'd been sent several opportunities to have another card so I'm sure Nicole had. It would have been very easy for her stepdaughter to intercept one of these, fill in the application form with Nicole's details but her own devised signature, and then make sure she was first to the post every morning until her card arrived.

So Cate had set up a line of credit in her stepmother's name and a second, confirming means of identity using the coincidence of initials and the fact that she could pass for 21 when she was only 17 or 18. But why?

I was distinctly unhappy. I somehow felt I couldn't ask Cate, that despite the search for the cufflinks I had been snooping. It seemed like I had done a lot of snooping lately and every time I had discovered something worse. I didn't want things with Cate to get worse. But I couldn't just pretend I hadn't seen the cards. They were there for a purpose and in the end, in ignorance of the facts, my nasty little brain would devise a purpose as awful as any reality could be.

I sat on, in the chair in the study, looking out at the dustbin and the brick wall and, in self-fulfilling prophecy, a monstrous train of thought began to pick up speed in the back of my mind. What were the chief uses of credit cards when you didn't have a home of your own and your allowance, while probably less than you wanted, was sufficient to buy clothes and records? You couldn't, as far as I knew, use credit cards for drink or drugs. What else did I use them for? Restaurant bills, but when I first got to know Cate it was obvious that she still regarded restaurants as an occasional treat, paid for by someone else. Hotel bills, but Cate was a schoolgirl, hardly able to slip away for nights unnoticed. Travel then: air fares, rail fares, petrol . . . and car hire. The train thundered towards me and I wanted to roll out of its path but I couldn't. Without a credit card, car hire is irritatingly complicated – if you want to pay by cash or by cheque then all sorts of secondary proofs are demanded, but a credit card will do nicely all on its own. And where had I seen a car hire receipt in the name of N.D. Makepeace? On the kitchen table in Corsica.

The evidence found by Cate that had led to Nicole's confession.

The train hit me.

The only authority for Nicole's confession was Cate. What if it was her, not Nicole, who had hired that car, who had driven from Heathrow to Stirton? It was like looking at one of those black and white pictures that suddenly stops being a flight of birds against a pale sky, transformed into white waves on a dark sea by a switch in the viewer's perception. None of the circumstances of the murder needed to be changed for the murderer to become Cate. All you needed was a change in perception to visualise Cate putting the sleeping pills into her stepmother's drink rather than the other way around.

I was sick. How could I be thinking this? Cate was the girl I loved.

Cate who brained her boyfriend and nearly blinded you, a small voice insinuated.

But they were spontaneous acts of passion. Not planned.

Those documents took some planning, the voice insisted.

Documents. Salvation. You couldn't hire a car without a driving licence. I steeled myself to go back upstairs. The box was still lying upside down on the bedspread where I had left it. Clearly empty. Was I going to search the rest of the room? I couldn't believe that I was.

I picked up the box and turned it over. The driving licence, tissue pink, innocent pink, being somewhat larger had wedged in the cracks between the sides and the base of the box. Nicole Deborah Makepeace; similar signature to the other two. I opened it out. Date of birth as on the travel card.

I sat heavily. It couldn't be. What was her motive, for God's sake? Patricide for money? Some extreme of jealousy? Then why hadn't she killed Deborah? She didn't bottle that girl at Cathy's ball, the little voice said, only the boyfriend, the one who had betrayed her.

Insane, I thought, but I didn't really know whether I meant her or me. I couldn't think properly in this poky, stuffy little house, I had to get into the cold, clean air. Action. I ran down into the hall and pulled on my jacket. A note to explain my absence? But what could I say?

I was unlocking the car when she came round the corner. 'I see. And where are you running off—?' She faltered, silenced by my expression. What must it have been like? 'What . . . what's the matter? What's happened?'

My mouth gave my brain no time for circumspection and to my amazement blurted out exactly what was on my mind. 'Did you kill Stuart?'

She stared at me for what seemed like an age, probably two seconds, and then, when I was certain her lips were forming the phrase 'What do you mean?', she stuttered: 'I . . . well . . . I didn't mean to . . . I just wanted—'

Chapter Twenty-Seven

I wasn't aware of getting into the Saab and starting the engine, only of taking that reflex look in the rear-view mirror as I pulled away and seeing Cate standing there, abandoned, on the icy pavement in her shiny aubergine parka, her shoulder bag collapsed before her. I drove to the A1 and headed south because I couldn't think what else to do.

How could she not have meant to, with all that meticulous planning? I kept seeing her, in her green jumper, looming over Deborah, the scarlet woman in a tart's nightdress, pinning her arms by her sides until the chloroform took over. Cate was certainly strong enough.

In some ways it rang truer than the same scenario with Nicole. The youthful avenging angel, passing silently through the still house, as she had done that first day she saw them, disposing of her . . . what? Rival? Rival in his affections? How did she see it? How had she twisted this up in her mind?

Wetherby.

Her voice, calling from the landing, was more plausible. A man, hearing his wife's voice while lying in her daughter's bed would panic, wouldn't he? Not calmly put on his pyjamas and dressing gown. But what about a man hearing, confusingly, his daughter's voice? That might have other connotations, going back years, of the child who had had a bad dream needing comfort and reassurance that everything was all right really. The child who might not know any better or understand what she had half-witnessed. That was a situation, for a smart, machiavellian operator like Stuart that, with a bit of luck, might be rescued. Restore respectability. Admit nothing. Soothe. Explain.

Thirsk.

What I couldn't see was her pulling the trigger. Not my beautiful, wonderful Cate.

'I didn't mean to . . . I just wanted—'

Just wanted to frighten? To show how upset she was, what lengths he had driven her to? Maybe the gun had gone off by accident as he walked calmly towards her, squeezed in panic.

Perhaps that was it. Like the thing with Henry and the book left out. She had tempted fate and the consequences were bigger by far than she had expected. If that was so then what she had done was wrong but it wasn't murder.

I stretched my neck in relief, taking my eyes off the road for what seemed like only a second but when I focused again I was virtually sitting on the rear seat of the car in front. I slammed on the brakes, narrowly avoiding shunting it onto a roundabout.

Where was I? Grantham on the signposts. Lincolnshire then. Now I just wanted to get home. Why was I sitting behind this complacent company Ford? I glanced in the mirror and began to pull out, swinging sharply in again as a BMW rushed past in a blaze of headlights and horn. He must have been in my blind spot. Or otherwise I was incapable of concentrating enough to get home safely. I no longer felt suicidal so maybe I should take a break and calm down.

I pulled off at the next Little Chef and, although I was not hungry, ordered myself some sort of all-day breakfast. The waitress brought a cafetière of surprisingly good coffee.

Suicide. Could I really ever have contemplated that? I doubted it. I suspected I was one of those people who, no matter how depressing circumstances were, would always see life as better than no life.

Without warning another express came straight out of that tunnel and hit me. If Nicole had not murdered Stuart, been found out, confessed, then why had she committed suicide? Others had assumed that grief was the cause of the depression that had driven her to it, but the only real evidence of her demeanour on the day she died was from Cate.

So had Cate confessed to her and she been so distressed by this that she had motored off and gassed herself? It didn't seem a likely reaction.

I remembered Cate when I had arrived at the villa, pouncing on me with the knife, assuming that I was Nicole, the murderer. But Nicole wasn't a murderer. So what was Cate so frightened of?

I tried to step back and wait for the black birds to replace the white sea. Perhaps Nicole had found the hire receipt or a statement from the forged credit card, deduced that Cate had committed the murder and gone out to Corsica to confront her? Why else would Nicole have gone? It could hardly have been a coincidence, her arriving there a day later.

A sliver of memory nagged. Something to do with Nicole's state of mind just before she went to Corsica. Bill Starling, at her funeral, describing his last meeting with Nicole the afternoon before she flew out, saying, 'I just didn't attach any significance to the phone call at the time.' I had assumed that call was from Deborah, prompted by my efforts to find Cate, but what had Starling actually said? That Nicole had been very quiet when she came back from the phone, that he had asked if it was bad news and that she had replied: 'I don't know, Bill. My stepdaughter. A mysterious little madam.'

What if that phone call had been from Cate at the villa? 'You must come. I know what happened to Daddy,' or 'I'm in trouble'; at any rate, 'Don't tell anybody.'

Nicole was the one person who could bust Cate's alibi for the murder. Perhaps Cate had decided to eliminate that risk.

The waitress put the enormous plateful of sausage, bacon, eggs and fried bread before me. 'Enjoy your meal.'

'Thank you,' I said mindlessly. Somehow I had jumped from absolving Cate of true responsibility for one murder to accusing her of two. How could I possibly believe that? I didn't want to but the train was clattering on. Could it have worked, could it have worked, could it have worked that way?

Nicole arrives at the cottage; Cate establishes that she has told no one of her whereabouts. Nicole gets drunk – that's a fact, confirmed by post mortem – plied with booze by Cate, exploiting her depression. Nicole took sleeping pills – another fact – but these could have been slipped into her drinks by Cate. She had done it before. When Nicole is virtually comatose Cate puts her into the Lada, with or without the inducement of a shotgun or a knife, and drives her to the headland. She straps her into the driver's seat – Nicole was found bolt upright with her seatbelt on – feeds the tube through the window and watches the car fill up with exhaust fumes. When she is sure Nicole is dead she returns to the villa. But, half an hour later, she hears footsteps and someone opens the door. In her heightened and suggestible state – it can't be easy killing someone even if you're a psychopath – she assumes it is Nicole, somehow risen from the grave, and charges at her with the knife. Except it is not Nicole, it is me.

Nevertheless, she has made a necessary murder into a convincing suicide.

'Is everything all right, sir?'

'Oh, yes, thanks.' I smiled at the waitress and she smiled uncertainly back. She might have been taught to make this polite inquiry of every customer but I could see that she was genuinely concerned. I looked down at my plate. None of the food had been eaten, but it had been dissected into tiny pieces and mixed up into a gigantic hash. 'I'm sorry,' I said. 'It's no reflection on your cooking. I thought I was hungry but I wasn't.'

She nodded and took the plate away but I could tell she was convinced I was a nutter. Perhaps she was right. I paid the bill and returned to the road, driving carefully in the slow lane, desperately looking for holes in the horrific argument I had so easily woven.

What if Nicole had told someone Cate had invited her out there?

Cate could still have used the whole story of finding the car hire receipt, she would just have had to use it on a wider audience than me. She must have expected to use it on a wider audience, only I willingly agreed to keep it a secret for Deborah's sake.

Suddenly, a hole the size of the crater. Me. I rang the villa, she picked up the phone, perhaps thinking it would be Nicole, and found it was Alex. Admittedly she didn't speak but she knew I thought it was her. How did she know I wouldn't fly out and interrupt her mid-plan? I nearly had, would have done had it not been for the impossibly-parked baker's van.

Thank God; she was off the hook. Wasn't she?

I speeded up, as if that would prevent further analysis, pushing through the fading afternoon sky, startled by the bright lights of the Hatfield tunnel. Then I was trapped in the London traffic and the argument was on again.

Cate would not have known I had a travel agent who could get me onto a charter, and there was only one morning scheduled flight to Ajaccio. If I had been on it Nicole would have seen me and said so. Ergo, I was not on the island and the plan could proceed. Cate had been very lucky.

Why did it have to be true? Hadn't I suffered enough? Losing my brother, my mistress and my father in little more than a year. And then finding that the compensation, the great love of my life, had been responsible for eliminating the first two. What next, a plague of frogs?

Stuck in the January sales furore on the Finchley Road I switched on the radio to blot out the self-pity but *Afternoon Theatre* could not compete with the unfolding story of my involvement with Cate that drifted through my head.

Cate scuffing along that Greek beach in her swimming costume with, apparently, not a care in the world other than the usual adolescent uncertainties.

Cate on the couch in my office, angry with herself for crying as she asked to move in with me.

Cate's arms around me for the first time when she passed her A-levels.

Cate bumping noses with young Hugo Beaumont over the New Year dinner table.

Image after image, all of them poignant until her face, aghast as she saw me on the sofa with Dervla McKenna, glimpsed only for a second before she slammed out of the house.

Given that less than a week later Cate and I had become lovers, I had assumed that seeing me kissing another, unknown woman she had suffered a fit of jealous pique. But was that right? What, exactly, had she seen? Not Dervla's face. Just a soft, pliant female body with long, black hair draped over mine. What would that have reminded her of? Had she seen Deborah? Deborah devouring first her father and now me?

All these wild suppositions, exploding in my head. I was as mad as Cromarty. Except that he hadn't been mad and I had the evidence, even the confession, that he would have given his eye teeth for.

I parked the car in the square. It was warmer here. No ice on the pavements, just drizzle under a darkening sky. A dank twilight. As I walked along the street to the house I noticed the fairylights flashing in the windows. Even in my own basement.

But I didn't have a tree.

I hurried up the steps, peering down at the winking red and green lights behind the glass, relieved to realise that all I had done was to leave the studio equipment switched on. Very dangerous, of course, as I had been away for four days, something for which I would normally have chastised myself for but hardly another burden to add to mounting insanity. As I fumbled for my keys I laughed. My head was so mixed up I even imagined I'd heard Cate laugh, a light, tinkling giggle against some background interference.

I closed the door and leaned against it, just as I had leaned on our return from Corsica, only then Cate had been leaning against me, filling my mouth with kisses. How could that ever happen again? In the instant before I put on the hall light I could still smell the faint residue of her perfume; the house must be steeped in it.

Turn off that recording gear. I went to the stairwell, down the first, short flight into the dark, round the corner, and down the final flight towards the faint glow of the Camberwell Road seeping through the window.

Something glinted in the gloom on the far side of the room and, alarmed, I shot my arm out and hit the switch, flooding the studio with harsh, white light which negated the incandescent green and red pinpricks as effectively as if they had been unplugged.

Cate was sitting, crosslegged, on an old amplifier, her sleeves pushed up for business, the largest Sabatier knife from the kitchen held loosely in her right hand, its blade resting against the heel of her boot.

'How did you get here?' I would hardly have been surprised if she'd claimed supernatural forces.

'The train,' she said flatly. 'It's quicker than the car.'

I didn't feel wary any longer. I flopped into the old armchair. 'I won't tell anyone,' I said. 'So you don't have to shut me up. But you might as well.'

'Actually,' she said, 'I was thinking of cutting my wrists.'

'It's supposed to be better if you do it under warm water.'

'Oh.' Her eyes were big, darting, their lids smudged with kohl, such a contrast from the economical voice. 'Before I try it, can I just tell you something?'

'Yes.'

'I think there's been a misunderstanding. To do with these.' She scattered the documents across the grey carpet. 'You think I literally killed Daddy.'

Back to Daddy. 'That's what you said.'

'I know. I meant, I was responsible.'

'What's the distinction?'

'Nicole killed him. I presume, just as she told me. As a theory it works, doesn't it?'

For a moment I wondered if she was mocking my poor impersonation of a detective but there was no hint of irony on her face. I nodded.

'The thing is, she wouldn't have done it if I hadn't told her what I saw. Told her I'd caught Daddy and Debbie screwing.'

'Why did you tell her?'

'I was angry . . . being compared unfavourably with Deborah, yet again.'

'And that's all?'

'I know. I am evil.'

'How did she react?'

'She went white as a sheet, and silent, and then she went berserk. Ranting and raving, calling me a filthy little cow who'd only ever wanted to split her and Stuart up, who'd ruined their marriage etcetera, etcetera. She slapped me and punched me. I kicked her back.'

'Then what?'

'Then she cried and I cried and she simmered down and asked when it happened. She even got her diary out and flicked through a few pages. Then I could see, in her face, she'd accepted it. She knew, inside, it was true. Not that she admitted it. She told me to say nothing. She'd clear it up.'

'Then what?'

'Nothing much. A couple of weeks later she came to my room, said she'd sorted it out and if I ever breathed a word to a soul she'd make my life hell.'

'And when Stuart was killed? You didn't suspect her?'

'Why would I? We were in a hotel in Heathrow when that happened.'

'And you never told anybody.'

'Not until I told you. Why would I?' she asked bitterly. 'Ruin my dead father's reputation? What good would it have done?'

It was almost convincing. I nudged the documents with my foot. 'What about these?'

She wriggled uncomfortably on her seat. 'Stupid really. It was hard to go into pubs for some of us, at school.'

Hard for Cate to pass as 18?

'It was a sort of group dare. Getting a forged identity with a false age. Debbie was down one weekend. Her driving licence was just sitting there in her open handbag. I used that to get the travel card. Meant to put it back but there was such a fuss about her losing it and Mrs Cuttifer had been in so I could hardly claim I'd found it on the floor.'

'And the credit card?'

'The application form was left on the kitchen table with the other junk mail to be thrown away.'

'What did you want it for?'

'I was going to run up a huge bill at her expense, like she did with Daddy's cards. Teach her a lesson. He'd have given her a really hard time. I thought it would serve her right.'

'And did you?'

'I bought one or two things. Stupid things. Then I got frightened. Thought they might catch me and it would mess up university and everything. It wasn't worth it.'

'What did you do?'

'Paid it off out of my allowance. It took months.' She smiled, a grim little smile. 'Cost me a fortune in interest.'

We sat in silence for a while.

Then, cautiously, she ventured: 'If you don't believe me, you could check, I suppose.'

'How?'

'Ask Deborah when she lost her licence. It was ages before . . . Someone would remember the thing at school . . . I expect.'

'Did Jane Clifford do it?'

She twitched. 'No, I don't think so. But I bet she'd remember.'

We sat in silence, facing each other, washed out by the lights, worn out by the day.

After a bit she said, 'Can we go for a walk or something, not just sit still?'

'All right.'

We went through the garden and into the park, not speaking until, in the subway, she said wonderingly, 'You really thought I'd killed him.'

Thought? Or think?

We passed over the manmade hillocks and down to the paved waterside where, astonishingly, in the bleak light from the tower blocks, a few hardened anglers fished on.

She sniffed. 'I know I was awful and I'm still not very nice sometimes but you changed everything for me. I'm a different person. You've made me better. If you don't want me then I don't care about anything else.'

I believed her about that. I knew about change because, I accepted, she had changed everything for me too. But what about the other stuff? I tried to picture the signature on that car hire slip but it was a blank. I could ring Deborah and Jane but I didn't think I would. In case the truth they told was not the truth I wanted to hear.

I wanted to trust the only person that really mattered. 'Can you live with my suspicions?'

She darted me a glance. 'Can you forget them?'

I nodded. 'Can you forget that I had them?'

'Are we playing word games?'

'War games.'

'Oh . . . you.' She punched me in the shoulder. 'Why don't you . . .'

She searched for a phrase and her eyes settled behind me '. . . go jump in a lake.'

I turned and stepped off the edge. It was surprisingly deep, up to my waist, and the water was agonisingly cold.

'You're mad,' she squealed.

'Oh, I'm sorry,' I said. The agony had stopped and a delicious numbness was rising through me. 'I thought you meant literally.'

She jumped in, landing beside me with a splash and a scream, clinging onto me, our faces close together. 'Don't patronise me,' she squeaked.

'I can't,' I said, sinking in soft, forgiving mud. 'I love you.'

'I love you too.' Our mouths met.

'Oi! Oi! What do you two think you're playing at, frightening the fucking fish.' A belligerent angler charged along the bank towards us.

'I thought the expression was frightening the horses,' I said, and Cate snorted. He loomed above us.

'I'm sorry,' Cate said. 'We couldn't help it. Could you give us a hand out?'

Walking back, slowly despite the freezing wet clothes, I felt calm. Love was redemptive. Everything would be all right.

I could even expunge the disquiet I had felt so long ago . . . no, that morning . . . when, rooting around in the bathroom cabinet at Atherton Street, I had noticed that Cate's little foil strip of pills seemed to have too many untorn days. But that was all right. She had probably forgotten to take one strip away with her or something and had to start another. She was too careful to have forgotten full stop, and I knew she didn't want to get pregnant. She had told me.